BROKEN LIKE THIS

BROKEN
LIKE THIS

Monica Trasandes

Thomas Dunne Books ☙ New York
St. Martin's Press

This is a work of fiction. All of the characters, organizations, and events portrayed in this novel are either products of the author's imagination or are used fictitiously.

THOMAS DUNNE BOOKS.
An imprint of St. Martin's Press.

Jacket photograph © Michael Heissner/Getty Images

www.thomasdunnebooks.com
www.stmartins.com

Design by Omar Chapa

Library of Congress Cataloging-in-Publication Data

Trasandes, Monica.
    Broken like this : a novel / Monica Trasandes. — 1st ed.
        p. cm.
    ISBN 978-1-250-00683-7 (hardcover)
    ISBN 978-1-250-01833-5 (e-book)
    1. Life change events—Fiction.   I. Title.
    PS3620.R3735B76 2012
    813'.6—dc23
                                                    2012034557

First Edition: November 2012

10   9   8   7   6   5   4   3   2   1

To Valda, Mamá y Papá, Mercedes y Fernando
with all my love
And for all the brave girls of the world

ACKNOWLEDGMENTS

A million thank-yous to my wonderful editor, Katie Gilligan, for her intelligence and thoughtfulness, and to my agent, Kristin Nelson, for her great advice and ideas, as well as to the Astraea Foundation for their early support.

I'm very grateful to the following people for their help over the years, sharing with me their edits, ideas, support, and/or red wine, as appropriate: Valda Lake, Mercedes Martinez Trasandes, Rita O'Neill, Laura Black, Christy Sumner, Molly Snow, Sarah Winman, Patricia Niven, Marolyn Krasner, Britt Enggren, Amy Heidish, Taji Marie, Jesse Torrilhon, Christopher Rowley, Chuck Hurewitz, Tina Lake, Pam Lake, Paul Brownfield, Fontelle Slater, Heather Stobo, Leanna Creel, Margie Gilmore, Dorothy Atcheson, Daniel Caudill, Kanna Place, Paco Sovich, and Tyler Colton.

CHAPTER 1
On a Road in Spain
1994

Stretched out in the backseat of the Peugeot, Kate closes her eyes and inhales slowly, deeply. She rests her right arm behind her head, the elbow at her forehead. Then, eyes still closed, she leans her face closer and licks the inside of her forearm. Will it taste the way the Pacific did when she was a kid in California in the seventies? It does. The Pacific and the Mediterranean are the same in the crook of her arm.

"I saw that," Paul says, and laughs into the rearview mirror.

"Did you?"

"Yeah. How was it?"

"Tastes like chicken," she says, and the boys laugh.

Paul allows himself to watch her in the mirror for just a moment. What a beauty—those big green eyes, the short dark hair, full lips. She looks like Ava Gardner or a character in a movie who starts trouble, then gets more than she bargained for. That's Kate—normally, anyway, but maybe not right now. She looks relaxed, peaceful.

"Hey, Kika?" he says into the mirror, and enjoys watching those eyes open.

"Yes?"

"You look happy."

"Do I?"

"Yes," he says, "you do."

"I'll take that as a compliment," she says, and closes her eyes, smiles.

Kate does feel happy right now. She's not seen the truck, about two miles away, and fears nothing. Just a few days ago, on a flight from Brazil, she had pressed the tip of her nose to the cold window, looked out at the infinite clouds, and thought, Okay, it's different now.

"It's different now. Or maybe I'm different now," she'd whispered, and the passenger next to her, an older lady watching a movie, had smiled and pulled out a single earbud, thinking Kate was talking to her.

She'd felt new and light, as if she might even start floating over the others on the airplane, like an escaped Thanksgiving parade balloon. Was that just a trick created by the airplane or by leaving Brazil? Was it an attempt to detach emotionally because she'd failed that poor girl? Or was it just her hormones? Now, today, in Ibiza, in the car, Kate feels the same way—entirely herself but also light.

Paul turns back to the road and sees something odd and a little startling. About a mile away, coming down the hill, there seems to be something white and boxy, probably a truck, and in their lane. An optical illusion, he tells himself, making it only appear as if the truck's in their lane, because it's now clearly on its own side of the road.

Liam, sitting in the passenger's seat next to him, isn't watching the road, but the scenery.

"What's up, boo?" Paul asks, and Liam answers that he can't wait to shower, put on his big thick robe, stretch out on the bed, and finish his Stephen King book.

"Sounds nice," Paul says, and rubs the back of Liam's neck.

Liam reaches into his burlap bag and finds the bottle of ouzo he forgot to open on the beach. They'd spotted it sitting on a shelf at the market downstairs from their hotel and planned to mix it with Coke, see if it would taste like Dr Pepper. Only they forgot, and now it's too hot to drink. Liam shoves his Greek sake into the bag and extracts a joint, which he lights, then passes to the backseat, but Kate doesn't want any.

Kate rubs the hair on her neck, then the side of her head, and watches a few bits of sand fall on her white cotton dress. She loves the way little pieces of a place will sometimes find their way into your suitcase, your shoe, even your hair, and come home with you. She thinks of the coves, or *calas,* in which they'd just been swimming, so blue and warm.

"I like the name Cala," she says.

"Yes, for a tall, pale lady with a very long neck," Paul says.

"Hmm, the gentleman does have a point," Kate says, then reaches over and snatches the smoke tucked behind Paul's ear. If she lights it, this will be her last. So many things will change in the next months. No more smokes. And she won't be able to dye her hair. Kate puts the cigarette under her nose, a long white mustache—the tobacco smells different here, like whiskey.

How Paul wishes his glasses were not so scratched. He can't be seeing things right, because that truck, or whatever it is, up ahead looks like it's moving in ways that just don't make sense.

"Can I borrow someone's sunglasses?" he asks. Liam says his are in the bag in the trunk. Kate hands over hers and Paul puts them on. Never mind they're ridiculously oversize seventies movie-star glasses. So Jackie Susann.

Kate rests her hands on her belly and smooths it, seeing if anything is visible. It's not. She puts her hand against her chest, presses down, and watches the skin there turn slightly pink. She caught the sun. Kate looks at the cigarette and whispers, "Bye, old friend."

"I just quit smoking," she says.

"Good for you," Liam squeaks through the second hit of the joint.

Paul loves the way Liam holds his lips tight after a hit, like a little kid, worried that everyone will laugh if he exhales too soon. *When* he exhales too soon, because he always does. The truck up ahead has just swerved; there is no denying or escaping this. "What the fuck?"

Paul says under his breath. He considers pulling off the road, but where? This two-lane highway hugs the coast on one side, and a steep embankment frames the other. No. This is just one of those moments of paranoia you have to breathe through, push through, that's all. When the two vehicles pass each other safely, then Paul will take a big fat toke of that joint to celebrate.

The Beatles come on the radio. Yes!

"Molly is the singer in a band."

Liam turns up the volume and he and Kate start to sing. The truck's about forty seconds away from them now.

"Ob-la-di, ob-la-da, life goes on, la la la la la la . . ." Kate sings, eyes closed, as she taps her feet against the window, whose glass, in just seconds, will come flying at her like a million little knives.

"I love music so much," says Liam, whose eyes are still closed.

"Oh no!" Paul yells as the front of the truck comes closer and closer toward them.

At first, there are so many sounds: their car horn, long and beseeching, yet resigned to its futility; tires screaming as they fight to keep hold of the asphalt; metal biting metal, three people gasping in surprise. Then a heavy thump and new sounds: mirrors and door handles detaching from the metal that held them as the car, on its side, skids on the road before righting itself again with another hard bam as deflated tires slam back down onto the middle of the road. Now quieter sounds: a lung collapsing, a vertebra snapping, a wrist detaching, a heart stopping.

The dashboard has been shoved up into Liam's chest, making him look like a baby who fell asleep at a table he's not quite tall enough for. Paul's pinned behind the steering wheel, his broken wrist hanging out the window, a limpness he would have detested in life, so many years spent using those hands and fists to beat away bullies. The big-girl sunglasses have mercifully flown into the backseat. Kate's head lies on the broken window frame, as if she'd decided to take a nap. But bits of her hair and drops of her blood prove that before coming to rest here, that same head hit the frame not just once but twice.

The truck, a Mercedes 814 hauling dairy products, lies some sixty feet down the hill, on its side, so that the bright yellow-and-orange sign advertising yogurt in new tropical flavors resembles a billboard on the grass, itself dotted with tiny yellow mustard plants. The driver, who has died of a heart attack, lies about twenty feet from his truck, in a repose that suggests a man napping after a very festive night, except for the hands bloodied by grabbing the rearview mirror, on which hung a photo of his wife and kids.

Not much sound now, apart from glass falling onto the road, Kate and Paul moaning a little—Paul less than Kate—and the trickle of gas and water falling onto the pavement. . . . The Beatles song still plays, not from the Peugeot, but from the truck, whose driver had been listening to the same station.

About ten minutes after the accident, a VW Vanagon stops. In it are Danish tourists. Kate's relieved to feel her body leaving the mangled car and its smells. Time becomes impossible to gauge. All she knows is that someone dragged her out of the car; now someone else is putting a garment under her head. Despite everything that has happened, Kate can feel the softness of this thing, probably a sweater, at the nape of her neck. Doesn't make sense, in this heat, but it does feel like a sweater. A woman's face appears above her—the garment's owner?

Soon, another car pulls over. Two women and one man huddle around Kate, asking in different languages if she's all right, some conjugating verbs in totally unique ways: "*Usted y yo aquí bien,*" says a woman, who, apparently, thinks Kate is Spanish "You and I are here well."

Kate does speak Spanish, once spent a year living in Spain. If she weren't lying in the middle of a road all broken like this, she would probably quip, "You here well, but I here *not* so well."

Is her dress covering her still? She tries to find the hem of the white cotton but can only feel the top of her leg. Before leaving the beach, she took off the wet bikini and tossed it into the trunk. Is her "secret," as her mother used to call it, displayed for the world to see? And where are Paul and Liam?

"Pauly," she tries to call out. "Pauly, where are you?" It's not very loud, her voice, doesn't carry as much as she would like it to, and when the woman leans down and pats Kate's cheek with that look of tremendous kindness and pity, it occurs to her that not surviving is a possibility—for the boys and for her. She should have told someone.

Kate's grabbed hold by a sense of fear and dread she hasn't felt in nearly ten years. Suddenly terrified of being by herself and of losing this little promise she's carrying, she starts crying.

The lady whose sweater lies under her head tries to comfort Kate. "Shhh, shhh," she whispers, leaning down.

"Listen," Kate says to the lady. Her voice is so weak. "Baby," Kate says, but the woman doesn't understand. "*Bebé, bebé,*" she says, but her voice fails her again. Kate stops and concentrates, says it as loudly as she can: "Baby."

The woman's face registers a look of connection, finally, but that's followed soon after by panic. "Baby?" the woman asks. "In the car?"

Kate feels an intense drain of energy. The panic starts to dissipate, but so does everything else. Is she passing out? She tries hard to focus on the voice and looks up at the woman, who's sitting there in a yellow blouse. Even the pain begins to diminish. She is passing out.

"*¿Bebé?*" the woman asks again, and points to the car.

"No," Kate says, but too late, the woman's misunderstood and yells something to the other rescuers. Two men rush to the Peugeot and look inside but see nothing. They then run to the hillside and climb down, furiously scanning the landscape for fallen babies. One of the men calls to the other that he doesn't see a child.

Kate hears sirens now and feels grateful. If an ambulance is coming, that means they're going to the hospital, and if they're going to the hospital, then they will be all right.

"Pregnant. Me, mine," Kate whispers, but this is barely audible.

The woman smiles down at her. "Yes, yes, you are a mother. I understand. You will go home to your baby," the woman says. "I am a mother, too," she adds, and cradles Kate as if she is the child in question.

Closer and closer comes the ambulance, with its European siren, which sounds like the first strains of "Somewhere Over the Rainbow," with its "na na na na."

"Na na na na," Kate whispers as she lets herself fall asleep.

"Shhhhh," the woman whispers back.

CHAPTER 2

On the Hill, San Francisco
May 1994

Kate and Louis live in the Castro, on Diamond, just below the Twin Peaks, the two hills over which the fog rolls every afternoon, blanketing the stately pastel-colored houses with its wet embrace before spreading out over the rest of the city.

Theirs is the top-floor apartment in a two-story Victorian painted light blue and white, with yellow doors and trim. Sometimes, when Kate drives up, parks, and looks up, she likes to imagine she's standing next to a huge senior citizen waiting for the early-bird buffet. But, mostly, she appreciates the cheerful colors.

Louis has come home relatively late, about ten, because he went directly from his office in SoMa to a Thai place near the Haight, where he met his friend Dave for dinner. He sees the blinking light on the answering machine but disregards it. God, the house is cold. Kate keeps the place so hot, their gas bill is twice that of any normal household. He's always acted as if having blazing heat represents his accommodation to her desire to wear T-shirts and karate pants year-round, but tonight he realizes how much he now enjoys a warm house.

He'll get the heater going after he feeds Madonna Ciccone, their cat. Keeping his coat on, Louis goes to a kitchen drawer, finds a can of food, opens it, puts on a kettle to heat the water, then, a few seconds later, pours water into the bowl.

"How'd you get so damned spoiled?" he says to the cat, who blinks away the insult, waiting patiently for her warm dinner.

They thought about changing her name to Madonna Ciccone Ritchie, or Mads, or Lady Madonna, after the Material Girl moved to England, but then decided against it. "You represent the single 1980s incarnation of the Material Girl, don't you?" Kate will still say, petting the blue-eyed Siamese, who meows so much that Kate is convinced she has a higher IQ than most humans. "You represent those crazy eighties, don't you? Remember how much coke you used to do?" she likes to ask the cat. "God, you were such a slut for the stuff."

Madonna Ciccone, knowing her role in this little act, always meows like crazy at this point, as if waxing nostalgic about her days at Studio 54, and Kate eggs her on to keep spilling those disco memories. Louis always used to laugh and assert that, no, Madonna Ciccone did not understand the question, but was simply responding to oral cues, like any Siamese would.

"Your voice goes up when you say 'Remember how much coke you used to do?'" Louis argued. "She picks up on that. She does not recognize the sentence itself, just the fact that it's a question."

"Why is it so hard for you to accept Madonna's linguistic skills?"

One day, they did an experiment. Louis asked the cat the same things Kate asked, but in a monotone and using passive verbs. "Would you agree that, in the . . . 1980s, you were . . . uh, what some cats would describe as a 'cokehead'? Would you also agree with the statement, quote, 'She was such a slut for the stuff,' end quote?"

To their amazement, that damned cat yowled and meowed so loudly, they both started laughing, and Madonna got scared and had to be put on the floor, in order to run away from these crazy, loud humans. That was it. Kate had been forever proved right and Louis wrong. This particular cat definitely understands English.

Louis throws away the food tin, washes his hands, and goes back to the hallway, where he presses the tip of his forefinger to the MESSAGES button as he looks through the mail. He hears "Calling from hospital in Ibiza. Very important to talk to you about Kate

Harrington. Please telephone nine seven one two-two two oh seven four."

Louis stands there looking at an envelope, pretending that did not just happen. He starts to feel flushed and a little nauseated, the way you do when something bad you've eaten begins to rumble inside you. He wants to call, to find out, but also to lash out right now. "Oh fuck," Louis says. "Fucking hell!" he yells, and pounds his fist on the bureau, which sends his keys crashing to the floor and topples a vase. The cat runs in from the kitchen and sits there staring at him. He knows he should pick up the phone and find out how she is, but right now he's too upset, knowing something has happened to her.

"Fuck! Fuck! Fuck! Fuck!" he keeps yelling, although he knows it scares Madonna Ciccone, and he doesn't want to do that.

CHAPTER 3
Encino, California
1982

Louis first meets Kate freshman year of high school, when they are both fourteen. He's a lonely kid whose only connection to anyone at all is through skateboarding, but even then, there's not much in common with the five other skater kids he knows, except that everyone else at the school thinks they're a bunch of weirdos. He spends a lot of time on his own, lying on the warm concrete of his parents' back patio, wondering when life will start.

One day, in pre-algebra, he decides to sit behind this girl who's tall enough to shield him from the teacher's gaze. He doesn't mind being called on and usually knows the answer, but it makes it far worse with the school jerks if you appear eager to collaborate with the authorities in this system of oppression called school.

His plan doesn't work too well, because Kate keeps turning around and saying things every few minutes—slightly rude but funny things. She's pretty, he notices, but nothing like the other people in class. She looks like someone who already graduated but came back for a visit—with makeup on her eyelashes and big green eyes. All the girls he knows have soft little eyes. She has kind of a big mouth, too, and doesn't wear pink on it like the other girls. She wears 501 jeans that are baggy, but with a tight T-shirt, which makes her boobs look like round cups big as knee pads. And she talks—a lot.

When the teacher gives them twenty equations to work on and excuses himself to go get coffee, she really lets loose.

"See that guy over there," she whispers, pointing to a football player with longish brown hair who's wearing his red jersey over a white T-shirt. "He has the longest tongue in this school. A girl I know French-kissed him, and she said it felt like one of those cow tongues they sell in stores. You know what I mean? Mexican people eat cow tongue. It's a delicacy."

"Yeah, I know," Louis whispers.

"But Josh, that's his name, he wears Old Spice, which I like. Do you wear a cologne?"

"No," Louis whispers back.

"My real dad wore Old Spice. It's an old-man smell, but I like it."

Louis feels uncomfortable. He's only halfway through the problems, and now the teacher is back, reading a *Newsweek* magazine and enjoying fresh coffee in the small cardboard cup with playing cards printed on the front.

"No scent. I kind of like it when a guy our age wears cologne. Doesn't your dad wear anything?"

"Brut."

"Gross. Let's go to the mall and get you something. And me, too. I like men's cologne."

It's only a matter of time before the teacher asks what is so important that it must be discussed in the middle of class. Kate apologizes so profusely and politely, the teacher calms down.

"They love it when you kiss up really good, using a big Mexican cow tongue on them," she whispers, which makes Louis snort, once again getting the teacher's unwelcome attention.

"You can't get caught if you wanna hang out with me," she says a minute or so later.

Her words jolt him: ". . . If you wanna hang out with me." Yes! I do, and I will learn how not to get caught.

And so their first outing, weirdly, improbably, is to the mall to buy cologne. She buys him Paco Rabanne, and Karl Lagerfeld for herself. They eat pretzels covered in hot mustard, pee in the wrong bathrooms, with Kate claiming she stood at a urinal and watched a man pee as she pretended to be holding her penis, which the man never even looked at.

"People believe what you want them to," she says as they smoke on the top floor of the mall's parking lot. "So what are you anyway—gay, straight, what?"

No one has ever thought to ask Louis that question.

"Straight," he says.

"But you're a virgin, right?"

Oh no, now this girl is going to make him talk about IT, the only thing anyone thinks about. He's tried so hard to put it out of his mind. Not easy when you're watching twenty cheerleaders stream into the gym at a Friday pep rally or in the morning, when your body wakes up before you do. But being with a girl, just to kiss, let alone sex, seems as likely as hopping a ride to Mars, so he's worked hard to push all such thoughts far away.

"Virgin on the ridiculous," he says, which he heard on some English show.

"I'll take that as a yes," she says.

Louis takes a huge drag and pushes the smoke through his nostrils hard. "Would a virgin be able to do that?" he asks. And they both laugh. "No, right?"

She's still laughing, so he does it again.

"Well, maybe I can help you with that problem," she says.

"Cool. Right now?" he says, and smiles at her lasciviously.

She punches his arm. "Not with me," she says. "Do you have normal genitalia?"

"Oh Jesus!" he yells. What a question.

"I'll take that as a no," she says.

"No. It's a yes. I have normal genitalia, yes. Why?"

"Just checking. There are people who have both sex organs, you know. I saw it in my mother's sex book."

"Your mother has a sex book?"

"Yeah. Don't worry, I'm not gonna ask to see your genitalia," she says, and uses her old cigarette to light a new one. Louis had never met a chain-smoker, never mind a fourteen-year-old chain-smoker.

"Have you had sex?" he asks.

"Don't worry. We'll find you a girl," she says, and pats his leg.

"I'll take that as a no," he says, but she doesn't answer.

That school year and the next and the next are all made so much better by Kate's presence. She challenges him at every turn to do everything from taking a hit of LSD to earning an A+ in at least two classes.

"As middle-class people with above-average but not extraordinary looks, good grades will be our only ticket out of Encino," she often tells him. She says it's a historical fact that middle-class people with high intelligence levels and ambition do well in life, but middle-class lazy people do not.

"Where do you get this crap?" he'll ask, and she will say something like "My middle-class brain tells me so."

If the school years are more interesting, then, well, summers become absolutely glorious, thanks to her. They live only a mile apart, although a few years ago, she would have been living miles away, in Malibu, and they probably never would have even met.

Kate's father had owned a seafood restaurant he'd inherited from his dad. He was a surfer and her mother, Georgina, had such a crush on him, she began working as a waitress just to be near him, although she had a degree in accounting. Eventually, she told him the truth.

"You want to do the books instead of delivering food?" he asked.

"You want to marry me instead of paying me?" she replied. They got married and she gladly left the kitchen to do the books and then have Kate.

They were a happy family. But her dad drowned six years after Kate had come into the world, and what a different life it became. Her mom lost the restaurant and struggled, and they started fighting so much, it became hard to say yes when asked, "Do you like your mom?"

Then, Kate's mom married Don Williams, who drove a new car ("Never drive something more than a year old," he liked to say) and had just bought a big beige-colored three-bedroom house that reeked of new carpet, had skylights in every bathroom, and even a big pool out back. When he moved them in, Georgina thought the appliances were light blue, had no idea that's what a new dishwasher door came covered in.

"You stupid woman," Don had said, and laughed as he pulled away the blue plastic. To Kate, who was nine years old, it looked like that trick of putting glue all over your hand and letting it dry, then slowly pulling it all off, in the biggest pieces possible.

"Wanna try?" Don had asked.

"Sure."

This was to have been her third-grade year, and she felt lonely away from kids at her old school and the friends from the restaurant, including all the stray cats they fed—eight of them, all pretty much called *gordo,* or "fat guy," by the cooks and busboys.

"Who will take care of the *gordos*?" she'd asked her mom.

"Nando and Hernán will feed them."

"But what if they go somewhere or forget?"

"Well then, God will take care of them."

"But he didn't before. They were skinny before Dad and I fed them, remember? So why would he now?"

"He didn't know about them before, but you showed him. Now he knows."

Not much of an answer, but she didn't know what else to do. No stray cats in this new neighborhood, or kids, either. From nine to fourteen, she spent a lot of time alone in her room, or sometimes not, which was worse. Then Louis moved in and sat behind her in math class.

Her house is less than a mile away from Louis's, but the streets couldn't be more different. On her street, every shrub is young. Some still wear the plastic green tag from the nursery with its name on it, like a newborn just home from the hospital. On his street, the trees have grown tall, and in the crooks of their branches, way up high, you find time capsules made of spiderwebs, hardened leaves, bird feathers, torn notes from lovers who've long forgotten one another. Her driveway and the sidewalks around it are flat and smooth, easy to roll on with a skateboard, and his are scarred by cuts made by fallen bats and tools, excavations to fix broken pipes, and a thousand proclamations that MK LOVES JB.

They hang out mostly at Kate's, not because of its newness, but because of the pool.

Louis is up by nine, makes his bed, eats a bowl of cereal, then tidies the house just nice enough that when his mother and father get home, they'll think, What a good kid we raised. Then he pulls on his surfer shorts and a clean T-shirt and heads to Kate's with a backpack on his shoulder, in which he carries his bathing suit, a book or two, and the music mixes he stayed up late making. They love English bands like The Cure, The Police, and Eurythmics. Even if Tim Donnelly at school did call it "fag rock," they still love it.

They spend most of the morning in Kate's room, reading and talking, wandering out at noon, yawning, hair mussed, to make B and C sandwiches, which she prepares by microwaving refried beans (the B), then spreading this thick fragrant paste onto toast, which she then tops with slices of Monterey Jack (the C) and bakes in the oven for exactly eight minutes. Not seven, not nine—eight. While she does this, he makes coffee for them, which makes them feel impossibly grown-up. Bean and cheese sandwiches, plus a mug of coffee. Nothing could be better.

By one o'clock, the "June gloom," as everyone calls the morning fog, has burned off and the sun's hot and toothy, feels like it's biting straight through the inflatables on which they are lying in the middle of the pool. They read and talk and laugh—Kate sprawled on the blue floaty and Louis on the pink, because she hates what she calls "gender specificity."

They talk, then doze, then talk some more, staring up at the palm trees on either side of the house, making plans for the future and college. He's surprised when she brings up the idea of law school.

"Law school?" he asks.

"Yeah," she says. "As a lawyer, you can have money, if you want it, or help people, if you want that. It's good to have options, trust me."

"We should live in Europe, too, though," he says.

"With your long hippie hair, you'll fit right in."

She loves to tease him about his decision to grow his hair a bit longer than most people their age do. Everybody needs a way to stand out and be different, and he decided a year ago that longer hair would be his way. She sort of likes his hair, but that doesn't mean she can't tease him, sing Creedence Clearwater songs to him, or ask him which European soccer team he plays on. He, in turn, makes fun of the eighties bands she likes, and the singers' short, fluffy little haircuts.

"Real men don't have feathers," he says.

"Real men don't get called 'ma'am' at the Vons."

How he wishes he'd never told her that story.

This is usually when he gives her a nice big shove right into the water, which is, admittedly, mean, because when you've been lying in the sun, sudden immersion, even in Encino pool water, is a shock. She, of course, immediately grabs his leg and separates him from his inflatable. They wrestle underwater, but he barely fights back, because Kate mad is a strong and frightening thing.

Then they climb back onto their inflatables and wait for the sun to dry them again. Louis sometimes puts on sunglasses and surreptitiously watches her skin, all bumpy from the cold, the nipples under the bikini erect. He loves watching her skin go flat and smooth again as the bathing suit dries and the heat feels hotter and hotter.

Lying on his stomach, nose pressed to the plastic, which smells like a balloon or a new four-square ball, plus sunscreen, he can feel his erection stirring. He shakes his head and sighs.

She slaps his arm. "What?"

"Nothing." He smiles at her. "Everything."

If you asked him why he hasn't kissed her, why he hasn't at least tried to make love to her, he wouldn't know what to tell you. He thinks about it every day, pretty much all day, so much that it's become part of everything, not even a separate thought or desire, but thoroughly entwined into every waking and even sleeping hour. Maybe, he sometimes thinks, it's not real anymore, or maybe it's so real that its failure—or, rather, his failure to keep her after the kiss, after sex—would kill everything the world now means to him. Loss of Kate and loss of life would literally be indistinguishable. So he daren't.

Four summers now, he's watched Kate's arms get so brown in the sun, the hair on them turns gold. Kate says her real father was Italian or maybe American Indian.

"Everybody wants to say they're part American Indian. Have you noticed that? 'I'm one-eighth,' they say. Kind of strange. Like do they have a blood test or something?" she often says. "Only I think I really am. Or maybe just Italian," she says. "But I would never say it because of all these other idiots saying it."

Kate's real father, the partial American Indian or Italian, had a goofy smile. Louis knows from the photos he's seen of him with Kate at a swim meet. She's in a bathing suit, holding a trophy in her right hand; her left hand, still pudgy like a kid's, sits on his shoulder. He's on one knee next to her, an arm around her waist, just beaming into the camera. He started her swimming when she was only four, and she was good. She gave it up years ago, but the trophies sit on top of her bookcase. Sometimes Louis catches her smiling up at them.

They turn over on their backs and he puts one hand on her leg, that glorious leg, and uses the other like a paddle to get them both moving together over to the diving board. She puts her hand on his and he tries to send a thought to her telepathically: The rest of my life, I'd like to go wherever you go. Wherever you are, that's where I want to be. Over and over, he thinks this as he stares up at the white-and-blue fiberglass. Will she feel something here, under the diving board, and know it's a message from him?

In the last months of high school, Louis begins laying the groundwork for what he hopes will be the day he states the obvious: I love you, Kate.

He wants to live with Kate at college as boyfriend and girl-friend, not just friends. And it will take something dramatic, like college, to do that, break the friend connection and make it new. They've both applied to Berkeley and plan to live together off campus, in an apartment with a balcony. Kate is set on having a balcony.

"Why?" he asks.

"I don't know," she says, but then she explains that she's always imagined herself on a balcony, one leg tucked between the rails, smoking and watching birds sail by, preferably seagulls.

"I don't know how many balconies there'll be in Berkeley, or seagulls, for that matter," he tells her.

"No, you don't," she says. "So just share my fantasy, will you please? Why do we always have to live in the real world?"

Kate's letter from the office of admissions comes first, and it's good news: She's been accepted. He rushes home to check the mail, but there's nothing for him. The next three days are excruciating. Finally, it's there, a letter with the pale blue rendering of the University of California's insignia. It's heavy, like hers, so there must be paperwork in it, information on financial aid—all the things her envelope held.

But it's not the same, because his starts with the words "We regret to inform you . . ." He's not been accepted to Berkeley, it says, although he is guaranteed a place at any of the other, less competitive UC schools. *Less competitive*—the words feel like a knife inside his belly.

That night, Louis steals a bottle from his dad's bar and drinks it in the darkness of their backyard, his spine hard up against the brick wall, his mother's stupid ferns hiding him in case anyone comes looking. Everything will change now. Kate will make a new life without him, with some man at college. No more boys. Someone real will come into her life now and replace the man Louis aches to become.

How the fuck is he ever going to find the courage to let her know what he really wants? Louis drinks more of the scotch, fighting the urge to gag. He lights a cigarette, smokes it fast, wanting the head rush to give him some new feeling, some sense that he's changed, become someone who can say those words.

"I didn't get in to Berkeley," he tells her the next day as they sit by the pool, shoulder touching shoulder, about to go in. He feels his tongue stick to the roof of his mouth, so nervous about saying the words. "I don't know . . . I don't know what happened. We have the same GPA, right? Your essay must have been better."

"I told you to say you were a black orphan," Kate says, but she doesn't even bother to smile at her own joke; instead, she runs her hand along his forearm, lays her foot, under the water, atop his.

"Honestly," he says, "I don't know what to think now, how to plan for the future if we're not together."

"I don't, either," she says, and they sit there staring at their reflections, at faces wiped blank by disappointment. Finally, after a few minutes, she says something. "We'll have to pretend it's the army or something, that you got sent to war. Maybe after a year, you can transfer to Berkeley. Or I can come back here," she says.

He turns and stares at her chin, which has the loveliest dimple in it. It's the last trace of childhood on a face that is almost always beautiful now, has gotten prettier every day since they met.

"You looked like a girl when I met you. But you don't anymore."

"You looked like a hippie when I met you," she says, and pulls on the end of his hair, "and you still do."

"What if I moved to Berkeley and got a job. I could be your

boyfriend for a year and sort of . . . support you or whatever. Keep trying to get into the school."

He can't believe he has actually said the word *boyfriend*. He can hardly breathe now, feels as if the chlorine might burn a hole in his brain.

"You have to start school now; otherwise, you might never do it. Remember that girl Nicky who was going to start a year late so she could get into a better school? She ended up getting a job at Ralph's or something and a car with a payment. She never went to school."

"I won't get a job at Ralph's," he says. "I don't want to be separated."

She's smiling at him and her shoulder sits firmly against his, lodged almost, as if it wants to stay there for years. What if he were to kiss her now? This could be the precise moment to transform themselves by kissing. But then again, this is the saddest day they've ever shared. Is this really the moment to express the love and desire he feels, both of which have become so intense and constant as to have become, in essence, the very definition of him?

As he watches her, weighing what could be gained and what could be lost, she climbs aboard her blue inflatable and pushes into the center of the pool. He could protest, or charm her back. He could maybe swim out to her and say "I love you."

"Come on, my Louis," she says, and pushes the other inflatable toward him.

All he can do now is spend as much time as possible with her and be as present as possible, enjoy every moment, which is why as the weeks go by, he begins to see what's been in front of his eyes this whole time. Louis is not the only man trying to savor the last days around Kate.

Her stepfather, Don, comes home at five every day, not six or seven like he used to. And everything changes. Right away, Kate goes inside and comes back with clothes on over her bathing suit. She gets quieter, mellower, even seems kind of angry. Louis will try to pull her out of that darkness and back to the joy of their "little blue lake," as they used to call the pool, but it's impossible. She will look at Louis with this sweetness and even smile, as if to say, Nice try, but there's no way she can be happy and free after Don's come home.

Don's always cast himself as the savior, and he loves recalling how Kate's father died without leaving anything: "Nothing in the bank, no insurance, nothing. Hell of a guy, huh? Guess he was hoping a wave would carry them into the future."

Thank God for Don—that's the central theme of most conversations—coming along as he did to save the widow and her nine-year-old daughter, the skinny tanned girl with poor posture, shoulders so far forward, you'd only rarely see her little breasts. Big eyes, though, and full lips already. These traits were maybe not obvious to the outside world, but they were certainly visible if you were the person who volunteered to take her to swim practice.

So many of those days, Don had stayed and watched from the car, where he could follow Kate—easy to keep an eye on, always a little taller than the others—watch her goofing around, all confident and playful among her teammates. It was hard to ignore what he saw. A desire stronger than him sometimes got the better of Don right there in the car.

At home, it became harder and harder to walk by if he happened to notice Kate had fallen asleep on the couch or on a lawn chair while her mother was inside or busy. Yes, she was still, technically, a kid, but you could look at her and know what she'd almost become. And she was so very lonely. Heartbreaking. When he got her the dog, she hugged him, actually hugged him. He held on and tried to show her how nice it could be. Maybe a little too soon, because she pulled away. But it was clear how much he cared, because he'd gotten her that dog she loved so much. And now the two of them, or actually all three of them, were intertwined. So much more came to pass after that, so much that was beautiful and incredible and painful, too, of course, for them both.

And now, she's leaving. A month from now, she'll be driving to Berkeley in that awful beat-up Honda. He's offered to buy her a car, but she won't take it, is even disgusted by the offer, looks at him as if he is the most pathetic creature in the universe.

Don doesn't want to hide how he feels. And he doesn't. Everyone can see what he wants, including Louis. One Saturday, when Louis and Kate get out of the pool, Don tells his wife to free up the lawn chair she's sitting on and come share his chair. Then he motions Kate and Louis over to the now-empty seat.

"Louis, you excited about college?" he asks.

"Yes, sir," Louis replies.

"Too bad about Berkeley," Don says.

"Yeah, thanks," Louis says, and looks back at him. Is that a slight smile on Don's face?

Kate's mom murmurs, "Never mind that," and asks what he'll be studying. As he answers, Louis watches Don staring at Kate. Unabashedly, openly desirous, all the while his arm draped around the shoulder of the very same wife, talking about how much she wishes she'd gone to a four-year college instead of a two-year one. What a difference it would have made in her life.

"You really think it would have, babe?" Don asks, looking directly at Kate.

"Yeah, I would have never met you," she says, laughs derisively, and takes a sip from her tumbler.

This is one of the strangest moments of Louis's life. On one level, he feels like Don's mirror image, sitting across from him, an arm draped around Kate exactly like Don's arm sits on Georgina's shoulders. And it feels good: Kate's wet hair against his chest, the top of her ear brushing his jaw. This is the first time he's acted like a boyfriend, and she's fine with it, has even tucked herself into him. This feels amazing and, at the same time, sickening. He can't help think this is exactly what Don wants to feel or maybe is feeling right now, through him.

"You'll visit often," Don says. "Or we'll visit you."

"Is that a threat?" Kate says.

Don laughs too loudly as Georgina jiggles her glass and stares into it disappointedly—all ice, no gin.

Louis hates knowing they'll be apart, but right now, in this moment, he feels some relief, too. Yes, by leaving Encino, she leaves Louis, but by leaving Encino, she also leaves Don.

CHAPTER 4
San Francisco
May 1994

Louis goes to the kitchen for a glass of water and to talk himself into calming down. He doesn't need to panic. Could be nothing, could be she has a concussion, a broken foot—small things. Why assume it's bad? He goes back to the hall and dials the number in Spain. But whoever has answered, a nurse maybe, doesn't speak English. He knows a little of the language, mostly from talking with the guys who work in the kitchen of the restaurant below his office—nothing you could or should use with a nurse in Spain.

He says Kate's name and the woman says "*Sí*." Then Louis asks "*¿Bien?*" and the woman starts speaking in these long and fast sentences. Louis interrupts her and asks, "Is she awake . . . uh *hablar?*" Again, the poor nurse goes into a long jag, and Louis just wants to throw the phone. What is she saying—that Kate is awake, or not? Can she talk? It's useless.

Louis apologizes to her in English and says, "I will call you back. Sorry, *perdón*." The nurse clearly has not understood, because she again starts speaking quickly. Louis just says "Bye," which, finally, the nurse understands. She sighs and responds with her own "Bye-bye."

He needs to find someone who can help him figure out what's going on.

When her phone rings, Angela is lying on the couch, watching the news. She wears a pair of thin maroon sweats with flared bottoms. They're so cheaply made, they shrank the first time she washed them, but she loves them because the cut makes her hips and waist look skinny, even if her ankles are hanging out. She wears a gray cotton sweater over a white T-shirt, and her hair, damp from the shower she took at the gym, is up, held loosely by a tortoiseshell banana clip.

"The Santa Anas are coming!" the weatherman says, and promises to tell the audience more when he returns.

She hears the phone ring but ignores it, too tired to talk with her mom, who, more and more, requires a level of cheerfulness that is hard to conjure after a long day of work. But when she looks at the phone and sees the 415 prefix, the feeling changes altogether. Could it be Kate?

She listens to the voice mail and hears a man's voice. "This is Louis, Kate's Louis. I . . . uh . . . needed to talk to you about Kate, but I'm not sure if this is the right number. If it is—"

She hits redial and gets off the couch, goes to the balcony door. Louis says he and Kate live in San Francisco. Did she know that? Does she remember him?

"Of course I remember you," she says. "How are you? What's going on?"

Louis explains what he knows: Kate had gone on a trip, first to Brazil, and then to Spain, for fun, with two friends—Paul, from San Francisco, and his boyfriend, Liam, who's English. Louis doesn't know about the medical condition of the guys, but someone called to say Kate is in the hospital.

"I don't really understand what's going on. The nurse kept talking and talking. Since you speak Spanish and since it's Kate, I thought maybe you could call over there."

"Yes, sure, I can do that," Angela says. She feels as if she can't catch her breath, so she goes to her favorite spot on the balcony, where, if you lean over the edge, you can see the Hollywood sign in the distance.

Louis tells her that Kate has just finished her thesis and has a teaching job at San Francisco State. Things are going so well, he says.

Angela can barely listen, just stares down at the apartment in the next building, where the insomniac lives with a teenage daughter. Angela hasn't seen Kate in so long, and the last time was far from ideal.

She goes back inside, to the kitchen, where a thick glass filled with pens sits next to a pad decorated with the smiling faces of the local Realtor, who wants badly to sell her apartment. He courts her with penlights, sewing kits, and other Realtor flotsam. She turns on the microwave light and asks Louis to repeat the number, then jots it down. Then she stands, mute, leaning on the new counters, whose hard and clean stone edges would have given her a small but certain sense of accomplishment only ten minutes ago but now barely manage the job of making her feel supported. In that modest little patch of yellowish light, as if painted by Caravaggio of the sad new century, she listens to Louis talk about Kate and how happy she is now, how much stronger and happier than ever.

"I'll find out what's going on and then call you back," she says.

"That would be great," Louis replies. "You're great. Thank you."

Angela decides to boil water for tea. She fills the plastic kettle that plugs into an outlet, pushes down its lid, a little off after one particularly hard dishwasher ride, then stands there staring, arms crossed. She reaches down and opens a cabinet, behind which sit her phone books. What's the time difference? How can she not know? Then again, why would she? It was her parents and family doing the calling when she lived in Spain, not her. And that was years ago.

Nine hours ahead. So it'll be about 8:30 in the morning. Angela stares at the kettle, which is emitting the first bubbling sound of its contents beginning to boil, then around her apartment, trying to come back to the way things were just five minutes ago. Forget tea; she wants wine. She was trying not to drink tonight, but everything has changed now. She pours a glass of cabernet, then goes back to the couch with the phone, ready.

Angela dials and waits for the foreign-sounding tone. The phone in that hospital or clinic rings and rings, but no one picks up. Angela hangs up and tries again. Still nothing. The weatherman was right about the wind. Already, Angela can hear the fish-shaped chimes clanging softly against one another outside her French doors. She looks at the plate of glass-noodle salad she just ate, empty except for a pile of lemongrass sitting there like so many tiny, discarded wind instruments, and she wonders what to do.

She redials, and again it rings and rings. Nothing. Then she pets the suede couch, looks at the *Elle Decor* on the coffee table, *The Economist* next to it—signs, symbols that say, This is your home, your hard-earned couch, your magazines. Still you, still your life.

Kate. Isn't it something, the way a person's name and the feelings they stir inside you can pull you emotionally out of whatever situation you were in and thrust you into a totally different and unknown place?

CHAPTER 5
In Madrid with *Las Meninas*
1989

Walking down Calle de la Princesa, Angela keeps her head down, nuzzles the purple wool scarf her mother knit for her, which Angela has wrapped around her mouth and nose. She's trying to stay upbeat and positive, but it's hard because the scarf smells of Cartier, the perfume her mother wears, and this makes Angela miss her even more. Maybe the smell rubbed off when she tried on the scarf, checking the length, or trying to see the garment the way her daughter would in a week's time. Or, knowing her mother, such a romantic, she probably took one of the little bottles she buys for five dollars at the Swap Meet and actually pressed its tiny round mouth to each end of the scarf. But it's backfired. A gesture probably meant to say Remember that you are loved only gives a sweet olfactory definition to this unbearable sadness Angela feels.

Stop walking and find a way to change the subject. Go look in the window of the bakery, at the square cakes dressed in children's colors of pink and green frosting—petit-fours—and the shiny caramelized peaches and strawberries on the tarts, glowing in the warm track lighting. Watch the old lady inside, who's picking out treats and wearing so much Pan-Cake makeup that she herself looks like a powdered doughnut. Close your eyes and breathe deep. Take in the smell of butter and sugar that have permeated the door, the windowsills, maybe even the welcome mat. Everything will be fine.

She'll meet Kate at Café Sur in a few minutes and talk it through. Everything will be fine.

Angela turns and heads toward Plaza España, forcing her eyes up to the sycamores. They're beautiful, their thick bodies covered in a patchwork of brown, cream, and gray, soft as suede. Three months ago, when she first arrived in Madrid, these trees provided a cooling canopy over the city's steaming streets. Now, the giants have nearly gone bald, barely holding on to a handful of brown leaves at the very top.

How could I be so stupid? Angela wonders. What will Kate say about sleeping with a married man she met in the Metro? He'd been so bold, standing there on the crowded train in his caramel-colored coat over a white shirt and dark tie, his dark hair curvy and shiny, a big smile on his face as he shamelessly stared at her, swaying in her direction at every stop. But he was handsome, and so brazenly interested that it made her chuckle.

"Latin men," she said aloud in English.

He shrugged, smiled, and said in English, "Will you join me for dinner? Or is there someone else? Another *Latin man?*"

Emilio, that's his name, took Angela to a *cava,* a small bar where they specialize in wine and tapas and where the rooms are decorated with pillows and lit with candles. He ordered enough food for a family of four and eventually asked to take her to a hotel with balconies that looked out on a lovely little plaza.

"It's beautiful, because of the yellow streetlights," he said. Then, in perfect English, he added, "The phosphorous light."

An hour later, on a bed bathed in phosphorous light, as promised, she sat next to him, cross-legged, gliding her hand slowly over his leg, stomach, chest. She once saw a program on the Everglades that showed a boat zooming above the mangroves. That is how her hand felt, partially submerged in all that hair, moving toward his chin.

"Yankee, behave," he growled, wanting to sleep.

What is it that people find so amazing about this—making love? It had been fine but not that crazy, magical thing other people seem to feel. Or was it him she didn't find amazing? Or is there something wrong with her that she finds no one amazing?

And now, here she is, on a Saturday six weeks later, walking along Princesa, heading to meet Kate, who will hopefully help her with this dilemma—what to do about the little piece of married Emilio possibly growing in her womb.

As soon as Angela opens the door at Sur, she's embraced by the smell of fried potatoes and onions—the *tortilla de patatas* perpetually cooking in the kitchen of any Spanish café.

Normally, the television loudly telecasts soccer matches from as far away as Mexico City, Manchester, Buenos Aires . . . and the regulars boisterously cheer their teams. Today, five old men in sweaters nurse drinks while watching a much more subdued repeat telecast of the Miss World pageant, from the night before.

Angela chooses a table against the wall, where she can see out the window, not have to watch the television, although you can't escape hearing all the contestants talking about how they hope to change the world.

When Kate walks in, the guys turn to watch. This is her neighborhood bar, so they know her.

"*Hola, maja,*" one calls out, and Kate waves and smiles at the group. She's as beautiful as any one of the women on TV but far less interested in winning a contest. She wears jeans, brown leather boots, and a sixties-style blue-and-green-striped jacket that's tight around her shoulders. Angela stands to greet her and Kate puts a hand on her upper arm and leans in, kisses one cheek, then the other. She smells of fresh, cold air, plus smokes, plus the lemon drops Angela suddenly remembers that Kate loves.

"Hello, stranger," Kate says, then begins struggling to get the coat off, which Jordi, the waiter, notices. He comes and helps free her, then asks if she wants a coffee.

She wears hardly any makeup, except for a little liner around those big eyes, and the thinnest layer of mauve-brown lipstick.

"I haven't seen you in ages," Kate says.

"I know, I'm sorry," Angela replies.

It seems important to acknowledge this quasi estrangement. Somehow, improbably, Kate had taken an interest in Angela those first few weeks in Spain in August, when they all lived together in the empty dorms.

Kate, the wild child, dragged her everywhere, from a dizzyingly fast motorcycle ride at four in the morning with a Spaniard Kate was dating to visits to the bathroom to smoke during art class in the Prado. But the most memorable were two Saturday nights at the giant disco, Sol, where, at 3:00 A.M., a huge bald African man wearing contact lenses that made his eyes look bright yellow, his body covered in oil and dressed only in chaps made of white feathers, would be lowered onto the center of the dance floor on a giant swing, from which he would jump, then prowl the dance floor like a cheetah in white as the Divine song "You Think You're a Man" would pound out, making the crowd wild from the joy of communal partying and also, just a little, from the fear evoked by the crazy man hunting his prey.

Angela danced and partied as never before, and she also obeyed Kate's command of "Open your mouth" and let Kate slip an ecstasy tab onto the center of her tongue.

It wasn't a bad experience—just the opposite. They danced for hours in what Angela thought of later as a warm orange-and-purple embrace of a world where everything was a revelation, from the taste of the olives and tonic waters they had for "dinner" ("Mustn't eat too much, or the high won't be as good") to the sound of Erasure and Pet Shop Boys on the sound system. Even the drag queens danced *sevillanas* at five in the morning, makeup thick as cake icing. All of it amazed her brain and made her heart fly. She felt as if she was quite literally flying over a very beautiful world, and she told this to Kate, who smiled and kissed her cheek.

"That's why they call it ecstasy," Kate said, looking at Angela's eyes. "Because it makes the world so lovely. From the inside out *and* the outside in. Right?"

"Right."

But, unfortunately, the next morning felt exactly as gray and cold as the night had been orange and hot and joyous.

"It's just postecstasy down, that's all. Can't have ying without yang. You'll be fine on Monday," Kate had told her in the cab on their way home. But Angela hated how sad and weepy she felt for days after, and she vowed never again to do something so foreign to her essential self. The more she thought about it, the more guilt she felt. A good Latina girl raised in the San Diego suburbs who'd had to earn every penny of her scholarships with hours of studying, now taking a drug that could kill her brain cells? A wild partyer? That wasn't her, not even here, in wild post-Franco Spain. She stopped going to Sol with Kate and even seeing her much at the dorms. When everyone moved to individual apartments, it became easy to distance herself even more.

"So, what happened? You dropped off the face of the earth," Kate says now, and leans forward.

How to say it? Can't lie and say exams kept her away. This isn't med school. I met a guy, fell in love? No. I went back to who I really am? I saw that your choosing me as a friend had to be a mistake, an aberration? I got scared of becoming someone who does ecstasy and stays up all night—that is, not my parents' daughter anymore, even though, allegedly, that's exactly why I came to Spain?

"I don't know," she says. "I . . . don't know."

Kate, head tilted, smiles a little, but her brow stays knit in bewilderment, as if trying to discern the real reason Angela drifted away. Finally, the coffees arrive, so she turns her attention to the sugar packets, the tiny spoon.

"So what's going on?"

"I did something stupid."

"Like?"

"I met this guy, married guy, a stupid banker, wearing a coat with big buttons. I met him in the Metro," Angela says, and taps her spoon on the saucer.

"Let me guess—you fell in love and now you're heartbroken."

"No. Not quite. I had sex with him and now . . . I think I'm pregnant."

"Oh," Kate says, and plucks a cigarette from the pack in her pocket. She doesn't have matches, so she plays with it, rolling it between her thumb and forefinger. "Are you sure?"

Angela nods yes. "I think so."

"Okay," Kate says as Jordi tosses a book of matches at her elbow on his way to deliver two coffees.

"I don't know what to do," Angela says.

"Well, I'll help you," Kate says, and smiles, but her mouth looks a tiny bit twitchy, which immediately scares Angela. What if even Kate doesn't really know what to do?

"What should I do?" she asks. "Tell me."

"Look, I don't know, but it'll be all right."

"Yeah?"

"Yeah, yeah, it's okay," Kate says. "Did it just happen?"

Angela doesn't understand the question.

"When was your last period?"

"Oh. About two months ago."

"Okay. Don't worry, then."

Suddenly, a roar of disappointment fills the bar. The girls turn from each other and look over at the guys. Miss Poland has won. A couple of the men stand, shrug on jackets, begin gathering leftover coins, putting the pipe tobacco into their jacket pockets. Kate turns back to Angela.

"Do you want to come stay with me tonight?" she asks.

Funny that it would even occur to Kate to ask. Angela lives twenty minutes away on foot, five minutes by taxi. Why would she need to stay with Kate? Because there's a dresser at Angela's on which sit photos of her mom and dad, her sister and brother—all the people in the world she loves yet feels so incredibly far from right now, more than ever before. So far away, she's scared she may never feel their love again.

"My roommate's gone to visit her family," Kate says. "We'd have the place to ourselves. Then we can get up early tomorrow and go straight to the clinic. I know of a private one near the Prado."

"That would great," Angela says.

Kate lives on Campomanes, a narrow street on a hill, one of five roads that radiate out from a small plaza in front of the Teatro Real opera house—a far more elegant neighborhood than Angela's. Kate explains that her roommate's a wealthy girl named Carla, whose parents own the building.

"You got lucky," Angela says, and tells Kate about her place, a studio with coffee-colored carpets and ugly linoleum, with nothing to boast of except two large windows in the living room and a claw-foot tub in the bathroom.

They walk up two flights to the top floor. A bright white hallway leads to Kate's room at the front of the house. It has high ceilings, a thick cream-colored carpet, and French doors that open onto a skinny balcony with a view of the building across the way, which its owners have painted dark orange, with white shutters.

"The only problem is that Carla's parents don't like to use the radiator," Kate explains as she turns on a space heater in the corner of her bedroom. "They think it's bad for the lungs or something. They have strange opinions about the human lung. But that little thing is powerful," she says of the heater.

Kate takes off her scarf and goes to throw it on the bed, then changes her mind and sends it flying onto a sofa chair instead.

"I'm going to make the bed. Had company last night," she says, and leaves the room.

Angela can't help but look at the bed for some clue about the guy. From the other room, Kate talks about Carla, who's shy and afraid of everything, starting with the human lung.

"I'm trying to bring her out of her shell," Kate says.

"You're a shell shucker."

"That's true. My Louis was in a shell until I got him out."

"Your boyfriend?" Angela asks.

"Not really, but . . . I don't know. The person I love most," she says, and throws a pile of fresh linen atop the scarf.

Kate tells Angela about this guy, Louis, she spent her high school years with. He swore he would come find her in Berkeley, and for two years he tried, but then he couldn't get accepted. Then he got a girlfriend and Kate fell in love with someone and then they both just stopped trying to find their way back.

"He's a computer genius," Kate says, and quickly pulls off last night's sheets, throws them beside the bed, and grabs the clean ones. "Help me," she says, and crawls to the far end of the bed to slide the new sheet around the elbow of the mattress. "I have my own married man, you know—James Wittinger."

"Yeah," Angela says. "I kind of heard that."

"You did? Really?" Kate leans back into the corner, waiting for a response. Has she gone pale, or is it the white wall at her shoulders? Angela feels terrible, seeing that, clearly, Kate doesn't know her affair is not very secret. James Wittinger teaches literature at the Complutense, in the Americans Abroad Department, and he's married. "Do a lot of people know, or just you?" Kate asks.

Angela hesitates for just a second too long. Also, Angela is not the kind of person to have information no one else has, and they both know this. Kate stares at the clean yellow sheet lying between them. In her moth-kissed sweater, hands on her knees, Kate looks like she might be considering explaining something—James, her reputation . . . something.

"Shit," Kate says, and lies down on the sheet, face resting on folded arms.

This is staggering. How could Kate not know? After watching her for a moment, Angela rubs Kate's back. "I'm sorry," she says.

Kate just looks at her and blinks a few times. Angela lies down the same way, face on arms, about five inches from Kate. They don't talk, just lie there listening to the occasional car head up Campomanes, the bakery door open and close, with its tiny bell, and eventually, finally, to Angela's tears falling on the bed.

Kate watches the rivulets form around the side of her nose, congregating at the ridge on her top lip for just a second, then tumbling over and onto the bed. Angela could turn away or make herself stop, but she doesn't. Eventually, Kate takes a forefinger and places it near Angela's mouth, creating a dam. The tears stop falling.

"Are you the oldest child?" Kate whispers.

Angela nods yes but can't answer because she's really crying now, finally. "I feel so close to them, my family. I love them so much and I'm always going away from them. I always leave. And now this."

"They'll take you back, little bird, they will."

"'Little bird,'" Angela repeats, and laughs a little.

"What do they call you? Your family? Do you have a nickname?"

"Ani."

"Okay, well, I bet they love their Ani just as much as you love them."

Angela nods her head and shuts her eyes, trying to think of some happy memory, but all she can think is *little bird,* which makes her imagine the baby she might be carrying, and now she cries even more. This is so embarrassing. Why is she crying like this? Why can't she stop? Fortunately, Kate doesn't seem to mind. She cups Angela's shoulder, then pulls her in so that Angela's head lies under Kate's chin, her ear flat against Kate's chest, that slow heartbeat reassuring. Angela allows herself to be pulled in this way and wraps her arms around Kate's waist. She's ashamed of how pathetic she might seem but also incredibly relieved not to pretend anymore. Kate holds her tight, the way you would a kid who's upset over the smallest thing, which you must take seriously nevertheless.

"I know, I know," she whispers into Angela's hair. "Close your eyes and you'll start to feel better." Angela does as told. Eventually, it works. This fear starts, at some point, to feel all cried out. Soon she's asleep, and so is Kate.

Three hours later, Angela wakes up, arms around Kate, who is spooned against her. She pulls back and sees a tiny mole on Kate's neck. Christ, she can't believe she fell asleep here, with Kate. Unbelievable. Angela pulls back a little more, which awakens Kate, whose head rises a little as she turns toward Angela. She looks confused, then smiles.

"Oh, hey."

"I . . . think we fell asleep," Angela says, feeling herself blush, or maybe she's just reacting to this intense heat. Kate wasn't kidding about the space heater. The room is like a sauna. "I'm sorry I was such a baby," she says as Kate rubs her eyes and lies back down.

"Give me five more minutes," Kate says, and turns on her side, hands clasped as if in prayer, lying under her face.

This girl is so much nicer than she seems, Angela thinks as she watches Kate sleep. So tough and strong at school, not suffering a single fool, ever, but privately sweeter than anyone would imagine. And she really is having an affair with James Wittinger. Why would anyone have an affair with a professor? James Wittinger must be forty-five, with long blond hair. He wears a blazer with his jeans but still looks like the guitarist in some rock band that only plays beach towns.

"What are you thinking?" Kate asks, suddenly awake.

Angela smiles and shakes her head, reaches for the obvious, inserting a pinkie into one of the holes in the sweater. "That all your windows are open," Angela says, and feels Kate's shoulder.

"I tutored this kid once, at Berkeley, and he wrote an essay called 'Life as a Whole,' but he spelled it *H-o-l-e*. I've never forgotten that," she says, hands shielding her eyes from the recessed lights above. "Don't make my holes bigger," she says, then quickly sits up, yawns. "Let's go get some food. We should eat. If we keep sleeping now, we'll be up all night."

As soon as they step outside, the wind zeroes in on any residual tears lying undetected, until now, on Angela's chin or next to Kate's ear.

"Holy crap, it's cold," Kate says, and grabs Angela's arm, starts walking fast, head down. They had planned to walk to the large store a few blocks away, but this wind makes that idea unappealing.

At the corner market, Angela suggests a dinner of french fries and eggs—for years her favorite meal. Back at Kate's, they move the heater into the kitchen and soon are in T-shirts. Kate, wearing really big black Elvis Costello glasses she says once belonged to her friend Louis, leans a book by Unamuno against a salt container in front of her. She has a philosophy final in a few days.

"Why'd you ask me if I was the oldest child?" Angela asks as she peels the potatoes.

"I studied that in a psychology class: Adler's theory about how your personality is shaped by when you were born. The oldest child sometimes feels a heavy responsibility to make the family proud. Maybe that's why this is hard on you, the, uh, possible . . . visit from the stork," she says.

"We're from another country, too, my family. Did you know that?" Angela says.

"Yeah, you're fluent right? Aren't you from South America?"

"Yeah, and good South American girls aren't supposed to . . . you know."

"Have sex with bankers."

"Right. Well, they are actually, but they're not supposed to end up pregnant," she says, and turns back to the food prep.

"No girls are, really," Kate says.

Angela finds a pan under the stove and sets it up, pours in olive oil. "What if I want to keep it?" she asks, and fights not to look down at her stomach.

"Then you will," Kate says.

Angela picks up a handful of potatoes, cut long and thin, exactly the way her mom taught her, and drops them into the oil. She closes her eyes and pretends to be in their kitchen in San Diego, the smell of sweet peas outside, tangerines always on the table, and her mom talking and talking about some story line on *All My Children* or about a romance novel she just finished as she slowly cuts the potatoes with a paring knife, each piece long and elegant and not too thick, so that it fries quickly.

"My mother is very cheerful," Angela says.

"Yeah?"

"Yeah. She's very charming and talkative. My dad isn't, but he's sweet. And hardworking. It would break their hearts to know this."

Kate closes the book and sets it down upright, then rests her chin on it, those big glasses sliding almost off her nose. "Well, is that . . . I mean, you can't do this now, just for them, right? Either way, right?"

"I know," Angela says. "Don't worry. I'm not saying I would keep it for her. I'm actually not sure what would disappoint them more. They're so proud of me, for the scholarships, for being here. You know?"

"Yeah, I know."

"I'm just missing her, that's all. What about you? Are you close to your mother?"

"No. She's not nice. I had a nice father, but he died when I was a kid. All I remember is the smell of Old Spice, the vanilla soft-scoop ice cream we had once, the smell of raspberries from the wax on his surfboard, and, I guess, the feeling of seaweed against my tiny little feet."

"He took you surfing?"

"Yeah."

"Those are nice things to remember," Angela says, and smiles.

"I hope they're real. You know how sometimes, when memories get really old, especially if they happened when you were a kid, you don't know for sure how much of it is real and how much of it is stuff you added? Not on purpose, but over time. So I'm not sure if it's real seaweed or seaweed in my head. Know what I mean?"

"Yeah. There was a radio tower at a park I went to as a kid, in

Uruguay. The park was on a river, and I remember standing next to the tower, and it was huge to me, like the Eiffel Tower. My mom swears there was no tower, but I remember it. Your dad took you surfing. How old were you?" Angela asks.

Kate shrugs. "Little." She gets up and goes to the stove to see how the food is looking. "See, we could have been friends all this time."

They eat, then study, sharing Kate's books and her bed until eleven, when they're tired and decide to drink wine and smoke. Lodged into the tiny balcony off Kate's bedroom, they spy on the family in the orange house, just now dining, their silhouettes barely visible beyond the gauzy white curtains, conversation lively. The girls can't hear the exact words, but occasionally, they do hear a perfect ring, the sound of silverware rapping against a plate, so clear, it's as if they are in the room with the family.

"What do you think they're eating?" Angela asks.

"Not potatoes and eggs."

"No. Truffles and rabbit?"

"Yuck," Angela says. "Really?"

"Yeah, I bet. Eating small animals makes the bourgeoisie feel special."

"Does it? I didn't know that about the bourgeoisie."

"Well, now you do." Kate laughs and slaps Angela's leg. "Are you calling me fucking pretentious? You who slept with a banker?"

Angela throws her head back dramatically, eyes closed. "I didn't know what he did until after I fucked him."

"Liar," Kate says. "You fucked him precisely because he was a banker. It seemed exotic to you."

Angela starts laughing in extreme embarrassment that Kate has pegged it just right and that, yes, it was exciting, in some ridiculous way, to sleep with a man who said he was a banker. "What do bankers even do?"

"I don't know. Transactions. Was it any good?"

"Not really. That's the weird thing. It wasn't bad but . . . just okay. Like potatoes without eggs."

"Sometimes it's like that, but sometimes it's amazing," Kate says, and raises her glass for a toast. "Here's to future amazing."

Angela lifts her glass and toasts a little hard, which makes Kate laugh. "Don't break the glass, woman."

"I was having such a nice time, and then you had to remind me about the banker."

"Sorry," Kate says, and she seems to feel genuine regret, but then she adds, "With big buttons. I forgot about the buttons."

"Horrible, horrible person," Angela says, and shakes her head. "So, what about you? Are you in love with James?"

"I hate to think of it like that, but yeah, probably."

Angela stares at Kate, her head resting against the wrought iron. She's never seen hair so short on a girl, but it suits her, with those big green eyes, and the brown–purple lipstick, which she must have freshened at some point tonight. Lipstick, in and of itself, is odd for women their age, and these shades, which no one at the university wears, make her so different. No wonder James went for her.

"Is he good in bed?" Angela asks, and lets out a giggle that embarrasses her.

"Yes. That's the problem."

"What makes a guy good?"

"Well, for me it's slowness. Superslowness, like tease me till I am begging. I love that. But everyone's different."

"Do you want him to leave his wife for you?"

Kate shrugs her answer. "Was it your first time having sex, with the banker?"

"Oh God, not the banker again. Can we go back to talking about the family's dinner, please?"

The wine, the talking, it all makes Angela feel as if everything will be fine, that nothing so bad is going to happen to her. Not with Kate around.

•   •   •

In the morning, they have coffee at Sur, where it's quiet this early, just people sitting alone at the counters, having a quick breakfast before catching their bus to work.

"Have you ever noticed that Spaniards use a knife and fork on their doughnuts?" Kate asks, but Angela can't pretend to care, just nods no.

"Do you want to walk instead of taking the Metro?" Kate asks as they step outside. The sky's turned a bright gray and looks thick, almost pillowlike, but the temperature feels warmer than yesterday.

"Yeah. Come on," Angela says, and starts off. She doesn't want to talk, because she doesn't know the answer yet to the obvious question.

They walk in silence nearly the entire twenty or so blocks. As they reach leafy Paseo del Prado, now only a couple of blocks from the clinic, a jolt of dread hits Angela, so powerful that she feels out of breath and needs to stop moving. She stands still, and so does Kate, arm entwined in hers. Angela has to fight the urge to run back to that warm room.

"What if I want to keep it?" Angela asks.

"If you want to, you will," Kate says. "It's not that complicated. People have babies every day. And if you don't, well, that'll be all right, too."

Angela steps closer and puts her gloved hands on Kate's coat lapel. Can I cry on your chest, on your lapel? She stares at the faux fur and thinks this might be what they call hyperventilating. She knows she looks panicked but can't help it.

"Take a deep breath, and come back to who you are. It's time to . . . You have to . . . you have to sort of stand up and hold that head up. You fucked a banker with big buttons. That's it; that's all you did. Not a crime, all right? You have to be more than that now. Come on, now. You'll know what to do."

"I will?"

"Yeah, you will," she says.

Angela looks at the trees, at the third and fourth stories of buildings above them, at the pine needles and leaves wet and shiny on the ground. She takes a deep breath and does start to feel like she's coming back to her body.

"Knowing doesn't mean anything. You'll just know. And you can do whatever you want after that."

Nice theory, but how many times in life has she done things because she thought she should? Was coming to Spain even her desire, or just something she thought would make her stronger? It hurts to remember how much she missed her family the first few weeks here. Why did she leave them behind, then? And if she doesn't know why she's here, how in the world will she know what to do?

She looks down at the sidewalk, then up at the sky, and finally at Kate.

"I promise that I won't let you do anything you don't want to do," Kate says.

The doctor's office looks like an embassy. A three-story-high gray building with an ornate facade, it sits in the center of a neat garden, an eight-foot-tall black wrought-iron fence around its perimeter. A brick walkway leads to two benches opposite each other, then to the door.

Inside, it smells like leather and wood polish, probably because of the huge mahogany desk that dominates the room, covered with plants sitting on small blue-and-white plates. The black leather couches make it austere.

"He spends all day looking at twats. I guess he needs to feel manly when he comes out here," Kate says, and Angela laughs.

The leather even creaks as you sit, none too pleased to accommodate visitors. They each pick up a gossip magazine from the coffee table, with photos of the crown princesses on the cover.

"This one studies poly sci at the school, you know," Kate says.

"Does she?"

"Yeah, one of her bodyguards always bums cigarettes. I asked him one time, 'Doesn't the king pay you enough to buy your own smokes?' He just laughed. I was serious."

Kate wants to take Angela's mind off of this, but there is no taking your mind off this.

Finally, a bored-looking young nurse opens the door and calls her name.

"Come on, come with me," Angela says, and Kate does.

The room reminds Angela of an insane asylum from a TV movie—high ceiling, with white tile floors and white subway tile on the walls, too much space to fill. A light blue Naugahyde table with no paper cover like those in American doctors' offices, sits to the right, near it a matching round chair, presumably for the doctor. Two silver exam trays loaded with equipment sit on either side of the table. A single high-backed wooden chair, as if from a dining room, sits about five feet from the exam area—for the person accompanying the patient, presumably.

"I used to go to the doctor with my mom when she was pregnant with my little brother," Angela says, and puts on the gown, as instructed. She's embarrassed to strip in front of Kate this way.

As if she knows, Kate walks around the room, pretending to examine the walls, the windowpanes, arms wrapped around herself. "It's cold in here," she says, and runs her hands over her arms fast. "I wish we had my heater."

Kate scoots the dining room chair closer to the examination table, then pulls from her coat the same magazine from the waiting room and starts reading aloud about the crown princesses and where they were seen on a recent visit to Portugal.

"Oh, they like Sintra very much," Kate says, and shows Angela a photo of the royals seemingly, yes, enjoying Sintra.

"I was worried they wouldn't like Sintra," Angela says.

"Me, too."

Finally, the doctor enters, distracted, reading from the file, ever so slowly closing the door behind him.

Finally, he looks up. "*Hola, majas,*" he says in a baritone that seems practiced. He shakes hands with each of them, though lingering a moment over Kate's. He has lots of thin silver hair that looks spun and a white beard and small glasses in dark frames. He wears a light blue shirt under a white smock with his name embroidered on the pocket: DR. GUILLERMO PAZ-GUTIÉRREZ.

The doctor comes to the table and leans against it, Angela's wrist in his hand, taking her pulse.

"What's going on?" he asks, and Angela tells her simple story, minus the *cava* and phosphorous light. Sex, no protection. Not her boyfriend, not even her friend—somebody else's husband.

"Well, that's his wife's problem," the doctor says. "But as for you, they don't have AIDS in America?" the doctor asks.

"Yes, they do. I just didn't . . . I wasn't thinking," she says.

"*Vale*," he says, and quotes some line from a poem about how love and thought rarely coincide. Time for the exam.

Kate pulls her chair closer to Angela, leans forward, whispers, "Think of Sintra," which makes Angela laugh just as the doctor is finding his way inside her.

"You're so easy," Kate says.

"I think we've established that, or else I wouldn't have this man's hand up my snatch right now, would I?"

Kate laughs so hard, her forehead ends up on Angela's shoulder.

"Girls, you're in Spain to learn Spanish, not to speak English," the doctor reprimands as his free hand, now cupped, presses down hard on Angela's stomach, pushing in, so that his manicured fingers look like they are kneading a small amount of dough. He's gentle enough that it doesn't hurt too much.

When it's over, he goes to one of the trays and brings back a tourniquet and a needle, puts the tie around Angela's upper arm, dabs her forearm with an alcohol-doused cotton ball, and says, "*Piensa en los pajaritos*," telling her to think of the little birds.

"Yeah, little bird," Kate whispers.

Angela's mom used to say the same thing, "*piensa en los pajaritos*," if Angela had a skinned knee that had to be doused in that cold camphor-smelling antiseptic spray. Or the first time Angela went to the dentist. Close your eyes, little birds.

When the blood test is done, the doctor instructs Angela to get dressed and go to the bathroom, get a urine sample, then join "her lovely friend" back in the waiting room.

Soon the girls are once again shoulder to shoulder and thigh to thigh on the black leather couch.

"Did he hit on you, my lovely friend?"

Kate shows her the business card, offered when Angela left the examining room. They laugh and turn back to the magazines, though neither reads much. Finally, half an hour later, the doctor summons them back to the room and declares, "We have nothing to worry about." Maybe the missed periods were caused by nerves or stress. He'll check the blood test for pregnancy and HIV, just as a precaution, but all seems fine.

"Sometimes these things . . . take care of themselves," he says. "Maybe some of them know better than to come to a world in which they are not wanted. Yes?"

Angela can't even look at the doctor, just nods in agreement.

They quietly gather their belongings, Angela pays in cash for the visit, and, coats in hand, not bothering to bundle up, just wanting out, they step outside. The air feels heavy and smells like rainwater, pine needles, and bus exhaust.

Angela's eyes fill with tears and she can barely manage to get her coat on. She's not sure if she's sad for the baby she'd already started imagining, the same one she doesn't want, the one she would have named Pablo, or if she misses her mother even more, now that there's no reason to go back home. Or maybe worse. Maybe after all this, she is exactly where she was two months ago, in the Metro, answering Emilio's question, "Will you join me for dinner? Or is there someone else?"

"No, there's no one else," she replied that day. And it was so true. There's no one else. Never has been.

"You okay?" Kate asks as she goes to wrap the purple scarf around Angela's neck, so tenderly. Angela can still smell her mother's Cartier on the scarf. She puts her hands atop Kate's gloved hands and smiles at her, noticing just how fleshy her mouth is, how strong her nose.

"Thank you for helping me," Angela says, and leans across their gloved hands and the scarf and kisses Kate's cheeks, just on either side of her lips.

"You're welcome," she says quietly. "I wish someone had done that for me."

"Yeah?"

"Yeah," she says, and pulls her collar up against the cold, looks around, and exhales loudly. "I have an idea. Let's not to go school. Let's go to the Prado. Want to?"

"You don't have to do that. You already brought me here. That's enough."

"Maybe I do want to. Maybe I'd like to visit my favorite girls. Did you ever think of that?"

"Who are your favorite girls?"

"I'll show you."

Soon they're walking arm in arm over the pink marble floors of the museum, enjoying its overheated air and warm lighting, which feels even cozier every time they pass a window and see that outside it's now really raining.

Kate leads them to Velásquez's *Las Meninas*.

"These are my favorite girls. I know it's common of me," she says. "Everybody loves them, but I can't help it."

In the painting, two little royals, or *meninas,* stand in a giant room that looks like a ballet studio, having their portraits made, as their entourage awaits.

"See that, over there? That's the painter himself," Kate says, and points to the corner of the work. "That's Velásquez, and that guy coming in, he's the, uh, like the secretary of state or head of affairs or whatever for the king. He seems dangerous to me, like he plans to diddle one of the *meninas* or something, because of the color of his clothes, and his eyes. Don't you think?"

Angela nods yes, although she's not so sure about this interpretation.

She spends the night at Kate's again, and when she cries again, even though she's not pregnant, Kate puts one arm under her neck and another over Angela's hip, gently pulls her in.

"What's wrong?"

"I kind of hoped I was pregnant."

"You did?"

"Yeah . . . babies make you . . . less lonely. Don't they?"

"I don't know. Maybe. Are you lonely?"

"Yes."

"Me, too," Kate says, and moves in closer, spooning Angela.

Now, tonight, in Los Angeles, a strong Santa Ana gust sends the fish chimes clanging against one another. Angela squeezes the hot cup resting on her stomach. She wishes the wind could blow away this horribleness, this feeling that her chest is falling in on itself. She starts squeezing the cup more and more. How much before it breaks? Not much, probably. Angela's afraid of cutting her hand, but not as much as she is of the feeling inside her stomach, of regret for the kind of mistake—like failing someone—that won't be easily excused or forgotten.

The liquid's hot and it hurts, pooled in her belly button. So does the porcelain in her hand, a big piece of which sits just under her thumb. It is painful, but in this weird, abstract way. Now at least there's a wall of broken ceramic and hot liquid between her and the other pain of not knowing what will happen to Kate.

CHAPTER 6
San Francisco
1994

Louis lights the pilot on the heater—the last thing he wants when he brings Kate home is for her to arrive in a freezing apartment—then goes downstairs to tell Mariana and Helen what's happened, explain he'll be gone for a few days or maybe more, however long it takes. They promise to keep an eye on things and cat-sit Madonna.

They can see Louis has had a few drinks, but they offer him a beer anyway, and he drinks it fast, goes back to the apartment, and promptly falls asleep on the couch. But at two in the morning, Louis is awakened by the cell phone lying inches from his head.

A man asks for him by name, then identifies himself as Ted Griffin from the American embassy in Madrid, calling with news about Kate.

"Yes, yes, it's me," Louis says.

There's been an accident, in Ibiza, involving Kate Harrington, the man says. He got Louis's number from Iberia.

"I know," Louis says. "I got a call from the hospital, but I don't speak Spanish. How is she?"

"She's had a head injury and some internal bleeding. They operated. It's touch and go right now."

"Is she conscious?"

"Not now, no, but I believe she was, uh, at some point," Griffin says.

"Good, good," Louis says, and runs his arm across his brow. It must be eighty degrees in the house now.

"I'm flying out later. I mean this morning," Louis says.

"Well, good. The airline, I believe, will contact any other family members," Griffin says. "But I wanted to give you a call myself. You were listed in her paperwork from the passport office as well as the airline."

"Right," Louis says, and starts thinking of Kate, sitting on their couch, laughing at her passport picture and his. Focus on this moment. Kate would not want anyone to call her mother or stepfather. Should he say something? It's so fucking hot in here and he's got a headache, a hangover. All the lights are on. Who is this guy? He pictures William H. Macy in a linen suit or maybe Anthony Hopkins in the same suit. "I'm sorry, what was your name?"

"Ted Griffin."

"Mr. Griffin, I'm her only family," Louis tells him, and sits down on the bed. He cannot wait to get off the phone to have water. "So it would only be me on the form. You don't need to call anyone else."

"Actually, a . . . uh, let me see here, a . . . Georgina Harrington was also listed in some paperwork. In Encino," Griffin says. "Her mother, correct?"

"She was?" Louis asks. He's surprised to hear that name. Not only Georgina but with her old name, before Don.

"Yes. But I'm sure the airline will take care of calling her."

"Yeah, well, see . . . the thing is . . ."

"Yes, go on," Ted Griffin says, belying a sliver of impatience.

"Well, it might be tough to hear that news from an airline. I can call her, though," Louis says, thinking it better that he intercept in some way. "I'll call her. I mean, she should hear it from me," Louis says.

The man doesn't say anything, so Louis keeps talking. "She's an older lady; she should hear it from me," Louis says.

"Certainly, if you think it best, perhaps you could call her," Griffin says.

"Yes, yeah. I'll do that," Louis says.

Griffin starts explaining that he's in Ibiza right now, coincidentally, on vacation with his family. "I'll be here another three days," Griffin says. "I'll be sure to check in on her tomorrow."

"Thank you," Louis says. "Tell her, please, that I'll get there tomorrow. I'll be there by seven or eight, I think. If I can get on the flight I saw last night . . . Tell her I'll be there soon, okay?"

"Will do," Griffin says. "Be sure to explain the circumstances to the airline and ask for the emergency travel discount. Most airlines offer this," he explains.

"Thanks, I will."

Louis considers saying something more about how he will take care of notifying Kate's family, but he doesn't.

Before he's even gotten off the bed, Louis hits CONTACTS on his cell phone and looks for Georgina's number. Her phone is soon ringing, but no one, thank God, answers. Louis takes a deep breath and thinks it through as he hears Don's voice on the outgoing message.

"Yes, hello. Sorry to call so late. This is Louis Ross here. Just wanted to let you know, Georgina, that there was an accident, a car accident in Spain, where Kate was traveling. She's okay though. Roughed up but okay and . . . I'm going. I'll be there tomorrow and I'll call as soon as I get there. Or have her call you herself. This is my number in case you need anything: four one five-five five five-seven six one zero. Don't worry, she's fine, just fine."

Louis goes to the shelf with the coffee mugs in the kitchen and grabs a red one, then walks over to the purifier on the faucet for water. Madonna Ciccone jumps up on the counter and stares at him, then yawns. She's like the dutiful wife who feels she must get up with her husband to make his breakfast, despite the ungodly hour.

He decides to make coffee and stay up packing, writing letters to her friends, to his business partner, Ken, explaining what's happened. Madonna jumps down to the kitchen floor but stays there watching him make coffee, meows up a storm. Louis goes into his room and gets the digital camera, comes back, and lies down on the now-warm floor beside the cat.

"Smile for Mommy," he tells Madonna. He used to laugh at people who told their pets to smile; now he is one of those people.

Louis gets up off the floor and goes into the bedroom, looking for things to take to Spain, to remind Kate of home. He walks to the bed and grabs the pillow, feels the softness of the celery-colored case with its ridiculously high thread count. It smells of the oil she wears, that concoction the old Japanese guy at the spa makes just for her, of white tea and ylang-ylang and whatever else. It's hard being Kate, wanting to buy ridiculously luxurious sheets, having studied anthropology and sociology, having traveled as much as she has, written a master's thesis on sex workers, learned, right up close, exactly how many condoms one two-hundred-dollar sheet could buy, because she ships them to Brazil every single month, and yet still wanting to buy those sheets. He strips off both cases, folds them, and stares at the neat little bright green square. It's going to be all right.

One minute, he's trying to conjure optimism, looking at the sheets and the photos of the two of them, her laundry strewn at the door of the closet, and the very next—it's different.

That intense worry over her becomes something else: hatred, located in his gut, very immediate and undeniable, like a fist smashing your lip against your teeth. If Don shows up in Spain, Louis will settle the score. Finally. Without a doubt.

CHAPTER 7

Third Floor, with View, Los Angeles
May 1994

Angela gets up early, makes coffee, and takes it out on the balcony. The insomniac in the other building is finally asleep and now it's the woman's daughter's turn to pad quietly around the apartment like her mother did all night, preparing herself breakfast.

But outside, nature fails to cooperate. A dozen or so parakeets, in their bright green outfits, fly over the building, squawking loudly on the way to the sycamores on Sweetzer or maybe the palm trees on La Jolla. Angela loves the wild parakeets that live in the palm trees all over the city. They're everywhere, and yet some locals claim to never have seen them. Angela once told some friends gathered around a dinner table that she sometimes feels the parakeets are the only thing keeping her in L.A.

"Thanks a lot," someone said, and she had to backtrack, make a joke. Her lovely friends *and* the parakeets. But the truth is, she doesn't feel connected to her friends the way people in books and movies seem to feel connections. Can she even think of anyone who has the sort of bond she wants? Sometimes, arriving at a mall parking lot, she'll see two women laughing in a car and she'll think, *That. That* is what I want. But then again, that is what she's always wanted and also what has always eluded her.

Angela goes inside and calls Spain again, but, still, no one picks up. Is this the right number? She could call Louis, but she doesn't want to wake him up, because, God knows, he seemed to need his sleep. Not wanting to miss any calls, she takes the phone into the bathroom and sets it on the back of the toilet while she showers.

As soon as she woke up this morning, that feeling came back in the pit of her stomach. Fear plus something else—dread maybe. To fend it off, Angela covers herself in that beautiful-smelling lavender body wash, chants the words *happy* and *safe*.

"Happy, safe, happy, safe."

Good job, good living, a nice apartment she owns, a couple of good friends, a family that loves her and lives just a few hours away. Happy and safe, you just have to remind yourself, that's all.

She looks around at the new tub, big and wide, and the baby blue glass tile behind it. Stupid as it may be, that tile usually offers a little hit of joy, reminding her how ugly the wall had been: layers of caulking curling toward you as you showered, revealing mold and mildew created years before by the heat of some stranger's bath. But Angela came along and scraped that all away, then added layers of beauty: fresh new backing—"hardy backer," the construction guys called it—and new wood over that, pine-scented and cream-colored, with faint brown-orange wood rings, and finally the tile itself, periwinkle and perfectly cut, like those marbles she treasured as a kid—cat's-eyes or something—completely clean and all hers. A two-bedroom, two-bath condo. What more could you want?

Fixing houses, refurbishing things—that's all anyone puts their energy into anymore, her friend Craig says, arguing that humans have given up on knocking down walls between each other and turned instead to houses, or even their physical landscapes, knocking down the old nose, the old muscles, rebuilding *them*—anything to avoid trying to penetrate another person's mind or, God forbid, her heart.

She puts her palm flat against the tile and winces. A tiny corner of the cut must have something in it, maybe a shard of ceramic. It may be pathetic to get joy out of baby blue Italian tile, but at least there's still something, some way to get happiness, or what passes as a decent replica.

This is the worst time possible to leave her job. A hiring freeze started three months ago; then the company stopped matching their 401(k) contributions, and most recently, she hears—and is meant to hear—a whispered warning in the unfunny jokes that Bennett, the magazine's new associate publisher, makes about overpriced employees, although he is, ironically, its second-highest-paid employee. Or when he talks about the demise of print journalism, of magazines, of everything save himself, of course. Angela could come back to find her job given to someone younger, who doesn't yet own a house or need as much monthly income as she does and who, frankly, will do a passable job for much less. To a world that, birdlike, chirps and tweets its thoughts, desires, and fears in forty-character messages every few hours, the very idea of a story told in two thousand or three thousand words, and on paper, is becoming about as quaint as a harpsichord.

She'll call Spain one more time, then head to work, put this behind her. Finally, someone answers, a woman. This phone, she says, is located in the hospital's arrivals area, the number probably provided by the ambulance driver. Angela's transferred to the ICU desk. She explains who she is and why she's calling and asks what room Kate is in, but the nurse doesn't say. "Is there a phone in the room? Could I get that direct number, please?" Angela asks. No, the nurse says, and anyway, it wouldn't matter, because no one can speak to Kate.

"Well, not now, but soon, hopefully," Angela says.

"*Bueno, no sé porque es que está en coma,*" the nurse says, explaining that Kate is in a coma.

"Is it . . . Is it . . ." Angela's heard of doctors medicating people into a stupor so that their body will heal, and she struggles to remember what that is called. "Did the doctors do this to help her heal? Is it medically induced?"

"No, I think she has been comatose since arriving. Are you her family? Are you coming? You should come soon if you are her family," the nurse says.

"Yes, but . . ." Angela doesn't know what to say, wants to argue with this nurse or ask her questions whose answers contain some form of hope, but she can't think how.

"I'm sorry. Good-bye," the nurse says, and hangs up.

Angela goes to the couch and looks out at the sycamores in the distance, wishing the parakeets would fly by right now. Angela dials Louis's cell, but the call goes to voice mail. She looks up the contacts list on her phone and finds Kate, stares at her name. Of all the people in that list and the dozens of people she meets every week, that name, those four letters, still have the most power.

So many times, she's wanted to call but didn't. She presses down on the button and watches as Kate's number appears on the phone display. This time, it's Kate's voice, a little raspy, sexy. Angela closes her eyes and fights off the urge to disconnect.

"Please call me, Louis. We need to talk," she says.

Car accident, Spain. Not a surprise, but it also cannot be the end, not for Kate.

CHAPTER 8
Madrid
1989

The day after their visit to the doctor, the girls get up slowly but early. Angela awakens first, at six, and goes and turns on the space heater, then gets back in bed carefully so as not to awaken Kate. In two days, this baffling yet strong sense of intimacy has emerged between them. So different, the two of them—archetypes, even: the classic good girl and the bad girl, the loud one, the quiet one, the one who loves and misses her family, the one who hates her family. Suddenly, Kate's eyes are open and Angela blinks away her embarrassment.

Kate smiles and says, "Nice."

"What?"

"The heater. Smart girl."

Later, seated at the kitchen table, with its plastic cover decorated with bright blue and green flowers, like a farm tablecloth, Angela watches Kate heat milk for their coffee. She's using a spoon to pull up the layer of fat.

"Are you really lonely, or did you just say that for me?"

"I said it for you," Kate says, and stares at her, daring her to believe this. "Why would I lie to you? Of course I'm lonely. I hate my family. Most of the *children* at school think I'm crazy for smoking and, apparently, for fucking James. Of course I'm lonely. Why are you?"

"I don't know. We went to the United States when I was little, six, and I left my grandmothers behind. One of them kind of doted on me. So there I was, missing her so much and stuck in this country where I didn't speak the language, totally lost. All I knew was that once a day we got to eat Oreo cookies and drink milk. My whole day was pre- and post-Oreos until I learned the language."

"It's like you were a deaf-mute for a year. That would make me lonely, too," Kate says, and carries the beat-up little saucepan to the table, pours the milk into Angela's cup. "Loneliness has left its indelible print on your little six-year-old heart," she says, and takes the pot back to the stove.

"I know you're joking, but that's a really nice way to put it."

"Well . . . the key is to know what hurt you and then kill it. That's the part everyone forgets, you know? They just keep going over and over it in their heads, the thing that hurt them; they wallow in that, instead of finding a way to bury it."

"Are you a psych major or something?"

"No. If you met my mother, you'd understand," Kate says. Then she sits and starts scraping peach jam from the jar, although there's really nothing in there to scrape. She's wearing the moth-eaten brown sweater again, and, ironically, the only jam on that jar sits around the mouth, perilously close to the sweater's arms. Angela reaches over and pushes up the sweater's cuffs.

"Thanks."

"What are you doing for the holidays?" Angela asks.

"Not sure," Kate says. "You?"

"I thought . . . if I was pregnant, I would go home, but . . . now that I'm not, I don't know. You want to go somewhere?"

"Like Portugal?" Kate asks.

"Yeah, like Portugal. I hear Sintra's nice."

Kate chuckles halfheartedly and stares at Angela, as if about to ask something.

"What?"

"Nothing."

They eat bread and butter with the paltry scrapings of peach jam and talk about the finals next week and the art class at the Prado, which hasn't met in two weeks because their professor's been sick.

"You know her real name is Delacruz, but she changed it to Delacroix to sound French."

"Seriously?"

"*Oui*," Kate says.

They walk to school together, arm in arm, like the day before, and sit near each other in the economics class, have lunch in the cafeteria with a group of Americans, but then go their separate ways.

When they first got to Spain and Kate tried to befriend her, it was Angela who pulled away. She's determined not to do that now. She won't turn to Kate at the most difficult of times and then discard her. Angela seeks her out at every opportunity, invites her to a play, to the opening of an art exhibit, all slightly more sophisticated events than most of their fellow students would attend, events she's proud to have found out about in the arts section of the paper. Kate seems happy to see her, but there's always a little hesitation.

One Wednesday, after Angela's finished teaching her English class, as she rides the Metro from Valdecarros to the city center, looking up whenever a man passes slowly, and wondering about Emilio, she decides to stop at Sol station and use a public phone. But instead of calling him, she calls Kate. And the strangest thing happens: Her heart starts beating faster and faster as she dials.

"*Hola.*"

"*Hola, guapa*," she says, and listens to the silence as Kate tries to figure who's calling her. "Hey, it's me, Angela."

"Oh, hey."

"Listen, I'm wondering, have you ever had a mushy Rodilla sandwich with a cold beer? It's the exact opposite of what the bourgeoisie would eat," Angela says. The chuckle on Kate's end makes her blush.

"Is it? How mushy?"

"Very mushy. Like mashed potatoes and gravy on bread."

"Ooooo," Kate says, but she laughs. "I've missed you, Ani."

"Well, come over, then, for sandwiches and beer. They make tuna and pea and carrot, corn, uh, creamy tomato, ham and cheese, of course."

"At your place?"

"Yeah, we'll catch up."

"That sounds nice," she says, and promises to try.

"Don't try; just do it."

"Well, I sort of had plans, but I promise I will if I can."

Angela goes to the Rodilla store, a place she discovered in her first weeks in Spain. It specializes in finger sandwiches of every variety, and reminds her of El Emporio, a shop Angela's mom delighted in visiting whenever they returned to South America, where ladies clad in pink dresses and matching bonnets would use silver tongs to load trays with pastry or sandwiches.

She'll tell Kate about the ladies in pink in South America as she presents her assortment of odd but delicious sandwiches. She chooses tomato and pimento, Serrano ham and cheese. Is Kate a vegetarian? Better get some others.

"*¿Algo más?*" the attendant says, impatient. A few more: tuna with peas and red pepper, corn and butter. She'll make a joke of this; "a banquet of mush, for you, madame!"

Angela then hurries home to tidy her apartment. How will this place look to Kate? The orange-and-yellow couch, so threadbare, but at least adorned with the satiny brown pillows, which definitely make it nicer. Well, maybe. But there's the glass coffee table with its gold base, hopelessly seventies. At least there's an alcove for her bed, so it doesn't protrude too much into the room, and inside it, Angela has placed a huge lamp she bought at the Rastro flea market, with a blue glass ball for a center. It's kitschy but cool. Or at least she hopes so.

"Are you cool or ugly?" she asks the lamp as she fluffs the pillows and smoothes the comforter, a nice big fluffy white one, sent by her mother at what must have been a ridiculous expense.

The apartment may be small, but she gets to live alone—no one who's afraid of the human lung telling her what to do. She lives alone. That must count for something.

Her books. Surely, Kate will walk over and inspect the books. This is how we announce our tastes, our worldliness, right? What would I think if I didn't know you, Angela? Edward Albee play, another by Mamet, a paperback copy of *One Hundred Years of Solitude,* a copy of *Rayuela,* by Cortázar, the Argentine deconstructionist. Angela fights the urge to pull at its spine so that it would protrude a little more than the others.

Kate, if she comes, will be the first person to have dinner here. Friends have come to pick her up, and one guy even spent a few nights, but no one's actually sat at the little card table covered in a white tablecloth, with a bowl of flowers in the center. Ages ago, her mother had read in a magazine that fresh flowers are "a gift to yourself." With that in mind, her mother tried, every two weeks, to indulge. A few times, her dad protested the expense, then surprised his wife with Friday flowers.

Angela tries to do the same, as a way to keep connected, no matter where she is or even if that week's check from the language school is tiny. Even if she's had to pluck the neck of an illicit lily, bending it carefully to fit through the chain link of a stranger's fence, there have always been fresh flowers. In Spain, with the power of the dollar and her relatively lucrative teaching jobs, she indulges weekly in something—maybe a handful of purple violets, four yellow tuberoses, four tea-colored roses. For tonight, she's chosen six orange tulips from the Netherlands. So proud of his imports was the vendor, he said it twice, "*Son Holandesas estas niñas, de Holanda.*"

Orange tulips, white tablecloth, decent floors, big windows, new comforter, lots of books, rich-looking satin-covered pillows on, yes, an admittedly ugly couch. Fine, good. Why the hell is she so nervous? Fuck it, I'll have a drink, she decides. She opens a beer and pours its contents into a glass, walks over to the window, and stares at the plaza. She wishes it had trees instead of its huge red swing sets. There are actually twenty of them—she's counted—five rows, four each. Angela imagines that Russian parks might look like this—far more concerned with quantity than aesthetics—eighty young comrades could swing there at the same time!

As much as she's indulged the excitement of having Kate over, as soon as the phone rings, she knows there won't be a visit tonight. She lets the phone ring and takes another sip of beer. Disappointed or relieved?

Kate says she can't come for sandwiches because James is coming over to talk.

"Doesn't his wife ever wonder where he goes?" Angela asks. "I mean, for a married man, he's hardly ever with her."

"Yeah, they're having some trouble," Kate deadpans.

Angela offers the leftover sandwiches to her neighbor Manuel, a computer geek and hashhead who's always inviting her to go for an evening walk. He thanks her and comes back in an hour with an offer of a walk.

They bundle up and go out, stop right away to light a little *canuto* of tobacco with hash sprinkled in the end. This propels them farther, all the way to Malasaña, the junkie neighborhood, gentrifying but still rough. She would never come here alone at night. They walk all the way back to the Legislative Palace, all lit up, so that it looks surreal, with its fountains of ice-cold, beautifully lit water.

She's completely stoned when she gets home, although not sure from what—the cold, the long walk, or the hash. Manuel tries to invite himself in. She gently says no but kisses him at the door anyway. He's trying so hard to turn her on, but all of it—his big hard kisses, the hash on his breath, which tastes of olive water—just makes her say good night again.

He's surprised and maybe a little angry. Really, good night? Maybe he thought the sandwiches were a green light.

Angela throws off the coat and the purple scarf, lies on the couch in the dark, and starts thinking of Kate. She imagines sitting in class and feeling someone behind her. Without looking, Angela leans back and finds herself pressed to Kate, who puts her arms around her, kisses her cheek. They stay like this a nice long time—friends but about to be so much more, the anticipation nearly overwhelming. Then Angela stands up and turns so that they're face-to-face. She puts her arms around Kate's neck and kisses her directly, openly. And that's where it stops.

Angela opens her eyes and goes to fetch water, looks out the window at red-swing plaza, the sky, closes her eyes and listens to the sound of traffic out on the road, and of Manuel strumming his guitar on the balcony. She goes to bed and wills herself not to think about Kate in that way, but the hash makes this impossible.

In the morning, as she opens her eyes and looks around the room, she realizes the feeling is very much still there but now presents itself as a strange brew of conflicting emotions. There's clarity and even relief—finally, she understands why sex with the banker or with so many handsome boys back home had felt so uninteresting—but also fear. She's not so much afraid what anyone would think, not here in Spain anyway. What scares her most is the idea of rejection. Could there be anything more humiliating than to see that look in Kate's eyes that says, Sorry, I'm not interested?

How would Kate react to hearing that her new friend is crushing out on her? Should she wait for Kate to do something? How can she signal what she wants? Because there is no more ignoring what she wants.

Maybe something will come to her when she next sees Kate, at lunch. As she walks downstairs to the smoke-filled cafeteria, which resembles a bar, with coeds smashed together, drinking coffee and eating tortilla sandwiches, Angela makes herself stop at the bottom of the stairs and look for Kate. She wants to gauge her first reaction as cleanly as possible—to seeing her, nothing else. She spots her quickly, since she's much taller than most women. Angela starts to ask herself if this is really what she wants, but the answer arrives even before the question's been asked. The way her heart comes to life when Kate spots her, that smile on her face, tells Angela everything she needs to know. Kate waves her over, then puts down her glass and practically runs toward her and kisses her cheeks. Her face is cold; she must have just arrived.

"What's going on?" Angela asks.

"Some good news. What do you want? A coffee?"

Kate orders it, then announces that she has great news. James wants to spend part of Christmas with her. He told her last night. They're thinking of going up on the twenty-second or twenty-third to San Sebastían, in the Basque country. Then, on the twenty-fourth, he'll have to fly to Berlin, where his wife's sister lives. It's not everything, but something good, right?

Angela's bitterly disappointed but hardly surprised. "That's great," she says sarcastically. But Kate doesn't want to hear that, so she doesn't.

"Sintra in the spring? Rain check?"

"Sure, yeah," Angela says. "And where will you go on the twenty-fourth and the twenty-fifth, when he's with his wife?"

"I don't know. I don't care. It's not like I had Christmas growing up, not, you know, a storybook Christmas. Just another day to me."

Angela nods. "All right. If you don't care."

"Why are you—? Where will you be?" Kate asks. "You won't be alone, will you?"

"No, no, I won't be alone. I'll fly to Paris and stay with my friend Julie. She's an exchange student there."

"Oh, good," Kate says. "I mean, we hadn't confirmed, so . . ."

"No, it's fine."

"I don't want you to be alone."

"I'm not," Angela says, and refuses to look away, even manages to widen her smile, as if genuinely happy for Kate and for herself, too. Yeah, Paris!

Of course she's alone. You don't just suddenly have all sorts of people around. Angela's mortified by this situation. What kind of person has no one to be with over the holidays? Home, San Diego, that's the only place where she's wanted and where she wishes she could be, but flying there would cost six hundred dollars she doesn't have. The second installment of her student loans don't pay out until February. Maybe her parents would have the money, maybe not, but even if they did, that would be money taken away from the Christmas gifts for her sister and brother. No way. It's just too late. She can't tell her mother the truth, so she uses the same story she told Kate. Paris for the holidays.

"Oh, good," her mother says. "Paris, how romantic, *mija.*"

She'll stay in Madrid, stock up on her favorite foods, get wine, get new books to read, buy herself a journal, write about Spain, something she's been meaning to do since she arrived. She'll sleep and smoke hash. She must remember to buy some from Manuel. It'll be lonely at times, but as long as she stays inside and avoids going out and seeing groups of happy friends and families, she'll be all right.

"Have a good time," she tells Kate on the twentieth, the last time she plans to call her before the New Year.

"You, too. When do you leave for Paris?"

"In a couple of days."

"When will you get back? I'll miss you."

"Who knows. I might stay until after New Year's," she says, which is so stupid. What in the world will she do alone in Madrid for ten days? But right now, she wants Kate to imagine her in romantic Paris on New Year's Eve, even if it means making the lie worse.

"*A bientôt,* then," Kate says.

Two days later, as Angela listens to a tape of Bruce Springsteen songs that her best friend back home sent, the phone rings. Kate says that James never showed up at the train station. She waited two full hours for him, but he never showed up.

"I don't think I've ever done anything more humiliating," she says. "I was going to call you yesterday, but then I was so fucking embarrassed. When do you leave for Paris?"

Angela looks out her window at the benches across the street, at the plaza, and the swing sets so big and strong, their tall red frames slick and shiny with rainwater. They don't look so pathetic now, but strong and protective of the children who spend thousands of glorious hours flying under their steady steel arms.

"Well, actually, my plans have changed, too," she says.

Kate and Angela decide first to shop for provisions, in case stores close all week. Who knows about wild but still-Catholic Spain. On the twenty-third, they meet at noon at an outdoor market near La Latina, then plan to walk over to Plaza Mayor, which is all decked out for Christmas with mangers and rows and rows of round yellow lights strung from one end of the impossibly huge plaza to the other.

At La Latina, Angela thinks she hears a particular excitement, people talking a little more loudly, wishing one another a happy Christmas, patrons taking the time to thank that merchant who favors them, gives them the best apples, the ripest tomatoes. They stop near a pile of fragrant tangerines and stare at the long aisles. Where to start?

"Should we roast something like a turkey or a duck?" Angela asks.

"No. You know what? I'm kind of a vegetarian. Do you mind if we find a way to celebrate but not by eating an animal?" Kate says.

"That's right. Only the bourgeoisie eat small animals."

"Do you mind? I'm sorry, I'm not one of those militants, but if there's any way . . ."

"No. I don't care. I've been so broke here that I never eat meat anyway. We can have milk, though, can't we? I mean cheese. You eat cheese and eggs, obviously, right?"

"Sure," Kate says. "I don't eat animals, but I'm all for stealing their milk and eggs."

They buy a big chunk of hard Manchego cheese and silver-wrapped triangles of creamy soft cheeses; exotic breads with rosemary in them and basil; tangerines and chocolate; tins of peaches and apricots; lots of wine. Then they walk over to the vegetable aisles, where it smells of red pepper, cabbage, and fish from the stands nearby. They buy large quantities of potatoes and onions. When Angela sees a pile of fresh peas encased in slightly furry green shells, she's thrilled.

"Do you have chard?" she asks the vegetable lady, who raises her arm, clad in a gray wool sweater, its sleeves soiled by the dirt in which her produce came to life, and points to a bin filled with the green-and-red leaves.

Kate frowns.

"What?"

"I want the same as before, just eggs and potatoes."

"We can't eat eggs and potatoes every single day. Especially at Christmas. I'm going to make you a pea, onion, and chard tortilla. My grandmother used to make it for me. You'll love it."

"Why can't it be the same?"

"Because it's Christmas," Angela says, and turns the chard so Kate can see its dark green color and red veins. She holds the leaves against Kate's face. "Look how pretty it looks on you. You'll love it."

"I didn't realize I was going to be wearing it."

"Well, now you know."

They're standing close to each other, in a not very romantic place, with a vegetable lady in red galoshes and dirty wool nearby, puddles of melted ice below, the air fragrant with the smell of oranges and wilted vegetables, but it's Kate's turn now to reach across gloved hands holding a bouquet of chard and lean into her friend.

"Have you ever been with a girl?" Kate asks.

The question shocks her, but she tries hard to keep the same look, though she feels her eyes widen a little. "No. You?"

"Yes," Kate says, and smiles mischievously.

Angela grows quickly embarrassed by this and turns to pay the vegetable lady, who is weighing carrots for some imaginary customer.

*   *   *

Carrying mesh bags full of provisions, they start walking toward Plaza Mayor, dodging the families hurrying to the plaza. Everyone in Madrid, it seems, has the day off and has come here. As they walk away from La Latina, up the hill, Kate reaches back for Angela's hand and pulls on it so that she must stop walking.

"What?"

"Sorry about James."

Angela stops and looks at her. "What about James?"

"Just a stupid choice. Should have done this all along, don't you think? You and me, not some married jerk."

Angela shrugs and looks around—wet stone, big clouds, smell of caramel corn and roasted peanuts, the big yellow lights hanging in Plaza Mayor, the smell of hay from so many fake mangers.

"I wish I didn't feel the way I do," Kate says. "About James. I know it's a stupid thing to do. And I'm not a stupid person."

Angela looks directly at her friend's face, a few inches away, at eyes that have gone vulnerable and a smile that appears uncertain. Angela's natural instinct would be to say something about James or make a joke, distance herself a little, but she doesn't, just keeps looking at Kate, who leans across and puts her forehead against Angela's, then slides her hand into Angela's pocket.

"Can we share? I forgot my gloves."

"What about your other hand?"

"It will have to be cut off when we get back to the house."

"Oh, okay."

Sharing a pocket, they start down the hill, heading toward Campomanes, careful not to slip on the slick cobblestones.

For the next two days, they cook and eat and get stoned, eat some more, read Kate's books, then, when they've run out, go to Angela's for more. They read aloud from *Myra Breckinridge* and Salinger's *Nine Stories,* and *Breakfast at Tiffany's,* even Hemingway. At night, they watch the family across the way, writing whole scripts for them from the safety of the tiny balcony, sipping wine. They lie in bed, enjoying the lack of homework, lack of activity, lack of worries.

For Angela, this is truly a first. She's not had this easy companionship in so long. Maybe as a teenager with her best friend, Vicky, but not in college, not in the last few years. And certainly she's never had this combination of friendship plus a quiet, nearly silent, yet amazingly constant physical desire.

"Will you see James again?" she asks as they lie on the bed the day after Christmas, both wearing shorts, testing the space heater to see just how hot it can get. Angela props herself on one arm and, before she's had time to consider what she's doing, runs her finger over Kate's belly from hip to rib, then back down and across, a bridge across her hips.

"I'd like to say no, but . . . probably I will."

"I don't get it. He's a married jerk. How can a woman as smart as you are, on paper, do something like that?"

"On paper, ouch. You certainly are becoming very honest, here in old Spain, aren't you?" she says, and raises herself up so that her head is now an inch or two from Angela's.

"Well, come on, Kate, he's married."

"You almost had the child of a banker," Kate says, and pulls Angela's T-shirt a little, so that they're even closer. Her breath smells of citrus—tangerines plus the lemon drops she sucks on all the time, sent from home by her friend Louis.

Kate lies back down, then takes Angela's hand and pulls it onto her face, stares at the fingers, the inside, then puts it atop her hip and turns so that they're facing each other. "Can you even have mindless sex, or would you fall in love?" Kate asks, then answers for her. "I know you'd fall in love. You think children make you less lonely."

"That was mean," Angela says, holding her gaze.

"Was it?"

"Yes."

"Come on, don't pout," Kate says, one arm around Angela's stomach. Angela can feel warm breath just under the chin. She's longing to kiss her but also absolutely certain that the best thing to do is refrain.

CHAPTER 9
An Apartment in Encino
1989

Kate's gone to live in Spain. Then his girlfriend, Jen, transfers to Berkeley, of all places, and Louis is, once again, completely alone. How did this happen?

He gets new roommates, but this time he doesn't bother investing so much time in them. They drink beer on Saturday and watch *SNL* together, throw the occasional party, but now his life is focused pretty singularly on moving out of Encino altogether.

New York, he's decided, will be the place for him to really start his life. Louis likes the predictability of computers and he likes the unpredictable nature of things like punk rock and art. He loves Rauschenberg and Lou Reed, the Ramones, wants to go to New York and pretend it's the seventies and the eighties, pretend he could run into these people, somewhere, somehow. He wants to be in a place where there's at least the possibility, even if tiny, that something great could happen.

With a job as a computer engineer, he'll be grounded but also able to explore. His parents aren't thrilled with the idea of his moving, but he knows that, as their only son, this is the time to go, before life calls him back to help them maneuver old age.

Louis enjoys the summer with them, although it's a struggle, sometimes, to stick around watching *MacNeil/Lehrer* when it's still warm out, the air pungent with overheated earth, thirsty plants, the chlorine smell of the neighbor's pool, which reminds him of Kate.

Sometimes he goes for a walk in Newport, along the harbor, stops at one of the touristy restaurants for a beer. Sitting at the bar, there's always at least one nice woman dressed in a silk skirt, her jacket folded on the stool next to her, playing with the pearls around her neck. She's too tired to be picked up on aggressively, so, ironically, Louis's low-key conversation, with no such intention in mind, works a treat. He could start something with lots of these women, but why?

Accompanying him always is the knowledge that nothing would compare. And anyway, he's moving in two months. He pays for her drink, whoever *she* is, smiles sincerely when he says he's enjoyed meeting her, and takes the napkin she slides over, with her phone number written on it. On a couple of occasions, he's gone to dinner with these women, then to a hotel. But in the morning, standing there, staring at an attractive woman in a hotel bed, watching her rouse as the breakfast arrives, smiling appreciatively that (*a*) her one-night stand didn't leave in the night and that (*b*) he ordered food, Louis always thinks of Kate, which is so wrong, you could call it cruel.

But then in late July, something happens that portends at least the possibility for change. Louis meets a girl named Sandrine Delanoe. She's French and went to the same high school they all went to, as an exchange student back then. Louis actually remembers seeing her around campus. They're both at a house party in a place that looks like his own parents' home—cottage-cheese ceilings, ugly carpets, thick Spanish tile everywhere.

He steps in the kitchen, where she's mixing drinks as if it's her house and with the confidence of a much prettier girl. Sandrine has slightly crooked teeth and small eyes, but also a womanly, or maybe just not American, type of confidence. She wears a low-cut top, but also a strange sort of pink jumpsuit and perfume. People come in and out of the kitchen, but not Louis, who's transfixed, watching her mix drinks. Three, it looks like, using tonic in two, soda in the other—quite the conscientious bartender. He considers leaving before she's even seen him. But something about her neck and the wisps of blond hair resting there make him stay. He goes to the sink, standing shoulder to shoulder with her, and fills a glass with water, then begins watering the violets someone is growing in the glass window box.

"You are a very nice one," she says, and the accent plus the strange construction make him smile.

"You're a very nice one, too, making so many drinks."

"Yes," she says, and hands Louis one of the cocktails.

Later that night, outside, when they're standing close and savoring the moment before the first kiss, Louis asks her to say something in French, and she whispers a blue streak right into his ear, her breath sweet and warm. Louis can feel an erection forming under his jeans.

"What'd you say?" he asks.

"The lyrics to 'La Marseillaise,'" she says, and he laughs.

Then she tilts her head and actually presses her forefinger to her mouth, utters a small "Hmm," then kisses him under the lone palm tree.

On their first real date, they plan to visit an Italian restaurant near Sandrine's home, but when he arrives, she says she's changed her mind and made dinner.

"Oh, all right," he says, and walks in.

They sit at a glass table with a scary seventies lamp above, eating what she calls "peasant food"—thick bread and lasagna, a simple salad. She makes him laugh with her description of the town she's from and its people, whom Parisians consider backward.

"Those ridiculous Parisians," he says.

"Do you know any?" she asks, taking him too literally.

"No, no. I just meant that . . . Americans don't imagine there are any backward French," he says.

"Well, there are," she says, and leans on the table as if to get a good look at him or maybe to offer him a better view of herself.

"You are funny one. I like you," she says as he feels himself getting excited.

On the couch, as they kiss, he thinks of Kate, but not in a way that replaces Sandrine. It's more that Kate is whispering "Slow down, slow down, be sure," even when that's hardly what he wants. An hour later, in her bed, straddling Louis, Sandrine begs him to finish. Hands cupped around her ass, he moves her body down toward him, her breasts in his mouth, a trickle of Chanel-infused perspiration running down the center of her chest and onto his cheek as he reaches up and sucks her nipple one last time and harder than before. As she climaxes, she delivers the tiniest drop of sugar into his mouth, a sort of thank-you.

Later, they lie together under her ceiling fan, slowly cooling off.

"That's never happened with someone else," she says. "Only by myself."

"Really? That's not just what French girls say to their men?"

"No," she says, and shakes her head a dozen times, smiling, or at least it looks like a smile in the near dark. Before he knows it, she's out of bed. Gone to the bathroom, he assumes. But Sandrine returns a moment later and is soon standing above him, holding the square pan of leftover lasagna, plus two forks.

"You're nuts," he says.

"I know!" she yells, and gets in bed, hands him a fork. "I am still hungry. I didn't want to look fat naked in case we made love."

The next morning and the one after and the one after that, Louis begins to feel cured, like a character in some Russian novel who had to go to the country for rest, who didn't hold out hope for his own recovery and is surprised to feel better with each passing day.

That's how he feels at night, with Sandrine, the air from the fan above cooling his still-moist brow, this lovely woman next to him. Even as she tackles the most mundane of chores, like angrily trying to make the remote do her bidding, its buttons old and stubborn, she's seductive. Louis runs his hand down her spine. She turns and smiles, air-kisses him before focusing again on the remote. *"Putain!"* she calls out, and she has to get nearly out of bed, leaning close to the television, before she can get the channel to change.

This is why it makes sense that, in early August, at a movie theater, right before a film's about to start, Louis leans into Sandrine's hair and whispers, "Come to New York with me."

Later, on the way home, she asks him about it. "Are you serious?"

"We'll never know what we're like as a real couple unless we do that, you know?"

"You think we might be a good couple, like a very good couple?" she asks.

"I do," he says in what finally feels like a man's voice, a voice speaking with conviction. "Come live with me," he says to Sandrine. "I want you to come live with me."

Within a week of arriving in New York, Louis gets a job with the School District as a data-processing specialist, taking care of the servers. It's techie work and not exactly the most exciting job, but then, New York was never supposed to be about the days, but about the nights, the music, the streets. And this job earns him enough money to pay the rent on a two-bedroom apartment in a decent area of Park Slope and only three blocks from the subway. This way, Sandrine, who, after all, left everything to move with him, can take a part-time job and not have to worry about money.

Their apartment sits in the middle of a slowly gentrifying street. Some buildings have been fixed up, but the majority are "four in the morning buildings," as Sandrine calls them, because they look the way people do at four in the morning.

Their building stands one story taller than the others, making it look like the slightly older brother of the block, and is made of brick, which gives it an elegant bearing, but the dusty hedges pressed against the brick often hide half-smashed gold beer cans or red McDonald's fries containers tossed by kids walking home from school—like rosebuds from the modern era. The window boxes in the front have fallen into the garden and you can see the remains lying there between mounds of accidental flowers, the latter attributable not to any human desire or design, but, more likely, to seeds dropped by birds.

"Thank you, birds, for carrying your seeds over Park Slope," Sandrine says sometimes when they're sitting on the front stoop drinking beer and talking about those flowers. "Say thank you to the birds, Louis," she says, and takes his hand, puts it on her shoulder.

"Thank you, birds," he says, which she repays with a smile.

She's happy in New York, in their big, sparse apartment. It's like an Edward Hopper painting, their place, with shiny floors and clean cream-colored walls. Good thing about the views and the floors, because they can't afford much furniture, just a couch and two beds, a bed frame for themselves, but not in the guest bedroom. Old tables flank their bed, which they painted in the backyard. Mismatched glasses sit on once-beautiful but definitely stained tablecloths. But all of it sits on shiny wood floors. The owner was so proud of the floors, which he'd had done weeks before they moved in—and not just one layer of the best varnish, but three. They laughed at the man, Samuel, but, as happens, have now taken on his pride. Sometimes when she opens a little-used closet, Sandrine can still smell the varnish, and she wonders if some tiny corner at the back will remain forever undry.

It's not just their new home they enjoy. Every Saturday, they take the train in from Brooklyn to the city, walk through the Bowery, the East Side, eat greasy Vietnamese spring rolls chased with sake, then green tea so hot that it burns the tips of their tongues but propels them out, heated and buzzed, to wander another two or three hours through music shops and thrift stores until they end up in SoHo at dusk. Standing in front of those huge gallery windows, lit up in creamy expensive lighting, its art and clients competing for attention, he imagines seeing Robert Rauschenberg or maybe Basquiat or Grace Jones arrive—never mind that Louis is pretty sure at least one of these has already died. Sandrine's mitten-covered hands hold his spring roll–shined fingertips, and the warm gallery lights beckon them inside, while the city, just as relentless and as buzzed as they are from the green tea, says, Stay out here. Keep exploring. Keep going. Don't go inside.

It's a good life, to be sure, but that doesn't mean doubt has no place here. Maybe Kate should be living here with me, he sometimes thinks after a few beers. She would love this place, with its big windows. She would love the rooftop. One night, after too many beers, he walks down to the corner bodega to tell her about them.

"You would love my new floors," he says into her answering machine. This feels like cheating, saying "my new floors," not "our new floors."

She doesn't call him back for weeks. She went to Spain to start a new life, and, apparently, she has.

CHAPTER 10
Fourth Floor, Also with View, Los Angeles
1994

Angela stands at the conference room windows, waiting for her staff to assemble. Perched atop a converted warehouse at the foot of the Hollywood Hills, their offices enjoy a prime view of so many gorgeous homes with patios and decks. On any given afternoon, you can look up from your computer and see a home owner leaning on his or her balcony or veranda, prosecco in hand, gazing at yet another lovely sunset.

A little cruel, too, if you think about it, to house a newspaper or magazine at the foot of the Hollywood Hills—the lowest paid literally at the feet of the highest paid and yet each, weirdly, wrongly dependent on each other. Without celebrities, her magazine would never get read. And without magazines and TV shows dissecting and applauding their every wardrobe and relationship choice, measuring every bump, they would not be stars, just people. Angela remembers the look of fear she once saw on the face of a star who came out of the gas station with a pack of Marlboros in her hand and no makeup on her face. Sheer horror at seeing Angela, who'd interviewed her the week before, as if this star had been caught in a bathroom stall with a syringe in her arm.

Angela wanted to say, Don't worry. The story's done and in the can. And anyway I could not ever be so cruel as to describe, in print, this look on your face.

Of course, life can offer worse than positioning you within envying distance of other people's lives. She runs a magazine with forty staffers, has made it more relevant and profitable in her tenure. At Christmastime, her boss slips a thousand-dollar check into her card. At election time, politicians traipse up and down the stairs to their conference room, jostling for an endorsement from the editorial board, but in the end it is Angela and her boss who decide— measures of success, surely.

And there's the trivial stuff that in this town often matters more than the substantive—tenth-row seats at the Taper and the opera, premieres and openings. Angela thinks of the press opening of *The Lion King* and remembers walking around with a very impressed friend—Lucia maybe, or Tom—marveling at the jungle within a tent that had been created, complete with a three-foot-wide river lined in savanna grass. Lamb chops passed by waiters, no forks, just take one and eat it as if you are the king of the jungle, wash it down with champagne. If you are here tonight, *you* are the king of the jungle.

So many things other people aspire to have been handed to her for the price of convincing herself and her staff to shackle themselves to their computers twelve hours a day. Convince them they are contributing to something "important," called journalism.

Angela fishes her cell phone from her pocket and tries Louis again. He doesn't pick up.

By 8:40, all of her key staff members have arrived and taken a seat. There's Jorge, the art director, whose tanned skin and handsome new watch make her think he's been to Palm Springs, stopped at the outlets on the way back. Next to Jorge sits Jack, in khakis and a white shirt, his hair wet and combed neatly. As copy chief, Jack embodies the exact opposite of Jorge's relentlessly visual point of view. To Jack, the layouts matter so little, simply function as vehicles for showing off the all-important words. He even argues incessantly with Jorge about photos that take up entire pages, headlines that, in twenty-eight-point type, take up half a page. How dare a photo try to compete with ideas? Next to him is David, the entertainment/

features editor in a gray T-shirt, hands tight around a cup of hot tea, probably hungover. He's a music buff who would like to work at *Rolling Stone* but for now toils here, and it's Angela's job to keep him covering everything, especially the film industry, which Dave detests. Then there's James, in a crisp pink shirt and new glasses. He's the hardworking, incredibly bright senior staff writer who manages to type out seemingly fully formed stories, on which never more than an hour has to be spent editing. Angela can see it won't be long before they have "the talk" and he tells her he's leaving for *The Nation* or some other publication. He's drinking a Diet Coke. Next is Margaret, their editorial assistant and note taker. She's so happy to have a job at a magazine, thrilled at almost anything really, only twenty-two. She's so perky, she even likes talking to publicists. Finally, there's Merrill, the magazine's fifty-seven-year-old news editor, who at first resented Angela for getting the position she was meant to have, then decided to teach her all she knew about L.A.'s history, eventually becoming her friend.

Each editor takes his or her turn going through the list of stories for the next issue and the issue after that, telling the room, but especially Angela, a story's status, what they're waiting for in order to send it to the next person. As Jack finishes up his list, the receptionist buzzes Angela and says that Louis is on the line.

"Excuse me," she tells the group, and turns to take the call.

"I saw you called. Any news?"

"Yeah, yeah. I called and they said that . . . they said she's not awake, really. And hasn't been. She wasn't ever conscious," she says.

"No, no," he says. "That can't be. I spoke with a guy from the embassy. He said she was."

"Well, I think he was mistaken."

"It can't be."

She doesn't know what to say to him.

"A coma?" he says, and it strikes her for the first time, really, what that means.

"I know it's hard to hear."

"Just can't be true," he says.

"She explained it to me."

There's another long pause, as if he's trying to find good arguments why it's not true. "Well, I, uh . . . I'll be leaving in a couple of hours. And I guess I'll call you when I get there, if you don't mind."

"No. I don't mind."

"Thanks, Angela. Thanks. Bye."

She can tell her staff is losing patience, but she's almost scared to turn around. The person she is with them isn't accessible right now and in her place there's seemingly nothing. Her face feels hot and she feels shaky from the inside, as if she's not eaten all day.

She turns slowly, to see her staff staring at her, not hiding their concern or bewilderment. Should they just leave? Are they dismissed?

"Everything all right?" Jorge asks.

"Yeah. No. Family emergency."

"You okay?" Merrill asks.

"Yes. Thanks for asking.

"Sorry, folks. I can't really . . . Why don't we meet again in a couple of hours."

Angela goes back to her office and decides to just sit and think. She turns her chair so that it faces the hills, leans back, and breathes deeply. This is what you're told to do in yoga. Deep breaths allegedly center you or ground you or do whatever else you're supposed to want in life. A new movie billboard is going up on Sunset; it's of a beautiful girl in tiny jeans. Her lips are being rolled on now, five-foot-high lips.

Angela opens the desk drawer where she keeps a manila envelope, inside of which sit clippings of newspaper stories that have touched her in some way. Some are so old, the paper's gone brown-orange and is on the verge of disintegrating. Even the staples feel thin and ready to give out.

She supposedly keeps these to remind her staff that all stories are about people, that issues and ideas can be accessed only through the stories of people. These are teaching tools, she tells herself. Looking through them now, she realizes it's been years since she cried over the story of the eight-year-old brother who died trying to save his baby sister from an oncoming train; the lonely woman who calls 911 once a month, thinking she's having a heart attack, although she's really suffering a panic attack over being left by her husband of forty years; the family separated by the INS—parents in Mexico, the kids living with an aunt in Los Angeles. The photo shows the oldest daughter, age ten, struggling to comfort her little sister, who, at seven, still cries for her mom every single night.

Angela closes her eyes now and thinks of a Polaroid of Kate at maybe ten or eleven, dressed in a bathing suit, arms to her side, shoulders back, chest way out front, her ribs showing through the flimsy material. Her head is tilted back, but her eyes are looking at the camera. From her smile, you get the sense that maybe she was told not to look straight into the camera but couldn't help herself. The smile on her is something—utterly uncontainable—as if the world's entire supply of optimism has been stored there for safekeeping.

"I wanted to be an Olympic swimmer," Kate said to Angela once, looking at the photo of the girl. "I was trusting and friendly. Everyone liked me. And I liked everyone, including my new step-dad. I welcomed him as if he were my real father. I didn't even mind calling him 'Dad.' I was excited to show him what a great new family he had married into."

"Yeah?"

"Yeah," Kate had said that day, and then she hid her face by placing it on Angela's knee. "I was so fucking trusting and happy."

Angela looks up at those hills, then picks up the phone and dials Louis's number.

"Louis, what if I went with you?" she asks.

"Oh. You would?"

"I could. I mean, would that be all right?"

He hesitates, and she knows why. But she doesn't take back her words or fill the silence in any other way.

"Sure. Of course. Kate would probably want that," he says. He feels bad for hedging like that, but then again, does he really want company? He closes his eyes and tries to decide. Fuck it, why not? "I'm sure she would. Yes, yeah, please come. Of course you should. Come with me."

CHAPTER 11
Ibiza
1994

Louis and Angela arrange to meet at the Iberia terminal's café in Madrid's airport. Louis's flight arrives at eleven and hers at two, so he will wait for her. Then they'll fly to Ibiza together. She gets out of the plane fast, walks quickly to customs, chooses the shortest line, makes a quick stop at the bathroom to brush her teeth . . . and here she stands, exhausted, looking at what is essentially a square area off one of the main-gate hubs, with about twenty yellow plastic tables with silver legs sitting in front of a bar that consists of a long glass case and counter manned by two women in white jackets and bow ties. Not exactly the mid-century leather and chrome hipness of other European airports. Spain is still Spain. It may be a more equal and established partner in the European Union than when Angela was last here, but it's still a little shabby around the edges.

Or maybe she has the wrong place. Maybe this is just a café, not the main restaurant in the Iberia lounge. Should I keep looking? she wonders, not yet seeing Louis, who sits at a table by himself, with a family of five nearby, the parents, exhausted, chatting quietly, seemingly oblivious to the energetic children buzzing around them.

Then she does see Louis, or at least a man who looks vaguely American. But this guy wears his hair short, almost shaved. That can't be Louis, can it? A sandwich sits in front of him on a white plate, a white porcelain coffee cup beside it. She watches him for a moment before approaching. He's also more muscled or solid than before. He's in jeans and a long-sleeved checkered shirt, worn open over a dark T-shirt, and black boots. Can it be him?

Louis doesn't fully recognize her, either. Her hair is shorter than when he last saw her, when it was long and curly. She's in flared jeans and a long-sleeved V-necked black top, nice black leather boots. She looks like she lives in L.A.

He looks up. She waves tentatively. He does the same, then stands. She hurries over, puts down her bags, and they hug awkwardly. It's odd, to be sure. They've never been friends per se. Their paths have crossed only because of Kate, but always with her present, a sort of moderator.

"Angela, hey, it's you," he says, and hugs her.

It feels a little awkward because she's never spent more than a few days with him. She defines Louis strictly through what Kate has said about him, the way he's anchored her life. She's formed this idea of him as selfless and good, like some sort of protector, but she doesn't really know.

"Are you tired? How was the flight? I— You hungry?" he says, and they both look down and notice that the napkin he'd had on his lap landed on his knee when he stood to greet her.

"You should eat something. I'm having this; it's not very good. I think you have time to eat before our flight, which is"—he pulls up his shirtsleeve and looks at a big chunky watch—"uh, in about an hour and a half."

Angela feels hungry but also slightly nauseated, which could be from hunger, so she goes to the counter and orders a slice of *tortilla de patatas,* the ubiquitous Spanish frittata made of eggs, potatoes, and onions.

Louis watches her, trying to see Angela as Kate might. She's tall—Louis didn't remember her being that tall—and thinner than he remembers. She was always kind of averagely pretty, but now she looks . . . better, more interesting. Should he say she looks good? No. He can't remember if she's the type of person who would say

"Thanks" or whether she might ask, "What do you mean by that?" and make him explain himself. There are a lot of people like that in San Francisco, always asking, "What did you mean by that?" Better not to risk it.

A minute later, she returns with a plate and a Coke with a straw in it. She tells him that she had to fight for a cold slice of tortilla, not heated in the microwave.

"Not big on doing things differently here."

"I think I've heard her say that. Kind of stubborn, the Spanish."

She thinks about sharing a story about a lady she once taught English to who refused to pronounce the *ch* in words because she didn't think that made sense, but before her jet-lagged brain can get out the story, the father of one of the carousing children suddenly yells at them to calm down, then just as quickly returns his tired gaze to the end of his cigarette. The mother barely looks up from her magazine.

Louis shakes his head, then pulls up and opens a black shoulder bag, from which he extracts a laptop, which he says he'll use to access information on Kate's medical condition.

"One of Kate's colleagues at San Francisco State has a neurologist husband, who offered to be on call for questions. He gave me a few things we can read to understand what's happening. She'll be fine," Louis says, and touches her wrist.

"How long has she been teaching?" Angela asks.

"About a year. Her students love her."

"I'm sure they do," she says.

Louis looks to see if she means this in a malicious way. She doesn't appear to.

"There's some interest in her thesis, might get published. It's called 'From the Me Hurt to the Me Healed Generation.' You know, as in the whole 'me' generation becoming the 'me hurt' generation. Waiting to hear for sure—about the book, I mean—but I think it's a slam dunk."

"I'm happy to hear that," Angela says, and when she looks at

Louis, she can tell he's relieved to know her smile is genuine. Haven't we always known that we both want the best for her? Even when it put us at odds with each other?

"Been a while since you two saw each other," he says, and picks up the coffee cup, though with no apparent interest in taking a sip.

"Yeah. Too long," she says, letting that regret show. Want to see it on my sleeve? Here it is.

"Too bad about the way things went. With you guys. Not that I know much. She didn't talk about it."

"No?"

"No."

Is he waiting for her to elaborate?

"She'll be happy to see you," Louis says finally.

She nods and sips her drink. "I hope so."

CHAPTER 12

Madrid
1989

Like all young people, they think they have all the time in the
world. New Year's Eve, first of all, which they've planned to spend
together, then maybe a weekend of skiing in the Pyrenees and then
a longer spring trip. They've even talked about taking a trip somewhere exotic, like Morocco or Greece.

"Forget Sintra. Let's lie together in warm water," Kate says
during that Christmas break, in the warmth of her room, with its
ridiculous radiator and the view of the orange house and its happy
family, at least as seen through a gauze curtain from a balcony.

"Yes. Let's definitely lie in warm water."

But then, the first day of school after the Christmas holiday,
Kate is called in to speak with Roald Layton, the head administrator
of the Americans Abroad program, and also sitting in that office is
James Wittinger, who looks like he's been crying.

The rumors have finally reached Layton. James has confessed
and agreed to be suspended from teaching for a year, and to seek
counseling. All that's left is the student herself.

"It would be best for you to go home," Layton says. "While I
realize the greater responsibility lies on the shoulders of Mr. Wittinger, who, as a person of authority, could have prevented this, had
he shown far better judgment, I think it would be difficult for you to
continue with your studies in . . . this environment."

"Everyone already knows," Kate says. "Nothing will change for me."

"And yet it would be best," Layton says. When Kate protests again, he finally clarifies that, actually, he hasn't meant to present it as a choice. "Upon close inspection, it's clear to me that your grades have been inflated by Mr. Wittinger, and possibly others, for obvious reasons. I'll have to invalidate those grades, which leaves your GPA—"

"Are you insinuating that—? You're seriously not, are you?"

"I'm insinuating nothing," Layton says as Kate stands.

"You certainly may stay in Spain, but not at the school in this program, although you could, if you wished, reapply for next year," Layton says.

"You complete fuck," she says, looking at James but meaning both men. "I earned those grades like everyone else." Her plea has meant nothing to either man. James, absorbed in the apparent bleakness of his own future, stares at his hands, and Layton at a silver picture frame on his desk.

Kate decides that she wants nothing more to do with Madrid, or anything that reminds her of all this. She calls Louis, who asks if she'd like to come stay with him in New York.

"Why New York?" Angela asks, watching her pack.

"I don't know. 'If you can make it there, you can make it anywhere'?" Kate says. But when she sees the sad look in Angela's eyes, she comes around and sits next to her, leans her head so theirs are touching. They are sitting slumped shoulder to slumped shoulder, ear to ear. She kisses Angela's hand.

"It's just so unfair," Angela says.

"I know."

Kate kisses her cheek, then her lips, gently pushes her back on the bed and kisses her again. The desire of so many weeks locks them together, and soon Kate is pushing her luggage off the bed and pulling at Angela's shirt.

"I want to feel your skin," she whispers as her hands work to undress Angela.

But the fall of the suitcase on the carpet with a muffled thud, the neat piles of clothes all around, the empty top of Kate's bureau, the shadows behind the pictures she hung on the walls so many months ago—all serve as reminders of just how fleeting this pleasure would be.

"Stop, stop. I don't think . . . I want to, but not like this. I don't want it to be sad," Angela says.

Kate caresses her legs. "Come on. Just enjoy it for what it is."

"What it is?"

"Yes."

"I can't. . . . I just . . . I'm the kind of person who thinks children make you less lonely, remember?"

Kate offers a small laugh and lies back on the bed, hand on her face, eyes closed. Her face is flushed. "Agnelli, I knew you'd fall in love," she says, and her eyes fill with tears.

"I couldn't help it," Angela says, and leans over Kate's face and stares at those eyes. "No one could." She wants this to be so much more. She wants this kiss to tell Kate that, despite men like Wittinger, she's hardly disposable, hardly someone you would fit in between now and Berlin with your wife. "Stay here. Get a job; play house with me. Let's turn this from sad to happy."

Kate gets so serious, doubting the invitation, or so Angela thinks. "Sometimes, that's just not . . . Certain people don't have that ability. Happy to sad, sure, but sad to happy . . . not really."

Angela leans down and kisses Kate with every ounce of gratitude and—what else can you call it?—love she can conjure. "You've changed my life from sad to happy," she says.

"Have I?"

"Yeah."

CHAPTER 13
Madrid to Ibiza
1994

An hour and a half after meeting in Madrid, Louis and Angela board a 727 full of young men and women in their late teens or early twenties, mostly German or English, going to Ibiza to party. They all seem to have thrown on at least one beach garment—a T-shirt or thong sandals—combined with jeans or a sweater, probably expecting the plane to be air-conditioned.

Angela and Louis are seated near the front, thank God, where it's quieter. They don't speak much at first, just read. Then Louis orders two scotches and, as they stare at the ice in the little plastic cups, wonder aloud what they will find.

What, exactly, was Kate doing these past few days, before the accident? Louis has asked himself this a dozen times since the phone call. The last time they talked, she sounded secretive, uncertain, as if she wanted to say something but then decided to back off.

"She was just in Brazil. It was tough on her, I think. She called and sounded, I don't know, like she wanted to talk. But then she was on a flight when I called back, so I missed her. Haven't had a chance to really talk for days."

"Well, you will," she says.

"Yeah. Was it hard to get the time off? From work?"

"No, although who knows if this will be a good excuse to . . . you know. Budgets are tight these days."

"Yeah, but you're at the top, so . . ."

"Yeah, the top." Angela finishes the scotch and sighs. "Good to knock off the balance sheet."

"Hey, Mary Sunshine," he says, and laughs.

"I know, can't help it," she says. "My job is essentially to entice people to turn the page and see the next ad so they can buy things they don't need, eat out more, buy CDs, go to movies. A questionable pursuit to begin with and now that no one seems to have much disposable income, it feels slightly criminal. Not to mention difficult."

"Come on, this is the Fourth Estate you're talking about, Woodward!"

"When Botox arrived, the Fourth Estate left the building," she says.

This, Angela realizes, is a sort of rehearsal for what she'll say to Kate when Kate questions why she's not a serious journalist, why she's not telling stories that matter, about Africa, about the Middle East, about immigrants in this country.

"Worse things you could do to people than give them something mindless to read," Louis says, and catches the flight attendant's eye. "Could we get two more scotches, please?" he asks.

"We're landing soon," she says.

"I know, but come on, help us out here," he says, and shakes the glass a little, smiles at her. She clearly finds him attractive. Angela finds herself wondering if he and Kate are together now. It would make sense, she thinks, and is relieved when the flight attendant comes back a few seconds later with two plastic glasses, a shot in each over ice.

"You're very kind," Louis says. People like to be told they're kind, probably because so often they are not.

"Don's a complete asshole. You know that, right?" Louis says, turning to Angela.

"Her stepfather?"

"Yeah. They might notify Don and her mother that she's in the hospital. They might, I don't know, want to come. If they do, it won't be pretty."

"What do you mean?"

"I won't let him near her."

"Who was she traveling with?"

"Two friends. Gay guys."

"I don't remember that much about her mother. Is she . . . Didn't she run a bar or restaurant?"

"Both, sort of. She was an accountant; then, after the dad died, she became a bar manager or something, when she met Don."

The stewardess comes by to collect their cups and tell them they must straighten their seats.

"Don, the great changer of lives."

"All-powerful Don."

CHAPTER 14

Brooklyn
1990

Finally, in February, Kate calls. She's leaving Spain early, not sure where to settle next. What would Louis think of having her come stay a month?

"That would be great. But it's not just me. I don't live alone," he says.

"You don't?"

"No. No. I live with a woman. You'll like her. You'll like each other," he says.

Sandrine says she doesn't mind if Kate comes to stay as long as she likes. But secretly, she wonders if this is a mistake. A man and woman who are best friends, pure friends, can this be?

Sandrine decides to make more of a mark than ever on the apartment, just so it's absolutely clear whose home this is. She starts visiting thrift shops in Queens and the outer boroughs, where she buys a crazy purple couch, a pretty bureau for the bedroom, a chair, some things that are interesting but not too expensive, things they can have reupholstered. She even buys material and does some of the upholstery herself with a staple gun.

"Genius," Louis says, and kisses her neck, her shoulders. "I love a woman who can use a staple gun."

He is so happy thinking she is welcoming his very good friend, when really she's only adding clear markers that this is her home.

Once she moves in, Sandine stops worrying. Kate's friendly but private. And she soon gets a job and is gone most of the time. Whether it's having his friend close or whatever the reason, Louis seems happier, which of course only makes their relationship better.

Kate feels welcomed by the little touches, the pillows Sandrine bought just for her, the chest of drawers, old and hard to shut but beautifully refinished. She appreciates that Sandrine is willing to share the kitchen with her, especially since she's in there almost every evening, braising short ribs, or roasting some poor animal's shoulder. Kate wonders if Sandrine, annoyed at having to share her home with a vegetarian, has become more aggressively carnivorous.

"Do you ever worry that if you were trapped in an elevator with her, she would eat you?" Kate once asked Louis.

"No. Unless I'd seen her put a saltshaker in her purse or something. She likes her meat pretty salty."

Kate is a polite-enough guest, buys food, cleans, is even respectful of Sandrine's role, always asking, "May I have this food?" or "Do you mind if I use these towels I bought instead?" She's polite, but like an aunt who's come to the house she will soon inherit and, though she pretends to like every little thing you have done, has definite plans to change every little thing you have done the minute you are gone. She's helpful, but in an already-apologetic way, as if making amends for Louis's feelings, which he tries so hard to hide.

"So you were dating a married man in Spain," Sandrine says to Kate one day as they stand in the kitchen, waiting for the coffeemaker to deliver a first pot, Sandrine leaning on one counter, Kate on the other.

"Yes. Not a great idea. I don't recommend it."

"No. I would not think so. Do you love him, your married man?"

"Well, no, and he's not mine, is he?"

"No. Right. That is your problem," Sandrine says, and smiles.

You don't know me well enough to be an asshole, Kate thinks, but she shakes it off. Don't, she tells herself. This is Louis's partner.

"No. But . . . Being rejected, to me, can feel like love, sometimes. Being wanted like something bad. I dunno, my wiring's kind of . . . faulty," Kate says, and smiles.

"Oh, yes," Sandrine says, "Louis has told me. Do you think Louis will ever ask me to marry him?" Sandrine asks.

Kate knows she's supposed to answer quickly and with assurance, act the part of conspirational woman friend, especially since she is Louis's best friend and would, presumably, know the answer to this question better than anyone. But the "Oh, yes, Louis has told me" tossed off so cavalierly has annoyed Kate.

"We don't . . . talk about those types of things, Louis and I."

"Oh, I see," Sandrine says, defiance immediately replaced by hurt.

Kate feels bad for the girl. And Sandrine does seem like a girl, most definitely, right now, so badly having wanted to injure her opponent, but shocked instead to find herself bleeding and bruised.

"It's nice to see how you are, you and Louis," Kate says. "When I see you guys doing something together . . . or when you bring him coffee or some food, and the way he looks up at you, it's sweet. It's nice," Kate says, frustrated at herself for this verbal hedging, this inability to reassure the girl. "I've never seen him so in love," she says finally, and she can feel herself looking beseechingly at Sandrine. Believe me. Please.

"Yes, of course, definitely," Sandrine says, and turns quickly to pour the coffee.

In the spring, Kate says she plans to stay in New York and starts looking for an apartment of her own, but both Louis and Sandrine say they want her to stay, so she does.

Kate and Louis have dinner together once a week, the night

Sandrine takes a business class. It's her dream to open an employment agency, like the one her uncle runs in the south of France. So, once a week, she treks to the city, to an extension program. And Louis and Kate have the night to themselves to go out or stay in, to make dinner or order pizza and plays cards—whatever they want.

At dinner, it feels like old times, plus a little more. He's more confident now, not afraid to show off a little. He's funny and nice. Interested in people. He asks questions of those around them, the waitress, the bartender.

"I like how you turned out. Sandrine has done a fine job," she says, and he smiles.

"What am I, made of clay?"

"Yes. You're a man; you are made of clay. And so am I. I'm made of clay and you shaped me those first years, didn't you?"

"I did. On that floaty in the pool, I shaped you and you shaped me. God, I wanted to kiss you then," he says, and blushes but keeps looking into her eyes. He knows he should look away, but he doesn't want to.

She smiles but changes the conversation.

"I think you should think about marrying Sandrine," Kate tells him another day, during dinner, and Louis stops chewing, puts his hand to his mouth, and speaks through his fingers.

"What the fuck is that about?"

"She's a nice girl. You should think about it," she says.

"Why are you saying this?" he asks, and takes a big mouthful of wine.

"I think she wants it. Normal girls want to get married."

"Oh, really? Is that what they want?" he teases. "Did you just read a normal-girl manual?"

"As it happens, I work with several of them and they all run to the bathroom all day and take secret hits of wedding magazine pages. They're all little addicts. They dream about it at night, the way you dream about music or computers or whatever it is you dream about."

"Kittens, I dream about kittens," he says.

"Right."

"I have an idea. Why don't I marry you instead?" he says, and meets her stare—slightly shocked?—with a smile, pokes at the ravioli on her plate, offers a smile that's sexy, and more than a little disarming.

"Watch out I don't take you up on that offer," she says, and smiles at him exactly the same way he's looking at her.

"Come on, tough guy, I can take it."

The dinner ends and soon they're in a cab, riding home in silence. But it's the most buzzed-up, euphoric, can't-stop-this-now silence he's ever experienced. He can't pass up this chance.

"Kate?"

"Yeah?" Her head's resting on the back of the seat, her hand on his leg. He puts his hand against her hip and leans in, kisses her. She touches his hair and pulls him in ever so slightly and the kiss quickly takes them far beyond friendship, leaving them firmly in a state of desire. He goes to pull her closer, but she resists ever so slightly, so he stops the kiss, although they linger close, as if considering whether to start again. They don't, but it's not gone, this energy. She walks up the stairs fast and he catches up midway, kisses her again.

"Louis, I don't think . . ."

"Stop thinking," he says, and puts the key in the lock.

And, as quickly and unexpectedly as it began, it's over.

"Hallo!" Sandrine calls, and jumps up from the couch to embrace Louis. It takes him a minute to find some normal-sounding words, to act as if nothing was about to happen. Sandrine doesn't seem to have guessed anything. Kate doesn't even look at him as she says good night and heads to her room.

Kate knows what she's playing at and she doesn't like it—oldest game in the world: wanting what you can't have. And, even worse, wanting to take away what another woman has. Kate has studied enough anthropology, read about enough matriarchies and colonies of women, to know the behavior's history and context—trying to take the men of procreating age, plus a spare or two. She won't let herself behave this way.

Just as she's been able to push away any desire to do things like eat a BLT, by choosing reason over base instincts, so, too, does she tell herself that Louis is a friend into whose heart she'll never trespass.

CHAPTER 15

Ibiza
1994

If they thought the plane was filled with young people, after arriving in San Pedro itself, driving to the airport, they realize every inch of the island is covered with twenty-something revelers.

Groups of ten or more girls stroll the sidewalks, sometimes laughing so loudly, it's obvious they're just trying to get attention. The boys use shouts the way the girls use their laughs, calling to friends across the street, sometimes even walking into traffic to cross over to a group of pals, which annoys their cabdriver.

"*Putos ingleses y alemanes,*" the driver says, thinking neither Louis nor Angela speaks Spanish.

"What's he . . ." Louis says, wanting a translation.

" 'Fucking English, fucking Germans.' "

Louis lays his head back and closes his eyes. He likes the way touristy towns get crowded with people hungry for a good time, and the smell of fried food meant to entice visitors ready to eat badly on vacation, the sound of disco music blaring from shops and restaurants, the aroma of bus exhaust and beer-drenched peanut shells. These are the smells of concentrated good times. He and Kate have been to so many such places. Kate always rails against the commercialism, the crowds of "cruise ship cows," as she calls them, mooing their way into tchotchke shops to buy junk for their loved ones back home to fake-smile at and then shove into a kitchen drawer. But Louis likes the sight of these tourists, for some reason. He likes their ambition. See! Photograph! Eat! Buy! Drink! Forget home! Remember this forever!

"Why don't you stay home awhile, skip the Brazil trip? Don't go to Spain this summer; wait till next year," Louis had argued. She didn't mind skipping Brazil but didn't want to let down Paul and Liam by canceling Spain. They'd never been and wanted her to act as a sort of guide.

Thousands of young English and German tourists flock to Ibiza every spring, summer, and fall, with its scrubby, barren landscape and reputation as the bad hippie girl of the three Balearic Islands. While Majorca and Minorca attract yacht dwellers in white who sip pinot grigio, Ibiza attracts the "better living through pharmacology" crowd that stays up until seven in the morning, dancing in cavernous clubs with swimming pool slides, rooms that get filled with foam or fake snow.

Kate and Liam and Paul wanted to see that but not partake so much. They, too, felt old among the kids, Kate told Louis on the phone only three days ago. And Kate said she wasn't feeling great, having some stomach problems. He told her to come home early. If only she had.

Their taxi pulls up to the hospital at seven in the evening, just as the heat is finally starting to diminish, the sky turning dark blue. A two-story seventies-looking building on the outskirts of town, it could be a bank or even a hotel.

"Is this the place?" Louis asks Angela, and she checks with the cabdriver, who tells her yes, this is it.

They pay the man and pick up their luggage, then walk to the entrance, where Louis stands, waiting for the glass doors to open up automatically, as they would in the United States. Angela takes the handle and pulls, which makes him laugh.

"I am so out of it," he says, and shakes his head.

The lobby isn't hospital-like at all—dark gray tiled floors, big potted palms, rows of black leather chairs, like an airport or the lobby of one of those fifties-style hotels in Miami Beach. And the air is heavy with overly perfumed water that someone seems to just have used on the floors. Not a bad way to be greeted by a hospital, but not familiar—none of the beige carpeting and framed Monet prints typical of American hospitals. Young-looking nurses in jeans and white lab coats stand chatting with one another at a desk.

Angela goes to the desk and asks about Kate and is told that one of the doctors should come to the desk momentarily.

"Ask if she's conscious," Louis says. Angela turns to do that, but most of the nurses have gone back to chatting quietly in a corner. One of them, with long, straight hair, hangs back a little and even allows eye contact with Angela, then moves back to the desk.

"*¿Si? Tienes una pregunta?*" she says, asking if Angela has a question.

"Can you just tell me the room number, and then we can go see her?"

"Yes," the nurse says, and looks at the desk, pulls out a chart.

"Has something changed? Is she all right?" Angela asks the nurse.

Although Louis doesn't speak Spanish, he senses a change in Angela's voice.

"No, nothing's happened. *Tranquila,*" the young nurse says, trying to calm her.

"The way she looked at us . . ." Louis says.

"I know, but she says it's okay."

After a few minutes of waiting, a doctor does indeed come to the desk, takes three files and opens each, makes notes. He seems about to leave, and the nurses seem in no hurry to stop him, so Angela asks him to wait, explains that they're here to see Kate.

He's about forty-five, with a shaved head but longish sideburns and a strong nose. Alberto Santillan is his name and he speaks in broken, British-sounding English until Angela tell him she speaks Spanish. "Oh, good," he says, "much easier."

The doctor explains that Kate has suffered an internal head injury as a result of the accident. That blunt trauma, in turn, caused her to have some internal bleeding.

"Acute subdural hematoma," he says in English. "We were able to look at the CT scan and locate the area of the bleed. The blood was causing pressure buildup in the brain and, we feel, was contributing to her altered state of consciousness."

Emergency surgery was needed to reduce that pressure within the brain. This involved drilling a small hole in the skull, which allowed the blood to drain and relieved the pressure on the brain. Fortunately, she hasn't had any seizures—common in this type of injury.

The doctor looks at them, notices their lost expressions. He takes out a pad and draws, then shows them the drawing. Angela can't help but notice that the drawing resembles a section of a grapefruit when it's peeled.

Santillan points to areas of the grapefruit drawing as he explains. "Here is where the bleeding was. Luckily, it was contained within this area and didn't press on this area—the breathing center of the brain. It also did not affect the speech center, so we are hopeful that her speech may return once the swelling goes down. This is where we did the surgery and were able to drain the blood."

"That's good," Angela says.

"Yes, yes. She tolerated the surgery very well. Her vital signs have remained stable. As a precaution, we are keeping her on some medication through the IV to prevent the buildup of pressure—also very common after brain surgery—and an additional medication so she won't suffer from seizure," he says.

"So why hasn't she woken up yet, if the surgery was successful?" Louis asks. "Is it because of the medication she's on?"

"No, not because of the medication. What you're referring to is a medically induced coma. We would go that route if she were to have seizures or have very increased brain pressure or the like. Fortunately, she hasn't had any seizure activity. We take that as a very positive sign."

"Was she awake? Was she ever speaking?" Louis asks.

"Not speaking, no, but she was making sounds, which is good, and she did react to pain. Her pupil reaction was good. She is in the middle of the Glasgow Coma Scale. It's how we measure this."

Angela and Louis take in this information. The doctor shakes his head, as if to pull away from the disappointment he can see he's caused them.

"Also, she is breathing on her own. We are giving her oxygen through the canula only as an additional precaution. If there were more severe damage to, say, the area of the brain that controls breathing—which we haven't seen any evidence of—we would have had to leave the breathing tube in. That she has been able to breathe on her own is very positive. With her age, in good health, as she is, there is a chance she will awaken. And hopefully without brain damage," he says.

This is meant as good news, but Louis had never considered anything like this: She *might* survive. She *may not* have brain damage. Maybe? He cannot, despite the best efforts of his own uninjured brain, make sense of this.

When Angela asks the doctor when they might expect Kate to wake up and if there's a way of measuring progress, the doctor says they'll do a CT scan tomorrow or the next day to check her status. But of course the ultimate proof of success is in her waking up, in her opening her eyes.

"The brain is very complex. We can't predict absolute time or response following an injury such as hers. But please, believe me. We are doing everything we can possibly do while she is here. We have to remain cautiously optimistic that your friend will recover. "*Y que veremos esos ojos bonitos finalmente abiertos,*" he says. "That we'll see those pretty eyes open," he adds in English.

"How do you know they're pretty?" Louis asks. "Was Kate awake when they first brought her in?"

The doctor nods no and his shoulders slump. "The next seventy-two hours will be very crucial in seeing how she does," he says, and starts to walk away.

"Wait," Louis says to Angela. "Ask him if they can operate again to relieve the pressure, if they can help her that way. Ask him if they would in a bigger hospital; ask him if they're lacking the equipment or money. Tell him we have money."

"Money is . . . not a cure," the doctor says in English. "If it was, no Americans would ever be sick," he adds, and smiles. "Another operation is not the answer at this time. Any more trauma to the brain causes even more swelling. What she and her brain needs is rest, not another surgery."

He puts his hand on Louis's shoulder. "Go to see her," he says in English. "Go to say hello and give to her your love."

Louis wants to say more, to argue and convince the doctor of something, but he is not sure of what, exactly. The nurse with the long hair steps out from behind the desk and offers to escort them to the room.

After walking down several corridors, she stops and motions for them to enter the room, but they both hang back, a little scared to see Kate like this. It's a small room but private and bright, with a window in the corner and two blue vinyl chairs. Next to the bed sits a heart and blood pressure monitor and an automated IV drip. Angela and Louis both step inside but stay near the door, put down their luggage.

"*Se pueden quedar por quince minutos, vale?*" the nurse says. They have fifteen minutes.

Neither one is sure what to do next. Louis steps inside first, but he stays about two feet from her. The back of the bed has been elevated, so that Kate's almost sitting up.

"She's so tan," Angela says, looking at those arms, so long and dark. She feels silly for pointing this out until she notices that Louis's shoulders have dropped a bit. He smiles at Angela and nods.

"Yeah, yeah, look at her. She's brown as a berry."

They both approach the bed now.

Kate's head is tilted just slightly to one side and is partially bandaged, not as much as either of them expected. Two clear prongs in her nose are giving her oxygen from a tank near the bed. Louis and Angela both stand there staring in silence, relieved to be with Kate, slowly releasing the fear they've been carrying—that it would be too late to ever see her alive. They're both oddly content at the moment, although also uncertain what to do with this silent Kate.

Words fail utterly to explain how bizarre it is to be standing next to such a still version of Kate Harrington. Even shut, her eyes command so much attention. Even with their lids drawn, they're huge—two big mounds lined in impossibly long lashes.

"No wonder the doctor said her eyes were pretty," Angela says.

"She found a Japanese spa where they tint her lashes with organic dye or something. So San Francisco," Louis says. "My little yuppie princess," he murmurs, leaning near her ear. Getting this close seems to give Louis permission to take her hand in his.

This feels right, finally, after two days of so many things that haven't felt right. Her hand, every centimeter of it, feels familiar, and he retraces the lines as if on a bed with her, the lazy exploration of a lover on a weekend morning. As the tip of his finger rounds each knuckle, he feels like he's going inside her heart, even looks to see if her eyes have opened as a result. He holds Kate's hand against his face, then turns so that his cheek rests on her wrist. Can he feel her heartbeat? In his mind, he can hear her talking to him as if from another room, so he rubs the beauty mark on her right hand, then runs his finger over the lines in her palm. Some tarot reader in Berkeley once told her she would live to be eighty-five and have five children because of these lines. Louis indulges the fantasy of her talking to him from the shower or the kitchen as he stares at the lines of her palm and tries to see eighty-five, not to mention five kids.

It feels so real, her hand, especially when he takes it and rubs his cheek with it, as if she were moving the hand, as if you could expect her to say, "The least you could do was shave, hippie boy."

He smiles at her as if she did say this, then turns to Angela, who looks thoroughly unanchored, like a kid on the first day of kindergarten.

"Brazil. That's why she's so dark," he says.

Angela looks surprised, his voice the last thing she expected to hear.

"What?"

"She was in Brazil, remember?"

"Oh, right," she says. "What was she doing there?"

"You can come closer," Louis says.

Angela leans in a little and puts her hand on Kate's shoulder, mostly feeling the baby blue gown in which they've dressed her. She can't imagine American hospitals washing and rewashing a garment enough to get it this soft.

"That lipstick," she says. Someone's put a dark shade of pink lipstick on Kate, probably a nurse trying to pretty her up for visitors.

"Yeah," Louis replies, and looks, as if for the first time, at Kate's pink lips. "Pretty garish." Angela feels physically unable to speak. She feels as if she and Louis are children whose father has passed out at Christmas, and they're coping by pretending not to see the nearly lifeless person in front of them. Angela can feel herself wanting to fall into that lifelessness.

"Fucking hell, Kate," Louis says, and shakes his head hard. "I'm going to get some air now." He slips out of the room, fast.

Angela, arms folded around her body, moves closer to the bed. Kate's bandages are clean, her breathing steady. That trace of pink covers her lips, making her look like a forties movie star, sick but glamorous as hell.

"Look at you," she says, and stands there for a long time, almost afraid Kate will open her eyes. She waits a moment, in case that happens, but it doesn't. In fact, Kate's eyes appear so resolutely shut.

"Kate," she whispers in her ear. "Hey, it's me." She doesn't know why, but just saying "It's me" makes Angela want to cry. She says it again, her voice hoarse. "It's me, Kate."

Stop, stop, stop. She reaches for something concrete, something she can see right now—Kate's hair. Around her ears, there's a tiny patch of gray. Angela's about to say something, tease Kate about going gray, when a different, older nurse comes into the room and begins speaking very emphatically about the need for Kate to rest. And anyway, visitors are allowed to stay for only ten minutes, and she and the gentleman have been here far longer.

"We were told fifteen minutes."

"No, no, it's ten," the nurse says, and gives a look that says, Don't try that on me.

Angela whispers to Kate: "We'll come back soon."

On her way out of the clinic, Angela stops at the desk near the door and finds the nurse with the long, straight hair. "Hi. Thank you for your help. My name is Angela," she says. Carolina is the nurse's name.

"I'm sorry about that. Where I used to work, it was fifteen."

"That's all right," Angela says. "Thank you for taking care of Kate."

"You're welcome," the nurse says, and smiles shyly.

Patients in critical care may have visitors three times a day—at nine in the morning, at three in the afternoon, and again in the evening, at seven, as long as the doctors don't prohibit visits, Carolina explains, like a child reciting times tables she's only recently memorized.

Louis walks up and asks Angela why she left the room.

"Asked me to."

"Oh," he says. "Please tell her we need to talk to the doctor again." Angela does but is told he's left to visit another hospital where he's affiliated.

"Which one?" Louis asks, and Angela translates, but Carolina doesn't give them the name. "He'll be here tomorrow morning," she says.

"Is there a better hospital here on the island? I mean, this is fine, but is there a bigger hospital with the best technology, the best doctors?"

"There's a hospital, but it's not bigger," Carolina says.

"Okay, thanks," Angela replies.

As Angela and Louis stand outside discussing the idea of flying Kate to Madrid, a man in his sixties, with white-blond hair and deep, deep wrinkles approaches them. He's wearing high-wasted jeans and a striped polo shirt with a dark blue blazer over it.

"Are you folks here to visit Kate Harrington?" he asks.

"Yes, yes," Louis says, and steps forward to shake the man's hand before Angela can. "You're Ted," Louis says, sounding excited.

"Right. Ted Griffin, duty officer from the consulate in Madrid," he says.

"I'm Louis Ross, Kate's husband," Louis says. "And this is her sister Angela."

Angela tries not to show surprise at the idea of Louis as husband and herself as sister to Kate.

"Oh, I didn't . . . I was not aware that you were married," Griffin says, looking comforted, maybe, by the information. "Wish we were meeting under different circumstances," he adds.

"Yes, me, too," Louis says.

"I think I told you on the phone, that we're vacationing here for a couple more days—my wife and I and our daughter. That's why we're here in Ibiza instead of Majorca. Well, anyway . . . I got a call from Madrid about Ms. Harrington. Asked me to check in, offer any assistance you might need, make sure the family's been contacted."

"We're her only family. I mean, apart from her mother, and I called her," Louis says.

"Oh, good." Griffin half-smiles and uses his forefinger and thumb to push up his glasses. "Have you been able to see her? Do you need a translator?"

"We did, we saw her," Louis says, and runs his hands over his head. "Listen, Mr. Griffin, what's the plan, because I think we'd like to fly her to Madrid, to a better hospital."

"This is a small island, true enough, but . . . they seem very competent to me."

"We kind of think we should have had her flown out right away, that first day," Louis says.

"That was only a day and a half ago, Mr. Ross. I was in no position to make that decision."

"I'm not saying you should have. Just that it might be good for it to happen now. That's all."

"Right, okay," Griffin says, hands on his hips, not sure how to break this impasse.

"Sir, is there a way you can find out?" Angela asks. "Even if it turns out we shouldn't do anything different, could we know the options? Or maybe someone can be flown here—an expert. Won't the embassy know if this is the best we can do for her?"

"I'll find out. I'll do that," he says. "I sure will. In the meantime . . ."

Griffin puts a hand on each of their shoulders and reassures them that in the morning they'll know better. This is like the coach trying to give you some bullshit strategy to beat the other team, the one that's never lost a game, just so he can still feel important and coachlike.

"Get some rest," Griffin says.

He doesn't know what to do, so he's resorting to clichés and stalling, Angela thinks. "What happened to the guys she was here with, Paul and the other guy?"

Griffin just looks at Louis for a second, as if he doesn't understand the question. "They were escorted home by, umm, the young Englishman's—Liam's—father, George. I understand they'll be buried in England, both of them," he says. "Their families didn't call you, then, I take it?"

"No, no. Or maybe they did, but we've been traveling, so . . . I didn't know them that well," Louis says.

Griffin seems confused—wondering, no doubt, why it is that Louis's wife was traveling around Spain with two men her husband doesn't know.

"Well, my condolences to you nevertheless," Griffin says, and hands Louis a card on which he's already written the address of the hotel where Kate, Liam, and Paul had been staying. "The embassy will pay for it if you want to lodge there," he says. "Or somewhere else is fine, too. Wherever you're comfortable. Just not a luxury hotel, please."

"We'll stay where they stayed. Thanks," Louis says, and shakes Griffin's hand.

"As I believe I mentioned, Ms. Harrington listed her mother on the airline contact form."

"Right, and I called her," Louis says.

"So did the airline. I believe they gave her my number, as well. I'll be sure to let you know if she's coming," Griffin says.

Louis doesn't say anything, just stares at him in a way that makes Angela nervous. "If she's coming? Why would she do that?" he says, exasperated.

"Well, the usual reasons a mother would fly to be with her daughter."

"This is not June Cleaver we're talking about," Louis says in a cold tone that surprises Angela, and Griffin, too, from the look on his face.

Angela puts her hand out to shake good-bye. "Thank you so much, Mr. Griffin," she says. "Please do let us know right away if she's coming."

"Certainly," Griffin says, and walks away.

Even after Griffin's left the building, Louis stares intently at the doors through which he exited.

"If Don comes here, to this hospital, to that room, I will kill him myself," Louis says, not the slightest hint of aggression or anger in his voice, only certainty.

111

CHAPTER 16
A Hotel Room in Ibiza
1994

The hotel where Kate and the boys had been staying sits off the beaten path, several blocks from the beach, on a plain street with four- and five-story seventies-looking apartment buildings. The cab starts to slow down as it passes a hair salon, several small boutiques, and a large pharmacy.

At first, Louis assumes the driver's gotten it wrong—there can't be hotels here, not when some balconies have laundry hanging from a line, when the plaza across the street has kids riding ancient-looking seesaws, and men and women as old as the playground toys sitting on benches, legs crossed, moving to the rhythm of the see-saw. But the driver stops the car and points out the window.

"Hotel Rondo, *aquí está,*" he says. It's a three-story white building with a small yellow sign over the door; underneath the name are three stars.

The concierge, a pear-shaped lady in her sixties with a pronounced limp, looks so sad when Angela tells her who they are. She says she will take them to the room where Angela and the boys had been staying.

"*Vengan, vengan,*" she says, and leads them to a tiny elevator with a rusted accordionlike grille you must pull hard in order for it to latch. Up they go, until they reach the third floor. The elevator makes a small but hard downward fall as it aligns itself with the door.

"This is not like Kate," Louis says. "Those guys must have guilted her into staying at this hotel."

The concierge leads them down a hall where at least one bulb needs replacing and opens the door, motions with her hands going round and round, as if polishing a floor, then points to herself and nods "no" fervently, trying to explain that she didn't clean the room.

"*Está bien*," Angela says. "*No importa. No se preocupe.*"

"*No limpiar,*" the woman says loudly, the way people sometimes speak to foreigners or the deaf. Although Angela has been speaking to the woman in perfect Spanish, the old lady hasn't computed this—something that used to happen all the time to Angela, Kate, and the other Americans living in Madrid. Because they looked and dressed like Americans, the locals sometimes took several minutes to understand that the gringas and gringos were speaking to them in Spanish, not English. Perception trumps reality.

Louis hands the concierge some dollar bills and she nods vigorously and thanks him several times before finally leaving.

Angela's relieved for the windows and glass balcony doors, and the rich brown wood flooring. Old carpets and dreary light would be tough to bear right now.

To the left of the door, abutting clean white walls, sit two full-size beds covered in brightly colored spreads—one magenta, the other yellow. Propped jauntily on each of the beds is a blue sixties-looking pillow with a large button at its center. Between the beds sits a square seventies end table and on it a large yellow ceramic lamp dotted with white porcelain roses. A thick water glass sits beside the lamp, in it two gardenia blossoms. On the right side of the room is a long credenza with six drawers and a light blue vinyl top. Nothing in the room is particularly well matched or especially lovely, but every bit has been lovingly cared for.

"Didn't the embassy guy say their stuff would be here?" Louis asks.

"Yeah, he did," Angela replies, and sets her own suitcase atop the yellow bed.

Louis walks to the right, where the bathroom is, and notices a closet door, opens it and sees Kate's suitcase there on the floor. He picks it up and carries it to the magenta bed, opens it.

A quick look reveals the stuff on top: shorts, a top, a bra, a bag with the word *farmacia* written on it. Liam's father must have been by and picked up his son's and his son's boyfriend's things, and put this suitcase away. But then Louis realizes he's wrong, because so many of the men's belongings lie here and there in the bathroom.

Angela takes the Stephen King book lying open and facedown on the table and closes it, then looks at the inside cover, where there's a receipt with the name Liam Randall.

"Whoever picked up their stuff was in a hurry or just didn't want to look around," Louis says as Angela eyes a pair of khaki shorts hanging on the closet door, surely not Kate's. "His father probably couldn't handle it."

"I guess not," Angela says, and rests her hand on her suitcase, like a kid at camp clinging to one thing with which she is familiar. Then she lies back and pulls up her legs. "Wow," she says, the pleasure of this simple act a revelation.

Louis wanders into the bathroom to wash his face, and as he leans over the sink, he inventories the contents around it like an anthropologist. To the left are Kate's toiletries, all Lancôme, pushed together so they resemble a white-and-gray office tower, then her makeup in a hot pink bag. To the right of the sink lie the boys' shaving creams from Kiehl's, and three toothbrushes, two that look alike and one he recognizes from their home. Louis thinks of picking up her brush, but instead he lifts the glass and looks at it, trying to ascertain how much toothbrush gunk is at the bottom.

"You've watched too much television," he whispers into the mirror, feeling like one of those postmortem detectives who wow audiences by picking up clues in the places most people ignore. Kate makes fun of these shows, and how each one positions its heroes as the main investigators. In one show, it's the cops who find the killer;

in another, the crime-scene investigators do all the work; in yet another, the coroner is firmly in charge. Kate jokes that she wants to write her own show, called *Follicle,* in which the mortuary hairstylist solves cases.

He turns the faucet and watches the water come out, then cups his hands and washes his face. On the pegs where towels should hang, Louis finds, instead, two shirts. He touches one and takes a deep breath, thinks he smells the smoke of a club mixed with men's cologne. They were airing the shirts out in here, but whatever Kate was wearing will be elsewhere, he thinks, and immediately knows exactly where.

Kate would never hang anything in a bathroom—God forbid a garment be touched in any way by mildew, one of her mortal enemies. At home, even in "San Frantartica," as she calls it, Kate insists the tiny window in their bathroom remain open at all times to prevent mildew. They argue about this sometimes, after Louis, in the shower, has noticed his nipples are erect from the cold air coming in through that damned open window. It is fundamentally wrong to feel chilly when you are standing under a torrent of boiling hot water, he contends.

Louis dries his face, then pushes his hand into the makeup bag—did she bring it? He feels a square glass bottle and sighs with relief, then takes it out and examines the small bottle of perfume he knows to be Kate's. She buys it at the same spa where she has her eyelashes dyed. Made just for her by the elderly Japanese owner, who has a crush on Kate, like most everyone else in her life, it smells of tea and oranges and patchouli or cinnamon . . . a little . . . sandalwood, maybe?

After stretching her back a bit, Angela decides to check out the balcony, see if there's any kind of view. Not really, but something maybe better than a view—a black dress hanging from a line running just above the door frame.

The dress has a low back and low front, and small pink beads along the neckline—a bold shape but sweet details. Angela turns and looks down at the street below, the other buildings with their satellite receivers, some balconies crammed with plants, others bare. She listens to unseen kids hollering as they plow down unseen corridors, their voices echoing until they spill into what she imagines is a bare courtyard somewhere. She takes the deepest breath possible, searching for the smell of the ocean, but also enjoying the peripheral view, pretending the dress is Kate herself. She tries to bring together those brown arms on the bed, so that they're here, too, those shoulders holding the dress, hand an inch or so away from hers.

How can one person you haven't seen in so long, from whom so many things have allegedly distanced you, still make you feel this way?

Louis steps out onto the balcony, carrying the perfume bottle.

"Hello, Kate," he says to the dress, "I knew you'd be out here."

Louis reaches out and touches Angela's arms. "May I?" he says, and holds up the perfume bottle.

"Sure," she says. "Is this on sale today?"

"Yeah, our best-selling scent," he says, and tips the bottle onto one of Angela's wrists, leaving just a dab behind. She puts that wrist against the other, waits for it to dry, then puts it to her nose. It smells wonderful.

"She's going to be all right. I feel it," Louis says.

"Do you?"

"Yeah," he says, and leans on the edge of the balcony, tips the bottle onto his own wrist, and rubs it against the other.

"And your feelings are pretty accurate?"

"I'm not famous for them or anything. No one's ever called me psychic, but . . . yeah, I think so," he says, and stares out at this view, if you can call it that. "Let's see how it goes tomorrow. Maybe we can move her. I don't want Don and Georgina to come here."

"They won't."

"Sure they will. He will. He wouldn't pass up an opportunity to see Kate all helpless and vulnerable, lying there—"

"Please, Louis. Don't," she says, and leans forward, her head heavy.

"Sorry. Fine. Everything is fine," he says, and rubs her back. "I'm glad you're here."

"You are?"

"Yeah."

CHAPTER 17
Spain and California
1990–1991

In Madrid, Angela decides to focus on her future, pick a career and not think too much about anything else. She's always loved the idea of reporting, of covering wars and fights. Unlike the United States, Spain at least has clashes and dramatic politics. When she hears of a demonstration in San Sebastián, mounted by Basque separatist sympathizers, she and her friend Eddie head there, cameras and notebooks in hand. They follow a few rowdy protesters away from the march and into the tiny, labyrinthine streets of the old part of the city, a tactic to draw in the police to an area where guerrilla fighting is easier, they soon realize as rocks and tear gas canisters fly over and around them. Scared, so out of breath that she thinks she might vomit, and completely uncertain if her leg is moist from sweat or something else, Angela knows journalism is the right choice.

She interns for a few months for a reporter from the Voice of America, who pushes her to become a stringer for *Newsweek,* and one of her stories—yes, three paragraphs, but a story nevertheless—gets published in the international edition.

She and Kate speak a few times and Angela writes her a dozen letters but mails only a few. Time starts to wear away the potential of Kate and Angela and leaves only the facts—a short but intense friendship between two women who were attracted to each other but acted on it only in the most modest way. It becomes too difficult, for

Angela anyway, to navigate the difference between what she'd felt and what had actually transpired, especially when she imagines how many people Kate will be meeting in New York.

If she graduates and stays in Spain, who knows, maybe she could become a reporter for *Newsweek*. Maybe she can branch out and try to cover stories in Portugal, even Morocco. But one day, as she sits outside, having a beer near the Prado under a canopy of leaves, she imagines how bare this tree will be in three months' time and wonders if it's time to go home.

If the point had been to grow up and become what your intrinsic characteristics and desires were going to lead you to become, as opposed to falling under the spell of family or cultural expectations, well, she's more or less done that.

So why not reward the homesick girl who'd conquered Madrid by letting her go home and graduate then spend some time with her parents? The more she thinks about it, the more she aches for the simple happiness of sitting at the table as Mom sets down a delicious meal, of saying yes to Dad's offer to go play racquetball at the junior high or wash the cars together in the intense heat of eastern San Diego County. Why not?

At first, she's not sure if she can fit again with the family she once so missed. Her sister, now nineteen, lives nearby; her brother, fourteen, lives with her parents. Angela rents a place just minutes from their home and gets a job at the local paper, taking ads and obits over the phone, chasing the occasional ambulance or fire truck.

She has dinner at her parents' often. On weekends, it's errands with her mom or her sister, then one long, lazy barbecue on Sunday. And in some way, they always make it seem as if they're still celebrating her return from Europe. Nearly every Sunday that summer, she finds herself nursing a beer and happily watching her father cook short ribs, her mother setting a salad on the table, along with red peppers and onions, Angela's favorite. It feels ideal, and she starts to think it can work.

She meets Alex, a reporter, who's mustached and tall, almost magazine handsome. Smart and confident, he's also funny and playful.

"You are so damned lucky," says her friend Heather as they sit at a table in a restaurant and watch Alex arrive, speak with the hostess, then start walking toward them, looking handsome and sexy but with a big sweet smile on his face.

I can do this, she thinks. She even takes him to dinner at her parents' home and they like him. He speaks some Spanish and clearly wants to ingratiate himself.

But she feels like such a fake every time she kisses him, especially when she begins to sense his interest in her grow. Only after quite a few drinks can she bring herself to make love. As he reaches for her afterward, his arms holding her in a loving, protective embrace, she kisses his arm and sighs so heavily, it worries him.

"You okay?"

"Yes," she says, and caresses his wrist.

She realizes that she'd held off making love to him in order to postpone this, the undeniable and absolute knowledge that it won't work. She has to be honest again. Strange, that the act of being yourself isn't one constant forward trajectory, or at least not for her, but a few steps forward, then back, then forward again.

Maybe she needs to move away again, in order to really be honest, although not as far as Spain. She looks for and eventually finds a new job two hours away, in Ventura, a town on the beach but not defined by it the way San Diego is. In fact, all around Ventura are little towns defined instead by the produce they grow—strawberries, cantaloupe, broccoli, citrus—nothing to do with the ocean.

And because of that need for migrant workers to plant and harvest these fields, the town's demographics are now half Latino, and the newspaper needs bilingual reporters to cover schools. No more obits on the phone, time to be a real reporter.

Her departure this time is easier on her family and on her, because the distance isn't so great. Angela rents a big studio apartment in an ugly seventies building on an ugly street but with a view of the ocean from the bathroom window, which sits, unfortunately, high above the shower. It's tough for her family to hide their disappointment.

"It's very clean," her mother says on her first visit.

Nearly every day, wearing a skirt in order to look professional and not gay, although she'd never admit this to herself, Angela treks out to school board meetings in Oxnard, Camarillo, Moorpark. Occasionally, one of her stories ends up on the front page, usually with a headline that says something like IMMIGRANT GIRL, SMUGGLED IN CAR, GOES TO STANFORD!

"This makes it sound like she rode to Stanford in a trunk," she'll argue with the copy editor.

"Newspaper shorthand, sweetie. Get over it," he says.

Despite its headline, Angela wants to feel proud of this, her first front-page story, so she sends the clip to her parents. And the next Saturday, as she sits on her futon drinking coffee, Angela watches a man in a red T-shirt and matching ball cap walk up the ugly stairs and down the corridor toward her, holding a vase with a dozen yellow roses, around the vase's middle a matching ribbon that looks like a sash.

"We're so proud of you," the card says.

She arranges her body around this little square of thick paper, as if it's something precious, even runs her forefinger along its glossy face. This is what we all strive for, right?

A few weeks after starting her new job, as she's sitting in the cafeteria, eating a sandwich from the vending machine, Angela looks up, to see Teresa Barnes, the head of accounting, standing above her in a nice skirt and suit, a powder blue shirt underneath. Texas-born, with long, curly hair and a beautiful mouth she paints red, Terry, as she likes to be called, looks like someone who would try to pretend embarrassment as she proudly told you that yes, she once was a cheerleader.

"I noticed you right away," Terry says. "But I couldn't figure out if you were or not. You are, right? 'Cause, if you are, then I'd love to take you to dinner."

So many ways to answer such an odd question, but Angela can't seem to articulate any one of them very quickly, just blushes and smiles.

"If I understand the question correctly, then yes," Angela says.

"Oh, I think you are understanding the question correctly," Terry says, and sets down her business card, uses a manicured hand to slide it forward.

Effusive, chatty, endlessly optimistic, Terry doesn't care much for politics, though she likes dating someone who does. And although bighearted, she doesn't take on anyone's worries for very long.

"Heart like a sieve," she says, and laughs, pulls her hair behind her ears. Angela finds her attractive, fascinatingly feminine, and something else: confident in a whole new way. "Cocksure," they might say in Texas, a theory she shares with Terry, who laughs and says, "I'll take the 'sure,' but you can keep the 'cock' part."

When she finds out Terry comes from money, she assumes that's the reason for her confidence. Whatever the cause, Angela likes being around someone so open and strong.

Within three months of dating, Angela has moved into Terry's place, a two-bedroom house on a hill with a deck and a proper view of the ocean, big flowerpots in every corner and teak lawn chairs. Angela laughs to herself every time she hears Terry tell someone the chairs are teak. So silly and also a little pretentious, the idea of identifying a type of wood, but even as she laughs about it, Angela knows she, too, is proud to have some emotional ownership over these six handsome teak chairs.

At night, she and Terry will sit out there and stare at the oil platforms in the middle of the ocean, sparkling like falling stars suspended just above the water. At times like these, Angela will sometimes think of Kate and wonder where she might be, how she might be. But it definitely feels like another era, even another world, something that belongs firmly in the past. When Angela looks at pictures from Madrid, taken just before Kate had to leave, she feels as if she's opened an album with a beautiful soft leather cover and the word YOUTH emblazoned on it.

And then, it happens. One night at eleven, her cell rings as Angela's driving home from a nighttime school board meeting, through the fields of Oxnard, with all its dichotomies: ocean air, plus sweet, fragrant strawberries and cantaloupe, plus, unfortunately, the sharp stench of chicken manure in which all that fruit grows.

Angela looks at the phone's display and doesn't recognize the number but picks up anyway.

"I found you! It's me," she says. "Kate."

Kate seems ready to spend hours recounting her life over the past years, as if she wants Angela to know every detail. She talks about having moved to New York with Louis and his girlfriend, and starting a master's program in anthropology, about the lap dancers she's writing about. She has a job, too, at a law office, and makes too much money and spends guilt-inducing amounts of time shopping, Kate tells her.

"I'm interested," she says, "in the correlation between consumerism and pleasure."

Angela laughs. "Are you really?"

"What?" Kate asks. "Are you saving the world?"

"Yes, I am," Angela says, "one school board meeting at a time. One peanut butter cookie at a time."

It's too much, talking to Kate again and driving and knowing how tired she is, and she has to get back to the office and write her story. And it's hard, talking to Kate after so much time. Hard to place her in the context of this life, her actual life, not some college-girl fantasy.

"I have to go," she says.

"Can I call you tomorrow?" Kate asks.

Angela hesitates long enough that Kate seems to understand it's not a great idea.

"Okay, well, at least now you have my number," she says. "Call whenever you want, okay?"

Angela assumes that, once again, weeks will go by and then months, and Kate will be more or less out of mind again. But two days later, on Friday, as she and Terry stand outside, having a glass of wine and debating whether to enlarge the deck, Angela hears the work cell ringing. She knows it's Kate.

"Strange," Teresa says. "On a Friday night? You should get it, probably an emergency."

Angela goes inside, checks, and sees that indeed it's a 718 number. She carries the bottle of wine out to the deck and pours them two more glasses. On a trip to Santa Ynez, they'd gone to a wine tasting at BV and Teresa bought two cases of this wine. If you like something and you can afford it, buy large quantities, she always says.

She tells Terry all about Kate and how she recently got in touch.

"Oh, really?" Terry says with a Cheshire cat smile. "The straight girl from Spain?"

Funny how quickly competitiveness can surface—*the straight girl from Spain*. This is probably meant to rile Angela a little, remind her that this girl is out of reach.

"Exactly," Angela says.

Kate starts phoning about once a week, knows which nights Angela has board meetings in other towns, so that she's flying through the dark strawberry fields of Oxnard or Camarillo, or taking back roads along the lemon and orange orchards of Santa Paula or on the longest drive of all, from the new L.A. bedroom community of Moorpark, a good forty-five minutes away.

She entertains Kate with stories about the rich moms who moved into these bedroom communities and now hold everyone hostage into the wee hours, trying to squeeze Harvard prep standards out of public school budgets. But these are the same mothers whose husbands head groups called Citizens Against Taxes.

"They want it all," Kate says.

"Yes, they do. And they usually get it."

Kate loves it when Angela tells stories that have a clear villain, like the white self-entitled parent, or the greedy farm owner. They reinforce the way Kate already sees the world: good people or bad people, nothing in between. Sometimes, Angela wishes she could, too, but journalism, with its commitment to telling both sides of every story, has already robbed her of the ability to stand firmly on any one side for very long. Or maybe she's always been most comfortable in the middle and she's lucky to have found a profession that encourages this.

Sometimes Kate talks her all the way home. Their conversations will meander from the mundane or silly to the far more serious.

"I can hear an earring against the receiver," Kate will say, sounding sleepy. "Do you wear earrings every day?"

"Just on meeting days. And skirts and heels, too. And silk blouses."

"Do you look hot, or just kind of frumpy?"

"Hot," Angela says, and Kate laughs.

"I wouldn't mind seeing for myself. Why don't you come visit me?" she asks.

Now it's Angela's turn to laugh. "You're all talk. If I took you up on it, you'd slink away."

"Me? Slink away? I don't think so. I've never slunk in my life. Or slinked. You should come test that theory," Kate says.

Angela laughs and changes the subject.

In the last seven months, she's come to have so much with Terry—lovely, charming Terry, who, by building a beautiful home with her and by being so welcoming to Angela's family, has given her such a gift. Angela's parents, who at first had a hard time accepting her orientation, are now fine with it. They even visit often, stay the weekend with them.

One weekend, Angela even asks her mother what she thinks of the life she's made.

"It's a nice life, sweetheart, a really nice companionship."

It doesn't bother Angela, the term her mother uses. A woman

of a certain age, born in South America, of course she prefers to imagine her daughter with a companion rather than a lover.

"With Dad, did you ever think it might not last, that you were okay but not perfect together?" Angela asks her.

"Sure," her mother says. "And he did, too, probably, but the key to a long marriage is moving past the times when you question things, when you think you're not in love anymore."

"Yeah?"

"Yes. I have ways, things. When he's being negative or moody, I remember how he looked at me when he asked me to dance our first tango at the birthday party. And I took a minute to say yes. I think of that look, like he might die if I said no. . . ." Angela laughs, and so does her mom, with more than a touch of pride. "How he looked at the altar. His eyes filling with just a few tears, not a lot, but just enough tears."

"Aw, Papi!" Angela says, and looks for her dad, who's having a tour of the garden with Terry. Angela watches Terry lead him back to the table, where she picks up the champagne bottle and refills his glass, comes and does the same for Angela's mom. She makes such a lovely fuss over them every time they come up, cooking a special breakfast, with mimosas.

Everything is perfect right now: the sunshine, ocean breeze, the food, the deck, with its pots of bright blue hydrangea. Angela's mom told Terry once that if you put rusty nails into the soil, the flowers will change color, become blue instead of pink. Terry did and now—surprise—blue flowers. It's Terry's home in every way, but she's tried to share, to make Angela feel part of it, as the now-blue flowers can attest.

Angela closes her eyes and takes in the tarry smell perpetually in the air on this part of the coast. Only a fool would throw this away.

"Explain to your parents that the smell isn't from the oil platforms, that it's natural," Terry says.

"It is. It's natural," Angela says, and starts to tell her parents all about the Chumash Indians and how they once used the tar that seeps from the ocean floor to repair their canoes.

Angela decides that it's her career she's not happy with. She'd expected that, by covering schools, she would be telling the stories of children, but since children don't buy papers, she writes about how tax dollars are spent, or misspent, and about the power plays of school board members and administrators.

A story has to have a hero or a villain—that's the way to keep the reader and get the promotion. Always good, but not necessarily satisfying. Not even the stories about heroes move Angela anymore. A follow-up on how hard it is to stay at Stanford when your financial aid gets cut and when your parents don't really understand why you had to go away to college in the first place gets shelved, and what runs instead is a piece titled "Farmworker Girl Going to Harvard."

Maybe, if she goes to grad school, Angela thinks, she'll find a way to tell the other story, "Farmworker Girl Struggles to Find Happiness Living in World She Is in No Way Part Of," or the even sadder "Farmworker Girl at Harvard Finds Herself Lost, Unanchored."

She's decided to stop covering schools, try instead for a different beat, either the city desk or the arts. Completely different directions, but interesting either way. Applying for new jobs seems to lift her mood, make her feel less restless.

Although sometimes, in the middle of the night, after she's gone for a drink of water and then gets in bed and Terry starts looking for her, to spoon, this feeling gets its arms around Angela, one that, if you dared attach words to it, might be "I'm not sure I love you." When that happens, Angela will turn and prop herself on a pillow, watch Terry sleep, examine every line on her face, even draw close and try to breathe in the smell of sandalwood oil that Terry dabs at the back of her neck, at the edge of her hairline. Angela is like a detective looking for signs, not of a crime, but of love.

One day, a warm October Wednesday, as Angela parks her car

beside the house, turns off the engine, and steps out into a balmy wind, she decides to do it. She goes into the garage instead of the house and finds a box of cigarettes stashed above the washer, lights one, takes off her jacket, grabs her cell, and, leaning against Terry's still-warm car, dials.

She can hear the water being turned on in the shower upstairs as, in her ear, a phone in Brooklyn announces her call.

"Ani!" Kate exclaims. "I've missed talking to you so much."

"Me, too," she says, and feels her own mouth creasing into a smile. She's so happy, and at the same time disappointed, about what she can no longer ignore.

She listens to Kate talk about her life and her schoolwork and how beautiful Brooklyn is and ask why she doesn't come visit, and Angela listens to the water run through the pipes. She imagines the house up there, clean and tidy, since this is the day the cleaning lady has come. The whole place will be spotless and smell of Murphy Oil Soap and Clorox. So as not to dirty the kitchen, they'll barbecue tonight. Terry will already have steaks or tuna marinading in a dish on the counter.

On the deck, next to the grill, will sit three fancy stainless-steel tools all ready to go. They will be done eating about eight and, a little high from the wine, they'll fall asleep reading or watching television. Then someone will awaken someone and offer a hand. Up you go. To bed and sleep. And then morning again.

Angela doesn't have to go inside to know all of this—the beautiful predictability of marriage, like a Swiss watch, coveted for its durability and precision.

"Why don't you at least fly out and visit me? Just a visit. What harm can it do?"

Angela laughs at this. What harm? They're not girls now; they know exactly what harm.

Angela waits, listening to the occasional ping of Teresa's SUV cooling, a bird skitting around just outside the garage door. Then she hears the water shut off, watches the last rays of sunlight filter through the cracks in the door and dust particles float around Terry's car antenna.

"Kate, I'm so different from you. I mean, can two people be more different than the two of us?" Angela says.

"I know," Kate says. "But, still . . . I don't know how to explain it. Something about us . . . is good and makes sense. I mean really good. And also . . ."

"Yeah?"

"I didn't ask you to marry me, Agnelli. Just to come see the Statue of Liberty."

Angela hangs up soon after this, but she stays put, leaning against the car, its body warm against the small of her back, the tiniest bit of tire rubber touching the back of her knee. She listens to the hum of their big square freezer, a gift from Terry's dad. Next to it sit the cases of the BV wine, and next to that, industrial-size containers of paper goods. Enough food and wine and paper plates for years to come. Above it all, on the highest shelf, the Christmas presents hidden in plain view, but in red-and-white Target bags, the words *Don't even think about looking* written in blue Sharpie. Terry told her to expect a Christmas tree covered in gifts. They might be small and they might be from the 99¢ Only store, but there will be dozens of them, because Terry loves to see people open presents.

In the house, Terry has put on music, is probably pouring them wine, has surely looked out the window and seen Angela's car out in front, will soon start looking for her.

Angela thinks of Kate, dancing in Madrid at that club, with that gigantic African drag queen in white descending on the swing, of the music she would play Christmas week, loudly, that they would dance to on her bed, her chair, the balcony.

The next day, on her way to work, she hits redial.

"We're thinking of going to New York," she says, and tells Kate that "they" will be in the city next month. Somehow, this seems safer, pretending she's traveling with her girlfriend, as if the existence of Terry will keep certain feelings at bay.

"Great," Kate says, but then she pauses for so long that Angela wonders if there's someone in her life now, a new man or woman.

"By the way, are you . . . dating anyone?"

"Not really," Kate says.

"'Not really'? What does that mean?"

"I'll tell you when I see you."

CHAPTER 18
A Room in Ibiza
1994

It's only nine, but Louis and Angela are both jet-lagged and tired. They leave the balcony and go inside.

"I think this one is hers," Louis says, and points to the bed with the magenta spread, on which lies a folded white dress and a book by Edward Gorey.

"Go ahead, take that one," she says to Louis, who plucks the items and wraps them in the dress, which he carries to Kate's suitcase on the bureau.

On the yellow bedspread lies a tube of children's sunscreen.

"Did they have a child with them?" she asks, holding the sunscreen.

"No, no. That's probably Kate's. She thinks sunscreen is kind of a lie—you know, fifteen, thirty, whatever. But she figures that they wouldn't lie about children's sunscreen, you know? 'Cause babies could get burned, so that's what she buys."

Angela takes these items and puts the pile on a chair near the closet.

"She's read too much Chomsky," Louis says, and closes his eyes.

Angela strips off the spread, pulls back the blanket, and lies on the sheet. "When did she get here, from Brazil?" she asks Louis, who waits long enough to answer, she knows he's about to fall asleep.

"Three days ago. Or four now. Maybe. I've lost track."

Jet lag awakens them early, at six. They each shower, check their e-mails. Louis brought a device that lets them go online from anywhere. The friend from San Francisco State has sent articles on cases involving head trauma, which they each read, although without coffee, it's tough to retain anything. They decide to walk to the hospital, get breakfast on the way. Maybe, arriving so early, they'll be allowed to visit Kate longer.

The streets feel empty—doesn't anyone work a normal day? Only occasionally does a taxi drive by with three or four passengers crammed into the backseat, heads back, mouths agape or bobbing forward, spittle certainly dripping from their lips, fast asleep.

Louis can't help but wonder what Kate's head looked like, in the car during the accident, her face looking up from the rear window. Was she ever conscious? Could he have flown here any faster? It's a torment, this question—Did you hesitate?—and yet also useful. He knows its effect from having asked it of himself so many times over the years. Did you hesitate, Louis? Rubbing salt in your own wounds may hurt, but it also riles you, fills you with anger and energy.

Their search takes them on a long walk, at least ten blocks into what Louis and Angela both surmise is a working-class area. Things are a bit more gray here—some buildings have broken windows up top; a bit more trash sleeps next to the curb. Even the trash cylinders look haggard, not the cheerful baby blue bins of their street.

Finally, they see what appears to be an open café, with a small window display of wine, bread, and several pieces of plastic fruit. They cross the street. Adorning the window, like a lacy window in some farm town, hang the ubiquitous legs of pork, from which *jamón* Serrano gets sliced.

"Is she still a vegetarian?" Angela asks Louis.

"Yeah, sort of. A bad one. Eats fish sometimes and a BLT about once a month. Thinks I don't know," he says, and shakes his head at the thought of this.

"Are you?"

"Not really. At home I am, though, because she's the one who cooks, so—"

"She cooks?"

"More or less," he says, and smiles. "Lots of coconut milk and tofu. You get used to it," he adds, and feels bad for Angela, and the look of regret in her eyes.

"I bet."

Before entering the place, they smell the coffee. It's a sort of bakery/café/restaurant, but with a psychedelic, sixties feel: low ceilings painted black and dark gray walls, a cement floor that someone painted cobalt blue. Another someone, or maybe the same someone, has used a can of silver spray paint to put up words like *ODIO,* which means "hate," next to *AMOR, LA GUERRE,* and even some German phrases.

"Don't they know all caps means shouting?" Louis says.

Behind the counter stands a pale and extremely skinny kid with a faux mohawk and fingernails painted bright pink. Three rings adorn his lower lip in exactly the center, making it, Angela thinks, impossible to ever get a decent kiss from that mouth. Probably the point.

In the glass case sit several salads and plates of tapas still covered in plastic wrap, but above these, on the counter, there are two wire baskets. One holds dozens of baguettes, the other croissants.

Angela asks the kid for two croissants and he takes a piece of wax paper and grabs each pastry as if his hands are sharp tongs, then rolls the bag closed and takes it to the register, which he clearly finds far more palatable than their faces.

"Dos cafés también," Angela says, and the kid looks at her with a thin layer of disgust, nods yes, and turns to get the coffees. Just the international language of angry kids, Angela thinks, the same look that any two people are guaranteed to get from any young counter boy in the world.

Angela inspects the sandwiches sitting on the doily-lined plates at the end of the glass case: simple, just Serrano ham and bread or cheese and bread. Nothing like deli sandwiches back home, so ambitiously stuffed with avocado and peppers, lettuce, tomato.

When Angela turns to ask Louis if they should buy sandwiches for later, she notices him lingering near the punker kid, talking quietly, or trying to express something.

"Were you talking to him?" she asks a few seconds later as they sugar their coffees.

"He speaks English," Louis tells her.

"Really?"

"Yeah, he told me to fuck off in perfect English."

"Oh. And what exactly did you say to get such a response?"

"Nothing," Louis says, and laughs.

"What do you mean, nothing?"

"Surly bastard," Louis says, and looks at the ground. She knows he's lying, but she can't imagine why or what he asked the kid.

The hospital is as still as the streets. Only a few nurses and doctors appear to be working. It feels as if more people have been here, because they've left behind perfume ghosts, coffee ghosts, the smell of hair gel lingering in the air. Finally, Louis and Angela pass a large conference room and see about twenty staff members sitting in chairs around a conference table, a dozen or so in the row behind them, and another dozen leaning on counters. All are facing and presumably listening to a short bald man in a white coat, who's standing at the front of the room, red bifocals perched off the tip of his nose. He reads from a piece of paper in his left hand; in his right, he holds an unlit cigarette.

"If they're busy, maybe we can hang out with her a little longer," Louis says, and they walk down the hall fast.

"Yeah," she says. "Why don't you go see her and I'll stick around for a minute, see if I can catch her doctor and ask about moving her," Angela says.

"Okay, good idea. I'll go to the room," Louis says.

As Angela stands in the hallway, listening to the meeting and wondering how her staff is doing in Los Angeles, she hears her name called. She turns around and sees that Ted Griffin has arrived. He's wearing the same high-waisted jeans as yesterday, but today he has on a round-collared red T-shirt. On his face is a stern look.

"Good morning, good morning," he says, and asks where Louis is.

"He just went in to see Kate. Why?"

"I'd like to talk with you alone," Griffin says. "I received a call from Ms. Harrington's mother. She was upset about her daughter, naturally, and also, she was rather upset when informed that Ms. Harrington is not conscious. Mr. Ross seems to have told her or . . . somehow created quite a misunderstanding about Ms. Harrington's . . . status. Her mother was under the impression that she was doing better, that she was awake and speaking. Is Mr. Ross . . ." Griffin hesitates then finally spits it out. "Is he in denial or suffering from a sort of delusion about his wife's condition?"

Angela is relieved that Griffin hasn't caught on to very much.

"No, no. I don't think so. I think he realizes . . . There was a lot of confusion about whether she was conscious or not. I'm sure he was just . . . confused."

Griffin nods as if he believes her, but he's clearly lost faith in Louis and maybe Angela, too. Yesterday, he trusted them, based on a few but important commonalities—Americans roughly his oldest children's ages, both well dressed, probably college-educated. He believed them.

But today, after the call from the mother and one from the police sergeant, saying hashish was found in the car and an open bottle of alcohol, well, now he focuses on their differences. A woman traveling with two men her husband doesn't even know. The drugs . . . These people are nothing like his children.

"We'll call her mother today and straighten it out. I'll call her myself."

"No need. She's on her way. She and her husband were hoping to make a flight that arrives . . . later in the afternoon," Griffin says, and looks at his watch. "I don't have the flight number with me. But I can call you when they arrive."

Angela tries to conceal her surprise. "Yes, please do call me. Were you able to find anything out about flying her to Madrid?"

"Oh, right," Griffin says, and tugs at his shirt collar. "Once the family arrives and you've all had the chance to discuss it, I'll be glad to," he says.

Angela feels her face grow hot, her eyes widen. What business is it of his, really?

"Her husband, Louis, is her family," Angela says. "What other family is there?"

"Well, if I may be blunt, are you really her sister?" he asks, rubbing the back of his neck. She can tell he doesn't want to be lied to right now. "Because when I mentioned a sister, her mother explained, well, that Ms. Harrington does not have a sister. So, of course, I'm rather confused myself."

"No. I'm a good friend. I said that because sometimes people are funny about who they consider family."

"Ah, I see. And is Mr. Ross really her husband?"

"Yes," she says. "He is."

"Well, fine. It's not my place to make these . . . Her mother was listed on the flight form, so . . . But I will call, I will inquire about Madrid," he says.

Griffin mutters something about joining his family. It's their vacation, after all, he says apologetically, then turns around. "Sorry, one more thing. The uh . . . the consulate can't pay to medevac anyone out of a country, so that will be your responsibility. I'm sorry," he says.

"It's all right," Angela tells him. "We didn't expect you to pay. I just want to know how to do it."

"Right, absolutely," he says. "I will call you as soon as I have an answer. You'll . . . talk to Mr. Ross?"

"Yes."

Griffin looks at his watch, then at her.

"Okay, bye, then."

She goes to Kate's room, where she finds Louis sitting next to the bed, holding Kate's hand and caressing her leg.

"It smells good in here," Angela says.

"I brought her perfume, from the hotel. Put it on her."

Angela goes to the other side of the bed and leans down, close to Kate's head. Louis watches her keenly as she carefully caresses Kate's cheek, like someone touching an article of clothes they once adored or a beloved toy from childhood.

"See here," Angela says, and points to the area just above her ear. "She's going gray. I can't believe Kate's going gray."

"I know. My old lady," Louis says, and kisses her hand.

"You were right. We need to work on moving her. I saw Griffin, and he's not doing anything about the medevac flights," Angela says.

"Yeah, definitely. If you let people do nothing, they will. Hey, boss," Louis says to Kate. "We're flying you out of here soon, to Madrid, where the doctors are going to get that marvelous brain of yours and that big mouth going again. Right?" Louis says, looking at Angela.

"Right," Angela says, and forces herself to look at Kate, more for Louis's benefit than anything. It's tough to imagine Kate can hear a voice, see a smile.

"You can kiss her, you know," Louis says, his voice catching with something like mischief.

"I can't," she says.

"Sure you can. Angela's afraid to kiss you, Kate. Tell her it's all right."

Angela can feel Louis looking at her, but she refuses to look at him directly. Does he really think that after being estranged for two years, she would just walk into a hospital room and kiss Kate hello? Do people get to forgive and be forgiven in a flash like that? As if broken bones and shattered glass have the power to erase the past?

"Sorry," he says just as Angela turns to look at him. He's now leaning forward, head in his hands.

CHAPTER 19

California
1991

It's been a week since she told Kate that she and Terry would be going to New York. On a Friday morning, an hour before work, they are in the kitchen, making coffee and toasting bagels. The fog outside gives the air a briny smell, but inside it's all French vanilla—making the near-weekend feeling even sweeter. A vase filled with bright yellow mums sits on the counter, under them an invitation to someone's fortieth birthday party tomorrow, to be held at a nice restaurant overlooking the ocean. Then, on Sunday, there's a brunch.

And, of course, on Monday, back to work. But you're not supposed to think of Monday now, are you? Blasphemy. It's Friday, glorious Friday.

"I'm going to a conference next month in New York," Angela tells Terry.

"New York, wow. I haven't been in years. Can I come?"

"Well . . . Three pretty full days, and I can't stay longer. Probably not a good idea."

"I know what you mean," Terry says. "I know how those conferences are. Have you ever been to New York, honey?"

"No," she says, and reaches for the coffeepot's handle, pours Terry a cup and then herself one.

"You'll love it. I'll make you a list of things you have to see."

There's no way she can be this person. Angela stares at the coffee, then looks at Terry to see, one last time, that look of confidence and pride. In a minute, those same eyes will be filled with the question "What's wrong?" And she won't lie about what is wrong and all of this will come crashing down—the future that right now seems so certain, beginning with that birthday, then the brunch, all the way to Christmas, months away, and all those presents in the garage, bought with so much hope for the future.

Two hours later, fog gone, the sun strong in the sky, they sit on the deck, Terry with her arms tight around herself, eyes red both from crying and from getting stoned to try to feel better. They both called in sick, but now don't know what to do with the rest of the day. Moments ago, Terry ate a tangerine and now plays with the bits of rind, arranging them in her lap like so many beautiful orange puzzle pieces.

Angela says she's just not happy. It's not about Terry, but about figuring out what will make her happy. But it's clear to Terry, who, just by virtue of being eight years older, understands this sort of subtext. Angela says she may look for a new job, or travel, maybe go to grad school. She says everything except the obvious.

Terry looks spent, nothing left to argue or ask. She says she's going to take a shower, dress, and maybe go see a movie by herself. She scoops up the bits of rind and stares at them like runes or dice, shakes her head no, and starts to cry again. "I knew that fucking straight girl would be trouble," she says, and sends the rind flying toward Angela like so many little pieces of betrayal.

The next morning, Angela offers to move out right away.

"I would hope so," Terry replies.

CHAPTER 20
A Hospital Room in Ibiza
1994

After a few minutes, Carolina, the nurse from yesterday, comes to tell them it's time to leave. They stand outside the hospital, waiting for some idea what to do next.

"Food," Angela says. "Let's get some things for now and for the room later." She has to tell him that Kate's parents are coming, but it doesn't feel right quite yet.

Louis and Angela find a nearby market and go inside. As they walk around, the contents of each shelf awaken the memory of hunger.

"We haven't eaten an actual meal in a long time," Louis says, left arm now formed into a basket he's filled with bread and tomatoes, oranges, bags of chips. Angela goes to the refrigerator and plucks out packages of cheese and ham, a white tray of six baked drumsticks.

"Do we have a fridge in the room?" she asks.

"I don't remember," he says. "Get it all, though."

At the counter, he sets down his items and grabs cold bottles of Coke and cigarettes.

They find an empty café table down the street and sit, hoping the owner won't mind if they eat here. Even at noon, there isn't much foot traffic. What a strange town.

They make sandwiches, cutting the bread with their fingers and eating the tomatoes like plums because they have no knives.

Only after they've scarfed the food and then lit cigarettes does Angela decide to tell Louis what she knows.

"They're coming. Don and Georgina are coming," Angela says.

"How do you know?"

"Ted came by while you were in the room. I guess the airline called. She put her mom on the flight information form."

"Okay."

"They know I'm not her sister. He asked me and I told him the truth, but I said you were married. Are you married?"

Louis just stares at her, his eyes darting around; then he sits forward, elbows on his knees, hands entwined, and lets his head drop. Eventually, he looks up and shakes his head no. "No. We meant to because of the diving. Sometimes there are accidents. You know, an eardrum busts, things like that. You have to get to a hospital, and we figured if we were married, it would make things easier on the other person."

"You don't owe me an explanation," she says, and puts the cigarette out in a piece of tomato sitting on the paper bag.

"Well, I wasn't giving you an explanation per se. I was confirming that we meant to but that we didn't get around to it. Unfortunately."

Angela's embarrassed now by her defensiveness. Kate wouldn't just marry Louis in case of a diving accident. It's much more than that, and they both know it. Angela lights a fresh cigarette. "What am I doing here, Louis? Why am I here?"

"I don't know. Why? I hope it's not to say good-bye." His face is challenging, angry.

"No. It's not."

"Good. You're here because . . . because it's you and me. It's always been one of us, always. Right?"

She still looks uncertain.

"I know it's strange. I know you guys have some stuff to talk about, but how would you feel if something happened and you weren't here?"

She shakes her head and leans back, fighting off a sudden urge to cry. She's tired. No good, can't fight the tears.

He puts his hand on her leg and squeezes it. "Look, it's Kate we're talking about, Angela. It's Kate. She loves me and she loves you. And that's pretty fucking simple."

"Right, simple," she says, and runs her sleeve along her nose. As if loving someone has ever been enough.

CHAPTER 21
California
1991

Angela moves out and goes to stay in a condo near downtown Ventura with Beau, a new friend who teaches piano for a living and has a sweet disposition. His place is clean and bright, and she's glad for his furnishings because, upon leaving Terry's, it became clear that she has so very few possessions. Moving in with Terry, she had thrown out so many of the cheap household items she'd bought on her comparatively measly salary.

Kate is so excited about her visit to New York. Or "their" visit, since she still believes they're both coming.

"I'm organizing a birthday party on the Saturday for my friend Paul at a little restaurant in the Village. You could come join us. That way, it's a group setting, you know?"

"Okay," Angela says. "That sounds good."

On the flight, Angela's so nervous, she has to remind herself that Kate will not be at the airport, that she has hours to go until they meet for dinner. She's rented a room at a hotel near Rockefeller Plaza. She sits on the double bed, which takes up nearly the whole room, and tries to talk herself out of meeting Kate. A bottle of water, a bowl with two bright green apples, and a Gerbera daisy in a long vase all share the small table next to the bed, which is covered by a soft suedelike bedspread.

Angela lies back and looks through the window at a billboard for a play. She'll go for a walk, then come back, shower, and dress for dinner.

As eight approaches, Angela's nerves get worse and worse. Her fingers, curled around a lipstick tube, shake like leaves and she has to take a few deep breaths before completing this normally simple task.

The restaurant is smaller than she'd imagined, with dark orange walls, a big fireplace, and French doors that lead to a patio. She doesn't see Kate right away, who sits to the right, in a group of about eight or nine people. But Kate sees her and stands, smiling in a way that says, I've been watching you. Finally, Angela turns to the right and sees her. Kate leaves the table of friends and starts walking toward her. She stops a foot or so from her and stands, head tilted to one side, inspecting her.

She's dyed her hair white, although it's still short. She wears a skirt, high boots, and a black sweater. She is so tall and those eyes are so green. Amazing, Angela thinks. Amazing how many thousands of people you walk by every single day without noticing. And how one person, *the* person, can immediately steal your breath like this.

"Where's your girlfriend?"

"She didn't come with me."

"She stayed at the hotel?"

"No, she didn't come at all. I'm alone."

Has there ever been a more triumphant smile than Kate's?

"Oh, okay," she says, and puts her arms around Angela, gives her the sort of hug that says, I am definitely here.

Kate's friends have grown quiet and are watching them. Obviously, they're thinking, So this is the friend whose arrival Kate has been anticipating. But as the women continue holding each other, everyone at the table begins to stir, uncomfortable witnesses to this never-ending embrace.

"Come meet everyone," Kate says finally, and takes Angela's hand the way your fiancée would when you arrive at her family home for the first time, or the night she's brought you to meet her very best friends in the world. Of all the things Angela has already done that are disloyal to Terry, this feels like the worst.

These friends have gathered to celebrate the birthday of a guy named Liam, from Manchester, who's visiting his new boyfriend, Paul. Also at the table are Stella and Joanne, who work at the law firm with Kate. Then Paul's nephew, a rugby player from Cornell, who looks about eighteen, then Petra, who looks dangerously thin, with wrist bones the size of walnuts and a pretty, apologetic smile. Next to her is Jack, chubby and with long, bushy sideburns and thick glasses. From his proximity to her, the protective way his body leans into hers, she thinks he's Petra's boyfriend.

Also at the table is a very white-skinned blond girl named Sandrine, and next to her sits Louis—the famous Louis she'd heard about in Spain. He's cuter than Angela had imagined—with longish hair and pretty green eyes, a little stubble on his face, but still a soft face. He wears jeans and a black Yazoo T-shirt with a tweed jacket over it. He smiles broadly and says, "Howdy, stranger. Heard so much about you. Good to finally meet you in person."

"You, too."

"Come here," Kate says, and pats the spot next to her, where she's decided Angela will sit. They eat and laugh and Angela enjoys that particular attention of people eager to like you. She can tell, from their questions about working for a newspaper or about Madrid, that Kate has told them about her. When added up, minor confidences your friend has shared with people over the years can make you sound pretty special.

Angela's grateful for her training as a reporter, knowing how to ask questions, how to listen enough that the follow-up question gets the person talking even more. Every few minutes, she catches Kate looking at her in a way that's . . . inquisitive and maybe a little relieved? It's as if she's thinking, Oh, good, you became someone I still like. A couple of times, Kate's smile and the look in her eyes even says, You became someone I like much more than I'd expected to.

A couple of hours and bottles of wine later, Kate stands and, looking at Angela, says she's going for a smoke.

"You still do that?" Angela asks. .

"Yes, I still do that. Come with me," Kate says, and offers her hand in a courtly way.

The patio's center has four tables, only one of which is taken, but off in the far corner there's a wooden bench under an olive tree whose branches have been dressed in white lights. That's where they sit. Somewhere, a water fountain emits a tiny gurgle. They both look around and Kate sees it first, points to the corner, where a tired-looking little angel sends water through his pursed lips.

Angela takes the lighter from Kate's hands, like James Bond or something, and lights the cigarette, as Kate drapes a leg over Angela's and leans in close, then pulls at the sleeve of Angela's sweater, black and V-necked, like the one Kate wears.

"Fucking dykes, always dress alike."

"Dyke? I thought you were bisexual."

"Yeah, I'm *bi sexual*—buy me something and I'll get sexual," she says in a thick southern accent.

"I remember that dumb joke," Angela says.

"I would certainly hope so. It's my best joke. Do you like my hair?" Kate asks. "I dyed it for you." She fusses with her hair, preens.

"I love it."

"I don't look like an albino?"

"Well, yeah, but . . . a beautiful albino," Angela says, and runs her hand along Kate's back, down her leg.

Kate doesn't say anything, just emits a low "Mmm" and comes closer.

It's amazing, the pull of physical attraction, what it stirs, what it erases. Looking at Kate like this is like turning the corner and seeing what, to you, is the perfect painting—say a Rothko or a Picasso—or taking a deep breath of some scent that pops all your synapses: apple blossom perfume, or jasmine, or a lipstick that reminds you of that first, best, most real kiss ever.

If beauty is in the eyes of the beholder, as the saying goes, then it must be true that for this beholder, Kate defines beauty. Angela leans forward and brushes her lips against Kate's. Kate responds by closing her eyes and leaning forward, giving her a quick kiss, then placing her hand on Angela's shoulder.

"You're not going to stop, are you? I mean you're not going to stop this, are you?"

"No, I don't think I am," Angela says, and they kiss, finally. It starts slowly, though not tentatively, and becomes something you feel through your center, pulling you toward the other person so much that you don't care how inappropriate this might be. They kiss like this again in the restaurant, then later as they wait for a cab, then up the stairs to the apartment, and, finally, on Kate's bed.

Angela teases and stops so many times that Kate's face glows hot, her breathing fast, her body moist. She flips Angela and lies atop, gently bites her chin.

"Okay, that's enough. You need to stop teasing me now," she says, and the kiss deepens.

It's like this all night—making love, followed by sleep, by eating, by showers, and then again. In the dark blue of Brooklyn at four, it's finally enough and they're ready for sleep. In this room with its smell of leather from new boots discarded at the door and dusty grapevines on the wall outside, and hours-old perfume, of sex, in this room of fleeting darkness and soft sheets, Kate and Angela lie side by side, staring at one another, though barely seeing each other's faces.

"I can't believe it," Angela whispers.

"Finally."

Angela awakens first, at eleven, and lies quietly, wondering where Kate has gone, touching the pillow where she'd lain. The heat's on and this bedroom must be eighty degrees. Isn't it funny, she thinks, the life patterns you see only after a certain age? Kate may have claimed in Spain that her room was hot because of Carla, afraid of the human lung, but now here they are, in yet another overheated apartment.

Angela looks around at the white curtains to the floor, all drawn. From the bed, you can see the red brick of the buildings around them. It's tasteful, the room, with its high ceilings and lovely molding, the big desk and handsome lamp. And the bedding feels so soft.

The door opens and Kate, in a towel, walks in. She throws the towel at Angela and moves to the full-length mirror perched in the corner, starts inspecting her butt, the back of her legs.

"What are you doing?"

"Looking for cellulite," she says.

"And what will you do if you find any?"

"Oh, haven't thought about that yet."

"I bet you're pretty confident you won't find any."

"Maybe."

Angela laughs as Kate keeps searching, finding only big drops of opaque water. Then she walks over to the bureau and plucks a cigarette from its box, walks to the window and starts telling Angela all about the Italian family that owns the brownstone behind this one. Angela loves the way she cups her hands around the cigarette to light it, even in stifling, windless Brooklyn.

The Leggios, who live back there, grow basil, tomatoes, and Concord grapes, whose vines climb so high up that Kate swears she can sometimes reach right out and take a handful of fruit. "Those are your favorites, aren't they?" she turns and asks. "Concord grapes, right? You had those back in South America, when you were a kid, right?"

"Yeah."

"I thought so," she says.

Angela decides not to tell Kate that she already broke up with Terry. She flies to New York three weeks after the birthday party and then again two weeks later. They stay at the apartment, in bed, leaving only once, for dinner with Louis and Sandrine, who seems sweet but uncomfortable around them, the insecure friend. Angela works hard to make her feel included, and mentions it later to Kate.

"She's jealous of me. She's a really envious girl, plus a girl who hates envious people, which makes it doubly inconvenient to be her."

"That would be tough."

"But she's really sweet with him, don't you think?"

"I guess. Is she?"

"Yeah," Kate says, and smiles in a way that makes it look as if she's put on a mask.

"Is that what you meant when I asked if you were seeing anyone and you said it was complicated?"

"No. Well, sort of. I mean living here, it's . . . hard to date anyone. Not that I want to. I don't want to. Especially not now."

"Oh?"

"Not now that sexy Madame Bovary is here," she says, and starts touching Angela.

Angela groans. "Not Bovary."

They kiss and fool around a little, but it's hard to feel carefree on Sundays. The bedroom's been made heavy by the knowledge of that flight to California later. Kate gets up and makes coffee, brings two cups back to the bed. She sets her cup down next to the bed and shimmies under the covers, then props herself on one elbow and blows small coffee-scented puffs of air on Angela's eyelids until she smiles and opens her eyes.

"You're not asleep."

"No."

Angela sits up and takes the coffee meant for her.

"Are you still lonely?" Kate asks, and Angela doesn't say anything. "I mean, remember in Spain, you said that once?"

"Yeah, I do. And yeah, I am. I think it's who I'm meant to be, in some strange way. I just think that's how I'm constructed. I don't connect that well with other people. Like you said before, I watch, take notes."

"I say a lot of shit you probably should disregard."

"And you say a lot that's true. My job is to ask people questions, and I listen carefully and write the answer on a notepad and then that's it. I walk away. I rarely remember the answer without looking at my notes."

"Really?"

"Except with you."

"You don't need to look at your notes with me?"

"No."

Kate smiles and kisses her. "When you're with me, are you just a little bit less lonely? Don't lie if that's not true, okay? I hate lies."

"I wouldn't," Angela says, and closes her eyes, thinks about it, then opens them and looks at those eyes of Kate's, that kid smile she gets sometimes, with the dimple on her chin. "I am less lonely when I'm with you, yes. That is very true."

"Me, too," she says. "And also, sometimes with us, it's pure, not touched by anything or anyone. You know?"

"Not really. Touched by what?"

"Oh, nothing. Not worth thinking about really, and it's a cliché."

"Are we talking about you? Because if it's your story, how can it be a cliché?"

"Listen, Agnelli, right now I am talking about being happy and feeling connected. I don't want to talk about *that*. I'm talking about the exact opposite of that."

"Maybe you need to tell me about the opposite of that."

"No. No. What if it changes how you feel?"

Angela shrugs and kisses her shoulder. "What if it doesn't? What if knowing you more makes me love you more?"

"Ah, so you love me," Kate says, and taps Angela's chin. "You just said you love me."

"Did I?"

"Yes, you did."

"I guess I do, then. I do love you, Kate."

"Mmm, you think you can distract me and make me open up, huh?"

"Would that be so bad?"

Kate seems to be weighing this question; then she gets up, taking the sheet with her, and goes to the bureau and gets something, brings it back and holds it behind her.

"What is it?"

She sits down and sets a color Polaroid on Angela's chest. It's of a girl, ten, dressed in a swimsuit, arms to her side, shoulders back, chest way out front, her hair in two ponytails. Her head is tilted back, but her eyes are looking at the camera. You get the sense, from her smile, that maybe she was told not to look straight into the camera. But she can't help herself. That smile is quite something—utterly uncontainable—as if the world's entire supply of optimism had been stored there for safekeeping.

"I wanted to be an Olympic swimmer. My dad, my real dad, taught me to swim, to love the water," she says, and shakes her head in mock, or maybe real, disgust. "Such an innocent little fool."

"Oh," Angela says, and looks at the girl's eyes—Kate's very same huge eyes, but open and dreamy. "Don't say that about her."

"I was so fucking trusting. I welcomed my stepfather as if he were my real father. I didn't even mind calling him 'Dad.' I was even kind of excited to call him that, to let him know that I was ready for a dad, you know? 'Cause I missed mine."

"Yeah."

"I was so excited to have a dad again."

"Yeah?"

"That's it. No more," she says, and looks at Angela sternly, a warning not to keep pushing: Stop asking. That is it.

"Do you really think this little girl was a fool?"

Kate, kneeling next to Angela, takes back the photo and holds it in front of her, trying to come up with an honest answer. She squints so hard, the top of her eyebrow twitches. And it's clear, from her bent shoulders, her fingers so tight around the edges of the photo, that this is not the first time she's looked to the faded Polaroid for answers. "I'm supposed to say no, right?"

"Right." Angela feels her eyes filling with tears, is embarrassed by it. She takes the photo from Kate and kisses the girl in its center. Then they sit there looking at the photo, until Kate lies down in her lap and, after a few seconds, starts crying softly.

CHAPTER 22

Ibiza
1994

Louis takes an orange and stares at its skin, then pushes his finger-nails into the top and pulls down. In three moves, he's got a naked piece of fruit sitting in the center of his hand, but he seems uncertain what to do next. He pulls apart the fruit itself and hands Angela the bigger part. "There have been people, yeah, but not people she loved the way she loves us."

Angela takes a piece of orange and pulls off the top part, like opening a Ziploc bag, pulls down the skin to reveal all the juicy, bright-colored nibs of fruit, tender and entwined, so vulnerable. She pushes the skin back over it and puts the fruit on the table.

"Louis, what—?" she starts to ask a question, then changes her mind, stares at the street, the cars, the striped awnings.

"What?"

"I haven't seen her in over two years and . . . I should go back. I have an important interview in a few days, a deadline. My job's already on the chopping block. . . . I don't even know if she'd want to see me."

"Come on, come on," he says, and grabs his cell phone. "If they're coming, we have to get her out of here tomorrow. No more waiting for our friend in the diplomacy business," Louis says, and pulls a wallet from his back pocket, plucks out a credit card, and dials a number printed on the back of the card.

"Yeah, sure, four eight three oh–nine eight seven six–oh eight nine seven seven two four one. Louis J. Ross. Yes, thanks. I have the platinum card, right? . . . Good, because I'm in Ibiza, Spain, and my wife's had an accident, a car accident. I need to fly her to Madrid. Can you increase my credit limit? I don't know. What is it now and how high can you make it?"

He nods a few times and tells the person on the line that his is a satellite phone, shouldn't be a problem.

"Okay, good. Thank you. Yeah, you've been very helpful," he says, and hangs up.

Angela watches Louis take two puffs of the cigarette and guzzle the Coke, still angry, nervous. He looks like he's going through a list in his head.

"Let's go," he says. "It's time to do this."

"Louis, I have to ask you something. . . ."

"What's that?" he says, one eye scrunched against the smoke rising from the cigarette.

"Think about it before you answer. Would she want to see her mother? Would she want that?"

"No," he says quickly, and shakes his head several times. "I know that for a fact," Louis says.

"Then why did she list her on the form?"

"I dunno. Could be a passport application from years ago. She traveled to Spain pretty young; maybe they keep that on file. I can tell you she doesn't want to see Georgina or Don. And I do not want Don to see her," he says, and throws the smoke to the ground. "Come on, let's go."

Of all places, they certainly don't expect to find Dr. Santillan in the waiting area just inside the hospital, sitting on a chair near the door, writing on a clipboard. Though not watching television himself, Santillan shares the room with some ten or so people, all waiting to be seen, who watch a segment of *America's Funniest Home Videos* on a screen in the corner of this hot waiting area, the volume turned completely off.

Santillan wears a yellow shirt and a tie almost the same color, khaki pants, and black athletic shoes. He ignores them for a few seconds, continues writing patient notes.

"*Doctor, por favor,*" Angela says, and he peers up. Because his glasses sit perched on the tip of his nose, she gets the first unobstructed view of his eyes, which are brown, and big. His mouth is thin, though, shaped, from above, like an *M* or a circus tent. Louis lacks her patience. He takes a step back and turns away from the doctor, as if interested in the show on TV, but really trying to calm down. The doctor is forcing them to cool off, to switch over to his biorhythms, not their own hurried American energies. Fine, we're the interlopers here, she thinks, and takes a deep breath, smiles.

"*Doctor,* may I have a word?"

He stands, holds the clipboard in front of this stomach, sideways.

"*¿Sí? ¿Qué pasó?*"

"We'd like to fly her to Madrid as soon as possible," Angela tells him.

"Why?" the doctor asks in English, and Louis turns around to face him.

"Look, Doctor, nothing against you, but we have to make sure she survives this . . . party island," Louis says, and uses his hands to indicate the waiting room, where nearly every person waiting to be seen is under thirty. "With its overdoses and drunk kids. I mean, come on. In Madrid, they'll have better equipment, right?"

The doctor shakes his head, didn't really understand what Louis said, switches to Spanish and addresses Angela.

"Americans always want to take action," he says, and Louis demands a translation, which, after hesitating, she gives him.

"I know, I know," Louis says. "I get it. I know the history of Yankee imperialism, but sometimes action is good. Action is how things change," Louis says.

"Your friend . . . Kate . . ." the doctor says uncertainly. Kate is a hard name for Spanish speakers to pronounce. "She and her friends were smoking hashish. The police think that was part of the cause of the accident, and that they were drinking, too. They found a bottle of ouzo on the floor and—"

Having understood the words *hashish* and *ouzo,* Louis leaps out in anger. "Are you blaming her for this?" he demands. "Are you saying she deserved this?"

"No, no, please don't be ridiculous. I am only saying that English and German teenagers are not the only ones who consume drugs."

"Oh, okay, good to know. Very important bit of information. You know what, Doc? We don't care. We need to make sure she gets to a bigger city and a bigger hospital, to Madrid. I mean, come on, why is she getting fluids? She's not supposed to be when she's got a head injury."

"You have been investigating."

"Yeah, I have. We have a laptop with us and we read some things about head trauma."

"Well, not giving the patient fluids is an old way of treating trauma. No fluids would slow the heart, which would send less blood to the brain. We want normal blood flow, good pressure. Other than a slightly rapid heartbeat, she is doing well. A move could compromise her breathing, her heart. The change in altitude, any unnecessary movement, that could put stress on her heart."

"What about a neurologic assessment?" Louis asks "You said yesterday you would do another CT scan. Have you? And what about measuring her intracranial pressure?"

The doctor shakes his head, looks down, takes a deep breath.

"I can't right now. The CT machine is not working. We are waiting for the parts to have it fixed. Or to borrow one—"

"Oh, great, great." Louis interrupts, trying not to look as if he knows he's won his point. "Well, then . . . right. Nothing more to discuss. We're getting her out of here."

"I wish I could help you, I really do, but it's not so simple. I think the family has to make this decision. I believe my boss received a correspondence from her father," the doctor says.

"From her father? Her father's not alive," Louis says. "You mean her stepfather?"

"I believe so. You should speak with Dr. Mendoza."

"Why should I do that? I'm her husband and you're her doctor. Why would we have to ask someone else?"

"Okay, I must go now," Santillan says, and walks away from them.

Louis watches him. "I bet it's Don. I'll fucking kill that old man," Louis says, staring at his left hand, which is closed into a tight fist.

"Please calm down. We don't need to piss off her doctor. We need him on our side," Angela says.

"No, God forbid you or I ever do anything to upset someone," he says. "God forbid we fight back. We're just gonna stand by and wait, right? No. No. She did everything she could to change, to become, I don't know, whatever, normal. Now it's our turn to be strong and to take some fucking action, all right? It's your turn and it's my turn," he says, and walks off, fast, angrily, pausing for the doors to open and then, when they don't, kicking them open.

She can hear him yell "I'm sorry!" as he walks away from the hospital.

CHAPTER 23
New York
1991

On Angela's fourth trip to New York, the question finally arises: What next? They're in bed, Kate's head against Angela's neck, cuddling like an old married couple.

"I don't mean to be cruel," Kate says. "But you wouldn't be here if you really loved her. And this can't be easy."

Angela looks away, focuses on the comforter cover, trying to take interest in the subtle white stripe she's never noticed before, runs her finger along the pattern. She hates lying to Kate about Terry, but at the same time she can't shake the sense that telling Kate she's free will change everything she's come to cherish.

Kate gets out of bed, goes to her desk, and pulls something from the drawer, comes and straddles her, pops a lemon drop in Angela's mouth, then one in her own.

"We're not too old for candy?"

"No," Kate says, and kisses her. "Come on, let's go to a neutral city."

"What's a neutral city?"

"Boston?"

"Boston."

"Yeah, Boston for the summer. There's a law firm there where I could easily temp. This lawyer I used to work for just moved there."

"I don't know."

"Come on, Agnelli. Be different. Take a chance. You know how you are."

"How I am?"

"You're a journalist. You watch things and then take notes, tell other people exactly the same amount about each side. Maybe you tell them because you hope they'll get it and go out and do something about it. But what about your taking action? You could miss out on your own life, being so objective."

Angela dislikes people who dislike criticism, but right now, the lecture has annoyed her and she can't hide it. "Okay, thanks for your thoughts, Ms. Harrington," she says, and bites down on the lemon drop so hard, it hurts her teeth.

CHAPTER 24
A Bakery in Ibiza
1994

Louis feels as if he has spent his entire life trying to push away certain instincts. Wanting Kate was wrong because it was the same as what Don was doing. Now he realizes that wasn't the right lesson to have taken, but it's the one, at eighteen, he unfortunately took, sitting there on that lawn chair, watching Don smiling at Kate, with Georgina tucked into his arms.

Right now, in Ibiza, walking to that bakery, Louis can almost feel his new instincts replace the old ones, and it feels good. No one has ever mattered more than Kate. No one has ever deserved more than Kate, even if no one has ever felt herself less deserving than Kate.

"This is it. This is it. It is this. It is this," he chants, like some prayer or mantra. As he pushes open the door, he can see, in the punker kid's quick look, the recognition. A girl stands next to him. In every way, she appears to be his polar opposite—chubby and wearing a pink sweatshirt, no makeup whatsoever. Their only link, visually anyway, is that the girl's nails are as glaringly pink as his are blue.

"¿Sí?" the kid asks when it's Louis's turn.

"Hey, listen, can I talk to you alone? I want to buy something that is not coffee or baked goods," Louis says.

The kid eyes him suspiciously, but when Louis starts walking outside and motions for him to follow, the kid does.

160

He goes down the street a bit, stands in front of what looks like an empty building.

"I need to buy a gun."

"I thought you wanted drugs maybe."

"No," Louis says. "No. Can you get me a gun?"

"I don't know," the kid says, and stares at him, bony shoulders rising as he puts his hands under his armpits. "Why you no buy something else? Coca-Cola? I can check if you are my friend," the guy says.

Louis hasn't had a hit of coke in years, but if any moment were ever right, certainly this one is. "Yeah, all right, fine. Here," he says, and hands the kid two twenties.

The kid reaches into his jeans pocket and pulls out a vial, unscrews the top, pulls out a tiny spoon, and gives Louis the first hit, then takes one himself. Then the other nostril for each of them. The kid puts away the vial and starts to walk back toward the bakery.

"Hey, find out what I asked you for. I'm at Hotel Rondo," Louis says.

"Okay."

"And if you know anyone who can use it, even better."

The kid laughs and looks at the ground. He didn't expect this. "Eh . . . like Mr. John Wayne?"

"Yeah. Just like."

"*Ya, ya,*" the kid says, and jogs off.

Louis decides to go somewhere, he's not sure where. He walks to the main street and hails a cab. When the driver asks where he is going, Louis shrugs.

"Please just drive me toward . . . the water."

If you have all the money in the world, where do you go? Where do you get the best advice? Where would you go if you had everything? Where you pay the most, of course.

"What's the best hotel on the island?"

"Mirador or Regent."

"Okay, good, take me there, please. Either one," he says.

The driver stares at him in the mirror a second longer than normal. Maybe Louis doesn't look like a Mirador patron.

"Hey, do you have a Hugo Boss or a Calvin Klein store?" he asks the driver.

The man exhales patiently, then shrugs. "Eh . . . yes, yes."

"Yes, good."

The driver takes him to the main street of the shopping district and pulls over in front of a tony-looking boutique with potted trees under a striped awning.

"Wait? Stay, stay, *por favor*," Louis says, exactly the way he'd ask a pet to stay put.

"*Sí, sí*," the man says, and points to his meter, then switches it off and lights a cigarette.

"Good man," Louis says.

He goes inside and grabs the first shirt he sees that looks like it might fit, and a dark jacket to go with it, but it's huge on him. He goes back to the rack and finds another jacket, gray pinstripe and a better fit. A little big, but at least it doesn't scream "Dad's coat."

The salesgirl, in tight black bouclé, walks over and stares at Louis, says something he doesn't understand.

"*Gringo. No ingles*," he says.

"I know," she says in perfect English, and hands him a pair of pants.

No pants. His jeans are okay. Kate bought them as a gift not that long ago, so they're probably hip enough still.

At the register, the woman says in English, "We have tailor bring back tomorrow after four," she says, and grabs at the sleeve as if with fingers made of scissors. He loves how women are in other countries, how bossy and brazen. She keeps her scissor forefinger against his wrist just a second longer than necessary, then smiles at him.

"Hopefully, I won't be here tomorrow after four," he says.

"Vacation over?"

"Yes," he says, and wonders if his nose is running, rubs it just in case, and picks up sunglasses with a big fat label on the side. He needs something that really says money. He puts the glasses on the counter, next to his credit card.

As the sale goes through, Louis takes off his T-shirt and puts on the new dress shirt, only glancing once at the saleswoman, who is quietly horrified by this. She pretends great interest in finding a fresh pen for his signature.

"Let's go," he says to the driver, who gives Louis a thumbs-up for the shirt and jacket.

He'll go to the hotel, act like he's a big shot, and find some help getting Kate off this island and into a real hospital. Louis is glad he's doing this, and he's really glad he's high. It's an artificial feeling of strength, but so what. What is it the AA alcoholics say? "Fake it till you make it." Maybe if you wait your whole life to become something on the inside, you'll end up waiting forever. Maybe you just need to wear the costume, like you're in a movie or something, and then you become that.

"Fake it till you make it," Louis says, looking at the sidewalk and the pretty views, the pretty people.

"¿Qué?" the driver asks.

"Nada."

As they drive past sidewalks jammed with people toting shopping bags, he feels certain he'll soon get Kate off the island. He doesn't believe in a predestined outcome to anyone's life, but he feels, in what you could call his heart or his soul, that it's not the time for Kate to go.

CHAPTER 25

A Neutral City
1991

Angela sits at a café table on Tremont, a cup of hot coffee in front of her and a poppy seed muffin resting on a brown bag. The *Boston Phoenix* rental section waits on a chair beside her, yellow marker atop, ready to help find the two of them a new home. She leans over just a little and takes in the smell of the coffee and the muffin, that thick vanilla and egg smell, rich as one of Proust's madeleines. She even thinks she smells the ink of the paper and other things: the fresh dirt someone put into the window box in the apartment just around the corner; the hair spray from the salon on the corner, whose owner now, because it's spring, keeps her windows open.

This reminds her of Spain and those torturous days of having a crush on Kate, which, though painful, had seemed to awaken all her senses, so that everything smelled good, from the men's cologne that every guy seemingly bathed in to the mothball tucked into an old lady's coat, released as she extracted her hand to press the elevator button, to the cigarettes everywhere. Even the steely, harsh smell inside the Metro was a reminder of this country where she'd finally, for the first time, fallen in love.

Now, finally, the first day in Boston, she can breathe in happiness. So much of the last few months has been spent trying to ease Terry's pain, a ridiculous task for the very cause of that pain to have undertaken, she now knows. This is real happiness now, no longer infused with guilt, but happiness through and through, pure and simple.

Angela has found an ad for a six-month sublease—May to October. It's for a loft on Harrison Avenue, just four blocks from Tremont, with high ceilings and brick walls, floors made of wide railroad planks painted white. When she goes to see it, the place smells of hay, and she wonders what in the world that might be, but then she sees that a green sisal rug covers the kitchen floor.

"Brand-new," says Joel, the owner, and points at the rug, then goes to his French coffeemaker and pushes down the press, asks if she'd like some. He looks like Bruce Springsteen, with messy brown hair and those nice, almost girlishly pursed lips, even dresses like Springsteen, in dirty jeans and a gray T-shirt that smells a little sweaty.

Mug in hand, he shows her the rest of the place, with its views of the bread factory across a weed-filled parking lot, the freeway behind that.

"There's a homeless center a couple blocks away, mostly drunks who use it just at night to sleep. Harmless, but I do carry Mace. You okay with that?"

"I think so," she says, and looks around at the loft—romantic as anything she's ever read about, complete with huge abstract paintings hanging everywhere. Done in muted grays, whites, and dark colors, but with a burst of bright color somewhere—yellow or magenta—they're Joel's art.

"Anyway, you said it was for two of you, right? So . . . is your boyfriend muscular like me?" he asks, and laughs. He's cute and clearly talented, but not muscular.

"My girlfriend," she says for the first time ever about Kate. "No, she isn't too muscular, no."

"I'm sure she has other attributes."

Angela's never thought to call Kate her girlfriend. "Girlfriend," she repeats for herself, but Joel seems to think she's clarifying this point for him.

"Yeah, no, that's cool. My sister's a lapper," he says, and they both laugh. "Is that the PC term for it?"

"Lapper. Yeah, I believe so," Angela says.

"Do you want it? 'Cause if you do, it's yours."

"I do," she says.

When it's time for Kate to move in, Angela considers doing the things you might see in a movie, like setting out a picnic in the center of the living room, a bottle of champagne chilling on the floor, next to some flowers, or just a card maybe. But in the end, it all seems too romantic for the two of them.

Instead, she goes to Tiffany and buys a simple key chain, asks them to give her a big box, then sets the key chain in the center of it. *Breakfast at Tiffany's* is one of Kate's favorites.

The reward is one of those kisses and one of those embraces that feel as if Kate herself is as new as their home—more open and available than ever before. She loves the loft, the fact that there's a Greek deli just downstairs and a bakery nearby. She loves Joel's artwork, even loves the drafty windows with the inch-wide gaps between frame and glass in some places, which someone has covered in thick plastic.

"I wouldn't want to be here in winter, but for the summer, it'll be perfect," she says.

They spend the afternoon cleaning the floors, so the place smells of Murphy Oil Soap, plus the sisal rug, plus vanilla candles that Kate was amazed to find at the deli. They buy olives ladled out of a cask, and hummus, pita bread, feta cheese, wine.

"Can you be a vegetarian just for a while?" Kate asks, and kisses her right there in front of the owner, a lady in her seventies, who quickly turns to look up at her shelves.

"I can do that, yes."

Kate goes to a fabric store and buys yards and yards of sheer white material to make curtains. She even buys herself a secondhand sewing machine, which she sets up under one of Joel's paintings.

She spends the entire first week at the sewing machine, dressed in a white T-shirt and her black yoga pants, the thick, heavy nerd glasses sliding off her nose as she sews enough curtains for a mansion.

"How many of those do we need?" Angela asks from across the room as she lies on Joel's green velvet couch, enjoying the warm wind that does indeed seep through all his windows.

"It's 'cause I'm not very good at it and keep screwing up," Kate says through the pins in her mouth.

"Sorry, what was that? I don't comprehend."

She takes out the pins. "I said, fucker, that I'm not very good at this. But . . . ta-da!" Kate stands and holds beside her the piece she's just finished. She looks like a kid showing off a project she can't believe is her own handiwork, her face bursting with pride and amazement.

"Brava! Fantastic hem!" Angela shouts, then applauds. "Who knew a white curtain could make someone this happy?"

Kate looks at the material, then at her, folds the curtain and sets it on the table, then walks to the couch very purposefully, takes the wineglass out of Angela's hand, sets it on the window ledge, and positions herself so that she's lying across Angela. She leans in, looking very serious.

"It's not the curtains that are making me happy," Kate says, and kisses her.

It all makes sense now, the songs, the paintings, the sumptuous buildings—the myriad extraordinary achievements she now realizes were probably inspired by this exact thing she's feeling.

One day as she's walking home from work through the Commons, it starts to rain, a warm summer rain that, as it falls on her jacket, triggers the scent of Kate's perfume somewhere on her—the collar or the sleeve maybe? Kate wore the jacket to dinner two nights before. Some people dash toward awnings; others hunch into their umbrellas, shooting her a look as they pass that says, Get undercover, fool. And *why* are you smiling?

To hear a beautiful woman say "I want you" is to feel a crown laid upon your bowed head. It changes how you see everything—yourself included. No wonder some men chase this night after night. And it doesn't end or diminish after the body's satisfied; just the contrary, in fact. Desire begets more desire, and not just for your lover but also for the world and nearly every little thing in it.

Normally mundane weekdays now taste of Italian coffee and corn muffins in bed, angel-hair pasta on the couch, and wine drunk while lying in a cold tub, because Boston can be so incredibly hot and humid.

Weekends are glorious. Often they rent a car or hitch a ride with new gay friends who are driving to Provincetown; if not, they take the ferry. They lie naked in the dunes, go back to the room and nap, then go for oysters and Kir royales at sunset or to the tea dances on the deck of the Steam and Anchor or one of the other restaurants overlooking the water, just as the sun starts to set. Surrounded by loud techno or trance and sweaty, beautiful gay boys who love to dance, it's the perfect celebration. Even the quiet Monday-coming resolve of that last ferry home on Sunday night feels joyous.

"We were right about Boston," Kate says, sitting next to her on the top deck, tired, sandy, a little sunburned.

"Yes, we were."

CHAPTER 26
A Hotel Room in Ibiza
1994

Angela takes a taxi back to the hotel, showers, and lies on the bed, wondering what to do next. Would Kate want to see her mother? Or her, for that matter? What is happening to Louis, this person who, after all, she doesn't know that well and with whom she essentially has only one thing in common—and what a hell of a thing to share—the fact that they love the same woman.

Staying feels wrong, but so does leaving.

As the wind pushes the curtain toward the bed, Angela rolls on her stomach and slips her hand down between her body and the bed, lets her head rest against the sheet, pulls up her hair so the wind can dry the nape of her neck.

"I want to go home," Angela says, alone in that hotel room in Ibiza, sweat and tears running down her cheek, scared to death that Kate will never wake up.

CHAPTER 27
Boston
1991

Angela starts wondering if they could stay beyond the summer. They can afford this place or another, maybe even something nicer. Kate's law office gigs pay well. Angela could keep freelancing for the *Phoenix* and waiting tables at the Museum of Fine Arts restaurant. Wealthy art patrons leave tips nearly as handsome as the view from the giant windows. At the end of a shift, she'll sometimes ride home with nearly one hundred dollars in her pocket, not to mention a few delicious desserts packed into her tote, since everyone's allowed to raid the pastry table at the end of the night. She showers off the smell of the kitchen and gets in bed, where they stay up late reading and polish off Courbet's crème brûlée or Titian's tiramisu.

"You realize we can't do this forever," Kate says, patting her still very flat stomach. "You'll have to get a job at a salad restaurant soon."

"Already applied," Angela says, and lays her head on that stomach.

Kate keeps reading, holding the book in her right hand. With her left, she absently plays with Angela's hair, pausing every few minutes to push the glasses back up her nose, then going back to Angela's hair.

Without really admitting it to herself, Angela starts playing with that special brand of magic called "trying to heal the pain of your lover's past." She starts by often asking Kate to tell stories about the good childhood, the one before her father died.

"He used to take me to the beach. He'd put me on his board, and we'd sit there in that glassy green water and wait for waves, me leaning against his chest. I think I remember what the back of my ears felt like against his wet chest. I think, but . . . maybe I'm making that up. You know how it is with really old memories—they're so old that you don't really know what's true and what you filled in."

"You said that to me in Spain once."

"Did I?"

"Yeah."

"Has the story changed much since then?"

"No. I don't think so," Angela says, and runs her fingers along Kate's back, over one shoulder blade, then the other, imagining them as waves.

"I must have it right, then. And then, after surfing, he'd take me for ice cream. Those big soft-serve things that smell super vanilla-y. Maybe that's why I like the vanilla candles."

"Maybe."

"That's it, that's it, all I got," Kate says.

"There's got to be more," Angela says.

"There was this thing he did. We had a garden behind the restaurant. And we grew zucchini, and he wrote my name on one, when it was little, so we could watch it grow. We'd go down and look at my name get bigger, until it was this huge, magical, edible sign."

"Did you eat it?"

"No. Because I thought it was real, that it was like a pet or something. I didn't want to eat it."

"And it was named after you."

"Exactly. So it just sat out there in the garden, and then I guess it went in the trash. I don't remember. Time to go to sleep now," she says.

"Come on, one more good memory. There's got to be more."

"No, ain't got to be nothing," Kate says in her old black jazz singer voice. "Old man died in the water. That's all little girl remembers." She sits up fast, scaring Angela. "Your turn now," she says, and pretends to play the piano on Angela's arms, morphing into Stevie Wonder. "Happy birthday to you, happy birthday," Kate sings in the middle of the night, and Angela indulges her with stories from a far longer and less complicated childhood, in San Diego.

Yes, there were layoffs that sent Dad into depressions and sparked a few fights, and there was Mom's cancer scare, but the sense of family and of communal strength never wavered. She thinks of her dad at her college graduation, crying. "*Qué orgullo, mi hijita, qué orgullo,*" he'd said over and over, telling her how proud she'd made them. Knowing your people are proud of you—what more could you ask from life?

It's bittersweet, the memory, because it reminds her that college paved the way for many more departures—Spain, then Ventura, now Boston. Once she got used to going away, it became easier and easier to keep doing it. She wonders if she's building a life almost irreconcilably different from that lived by the rest of her family, not unlike the farmworker's daughter she wrote about, who went to Harvard. How proud of me are you *now* that I am completely different or gone?

She sighs so hard, Kate looks worried. "What's wrong?"

"The distance."

"What distance?"

"Nothing," she says, thinking this is nothing compared to what Kate must feel. Ironic that she struggles to hold on to her family as Kate works to let go.

Angela knows she's the lucky one, the toy that isn't broken, so she keeps trying, in this summer of theirs, to essentially commingle their pasts, as if pouring the contents of two separate beakers into one bigger one, hoping the contents of one can dilute the power of the other.

Angela tells her how her father once, overcome with happiness after the tumor in her mom's breast was found to be benign, walked around the house, pointing out everything his wife and their mom had bought or made. He'd acted a little crazy, honestly, and scared Angela's sister, but it was the energy of a man who was suddenly feeling the full intensity of his good fortune.

"See that couch covered in that beautiful blue fabric! That's because of your mom. And that vase, too! The flowers in it. Everything!"

"Your dad sounds sweet."

"He is."

She tells Kate about how her parents gardened together, dredges up details about her mother planting sweet peas, especially purple ones—everyone's favorites—and about her dad planting tomatoes.

"Hey, should we try to plant something back there, behind the parking lot?" Angela asks.

"Is there dirt back there? It's not soot?"

They plant a basil bush and four tomato plants. Knowing full well she's being too literal, Angela buys a bag of zucchini seeds, which she tucks into a single long row. They drag home a card table someone left for the garbagemen, cover it in a red tablecloth, atop which they set a big white pot filled with herbs. Angela even puts a few strings of tiny pink lights around the one real plant—a single huge sunflower.

"It looks like a sad little gay bar in the Naples back here," Kate says.

"Yes, it's called the Secret Sunflower," Angela says. They heard a comedian making fun of the fact that the names of gay bars are always in code and either sound dark and scary or refer to Judy Garland.

"The Leather Sunflower."

"Somewhere Over the Sunflower."

"Stop it!" Kate yells, but they keep it up all night, even in bed.

"Did you ever read that book?" Kate asks, and pauses long enough that Angela knows what's coming and can jump on her joke.

"The Well of sunflowers?"

"Oh! You got me."

"Yes, I did," she says, and pulls her close. "I did."

CHAPTER 28
A Hotel Room in Ibiza
1994

Louis walks into the room at three, still wearing the new jacket and with the sunglasses perched atop his head. He carries a paper bag under his arm, the contents of which he spills onto the credenza.

"What happened to you? Where did you get . . . that?" Angela asks.

"There's a little market right across the street. Doesn't sell real food but has some things, like this," he says, and pulls a bottle of vermouth from the bag.

"I mean your clothes. What are you wearing?"

"Oh, I forgot," he says, and looks at his jacket as if someone else put it on him, then opens it to show off the look. "Do I look rich or what?"

"Yes, you look rich."

"I didn't bring anything nice, and I thought I should try to look kind of money," he says, and holds the bottle up as if it's a rare champagne. "Cinzano. She used to say you taught her to drink it. Your family drank it or something?" he says, then sets it on the credenza and starts to unscrew the top.

"Well, yeah, not as a rule, not all the time, but yes, at parties, weekends."

"Plus a lemon twist?"

She nods yes, and Louis pulls two lemons from the bag, then

looks for and finds a Swiss Army knife on his key chain. "Times like these, it's good to be a gadget geek," he says, sitting on the credenza and starting to peel the lemon with that impossibly small knife. Louis's hand shakes just a little as she watches him try to cut one long ribbon of rind.

"You don't really have to use the whole lemon, just a little piece of rind," she says.

"Think rich, live rich," he says, and tears the rind ribbon in half and twists each piece to release the flavor, then runs one over the lip of its glass, tosses it in, does the same with the other, then pours a good three inches into each glass, so that the fruit's skin rises to the top.

Louis comes and sits on the bed opposite Angela, hands her the glass. She should probably be self-conscious, in her underwear and a tank top, but she isn't. Across from each other, so close that their knees nearly touch, they toast, then drink.

"Your eyes are swollen," he says.

"Did a little crying."

"I see," he says, and takes one sip, then another, his hand still shaking a little.

"I put some of her perfume on," Angela says. "I hope you don't mind."

"Course not," he says, and reaches for her wrist, puts it to his nose, and takes a deep breath.

"So, where have you been, rock star?" she asks. She's staring at that big label on the sunglasses atop his head.

"I went over to the best hotel in town, right, told them my wife had an accident, needs to be flown out. I actually asked for the manager, and I said, 'Hey, listen, I've been coming here for years. I must have spent a hundred thousand dollars with you over the years. You remember me, right?' And he said, 'Of course, sir, I remember you well.' So I said, 'Tell me the truth. If it was your wife, if your wife had had an accident and had, you know, a head injury, would you fly her to Madrid, or would you trust the doctors here?'"

"You did?"

"Wealthy people don't just follow the rules, you know? 'Oh, this is how we do it. Okay, then.' No. They figure out the best way to get what they want, the best *best,* and they do it. So this guy, the concierge, he says, 'Yes, sir, I would fly her to Madrid. I definitely would, and then maybe to London. I would not delay. We sometimes have a pessimistic spirit here in Spain. Because of Franco.' The guy said that."

"Really?"

"He says Spaniards don't always think big, you know? It's like they don't say to themselves 'We can do it; we can save this woman.' 'Cause of all the years of dictatorship, they kind of roll over and wait for the father or the dictator to dictate. Lack of self-determination. How about that? Politics as medicine? She'll love that."

"She will," Angela says, and takes a deep breath.

"So he gave me the name of the medevac company and of another guy who has a Learjet and basically rents it out for a lot of money. That guy will take anyone who pays, with or without permission."

"Oh, okay," she says. "So you're thinking of sneaking her out of the hospital and putting her on a nonmedical flight?"

"No. No. I'd rather use the medevac, but if worse comes to worst, it's good to know we have options."

She takes a few sips, shakes her head, and looks down at her feet. "Oh, God, Louis. This is all so crazy."

"I know, but we don't have a choice. We have to get her out of here. Will you call the medevac guy and find out what they need? Please?" He sets a card on her knee.

The card says "Lalo Rodríguez, Transporte Médico de Europa." She dials and explains the situation and the man says he'd been expecting the call.

"Federico called me," he says.

"Federico?"

"From the hotel."

"Oh, yes."

The man explains that he'll need a few simple things: an ambulance that will deliver the patient to the airport, with a doctor and nurse who will fly with the patient. Confirmation that an ambulance will be meeting the plane in Madrid and, of course, the name of the clinic where the patient is going. Paperwork transferring responsibility for the passenger's health from the discharging hospital to the in-flight doctor must be signed and notarized. There is a notary service at the hotel, he says, and he can fax the paperwork.

"Listen, what if . . . I'm not sure her doctor wants her to fly. Can we do this without his permission?"

"Oh," he says, and pauses. "There is a release from the doctor that says the patient is flying 'against medical advice.' But, of course, this is not the best option. It's better to have the doctor with you," the man says.

"Yes, that's our hope. We will have a doctor, but I just wanted to check."

"Good, because this is important. I will fax the forms to your hotel."

"No, you know what, I'd prefer to get them from you myself. I'll pick them up," she says, and gets his address.

Once all is signed, wheels can leave tarmac by the next afternoon, he says. She asks him for the best clinic in Madrid and he says he doesn't know.

"Where are most people taken when they arrive in Madrid?" she asks.

Many different hospitals and clinics, he says, then asks her to wait a moment. "Clínica Ruber—that's where we took a lady a few months ago who'd had an accident. Head trauma also," he says, and gives her the number.

"Good, thank you so much," she says.

As she dials the number in Madrid, the door opens and Louis steps in from the balcony, where he'd gone to smoke. He goes to the credenza and pours more vermouth. This time, he squeezes the lemon right into the liquid, then just throws the entire piece of fruit into the glass, drinks it down fast, grabs the bottle, and comes to sit near her.

Angela tells the woman from Clinica Ruber that her sister has had a car accident in Ibiza and that they're having her flown to Madrid tomorrow. Who is the best neurosurgeon, she asks, and the receptionist gives her the names of two doctors: Dr. Pedro García Ruíz Espiga and Dr. Carlos Mantela.

Angela asks what needs to be done for these doctors to take her sister on as a patient, if it's as simple as reserving a room for Kate. The receptionist says to have the doctor in Ibiza call.

"I'd like to make the arrangements myself," she says, but that's not an option for this nurse.

"Just have the doctor call. They have to plan the transfer together," she says.

Angela takes a deep breath, thanks her, and says good-bye. "We're going to have to convince Santillan to help us," she tells Louis.

He nods yes and stares at her. "We will. We have to."

"Yeah?"

"Yeah. He's coming for her, Don is. Just like we did."

CHAPTER 29
Boston
1991

The six-month lease has hung an invisible clock on the relationship. Hurry up and build memories to sustain you when winter comes.

One evening, Angela takes her to the garden to show her the first zucchini of the crop. Immediately, she regrets having done it.

"Lovely, so sweet," Kate says, staring at the garden. When she turns to go back up to the loft, the look in her eyes is both melancholy and cautionary, as if trying to say, Don't remember some of the things I tell you. And don't experiment with things you don't really understand.

That night, neither one can fall asleep. It's a particularly hot, sticky evening, and despite the late hour, the shelter men seem energized. You can hear some laughing or arguing as they clang down the street, preparing to stow or hide the carts filled with recycling they're counting on for tomorrow's drink.

"Must be a full moon," Angela says, and decides to just go ahead and be awake. She turns on her side and watches Kate. "You're beautiful, you're smart—" Angela says, then stops.

"Go on. I totally agree so far." Kate smiles and takes a bit of Angela's hair between her fingers and uses it like a brush against her upper lip. "I used to have blankets, when I was a kid, with these flecks on them and I would rub them on my cheek until I fell asleep."

"Am I your blanket?" Angela asks.

"No, not at all, but there is something about you that's . . ."

"What?"

"I don't know what it is. It's like—and this is going to be weird—it's like I can feel this strength that, honestly, I don't see in you just from looking at you. You're so gentle and peaceful . . . but there are times when . . . you're stronger than you are, if that makes any sense."

"It does."

"Yeah. And—now this is important," Kate says, and stops to look at the bits of Angela's hair she holds between her fingers. "That's how pompous professors say it—'This is important,' they say; then they pause till you pick up your pen."

"I don't have a pen," Angela says.

"Sometimes I get it, what it means to want someone inside you, to want to keep the person there. You know? When we're making love, I want to keep you inside me."

"I feel the same way."

"I know you do," Kate says, and rubs her cheek with one finger, then offers the saddest of smiles.

"Why is that bad?"

"Because it's like . . . I want you deep inside, but I also don't."

"Why not?"

"Because it's like this: All the best and all the worst, it all lives in the same place. You know? It all lives in the deepest place in me. That garden downstairs, it grows next to my dad's garden, but they both kind of grow in Encino."

"Why can't this be separate? Have its own place?"

"I don't know. It's just all so intense that it . . . all lives together—the good and the bad."

"Maybe we can chase it away, so that it finds its own home, separate from everything else," Angela says.

Now Kate's smile is even sadder, the look far away, and Angela knows why.

"That's what I want."

"That's what we all want," she says, and curls herself in Angela's arms.

CHAPTER 30
Ibiza
1994

Angela takes a cab to the hospital and arrives at seven, intent on finding Santillan, in order to convince him to do the paperwork for Kate's release. Just as she's about to ask the nurse where he might be, she hears Ted Griffin's voice. He's speaking in English, with a tone of helpfulness like that of a museum guide. Even before looking up, she knows that Kate's parents have arrived.

"Ah, Ms. Agnelli, there you are."

Ted Griffin is walking toward her with a blond woman in her sixties who's wearing a maroon pantsuit. Next to her walks a tall man in khakis and a dark blazer.

"Ms. Agnelli, these are Georgina and Don Williams, Kate's parents. But maybe you already know one another?"

"Hello," she says, and shakes hands with Kate's mother first.

"Well, hello," the lady says in a voice that makes her sound like Florence Henderson, a studied, practiced friendliness. "I remember hearing Kate mention you. From Spain, right? You met in Spain, didn't you?" she asks.

Angela would never have pictured Kate's mother like this—so fair and white. All these years, she'd pictured Liz Taylor or Ava Gardner, not the Mia Farrow of Encino. The woman's attractive, with pretty little blue eyes and the slightly teased blond hair Angela associates with school board or city council members who golf and drive white Lexuses with gold trim. Pretty, but so different from Kate's elegance and strength. Nothing of Kate's bearing. Instead, she has the sort of rough, pinkish skin and compact features Angela associates with snowy winters in Boston or Philly.

"Right, yes, Kate and I first met in Madrid. That's right."

"Yes, yes," Georgina says, and looks down at Angela's hand, which makes her look at Georgina's jacket sleeve. It's made of expensive-looking maroon wool, Georgina's suit, but the sleeves hang way down, nearly to half her thumb, and she has white-tipped nails, a French manicure.

"Donald Williams," the man says, and extends his hand to Angela. When she takes it, he places his other hand atop hers, making her hand feel, for just a second, trapped. He wears the sort of huge college ring that makes her think of winning football coaches. He shakes her hand only a couple of times, then releases it. He smiles kindly as he stoops a little. He must do that a lot, this man who, when he straightens, seems to be at least six four or five. Don has one of those big dimpled chins and high cheekbones covered with the pinkest of cheeks, like a character drawn by a child with new crayons. He has small eyes, like his wife's, and they are just as bright a blue as hers. He hasn't lost his hair, but he wears it short. And near the hairline, you can see the sun-marked skin on his scalp.

So this is Don. This is you! She would love to say that and just stare at him for a few minutes, trying to examine, inch by inch, his physical presence, study him to see if anything about him offers clues to the past.

"How are you, dear?" he says. "We sure do appreciate how quickly you got here."

That "we" is so preposterous. We, the family? You're not the family, she thinks, and feels a little of Louis's anger, as if he's there with her, at her back. *We appreciate your getting here so fast, even before us!* You wouldn't be here at all if not for the fucking flight forms, she thinks.

Angela may not be part of Kate's "we," of her daily life, but she's certainly not as estranged as are these two people, which makes it all so puzzling. Why in the world did Kate list her mother on the flight form?

"Good to finally put a face to your name, after hearing about you for so many years," she says.

Don chuckles with fake amusement, still in control but wondering about this comment, this girl in front of him. Kate would not have talked about him fondly. He knows that, and so does Angela.

Ted Griffin, in khakis that make him look like Don's golf partner, seems energized. Or maybe he's just relieved by the prospect of returning to his vacation. Mother and father here—great! Kate is now that much less his problem. He begins talking about the doctor and how competent he is, how confident he is that Kate will soon awaken.

Georgina listens with her head slightly down; her hands, fingers laced together, rest against her chest. She has rings on about four of her fingers, one with emeralds, a silver band with a diamond, behind it a simple band, then another with several different stones, all various colors. Don's head is slightly bowed, too, but he nods yes at everything Griffin says, as if he's already thought of all this.

Finally, Angela thinks. Finally, I'm here, next to you, this man I've never met but have hated for so long. She even takes a deep breath to get a stronger sense of him, and smells mint. Is he chewing on a mint? She watches carefully. Yes, he is, but in a subtle left or right shift of his jaw. You can only tell, really, if you watch him awhile.

"Can we see her right now?" Georgina asks.

"Let me inquire," Griffin says, and goes to find Santillan.

As they're all watching Griffin leave, Georgina suddenly shouts, "Louis!" Angela and Don watch Georgina throw her arms around Louis's neck, pull him close, and hold him for a long time. When they pull away, both have tears in their eyes, and since they both wear glasses, each has to do the same thing: pull off the frames and wipe underneath. The hug stuns Angela.

If he hates Georgina, why this?

Georgina grabs Louis again and cries in his arms as Don, uncomfortable, moves to the front doors and looks out, as if expecting someone else to join them. What is he looking for? Angela wonders. Finally, Georgina lets Louis go.

"This is terrible," she says.

"I know, but she's going to be all right," he says.

"I know," she agrees, and rubs his arm. "Look at you. You're a man. You're so . . . strong now," she says, and squeezes his upper arm.

"I grew up," he says.

"Louis, Louis," she says, trying not to cry more. "I wish it wasn't like this. We haven't even seen her yet. Just got here."

"Yes, yeah, but don't worry, she's on her way back."

"You know when you called me, the message you left . . . I thought she was fine. I didn't know," Georgina says, seeking forgiveness for misunderstanding his message.

"Oh, no, it's okay," Louis tells her.

Don finally turns, as if he only just now heard Louis's voice. "There he is," he says, and comes back to the group, hand extended. Hale, the man is trying to look hale, Angela thinks. Don reaches for Louis's hand and pumps it a few times with such false joy.

"Don," Louis says.

It occurs to Angela that there's history here she doesn't know a thing about.

"That message was very confusing. Good thing I had my attorney call the hospital, or we never might have made it in time," Don says.

"In time," Louis says, and moves closer to Don. "For?"

Don bows his head and Georgina comes closer, already called upon to smooth something over.

Then Griffin returns, oblivious, buoyant. "Ah! So you've all . . . Wonderful, you're all here now, together. This is good," he says.

"Yeah, all good," Louis says.

"Well, the doctor is doing rounds, but the nurse says you can go in to see her. I asked if perhaps the chief surgeon could also come and meet with us, have a word. They said they would send him, Francisco Carreras Irrigatu Mendoza, to speak with us. "Everyone in Spain has two surnames, but doctors, of course, sometimes have three," Griffin says to Don, who chuckles.

"Why would we need to speak with him?" Louis asks.

"Well, to advise us. I know you were interested in having Ms. Harrington moved and—"

"Moved. Why would we want to do that?" Don asks.

"So she can get better care," Louis says.

"This seems like fine care. They saved her life, after all," Don says.

"Not that it's any of your concern, but (*a*) you just arrived, (*b*) it's been seventy-two hours and there's been no change, and (*c*) it's none of your business, Don," Louis says.

"None of my concern?"

"Exactly. She doesn't live in your house, not your kid."

"This is her mother."

"Oh, I know that."

"Folks," Griffin interjects, trying to avoid further conflict. "The, uh, the nurse said to go on in. Time is limited. Why don't we do that," he says, turning to Georgina. "Would you like to go in and see her?"

Griffin, of course, is speaking to Don and Georgina, but there's no way Louis will allow them to go alone. "Sorry, sorry. Come on, yes. I'll take you in to see her," Louis says, and leads them down the hall, heading toward her room.

Ted Griffin's not at all sure about this arrangement. How many visitors are allowed at any one time? But Louis is already so many steps ahead. They all follow.

Once there, Louis positions himself next to the bed, using his body to ensure that neither Don nor Georgina will get close to Kate.

Angela hangs back, outside the door, hoping Santillan will show up. Or this new doctor. She wonders if he'll be more amenable to getting Kate to Madrid. Maybe this man will think it a good idea.

Georgina goes to the right and pats Kate's head gently, stares at her daughter's face, shakes her head slightly, then puts her hand against her mouth and nose, as if trying to suppress tears. Don approaches the other side of the bed but stays a foot away. Louis watches the old man intently, his body straight, fists clenched, ready to fly at him.

The old man doesn't kiss his stepdaughter, just touches her arm and stares at her as Louis stares at him. Don looks befuddled now.

Can't believe she's unconscious, or that you're this close to her again? Louis wonders.

When Don leans in as if to whisper in Kate's ear, Louis takes a step toward him. "Don," he says, and the old man takes a step back and looks at his own feet. But then he straightens and looks at Louis in a way that says, Okay, fine, this point is yours, but the match will be mine.

Louis clenches his jaw and squints ever so slightly.

Angela's relieved to see Dr. Santillan approach the door. The doctor stops and turns, as if to walk away, give the family more time with Kate, but Angela reaches out and pulls at the sleeve of his jacket.

"*¿No me haría un favor?*" she asks, hoping he will do her a favor. If you could go in and tell the family to leave, that would be a help, she tells him.

"*¿Pasa algo?*" He wants to know if something's wrong.

The usual. Family drama, she tells him. He stares for a moment, unconvinced, wanting to know what this means, exactly.

"The father asked to speak with the chief of surgery—Mendoza?" she says, and Santillan immediately expresses his surprise.

"Oh? Why? Do they want to move her, too?"

"I don't know," she says. "I thought you might know."

"No, I don't." Santillan then nods yes, as if to say, Fine. I can't do a lot, but at least I can do this.

Santillan enters the room and tells everyone that he's very sorry but he must examine Kate now. He says they can come back later, in the evening.

"Can we speak with you about her condition?" Griffin asks. "Her parents would like to know what to expect."

"Well, it's hard to know what to expect," the doctor says. "We must continue waiting. I must examine her now and you must, please, wait in the hallway," he says.

Angela tries to catch the doctor's eye to thank him, but he never looks at her, so she just ushers the family down the hallway to the waiting area.

They walk slowly and quietly. Every couple of seconds, someone seems on the verge of a word but then refrains. When they arrive at the main lounge, Ted speaks up first.

"I've prepared a list of hotels where you might be comfortable. All are close to here. Louis and Angela are staying at the hotel where Kate and her friends had been staying. I'm sure you can arrange with them to . . ."

Louis tugs at Angela's arm and pulls her to him. "I'm going to the airport," he says quietly.

"Wait for me. We'll go together."

"No. Stay and talk to the new doctor. And make sure Don never gets to see her alone, yeah? You need money to . . . give people?" he asks, and before she's answered, he puts cash in her hands.

"Yeah, okay," she says, and looks at him. He hasn't shaved in the last day and she can see a touch of brown stubble on his cheek.

Maybe he senses how unmoored Angela feels, and alone, because Louis hugs her, whispers "Soon, soon" in her ear, then kisses her cheek. He lets her go and turns to the group, offering the friendly wave of someone who must, unfortunately, leave the picnic a little early. Work obligation, so sorry.

"Got to go. See you all later," Louis says, and walks quickly out of the reception area, then out of the clinic altogether. Griffin and Kate's parents watch him go. Georgina looks slightly perplexed.

When they ask where he's gone, Angela says he mentioned having a terrible headache, probably went back to the room to get some rest. Don doesn't believe her.

"They're so close," Georgina says of Louis and Kate. "Best friends since age fourteen. He loves her like—"

If Georgina keeps talking, Griffin will soon know that Louis and Kate are not a conventionally married couple, so Angela jumps in.

"He was going to join Kate here, on this vacation, but he had work back home, so . . . He's beating himself up over that, because he feels that he wasn't here to protect her. You know?"

Griffin nods in agreement, Georgina more slowly, and Don just stares at the doors Louis went through, maybe curious where he really went. We're all pretty good little liars, she thinks.

"Well . . . it was an accident, after all. No one's fault," Don says. "Except the other driver. Is that right, Mr. Griffin. Was he at fault?"

Griffin folds his arms around his chest and looks down at the floor, then uses one of his fists to push up his glasses. "Well, yes, in a sense, although the driver of your daughter's car, or rather, well . . . alcohol was found in the car. And, uh, some hashish. We don't yet know if the, uh, driver, if uh . . . he was impaired or if something else was at play. But the driver of the truck had a heart attack. He died at the scene, as well as . . . We'll know more soon."

Griffin starts sputtering out information about the driver. He had a heart condition, had been warned not to drive, was trying to pay for a second-floor addition to his house by doing extra shifts.

"I'd be interested in seeing those toxicology reports on the driver of my daughter's car," Don says. Griffin doesn't seem to know how to respond.

"Sure, of course."

"I'll let you know where we're staying and perhaps you can have a copy run over to us."

"Certainly," Griffin says.

Once again, Angela feels slapped by the indignity of this. Who is Don Williams to ask to see a toxicology report on behalf of a woman who is in a coma right now and who detests him? And why the hell would Griffin agree to it?

Griffin explains that he has to go now, to be with his own family, but that he'll be back tomorrow. He really hopes the chief of surgery can come and explain to them what was done and what should happen next.

"What were those three names?" Angela asks.

"Oh, uh, Carreras Irrigatu Morelos," Griffin says.

"I believe it was actually Mendoza, the last name, was it not? Mendoza, not Morelos," Don says.

"Ah, yes, yes, good memory," Griffin replies.

"One of the few things left now," Don says.

Angela looks at Don and he at her, a sort of *Gotcha* in his eyes, as if to say, Glad you're paying attention, because I certainly am.

As soon as Ted Griffin has walked through the doors, Don turns and asks Angela about visiting the hotel where she and Louis are staying.

"We'd like to come by, if you don't mind, pick up some of her personal belongings, and so forth," Don says.

"Why would you need her personal belongings?"

Don's head literally jolts back, surprised to be questioned, although his smile projects bemusement. "Well, this is her mother, after all."

"Right, yes, I know Georgina is her mother, but Kate's very much alive and those are her belongings, so why would we divvy them up as if she's not?"

"I didn't mean to imply . . ."

Georgina puts her hand on Angela's arm. "We were just hoping to having something of hers as a way to have her close," Georgina says, and her eyes fill with tears.

"My apologies," Don says, and looks guiltily at Georgina, like someone sorry to have caused his wife more pain.

"Maybe you can stop by tomorrow," Angela says. "That would be better. Since Louis isn't feeling well," she adds.

"That's fine," Georgina says.

"I could bring you some things, if that helps," Angela says.

"No," Don says, "but thank you. Tomorrow's fine. We can wait until tomorrow."

Georgina gives Angela her cell number as she walks outside with them.

"Shall we share a taxi?" Don asks, and offers a confident but kindly smile, his eyes projecting warmth. "By the way, we're prepared to pay for all of the expenses," he says, "so please let me know if you'd like to move to another hotel or if you need anything."

"Oh, that's very nice, but I don't need anything at all, thank you," Angela replies. Funny, in most people, a manipulation would be visible in the eyes, where true intention often makes itself visible, but looking at Don, you can see the attempt at coercion in the smile—so cheerful and strong one second, then gone the next.

Don hails a cab, but just as the car arrives, Angela pretends to just now realize she should visit the restroom. "And anyway, I can easily walk back. You go on ahead," she says.

"Oh, okay," Georgina says, and, as if this last unexpected turn is just one too many, her shoulders surrender any attempt at posture, her cheeks lose air and become more sunken, and her eyes dull with disappointment. Is nothing predictable or simple anymore? her fallen face seems to be saying.

Angela watches the taxi drive away. Louis is right that Don does want something. Waving to her from the backseat of the car, he also doesn't seem to mind showing Angela that he's confident of winning.

CHAPTER 31

Boston
1991

As predicted, once summer ends and October nears, the plastic window covers that once let in a nice breeze now prove futile against winter's looming chill. Like the weather, their relationship starts to change, with far-away looks, long baths alone, no invitation to join.

One night, Angela asks if they should talk to Joel about staying longer in his loft, or look for another place together.

"Trade the dunes for snowbanks? I hear they cover the trees in the Commons with Christmas lights, these huge garlands of lights." She keeps adding layers to bring Kate back, but she looks as if Boston is the last thing on her mind. "Each tree a different color."

"Sounds beautiful," Kate says finally.

"Is this going to work?" Angela asks her, and watches Kate try so hard to come up with an answer she can give without lying to Angela or herself. Silence.

"We have to find a way to talk about this, either way."

"I know. We will," Kate says.

One day, Kate tells Angela that she has to go to New York to see Louis. No invitation for Angela to join her.

The day Kate's leaving for New York, Angela goes to the garden and pulls up the remnants of tomato plants and zucchini. Even the basil, still green and leafy, gets yanked from the soil. She doesn't have to do this at all—no one cares if that piece of dirt behind the parking lot is filled with dead plants. But she wants to indulge in the symbolism of it, of pulling up what once flowered and gave fruit but is now, seemingly, done.

CHAPTER 32
New York
1991

When Kate's in New York, she asks Louis to go with her to dinner alone. This angers Sandrine, but this time, Kate doesn't care. They walk to a bar down the road and order grilled cheese sandwiches and beer.

"I'm moving to Boston permanently," she says.

"Are you sure?" Louis asks, looking at the table. He'd hoped she would return to Park Slope in the winter and that, finally, he would have the guts to end it with Sandrine, start a real life with Kate. He's sworn to himself that if he gets another chance with Kate, he won't blow it.

"No, of course I'm not sure. She's a good girl, comes from a nice family. It doesn't make any sense. Right?"

"Is she trying to fix you?"

"No. She's smarter than that."

"You love her, don't you?"

"I do," she says.

He takes a drink of his beer, then another. "As in 'for real.'"

"For real."

"Well, then, you have to try," he says, still not looking at her.

"You okay?"

"Yeah," he says, and smiles, but still unable to hide his disappointment. "I just . . . I'm ending it with Sandrine."

"You are?"

He looks guilty and tired but also a little relieved. "It's not nice to pretend. I love her, but not the way she loves me, and that difference, I dunno, it feels unfair now. I can't pretend anymore."

Kate sighs and touches his hand. She could ask when he decided or if he's sure, but she doesn't want to ask, because she suspects he decided tonight and she knows he's sure.

Louis raises his glass. "To a new life."

After arriving in Boston Monday night, Kate stops at an Italian takeout and gets veggie lasagna and a bottle of Chianti; then she stops at two different corner stores for flowers. They're ugly, but at least there are a lot of them.

"Are we done with the tour yet?" the cabdriver grouses.

"We're almost there," she says, and looks at the city streets, all lit up even on a Monday. It's grown on her, this city, especially the South End, with its little eateries and boutiques, its bougie food shops.

But then as she unlocks the downstairs door and climbs the stairs, the cold, damp smell makes her reconsider. Maybe they could move to an apartment over on Beacon Hill, all cobblestones and quaintness, or to another loft, but a newer one, with better windows.

"Hey, beautiful, I'm home," she announces, pushing closed the heavy loft door. Before even turning around, she knows that something's changed, because it's cold in here, and if Ani was home, the heat would be on and it would smell like food, mint tea, or at least a lit candle, something. She looks at her hands on the door, turns the lock, takes a deep breath, and turns to see the card, with her name written on it, propped against an empty vase.

The night Kate left for New York, Angela started to wonder if she should leave, too. When Kate called on Sunday to say she was delayed and wouldn't be back until Monday night, that was the final turn. Angela packed her belongings into two big boxes and had them shipped via UPS to an address in Los Angeles, where her best friend from high school now lives. Then she took a cab to Logan and bought a ticket for a flight that left in three hours, went to a lounge overlooking the runway, and drank too much.

CHAPTER 33
Ibiza
1994

Watching the taxi drive off with Don and Georgina in it, Angela feels exhausted, as if she could go back inside, lie down in the middle of the floor, and fall asleep.

She goes back into the lobby and turns right, into the reception area, goes to the same corner where they'd found Santillan in that black leather chair against the wall, abutting the plant. Angela slumps into the chair and tucks her feet under her, then rests her head against the wall and reaches for one of the big round leaves of the rubber plant, presses her fingers down onto its thick center, which makes it look as if she and the plant are holding hands.

So many hours have passed since she left her home in L.A., the condo, with its smell of suede from the couch she's proud of having found, on sale, at Helms; the gardenia candles from Illume, a gift from—she can't remember; the ginger soaps and washes in the bathroom; the smell of clean sheets. Home. She longs for it right now.

And then, longing turns to a sick feeling. Things comfort her now, not people, not really. She loves her family, looks forward to seeing them, but what about the love of a partner? Does she even think of that? She aspires now to . . . what? Paying off the mortgage, stocks for the future, maybe someday a vacation house in Palm Springs? When did she stop hoping for people?

The intensity of that longing, first felt in Madrid, made her a little crazy. Then, while still with Terry, the excitement of knowing she'd soon see Kate, it was an excruciating mixture of guilt and excitement, pain and joy. Not easy to maneuver, those feelings, but so strong and real.

When did she stop hoping for and wanting other people? When did she turn her attention instead to success? On takeoff from Logan Airport, she wondered what Kate would do in that draughty loft all alone—if she even ever went back to the loft in Boston. It hurt so much to imagine what Kate was feeling that she forced herself to stop thinking about her altogether.

Angela looks at the plant, so shiny and strong, runs her fingertips over the leaf, grateful, then stands and decides to go see Kate. No one stops her or even notices her, really. The hospital seems at times to be sparsely staffed.

Angela pauses at the door and watches for a moment. When no one approaches, she enters. She stands close and touches the top of Kate's hand, rubs the circle of bone at her wrist. Is it protruding more? Has she lost weight?

"Hi, Kate; hi, beautiful," she says, and pulls the chair toward the bed. "We drank vermouth, Louis and I. He said you told him about it, how we drank it here." She puts her leg on the chair and uses it as a sort of pew for one knee, not sitting, not kneeling, but getting support.

Kate's gown seems unfastened, its strings lying on the bed, near Kate's neck. Ever so briefly, she sees Don's face. Certainly it was a nurse who came and left it that way. As if to confirm this, Angela pulls on the top right of the gown's collar, using her forefinger like a hook. It comes away from Kate's skin, so that her clavicle is visible. The skin looks dark. Bruised? Just slightly.

If she was just bathed, her skin will smell of hospital soap, probably less flowery than regular Spanish soap. Angela thinks of the vanilla candles in Boston.

"What kinds of candles do you like now?" she whispers into

Kate's ear as she caresses her hand—no smell of soap. She runs her finger up from clavicle to neck to earlobe and up to those gray hairs.

"I'll count these," she says, and does. "Fourteen. You have fourteen gray hairs, madame," she tells Kate, and leans close enough to kiss her.

"I still can't kiss you. I wonder why that is. I don't know. I guess I still don't know if you would want me to," she says, and feels a slight movement in her hand. Angela looks down at Kate's arms. She stares at her hands. The fingers do seem to be moving ever so slightly. When she looks up to see if maybe the nurse is in the room and has witnessed this, she sees something more amazing: Kate's eyes have opened.

Her eyes are open, right here in front of her. Angela is so shocked, she doesn't know what to do, how to react. She starts to speak, sending a tiny drop of spittle flying onto her own hand.

"Kate. It's . . . me . . . Angela. You're in Spain; you're going to be all right," she whispers, and leans forward. She feels Kate squeeze her hand ever so little, just a touch, and it sends tears down her own nose and then down Kate's face, around her chin, and down her neck.

"Sorry, sorry," Angela says, and puts her hand against Kate's cheek, dries it.

The look in Kate's eyes is odd, blank but not quite, intent but not quite right, as if she's looking at Angela but not seeing her. But then Kate blinks a few times and her lips rise as if in a smile. Recognition.

"Oh my God. Hi, hi, beautiful," she says, and finally kisses Kate, who responds only by fluttering her eyelashes.

"In Spain, you're in Spain, Kate. And we're here, Louis and I are here, and we're taking care of you. You're coming back; you'll be fine."

Angela's so shocked, she doesn't know what to do. Kate nods yes as her eyes start to flutter again. "Don't worry. Everything will be fine. You're getting better," Angela says. "You're going to be fine. Oh my God."

Kate's eyes close again, but she seems to have the slightest bit of a smile on her face.

Should she call Louis right now, get him here fast? But she doesn't want to get caught using a cell and get thrown out of the room. She doesn't want to leave right now. Maybe she should text him.

Angela wipes the tears from her face and looks at the outgoing calls. "Hey, come on, let me see those eyes again. Come on, Kate, open your eyes," she whispers as she finds his number and starts to text, but Kate's eyes are closed again. She stops texting, talks to Kate instead, not a whisper now, but a proper voice. She talks about the room, about seeing her dress on the balcony, about the scent on her own wrist, about Louis and how he is. She talks and talks and talks, but those eyes won't open.

Should she call Louis to tell him to come, because if Kate is going to come back, it might be right now? But this could only make things worse if she doesn't: knowing Kate's eyes were open and now aren't.

Fortunately, it's Carolina who walks by, sees her at Kate's bedside, and comes in to say visitors are not allowed right now.

"She opened her eyes," Angela tells her. "She tried to talk."

"Moan or talk?"

"Talk. She tried to talk."

Carolina says that's promising.

"It's more than that. I think she recognized me."

"I am glad, but this does not mean—"

"It means she's got full . . . recognition. And she tried to speak; she smiled at me," Angela says. "How can that not mean she's coming back?" she asks.

"Okay, yes, maybe she is improving," Carolina says kindly.

"Can I stay for the test?"

"No," she says. "I'm sorry. You must go now. Please."

CHAPTER 34

Ibiza
1994

Don is not at all surprised that Angela chose not to get in the taxi with them. She's Kate's friend, so she can't be trusted for anything. His wife sighs deeply, her face turned to look at the sidewalk, her hand on the seat between them. Wouldn't she be greatly comforted by having some of her daughter's belongings in her possession right now?

"Why don't we just pop by and see if Louis is in the room," Don says.

"We said we would wait."

"I know, but she is our daughter. No harm asking."

Georgina nods yes. She is so tired from the flight and the heat, but she knows this tone in his voice. "Fine."

"Señor," Don says, and taps the driver's shoulder, hands him the card with the hotel address.

"¿Quiere ir aquí?" the driver asks.

"Sí, aquí, aquí," Don says, and pushes the card closer to the driver's face.

"Vale," the man says, and makes a U-turn.

Don knows that Louis hates him. Men like Louis always hate men like Don. Raised in a home where both mother and father worked, they don't know who to be. Their fathers, cowed by the guilt of not earning enough to support the family, never modeled real strength. Taught at home to see their mothers as equals, taught in college to be soft if they wanted to sleep with the pretty girls, men like Louis are so confused. They want to take, but instead they ask.

And Kate, of course, has only made it worse by making Don the enemy, giving Louis something to protect her from. For a long time, she kept it private, but then something changed and she started to talk about it, and angrily. Thank God Georgina never quite believed her. Still, Kate never comes for visits anymore, nor was he allowed to visit and see her at college or anywhere.

How things changed. The little girl who knew he was in charge, who understood the rules and for whom he had the utmost consideration, whenever possible, now thought herself most powerful and righteous. Where he had been gentle and thoughtful, she was now angry, as if somehow he was a fault for what he felt.

What he feels. God, it's all right back again. There is nothing harder than seeing her in that bed and knowing he can't be alone with her. If he could, he would lift the sheet and lay his head against her breast, kiss her the way she never allowed him to before. Touch one last time that beautiful body he's been kept away from for so many years. So unfair that God would gift him with so much desire and love and make it seem wrong to nearly everyone.

"You okay?" Georgina asks.

"Yes. Fine. You?"

She sighs deeply and looks at the street from the car window. If not for her, he never would have met Kate, which has also kept him next to her all these years. If there was any chance at all, he had to stay next to the one connection point they shared. And after all, children love their mothers and always return to them. Or, as it has turned out in this case, in times of need, their mothers must go to them.

"She'll be okay," he says, and takes his wife's hand in his and smiles at her. It'll be over soon. And he will find a way to say good-bye properly.

CHAPTER 35
Brooklyn
1991–1992

When she returns to Brooklyn after Boston, Kate is circumspect about what happened. When Louis asks her about it, she mimics his line: "It's not nice to pretend."

"What happened?"

"Nothing. Everything. I don't really know," Kate says. "It's okay. Honestly, I can't stand another loss or to be the cause of a loss."

"So this isn't a loss?" Louis asks, sitting on her bed as she hugs a pillow painted by a river of tears and mascara. Her makeup's gone, washed away hours ago, eyes red and tired, and her mouth is lined in remnants of the Coke she drinks to stay up late and think. And all of it in an eighty-degree house.

"Yeah, it is," she says, and holds the pillow tighter, nods, and closes her eyes. "I think I'm meant to be the bride of Derrida. I can deconstruct but not construct. I've got the soul of a stick of dynamite," she tells him, opening her eyes.

"Is that right?" he says. "Dynamite?"

"Yeah."

"You blew up Boston?"

"I guess I didn't give her much faith. 'Cause I don't have any to give." With that, Kate can't hold it in anymore; she starts crying hard.

He puts an arm around her, pulls her in, kisses her head, and rubs her arms until she calms, then falls asleep. As much as he'd like to be with her, Louis knows she's too fragile and too in love with Angela still. He tells himself that it's all right. Whatever happened that night, when they kissed in the cab, then came charging up the stairs and found Sandrine waiting, it's still there. He just has to wait.

Kate starts a master's program at the New School in the fall, planning to study anthropology and write a thesis on strippers and sex workers. She even gets a job as a cocktail waitress at one of the clubs in order to study her subjects up close.

Louis worries when he sees her in the bright morning light, sitting in their kitchen, a laptop in front of her, a pot of coffee gone, another one brewing, as she finishes up her notes from the night before. If she's fallen asleep, he reads over her shoulder. It's tough, the details she carefully collects and records, interviews and conversations with the strippers and lap dancers: the minutiae of sex work or "dancing," or whatever the girl calls it. Many times, the men explode in their pants or on a dancer's leg. It's part of the job, Kate writes, but Louis can tell, from the strong smell of Zest rising off her arms, that she scrubbed harder than a person should after a night of simple research.

"Stop doing it. You have enough," he says to her, but she argues that's not true.

As much as she says she's studying other people, writing about "subjects," Louis knows this is something more. As he peers over her sleeping shoulder at those details about the guy who tried to kiss her, the one who asked to marry her right before he said he couldn't tip because all he had was a twenty, he realizes that so much of this is Kate's working out what happened with Don. Every friendly guy, every asshole who has to be escorted from the club, every old wretch who stares and stares and never speaks, each of them is some form of Don.

Louis kisses her head and watches her begin to stir, then closes the computer, pushes away the coffee, and takes her hand. He watches her wipe drool from her mouth, one eye still clinging to sleep.

"Come on, Popeye, time for bed," he says.

Then Louis will stand her up and walk her to bed, or sometimes carry her if she seems particularly tired.

It takes time, but slowly her mood starts to change. On weekends, she writes furiously, until eleven or so; then they order Chinese food and sit up eating sweet-and-sour shrimp, drinking beer, and playing cards or Monopoly late into the morning. Every day, she seems just a little happier and stronger. She even starts to feel optimistic enough to envision a whole new kind of life, in San Francisco. "Why there?" he asks.

"It's kind of like New York, as a touching-stone destination. The Haight, the Castro . . . I've pretty much met and sucked the life story out of every sex worker in these parts. Maybe there I can find that last little bit of inspiration to finish."

"But you hated it when you lived there."

"I lived in Berkeley with two southern women. This would be different."

Different, he thinks, and looks at her, then comes and stands behind Kate, rubs her bare shoulders, then her neck. She reaches up and cups his head, pulls it toward her ever so gently. It's becoming something different now, really slowly, in tiny increments, but definitely moving toward something new.

Louis asks everyone he knows about jobs in the Bay Area; he sends out résumés and gets an interview—all without telling her.

"I'm going out of town Thursday," he says one night.

"Where?"

"Surprise," he says.

She stops typing, takes off her glasses. "What you talkin' 'bout, Willis? What do you mean, 'surprise'?"

"Just a surprise, that's all."

"You're not . . . Are you moving somewhere?"

"Am I?"

"Yeah. Are you leaving New York?"

"No, I am not. Not alone, I'm not. I might leave with you. But not alone."

"Is that right?"

"That's right," he says.

Louis flies to San Francisco and meets over lunch at a nice restaurant with Kenyon Walker and his business partner, an attractive woman named Delia Blankowski. They're about to open three new private charter schools in the Bay Area and need a computer system installed and run, a two-year commitment that pays $150,000.

As they're walking toward the door and Walker is telling Louis that he "highly recommends" having a beer at the airport microbrewery, he says, "Also, listen, if you want it, the job's yours."

"I do want it," Louis says, not even thinking about it. They shake hands and soon Louis is in a cab on his way to the airport. Maybe he can catch an earlier flight, or not. Just have a beer or two. Then he looks out the window, sees a sign for a barbershop, and has a new idea.

"Hey, pull over," he tells the driver.

When he gets home, he doesn't want to look for his keys, so he rings the buzzer. Nothing. He takes off his gloves and cups his hands around the small windows of their front door, then rings again.

Finally, he hears the growl of a door scraping against the floor. Made of old oak and heavy as an ox, it's never fit right in its frame. Kate will have to use her shoulder to push it open.

"Stop, hey, stay in there. Stay," he hears her say to the neighbor's dog, Samantha, whom she sometimes sits, especially when Louis is away. A young pit mix with equal parts strength and energy, she's not about to let an open door go unused. Louis watches Kate try to coax her back inside as she looks down at the door hopefully.

"It's me," he says.

"Louis!" she yells. "Hold on. Stay here, you little fucker," she tells the dog. "Stay. It's cold out there."

Just to be a jerk, he rings again. She laughs and lets the dog fly down the stairs as she comes skipping down, too.

He wipes the glass and watches her come down the stairs— beautiful Kate, in jeans and her favorite gray wool sweater, eager to see him, smiling as she hurries toward him. Has there ever been a more beautiful sight than the woman you love, a woman who shows nothing but strength to the entire world, skipping down stairs to see you? Letting it be known she's chosen you as the one person in front of whom she's vulnerable, happy, and hopeful?

She's so warm to the touch, he imagines the apartment will be a sauna.

"I missed you," she says, and pulls back, smiles at the wool cap on his head. He never wears hats or caps. She looks at his face quizzically, like she's figured it out, then pulls off the cap. Her eyes widen to her ears and she covers her mouth, which stays agape.

"Oh my God," she says, and leans forward, rubs her cheek against his newly shorn hair, no more than an inch high now. "I don't even know what to say. Can I touch it?"

"You're already touching it."

"Wow," she says again, and caresses his head. "I knew you'd have a nice scalp."

She even pulls the glasses off his face and, holding them gently, leans back and shakes her head, as if marveling at a sculpture in a museum.

"Look at the bone structure," she says, running her hand along his jaw, then over his lips.

"I feel I'm being objectified," he says.

"You totally are. You look so handsome with short hair, and your eyes are so blue. I had no idea they were so blue," she says.

"Didn't you ever look at them?"

"I thought I had but . . . apparently not."

She takes his hand and they run up the stairs, open a bottle of wine, and finally he tells her the news—a great job, and in San Francisco. A chance at a fresh start.

CHAPTER 36
Ibiza
1994

After only a few minutes, the taxi carrying Don and Georgina pulls up to a white building with maroon-tiled stairs. Hanging modestly on the facade is a yellow sign that reads HOTEL underneath four stars. Ambitious. Don doesn't have a satellite phone and he doubts his or his wife's cell will work here, which is a shame, because if Louis is not here, a quick call to the American consulate could ensure entrance into the room.

When she sees this couple, the concierge watches for a moment before turning down her television. These people are not dressed for her hotel. They're not at the right place and will realize this shortly, then turn on their heels and go, before she has to lose the plot of her show. But they don't leave; instead, they linger near the window her husband, Gregorio, constructed, the small counter. Finally, they see the yellow button on the wall and press.

"*Allí voy,*" she says, and lowers the volume.

They don't speak Spanish, but they have a room number, which she explains is for a room that is taken. Americans, she says, two of them, and before these two, three others. In an accident, that first batch. Poor Americans. The man, so tall and with such sweet eyes, keeps talking and talking.

"*¿Teléfono?*" he asks.

"*Sí,*" she says, and he reaches out as if she's holding a phone right now that he would like to take.

She leads him into her apartment and shows him the phone. And he, in turn, shows her the card in his hand, for Theodore Griffin, American Consulate.

"*Ah, sí,*" she says. "*El consulado. ¿Os mandó el consulado?*" she asks, wondering if the consulate sent them.

"*Consulado,*" the man says, then "Kate Harrington." Then he says, "Mama," and points to the woman. What in the world are they trying to say? Kate—was that the name of the girl in the accident? The concierge opens the small blue case in which she files all of the registration materials and finds the card filled out by the Americans, the first group. Yes, Kate Harrington.

"*¿Usted es la mamá?*" she asks the lady, who's tall and wide-shouldered, as Americans often are, but also tired and weak, as Americans rarely are.

Maybe they should be allowed in the room. No harm as long as she accompanies them.

CHAPTER 37
An Airport in Ibiza
1994

In the hospital, it wasn't too difficult for Louis to pretend, to act like the best friend, the kid they probably remember from Encino before the muscles on which he still feels the memory of Georgina's fingertips, before the shaved head, the grown-up clothes. Of course they'll want to think of him as the quiet kid, the innocuous young man who hung out and kept quiet.

Now in the taxi, Louis feels his blood boil, remembering how Don asked why they would consider moving Kate. As if anything about Kate is that old man's business. Louis closes his eyes and imagines shoving Don against a wall and quickly, quietly ending the man's life.

At the far left corner of the airport sits a small terminal for noncommercial flights—cargo and medevac, and there it is, a sign that reads TRANSPORTE MEDICO DE EUROPA. Louis asks the driver to wait, then straightens his jacket, preparing to stride into the office and get exactly what he needs.

The green tile smells clean, the white Formica counter cool as Louis places his fingers on it like a pianist getting ready to perform a song he's done a million times. A man with curly hair and a pregnant belly, dressed in a white shirt and jeans, is sitting at a desk, staring off into space, maybe looking at the sky outside the big windows, maybe imagining tonight's dinner, who knows.

"*Hola,*" Louis calls, and the man swivels in his chair and stands.

"*¿Sí?*" the man says, pulling up the bifocals hanging from his chest.

"English?" Louis asks. He hates having to ask this of people. I don't speak your language, but I bet you speak mine.

"Yes," the man says. "How can I help you?"

Louis puts out his hand, gives the man a firmer than necessary shake. "You can help me save my wife's life," Louis says.

"Oh, well, yes, sir. Yes, yes, absolutely. Let's do that. Where is your wife going?"

Half an hour later, Louis leaves the office with the release that must be signed by the doctor at the hospital. Louis has also got to ensure that a doctor and nurse will be on the flight, because of the head trauma. It's a lot to hope for—that Santillan will sign and accompany them, but if not Santillan, someone will.

Louis pays the man a fifteen-hundred-dollar deposit, then, on the ride back to the hotel, allows himself to pretend this is as good as a guarantee that everything will work out. He knows, as a business owner, that once you have a deposit, in your mind that money is half spent; no way will you delay final payment. That Learjet has as good as lifted off the tarmac.

He looks at his watch: 8:00 P.M. He'll go to the hotel, take a shower, eat something, and get ready, mentally, to convince the doctor. As he rides back to the hotel, Louis tries to imagine his conversation with Santillan, the doctor saying yes. He pictures it happening, just the way he did with the medevac man. It's a hell of a bigger stretch, but they say that if you can imagine something, then it can happen.

As they pull close to the hotel, Louis decides he wants to drink and smoke, but no more of that vermouth. He wants beer. He ducks into the market across the street from the hotel. They sell Carlsberg, so he picks up two big bottles. It reminds Louis of his dad, and the Father's Day present he once gave him—four plastic mugs that would get frosted if you just put them in the freezer for a few minutes. Had

Louis ever seen his dad happier than the day he came home for a weekend visit and his father suddenly remembered, ran into the kitchen, came back with a mug for each of them?

As Louis watches the guy at the register slowly count out his change, he looks out through the window and glimpses a whole different type of father. Don is exiting a taxi, followed by Georgina.

"Fucking hell," Louis whispers, and the convenience store man looks up at him.

What to do? Would that concierge take them to the room? Louis thinks of her appreciation for the ten-dollar tip he'd given her when they first arrived. Surely, Don from Orange County will produce a lot more than ten dollars.

"Can I leave this here?" he asks the man, who doesn't understand.

As soon as he's walked outside, Louis realizes he's exposed himself. If Don and Georgina see him, they'll want to be taken to the room.

Louis walks down the street, head down, away from the hotel and the shop. He'll cross at the light and walk down, see if there's an alley behind the hotel or the street onto which their balcony faces. Is it an alley or a road? He can't quite remember. As he reaches the corner, Louis runs down the street, sees an alley. He goes down it, but when he's halfway down it, he realizes the hotel building is thicker than these others, reaches all the way onto the next street. Shit. Will he have to go all the way down to the main road? No. Louis runs back the way he came, but two buildings down from the hotel, he finds another narrow alley that leads to the street. He runs down it, makes a right, and reaches their hotel within seconds. He looks up and sees the dress on the third floor. No way will he let them take her things.

Louis looks around for stairs, a door. He spots a piece of white metal the same color as the building that is a few feet down on the left side. No handle, but it is a door. He slides his nails along the edge, trying to pry it open, but it's locked. He yanks hard, but it barely moves. Louis hears footsteps coming down the stairs, and a moment later, the door opens and two shocked teenage girls stand at the door, looking at him, scared.

"Excuse me," he says, and pushes past them.

"You can't go in there," one of them says in English.

He climbs the stairs two at a time, then three at a time when he hears a groaning noise that sounds like an elevator. He tastes the salt of his sweat falling from the end of his nose to his upper lip and licks it away as he shoves his hand into his pocket. There it is, the key. He runs to room 314, shoves in the key, and looks around. No one there. He goes to the closet and grabs a chair, shoves it under the door just as he hears footsteps in the hallway. Louis runs to Kate's suitcase and takes all the underwear, throws it on the bed. Next, he grabs the bag with FARMACIA printed on it, the Edward Gorey book. Whatever she had with her that last day, he wants it in his possession. What else? Bras, a pair of black shorts she wore around the house. What to do with this? He goes into the bathroom and grabs her perfume, a makeup brush, takes it all into the other room, opens Angela's case, and shoves it in there.

Someone is trying to open the door. Failing this task, they decide to knock.

"Yeah? Who is it?" he yells.

"*La señora Lola. Abra la puerta, por favor,*" she says.

"Sleeping," he calls out. "*Dormir.*"

"*Es que tiene visita,*" the lady says.

What else? The dress that guided him up to the room. He goes to the balcony and pulls it off its hanger, takes it and reopens Angela's suitcase, shoves it in there. What else? He feels sick to his stomach, as if he's at an airport, holding Kate, slowly saying good-bye, only to hear an announcement that her flight is boarding, that she has to go right now. Right now. He has to say good-bye to Kate yet again. The things he leaves out of that suitcase will be taken by them, gone forever.

"Louis, it's me, Georgina. Please open the door."

"Georgina," she said, not "Georgina and Don." They're of a piece, these two collaborators, each as guilty as the other.

"Georgina, what are you doing here?" he says through the closed door, and takes off his jacket and shirt, goes in the bathroom and puts water on his face, dries it with a towel. Eyelash curler? He shoves it in his pocket and goes back to the room, locks Angela's suitcase. Hopefully, she has the key with her.

Finally, Louis opens the door.

"Sorry," he says. "I had a beer at lunch and . . . jet lag. I was out."

"That's all right," Georgina says, holding her breath.

"Don," he says, and opens the door nice and wide.

"We were wondering . . . would you mind if we took a few things of hers, from her suitcase?" Georgina says.

"Why would I let you do that?"

"I just want a few things, to remind me of her, that's all."

"She's in a hospital, Georgina, but this is still her stuff."

"I know, but she's so very seriously ill, Louis. She may not . . ."

"So you don't expect her to live and you've come to claim your inheritance?"

This is too much for Don. "Do you mind? Could you behave like a gentleman for just one moment? Would that be too much trouble? Her mother is in a great deal of pain right now."

Louis stares at the old man and shakes his head. "Unbelievable, the way you care for and protect your loved ones, Don. A real example to us all about what it is to be a man."

"I can do without the sarcasm."

"I can do without seeing your face ever again. I know why you came here."

"Please," Georgina says, and starts to sob now.

"You know what, that one there is hers. Take it," Louis says, and points to her suitcase.

"That one?" Don asks, already suspicious.

"Yeah. Got her name on it and everything. Take the whole suitcase and get the fuck out of here," Louis says.

"With pleasure," Don replies, zipping up Kate's case. Triumphant Don with his wet-nosed wife, who's whimpering in front of Louis.

"Why are you so angry at us?" Georgina asks.

"Do you really need me to say it, Georgina? Really?"

"Come on, honey. We don't need this," Don says, and takes his wife's hand and leaves the room.

The concierge looks truly scared. "*Perdón,*" she says to Louis.

"Yeah, bad idea, letting a stranger into someone's room," Louis says in English.

"*Perdón,*" the lady says again, and goes seesawing down the hall, struggling to catch up to Don and Georgina.

Louis closes the door and presses his back against it, lets his head go flush against the door, so that the skin covering his skull has to accommodate the yellow tack holding the room-information sign. His right hand squeezing the now-locked door handle, he leans back into the tack's sharpness.

CHAPTER 38
Golden Gate
1992

Louis gives notice at work and they pack up the apartment, then decide to drive, take that big American road trip. They buy an old Chevy Malibu station wagon with decent tires that seem able to make it at least halfway across the country, if not all the way. They choose the southern route, even if it means Texas. But they make a detour to stop at the Grand Canyon. And it's there, at a Starbucks, while checking his e-mail, that Louis learns the job promised him has fallen through. A large investment from a venture capitalist has been put on hold, so they can't hire anyone for a month, maybe two, tops, Kenyon writes, ever so apologetically.

Amazing. One minute it was all set—not just set but golden—and then, suddenly, gone.

The unhurried amble turns into a dash to get to this new city and set things right again. A day later, they find themselves standing in the middle of their huge, new, and empty two-bedroom apartment on Diamond Street.

"Beautiful floors again," Kate says, and smiles at him.

"Indeed. I think you'll be happy here," says the new landlord, Lyle, a sweet older man who's clearly proud of his renovations. "Any kids?"

They both stare at him, confused. "Oh, I'm sorry, I shouldn't pry. Not everyone can or should have kids. Pardon me. Nosy old queen."

"No, it's fine," Kate says. "Maybe someday," she says, and smiles at Louis.

It's an odd place to be—more than friends, but not exactly lovers, either. It's as if the memory of Boston, whatever that is for Kate, needs to be erased or somehow replaced before anything new can begin, anything that has a chance anyway. He just hopes he will know when that moment does arrive.

"We should get to work on those kids," he teases her when Lyle is gone.

"You, so industrious," she says, and goes off to start unpacking.

How the hell are we going to pay the second month's rent? Louis wonders. Nothing coming in, and nearly nothing in the refrigerator except what they just bought: milk and cereal, a bag of coffee, a bag of sugar, and a dozen 99¢ Only store ramen cups.

That's how the panorama looks for days, even weeks after their arrival. Those paltry provisions all sitting in the fridge because Kate, thanks to New York, is wary of cockroaches.

That first week, Louis doesn't sleep very well, wondering what state of stupid hopefulness he was in when, here in San Francisco, his future was being decided. Was he staring at the Grand Canyon, a big dumb smile on his face? Or was he in a Jacuzzi, in New Mexico, eyes closed but listening to Kate chat up two German waitresses in their sixties, best friends since high school, vacationing together for thirty years? Was he trying hard not to smile whenever Kate reached under the bubbles and pinched his leg because one of the German ladies said something she found interesting or funny? When did his luck change, unbeknownst to him?

Those first weeks, they start going to gallery openings every Friday, to the Whole Foods every Wednesday for wine and cheese night.

"One day, we'll buy something," Kate tells the young guy at

the cheese table, a just barely cleaned-up skater or maybe musician, who couldn't care less if they ever buy anything.

"We'd better not get lactose-intolerant," Louis says as she hands him a peppered cracker with a mountain of goat cheese atop.

At least, thank God, after putting an ad in Craigslist for computer tech work, he's soon busing around town to people's homes to revive their hard drives or install software—little nothing jobs that bring in no more than one hundred dollars a day, barely enough.

Kate decides to wait to register at Berkeley and to take a job instead.

"No, I don't want that," he says. "I want you to go to school and enjoy life, just study and write. That's it."

She argues that the paperwork from the New School hasn't come through. And anyway, she can start her research at a strip club, doesn't have to be enrolled to work on her thesis. She'll temp in the day at law firms and waitress at night at one of the clubs.

"I don't want you in there now. I want you to have a fresh start here, without the girls, without the club," he says. "Please, just enjoy this new life for a minute before you start the research." Surprisingly, she agrees.

He starts to fix computers for companies, and there's no shortage of customers, but unfortunately, they are customers without much money. Kate manages to stay optimistic about it all. She visits tiny Chinese grocers and buys small, weird vegetables and fruits.

"What the hell is that?" Louis will ask about some root vegetable that looks like a giant model of a tooth.

"I don't know, but it was only twenty cents," she will say, and start to open that can of coconut milk she pours on everything.

They both lose weight, which makes Kate look only more beautiful. On days when she has temp jobs, it kills him to watch her leave the house in her charcoal Chanel suit and sexy blouse, the boots with the heels, her dark red lipstick.

Kenyon says it'll be more like three months before the capital comes in to fund his job. Louis looks for other jobs, but, for some reason, he can't conjure his own alchemy the way he did in New York, landing that position at the school district right away and getting promoted quickly. He remembers with pride hearing Sandrine report gleefully to her mother on the phone that she only had to work a part-time job, or no job at all if she wished, because Louis made so much money.

"He just wants me to enjoy the city," Sandrine had said. Louis knew that this was, in part, Sandrine talking up a relationship her mother always doubted would lead to marriage. But it was also the pride of a woman who can support herself but is made to feel special when a man cares for her both emotionally and monetarily.

Louis wants, more than anything, to do this for Kate, but like the things he's ever really, really wanted in life, it sits just out of reach. At every job interview, it's as if there's a wall between Louis and the man or woman interviewing him, no way to connect. And connection is all they want. Kate tells him this, and she's right.

"The people interviewing you, they know you can do the work, because you have a four point oh from a UC school and you've spent years working at a huge school district," she'll say. "What they really want to know is how you'll be at lunch, at bowling, at fucking karaoke. Will you be cool? Will you think they're cool? That's the most important one. You have got to learn how to get that look in your eyes that says, You're so cool."

"*Cool?* Is that even a word anymore? And karaoke, that's my problem?" he says, arguing with her but knowing she's right. He can no more envision himself singing a Nirvana song at karaoke than flying over the Golden Gate using only his arms.

"What do you do on weekends?" a man named Peter, with thick glasses and bushy sideburns, actually asks during a job interview.

"Get together with you and play pool," he probably wants to hear. Or maybe "I don't know. What do you do? Tell me what you do and I'll mirror that back to you, get this job, be done with it."

Louis shrugs. What do I do on weekends? I don't know.

"You might have to start your own business, Howard Hughes," Kate says, sitting at the kitchen table, still in her fancy New York coat. She's set her leather bag atop the table for some reason he doesn't understand until she tells him there's a surprise in there for him.

"Open carefully."

"What?"

"Open my bag, but carefully," she says.

"I'm not in the mood for magic tricks," he says.

She starts to pout.

When he finally opens the bag, Louis finds himself looking in at a two-inch-by-two-inch triangle covered in orange-and-white-striped fur, with a tiny pink tongue and two lines where one might expect to find eyes.

"A blind cat?" he says.

"A daughter," she replies, correcting him.

Kate says she found this tiny orphan in an empty lot in the Tenderloin, took it to work, and fed it heated Coffee-mate with an eyedropper.

"Her eyes do open," Kate says, and explains that she's used hot compresses all day. Tiny and sickly as hell, the cat's eyes may not be the best, but she's got the voice of three cats, and yowled so loudly for help that Kate was helpless to walk away.

Just what we need, another mouth to feed, he thinks as Kate hands him the, for all practical purposes, blind kitten.

CHAPTER 39
Ibiza
1994

After Kate's parents have left, Louis goes to the bathroom and splashes water on his face. He then goes to the main room, lights a cigarette, and drinks the last ounces of vermouth. He would rather have beer but is in no mood to go downstairs.

He goes to the suitcase in which he stowed Kate's things, looks for the key but doesn't immediately see it, pulls on the lock. He locked her things away from Don and also, unintentionally, from himself.

He wants to smell that perfume of Kate's, hang the dress back up, look for something to make him feel close to her again. He sees the paring knife he bought for the lemon rind and thinks about using it to slice open the luggage. Just buy new luggage for Angela. But just as he's about to do this, he sees a key on the far right edge of the credenza, next to a bracelet and some money. He tries the little key and it works.

As he opens Angela's case, the smell of wool meanders up. New socks? Yes, right there, the paper label still hugging the socks. Louis reaches down into the cotton belly of the case and feels for where he shoved Kate's things, brings up a handful that includes the white bag from the *farmacia* and some of Kate's clothes.

Louis gets out the dress and holds it up, gives it a good look, then takes it back to the balcony and hangs it up again. What the fuck do I think this will accomplish? he wonders, but he does it anyway, hooks the hanger to a bent nail, and there she flies again, Kate's sexy cocktail dress. And it does make him feel better, the symbolism of it, the *Fuck you* of it.

He comes back and sits on the bed and stares at the pile of her things, reaching hard for some kind of comfort in the makeup, the perfume bottle. He takes the *farmacia* bag and turns it in his hands, smells it. It has that vitamin/candy smell of pharmacies in other countries—the way Woolworth's candy counter used to smell.

When he first looks inside the bag, Louis assumes the square box holds tampons, but he turns it over anyway and shakes out its contents, thinking maybe there will be something else—a packet of gum or Spanish lemon drops, a list of things to pick up later, in her writing, or her change purse with the tiny photo-booth picture of them. It doesn't really make sense that these things would be in a paper bag from the pharmacy, but that is what he's thinking when the square box slides out of the bag and onto the magenta bedspread. It's white, with the words EXAMEN DE EMBARAZO in pink and blue. The *o* in EMBARAZO has been flown in by a stork. Pregnancy test. He picks it up and sees that the carton has been opened. Suddenly, he can hardly breathe. The box is open.

Louis pushes himself up and forward and, in about ten steps, is in the bathroom. The wastebasket is full. The room hasn't been cleaned, first because of the accident and the fact that the concierge didn't want to disturb anything, then because he and Angela have been in here every time the maid came around and they eventually told her not to worry about cleaning.

He overturns the basket and pushes aside spent tissue and candy wrappers, a razor caked in soap and tiny bits of hair, until, as if appearing in a clearing of refuse, there it is, a thin strip of white paper.

He gets up and runs back to the box, looks on the back, where it says ROSADO = EMBARAZO. Pink equals pregnant. Blue means not pregnant. But days have passed, erasing the answer.

"Kate," he says, and stares at the strip, then outside at the dress. "Jesus Christ, Kate."

CHAPTER 40
San Francisco
1993

It may be old school, sexist, whatever, but he wants to take care of Kate, give her time to finish that damned master's thesis and start teaching, move away from the research. No more temp work or law offices. Just teaching, writing, and home. She deserves this.

Yet he can't make it happen, not the way he wants to.

One night, as Louis stands at the window and watches Kate arrive home in a taxi from dinner, something inside him quiets, really just shuts down to a level of total stillness. He watches a man, fiftyish, in a dark suit, a bright pink shirt, exit and help Kate out of the car. Dr. Marcus Scoletti, as he prefers to be called, is a professor and the head of some department. He's also wooing her. Oh, not openly, since he's married. Openly, he's interested in her "work," her thesis. But Louis knows this guy will do everything in his power to seduce Kate.

He watches them talk, watches Scoletti offer her a cigarette, light hers, light his own. Marcus is charming her, surely flattering her, which Kate is smart enough to see as a tactic, and yet he's disarming her just a little. He can see this from so many feet away.

I'm so fucking tired of this, Louis says to himself. That night, after she's gone to bed, Louis redesigns his business card, making it much simpler and a bit colder—dark gray with a sixteen-point brick-red type. Just his name and phone number and the word *digitally,* then a plus sign, and then the word *connected*. Simple, deconstructed.

Then he calls Marta, an executive at a tech firm that hires him a lot. She mentions a party thrown by a dot-com. Louis puts on what he knows to be an ironic T-shirt, with a Japanese children's book character on the front, throws over it a black designer jacket with two bleach spots he has to Sharpie over, and jeans Kate made him buy, with a tiny English flag on the back, which makes them "hip." At the party, Marta pulls him into the bathroom and they do two lines. After that, he has no problem handing out his card.

He hopes Marta's a lesbian, but at the end of the night, as he drops her off, it becomes clear she isn't, and he wonders how long he can keep this up while not sleeping with her. The very next day, she calls and invites him to another party.

Marta's definitely a party girl, and Louis knows enough to make himself switch out the lines for two vodka Red Bulls, which helps him fake small talk. Usually, after half an hour, he'll see an opportunity. Standing next to a window, nursing a single beer or smoking, usually wearing one really expensive item of clothing or a fancy watch, there will always be the creative who runs an agency or a campaign. You can tell from the steady stream of people "slyly" trying to sidle up and throw out a line of clever banter they've practiced for hours.

When introduced, Louis doesn't try to impress; he acts polite but slightly distracted, a notch below the creative in terms of status. He's the opposite of the guy you want to karaoke with—in fact, he's the guy who, when the creative's assistant calls, quotes relatively high rates and says, "Sorry, Louis is out of the country for two weeks," which kind of makes him the guy you'd be lucky to hire.

You do need to mirror people, but it's all about picking the right people, not the Kenyons or Bobs of the world, the guys who want to have a beer, but the guys who have a lot resting on their shoulders, the creatives who are expected to be on the cutting edge but secretly rarely feel up to it. There's this whole new world that the guy at the window is terrified to admit he doesn't really understand, and if you can walk him through it and coach him so that he can give a good three-minute talk at lunch or a seven-minute presentation and look and sound really assured, that's it. The creative feels like a star, like a cutting-edge leader. But he knows he can't do it without you, so now you're the drug, you're the line item that can never be cut, and your karaoke skills couldn't matter less.

"I'm the tech whisperer," he tells Kate.

Computer skills have made not just Louis indispensable but all techies. Some of them can't handle it and, after a year, will disappear on some six-month hiking trip to Nepal or a retreat in Kauai. Gone, like the images on a broken screen.

Louis comes up with the idea of starting an agency for designers, programmers, Web architects, editors, a shop called Seven Point 0. He looks for and finds someone talented who can bring in lots of business in that crucial first year. Ken Larson is a redheaded, skinny as a reed, quiet as a mute genius who also wants to make oodles of money and move to Idaho but is willing to wait until he's forty. Louis then finds a two-thousand-square-foot loftlike space on the third floor of a building in the gentrifying South of Market, or SoMa, area, the rent for which is astounding for a brand-new business. Ken thinks Louis is crazy. For a hell of a lot less, they could rent a space two or three times the size, in Concord or Pleasanton, with fluorescent lighting already in, probably even built-in cubicles. This place Louis has chosen necessitates buying desks and lighting.

"Sanding and redoing the floors," Louis adds.

"What? They're fine like this. You're fucking ridiculous."

"No, I'm fucking right. It's an image. It's a brand."

Kate gets it, says the high ceilings and big windows will help his stable of techies at least enjoy the idea of living a life, even if their heads are buried in a computer fourteen hours a day.

"Am I turning into a dick?" he asks Kate.

"What would I know? I love my Chanel and my Lancôme, remember?"

It's true that he's picked that floor and that building because it looks like a loft, and he knows he'll get better designers if the place looks hip and cool, if it fits with the way talented people want to see themselves. Nobody is who they are at any age; we're all just in the process of becoming something else. It's who you want to be that counts, he thinks, writing a check to the broker for eight thousand dollars.

When the broker leaves, they open a bottle of champagne.

"I'm so proud of you," Kate says as they sit on the huge windowsill, smelling that cool wind that carries with it a little bit of hour-old rain on pavement, tempura from the restaurant below, and just a bit of leather from the shoe-repair shop next to it. Kate's leg lies over his and she holds a plastic glass of champagne in one hand and his hand in the other. Louis smiles, takes her hand, and kisses it.

"I love you, Kate," he says. "All of this is for you. And much more."

She lets the words in, even smiles proudly, as if she actually believes him.

"I love you, too," she says, and leans back and looks at him in a way she never has before.

The company does well. Soon there's an extra five thousand dollars in their bank account, and within six months, an extra twenty thousand, and the credit cards are all paid off. Madonna goes from Iams to some homemade organic cat food you can find only in San Francisco.

"Have you noticed? Our cheeses come from regions now, not just countries," Kate says one day as she's photographing their fridge, which is filled with expensive-looking square take-out boxes.

"The more money you have, the more specificity you crave?"

"Plus the more money you have, the more likely you are to have gone to the country, so now you need more; you need regions. Have you noticed? People with money don't go to France; they go to Provence or Bordeaux."

"Ah, *oui*," he says, and stands there watching her.

"This looks like Le Corbusier in white," Kate says of the boxy architecture of their bottom shelf. "That's how you know you've made it: take-out boxes filled with expensive food."

"We always eat it," he says, and pulls out a box of three-day-old pad Thai, opens it, and digs in, just to prove his point.

Kate has been fascinated with the contents of the fridge ever since they moved to the city. Like everything in life that interests her, she commits 500 percent. Not even the refrigerators of strangers are off-limits. It's embarrassing sometimes to be with her at breakfast and hear her ask the waiter, "Do you mind if I ask you a strange question?"

"Oh God, I mind," Louis will interject, but she'll just tell him to be quiet, and an hour or two later, there they are, in the waiter's apartment, as Kate snaps pictures of his fridge.

Marcus Scoletti, naturally, finds this fascinating. He loves the concept and shows Kate's photos to a friend who owns a gallery. Scoletti next sets up a lunch for him and Kate with the owner of the gallery.

"Terrific," Louis deadpans. "Where you having lunch, his house?"

"No."

"Hey, Kate, listen. I like your photos a lot, okay? So I'm not being an asshole by asking this, but this guy, this Marcus Scoletti, he's going to put the moves on you. You know that, right?"

She shrugs. "His wife is beautiful."

"So what? When has that ever mattered? And furthermore, so are you."

Kate smiles and says, "He can try, but it won't work."

Sure enough, Scoletti takes her to lunch with his gallery owner friend, a pretty woman in her fifties, who has to leave early. But as Kate and he are finishing their meal, she calls and tells Marcus that Kate can have a show if she wants it.

"And do you want it?" Louis asks as she tells him about it while making dinner.

"I might. How's Martyr, by the way?" Kate asks.

"Who?" he says, although he knows perfectly well she means Marta, whom he has not seen in a month because she has a boy-friend.

"Martyr, your techie girlfriend."

"Oh," he says, and smiles as if embarrassed. "She's good. Great. Why?"

"Oh, good, so very glad to hear it," Kate says, and walks out of the kitchen.

CHAPTER 41
Ibiza
1994

By the time Angela has returned to the hotel, the strip has been put back into the box and the box back in the white *farmacia* bag. Louis lies on the bed, a bottle of beer propped between his stomach and his raised legs.

"You missed a lot of action," he says.

"Oh yeah, like what?"

"Well, the grieving family popped by to steal a few things," he says, and takes a sip. "I tried to explain that she's still alive, but that didn't work."

It's stupid, but he does enjoy the tiny glint of surprise in Angela's eyes. Do you believe me now?

"They asked me and I said not today."

"I hid anything we would actually want in your luggage," he says, and points to the open suitcase. "Hope you don't mind."

"No. I don't . . . care." Angela sits on the bed and shakes her head. At least it's good to know that Louis was right. "They didn't get the black dress, did they?" she says.

He points outside, where the dress moves in the wind, a flag from their very own country.

"They actually came. I can't believe it. They said they wouldn't."

"The lady, the concierge, she was gonna let them in, too."

"I'm sorry," Angela says. "I shouldn't have trusted them."

"No, no, definitely," he says. "But do you get it now? It's about control for Don. Always has been."

"Why would they want . . . her things? I mean, what would they want, exactly?"

"I don't know. Just for control, probably, to say they can. For Don anyway, I'm sure that's a big deal."

She sits back on the bed next to him. "It's all so crazy," she says, and considers whether to tell him that Kate opened her eyes. Would it make things worse for him? Harder?

"There's something else," Louis says.

"What?"

Louis reaches under the pillow behind Angela and takes out the pregnancy test box, sets it on Angela's lap.

"What . . . is that? . . . that's hers?"

"The box was in her luggage and it was open, so I went and looked in the trash. She took it, the test. I found the strip."

"No."

"Yeah," Louis says, and places the box on the bed between them. "No color now, but she took the test," he says.

For a second, she can't believe it, thinks it must be a mistake, but then she turns the box in her hand and looks at the words long enough to believe it.

"She's pregnant?"

"She thought she might be," he says. He shimmies off the bed and stands there, hands on his hips. "I'm gonna go out there," he says, and points to the balcony.

CHAPTER 42

San Francisco
1993

"Do you want it?" Scoletti has asked Kate, referring to the exhibit at his friend's gallery but meaning much more, of course. She doesn't, actually. The only work that's ever mattered is her master's thesis. It's not unrelated, though, to this moment, having Marcus Scoletti standing here, using his power, or so he thinks, to offer something he believes she wants.

"Have your friend call me and I'll talk about it with her," Kate says.

"I can set up another lunch for all three of us," he says.

"Just have her call me directly," Kate says, and thanks Scoletti for lunch, then leaves.

The gallerina does call and does seem genuinely interested in showing Kate's photos. So Kate gives each image a name, then signs them, thinking the whole thing's silly.

"I Am What I Eat: A new exhibition by Kate Harrington" ends up hanging at the gallery near the courthouse, and on a warm October night, there they are, Louis and Kate, all dressed up, in that golden gallery lighting, watching people saunter up to her photos and nod approvingly, some posing hard, trying to look arty and cool, but others, you can tell, truly interested.

"That's not art, just a refrigerator," Kate says to one guy, who thinks about this, then nods in quasi agreement, because he seems to like the picture, this woman's opinion notwithstanding. Louis can tell she's proud of herself.

"This is important, symbolic," she says to Louis, and points to the picture. "We came here with nothing, and look at us now. The best hummus money can buy."

"True," he says, and lifts his glass for a toast. They touch glasses and kiss, just a peck and then a longer kiss. He knows Scoletti is somewhere in the room and that maybe the kiss is related to his courting of Kate, but it doesn't matter all that much.

That night, in the cab home, it feels like Brooklyn all over again, except this time there's no one else to hurt.

As she's about to go into her room, he takes her hand and pulls her in, kisses her. She kisses him back, then stops.

"I don't know. I just don't . . ." she says, and kisses him quickly, then goes into her room.

The next morning, ensconced in the comforter on the couch, newspaper pieces everywhere, she looks up at him and smiles as he stands there, two mugs of hot coffee in his hands. She takes off her glasses and pushes off of the comforter, stretches, being overtly sexy as she stares into his eyes.

"Mmm," Kate says. "Come here, why don't you."

He puts down the cups and she pulls him down next to her, then turns so that her back is against him, puts his hand under her T-shirt. Soon, she's pushing into him as he caresses her while kissing her neck, her ear. She reaches back and touches him, then pushes her herself into him again.

They stay here a nice long time. It may have been years ago, but he remembers what she told him when they were younger, about making love to girls and the importance of teasing. The idea that you may not do what she wants will make her want you all the more.

Finally, she turns around and starts kissing him. It becomes passionate very quickly and soon their bodies are locked together, each pushing into the other. She pulls off her tights and reaches into his pajama pants. He runs his fingers over the front, then the sides of her G-string. She moans and tries to pull him in. He wants to, of course, but then it occurs to him how much is at stake.

He stops and moves away, then gets off the couch. "Fuck, Kate, this . . . What are we doing? We should be careful here."

"I know, but . . ." she says.

"I don't want to stop, but I don't know," he tells her, and goes to the bathroom. And although it's a cliché, he turns on the shower.

A minute later, she comes in and sits on the toilet, watching him through the clear curtain. He has a beautiful body. How is it that she's never really looked at him?

"Is it crazy?" she asks.

"Maybe. I don't know. But it also makes sense."

"What are we worried about?" she asks.

"This story, people getting together, has two endings, right? You're either together or it's over."

She stares at him, trying to decide. "It won't be over," she says, and gets into the shower. "I want to do this." She puts her hand on him. "And so do you."

It's not easy to go slowly, and in the shower they nearly finish. In bed, he kisses her breasts a long time and runs his hand over her thighs, then cradles her center with his palm, rocking gently. He sits her up and uses his free hand to reach back. Every part of her is being touched right now. She whispers, "Please."

He tries to go slowly, more no than yes, slowing, then pushing harder.

"Stay inside me. Please," she says. Sweat covers her neck and chest, and she pushes his mouth back to her breast. As he quickens, she moves into him in equal parts. It feels perfect, a complete give-and-take. Finally, he gives everything he wants to give. And it feels like exactly what she wants. She climaxes so loudly, they both laugh. There's no way the neighbors did not hear that.

They lie there in silence, just looking at each other and laughing, then kiss again.

"Is this really us?" she asks.

"This is us," he says. "It's us, Kate, it's us."

They sleep awhile, then wake up, and she suddenly gets a hankering for both water and ginger cookies. She sets the water and cookies on the small nightstand, then gets back in bed. She pulls off the blanket and straddles his leg, her inner thigh just grazing the top of his kneecap, and stops right at the center of him and gently blows on his chest.

"My little wind machine," he says, and runs his fingers along the sides of her arms, then the side of her body, along her shoulders as she leans down closer and closer and blows on his hair, cut a little too short for her liking.

"When I blow on your chest hair, it looks like a wheat field. I feel like I'm a helicopter flying over a wheat field in Kansas."

"Is that right?"

"Yeah."

"Cool, 'cause that's all I've ever wanted to be," he says, and opens his eyes. "Your pretty little wheat field in Kansas."

CHAPTER 43
Ibiza
1994

Sitting on the bed, Angela feels practically unable to move. She stares at the back of Louis's head. He's sitting on the balcony floor, leaning against the glass door, smoking.

She thinks of Kate drying her tears so many years ago in Madrid when Angela thought she was pregnant. Then she remembers once, in Boston, when they babysat for a neighbor. Kate was absolutely undone by the thrill of hearing the baby laugh, of seeing him close his eyes every time she kissed his cheek.

"Look, I guess we all close our eyes when we get kissed," she said, and did it again. And again, the baby closed his eyes. "What a precious little one you are," Kate told him, and kissed his balled-up fist, still covered in just a bit of newborn dry skin.

Angela had gotten out her camera and taken a million photos of the child's fingers, the tiny nails and tips, which looked like peas. Kate kissed those baby fingers over and over again until they both fell asleep that way, the baby's hand resting on Kate's cheek.

Do I still have those pictures? she wonders, then gets up and walks to the bathroom. She finds Kate's perfume and dabs it on her wrists, then goes back and lies on her side in the center of the bed, nose pressed against the inside of her arm. This perfume is different from the one she wore in Boston, but it works.

She's had three people in her life you could call lovers, in addition to Kate. And the best memories of each can be triggered by certain smells. Clean, bright-smelling soaps remind her of David in San Diego; the ocean and Nag Champa incense remind her of Jennifer, a girl she dated in L.A. a couple of years ago, who lived in Venice Beach. And Terry, the only person other than Kate she's lived with, left a treasure trove to choose from: the cappuccino she loved to have after dinner (and still slept soundly), the lilies she bought every single Friday, the slight scent of expensive perfume plus perspiration that had become imbedded into her silk shirts over so many years that you could never hope to separate the two, and that drop of sandalwood oil way back at the nape of her neck.

But of all the details she's happy to carry with her about anyone she's loved, Angela's most grateful for the memories of Kate. Lying on the bed in Ibiza, watching the wind blow the curtains away from the open balcony doors, she thinks of one particular Saturday in Boston, after a wedding.

It had been a fake wedding between an American and a Brazilian friend in danger of being deported. Since both were gay, everyone was asked to try to "look the part" of a heterosexual couple. "No offense, but they have to look straight, and so do their guests. So, if you're a girl, a real girl, wear a dress." Kate, with her love of beautiful things, including fashion, didn't have to be told twice. She went out and bought two dresses, spent as many days figuring out which to wear. As the maid of honor, she claimed it was her duty to look good. And she did.

"You're not supposed to outdo the bride," Angela said as Kate finished applying her lipstick, rolling one lip over the other slowly, dramatically, knowing she was being watched. She grasped the sides of the sink, leaned in, and looked at the mirror the way a woman will when she knows she looks fantastic.

"She's not a real bride, though, is she?" Kate said, and savored the reaction from Angela: a huge smile and a shake of the head.

"No, she is not."

They came home tipsy and a little sweaty, ripped off their panty hose, and made love while still in their dresses, then lay there like two spent bridesmaids, kissing and drinking more champagne.

Hours later, as everyone else in Boston was going to sleep, they got up and made sandwiches, which they took to the tub. It was such a hot and humid night. Kate brought out an old paint-splattered boom box she'd found under the sink and a favorite CD. They belted out the words to their favorite song, "Blue Savannah," singing loudly and badly.

The CD might have been corrupted, or the boom box broken, but only that one song would play.

"Again?"

"Again!"

Cradling Kate in that tub, the pink glow from the twinkle lights around the neck of the sunflower reaching all the way up there, her fingers resting on Kate's stomach, the same great song playing over and over again, the world was undeniably perfect.

Angela opens the door, steps out, and sits down beside Louis. She can hear a conversation somewhere on the street below. Two old men who apparently haven't seen each other in weeks are trading details of their and their spouses' latest doings.

"Is it yours, then? I mean, do you think it's your baby?" she asks, and turns to face him.

Tiny lines of water run through and around the red-and-brown bristles on Louis's face, not straight lines, but little broken streams, like those glimpsed from an airplane flying over a forest.

Louis nods yes.

She takes a deep breath and closes her eyes. This is not a surprise, not really, so why is it hard to hear?

Louis rubs his head and pushes it down far into his chest. "I'm sorry. Does it hurt you to know?" he says, and exhales.

"Sort of," she says. "I didn't think I could lose her any more than I already had, but I guess there was a little bit more left in there. If that makes sense."

"Yeah, it makes sense," Louis says, and pulls Angela's hand toward his chest. "There haven't been many guarantees with Kate. Right? Except that it's always been me and you. Just us," he says.

"If Santillan knows she's pregnant, he'll help us, don't you think?"

"Definitely. And if not him, someone else. Let's not forget who Kate is, right? You know? The girl who's transcended so much."

"Right."

"The girl who survived an accident that others wouldn't have."

"Right," she says, and smells her wrist. "They didn't get the perfume, did they?"

"No," he says.

Angela looks up at the dress and thinks of Kate's smile today. Would it be cruel or kind to tell him that Kate opened her eyes? Louis has so much, but at least she has that.

CHAPTER 44

At Home on a Hill Where the Fog First Embraces the City
1993–1994

The morning after Kate and Louis made love, Monday, he gets up first and makes coffee, stands there waiting for it to brew. He can hear her in the room, shuffling around, and suddenly, there she is at the door, wrapped in a towel, her three or four inches of hair pointing every which way. She cringes at the bright sunshine, but then comes and sits on his lap, starts drinking his coffee.

"This is definitely strange," she says. "But I like it."

"Me, too."

It doesn't stop. This new way of being together, as lovers, feels like a new toy to both of them. It's odd to find themselves kissing at a restaurant or on the way home, and then to end up in the same bed night after night. It's even stranger to go to dinner with friends and touch each other under the table, taking months to work up the nerve to tell them that something pretty major has happened.

It's hard not to want to do everything at once—all of it. Now that they're lovers, it's as if he has a green light to do and say so many things that before felt off-limits. He likes the idea of them as a family. One day, as they pass a pet store where they have an adoption day, he suggests getting a dog.

"Madonna won't mind, especially if it's a puppy," he says, but she just shakes her head no. "Let's go look at them. They're all from different pounds. Let's save a life and get a son."

"I can't. I really can't," she says, and takes on a sullenness he's seen a few times in their life together.

"Why not?"

"I don't want to talk about it. Let's just go. Please."

"Sure."

The rest of the day, she's serious, not present.

"You need to tell me," he says that night after dinner.

"No. I don't."

"You do. What is it?"

"I had a dog in Encino. Pete. I lost him."

"That's it?"

"Yeah."

"No, it isn't. Come on, Kate. What is it?"

"Well," she says, and pushes her hand through her hair. Her eyes fill with tears. "He was so sweet, you know? A big old sort of collie mix of some sort, black and white, with the softest ears. I loved him so much. My best friend the first few years in that house. He was my only friend," she says, starting to cry now.

"What happened, Kate?"

"One day, I took him for the longest walk—I mean miles—and then I tied him to a pole and I left him there. He barked and barked for me to come back, but I didn't."

"Why did you do that?"

"He didn't know why I left him."

"Why did you?"

"I thought that . . . I thought he was the reason Don did the things he did. Because the very first time it happened was the day Don gave me Pete. He gave me the dog and then he hugged me and then . . . So I left him there all by himself. I left Pete all by himself."

She's sobbing now, and all he can do is hold her. She nearly chokes while trying to speak, has to slow down, coughs. She cries like this for so long, he starts to worry about her. Louis just holds her and kisses her until it eventually slows and stops and she curls up and falls asleep.

CHAPTER 45

A Room in Ibiza
1994

That night, as they're making a plan to find Santillan the next day and tell him about the pregnancy, there's a knock at the door.

"Ted? Or maybe her parents?" Angela says.

Louis stands and goes to the credenza, grabs his wallet. "I think I know who it is."

"Who?"

"Don't worry about it," he says, and puts on a T-shirt. "I'm just gonna step out, but I'll be right back."

"Who is it?"

"A new friend," he says.

"A new friend?"

"Yeah," Louis says. He goes back to his suitcase, grabs a sweatshirt, and leaves the room. "Back in two minutes," he tells her.

He probably shouldn't have given the kid his address. But he did, and now he's here, hopefully alone. Louis opens the door just a few inches and sees the kid in the hallway, nervous, arms so skinny, that face and the rings through his lip. The kid has a pair of cheap aviator-type glasses on his head, and somehow this comforts Louis, even though it could be the same trick he just used. Those glasses make Louis think the kid just sells a little powder on the side to finance a rock band, maybe, or a new car, or just food and shelter.

"Hey," Louis says, and steps out. "I'm not alone." He tilts his head toward the room.

"Oh, well, out here, then?" the kid asks. He shifts a little to the left and Louis can see he's carrying a dark green backpack.

"Sure. Fast, yeah?"

The kid nods, looks around, and pulls the backpack around to the front of him, then unzips and pulls out something wrapped in an orange dish towel.

"Is it your mother's?" Louis asks, and the kid at first looks irate but then laughs a little.

"My grandmother. Fuck you," he says. "Three hundred."

Louis pulls money from his pocket, placed there just for this sale. If it's dangerous to pull out a wad to buy tchotchkes in foreign countries, what would *Lonely Planet* say about this?

"Is it . . . does it belong to someone with a record, a criminal?"

"I think it came from a robbery, a house here. I don't know. I don't care," the kid says, nods his good-bye, and heads for the elevator.

"Hey," Louis calls after him. "Do you know how to use this, in case . . ."

"Yeah," the kid says, and hits the elevator button once, twice, three times. "I do." The doors open and he's gone.

"Who was outside?" Angela asks.

"Someone who will help us if there are insurmountable obstacles in our way."

"What are you talking about?"

"Nothing, don't worry."

"Who was it?"

"Come on, you don't want to know, don't really need to know," Louis says, and takes a swig right from the bottle. "Let me just take care of it, quietly."

"What are you, the Mafia?"

"Yeah, that's me," he says.

"Come on, who was it?"

"An unsavory fellow who has dabbled in crime," Louis says.

"I didn't come here to end up in jail. I came here to help Kate," she says.

"I know, and we will."

Angela knows, and so does Louis, that Kate had talked about, dissected, even studied what happened to her with Don. She'd shone a bright, bright light on it. Which is how she broke away. How can they now link her to him again, simply because Don came to Ibiza?

"Louis, listen, I just don't know if this makes sense. She was all about letting go of the past. . . . Come on, her thesis was called 'From the Me Hurt to the Me Healed Generation.' She's not defined by what hurt her."

"How do you know the title?"

"She sent it to me."

"She did? When?"

"A few weeks ago."

"You were in touch?"

"My point is that Don does not define Kate."

"Not define. I didn't say define, but . . . we can't pretend it didn't affect her. Or us. Don ruined a lot of things, like her ability to trust anyone. Like me. Or you."

"The past, it has nothing to do with this . . . accident. Just an accident. You can't fix her now by fixing what happened. As if that's even possible."

"It is possible."

"How?"

"By making things right. We're going to make things right."

Angela thinks about arguing, but she stops and just takes in his face, his eyes. He normally looks gentle. Not now. His chest, his arms look ready, like he very badly wants to break something in half.

"I don't know, Louis. This is just too much. I don't know if I can," she says, and gets up, slips on flip-flops, and grabs money from the credenza.

"When's the last time you saw her?" he asks.

"A long time ago."

"What? Days? Hours?"

"Come on now, don't do this. I'm going to the store. Want anything?"

"Some smokes. Please." He thinks about saying more, then doesn't.

CHAPTER 46

Los Angeles
May 1994

The elevator doors open onto the building's lobby and Angela's greeted by the smell of cleaning liquid—as sweet and concentrated as a freshly cut green apple. The janitor mops the gray slate flooring every Friday, Windexes the mirrors and windows, and polishes the leather bench opposite the mailboxes. Perfuming the lobby even more is a vase filled with pink and white lilies sitting on the table next to the door. Someone is probably selling their apartment and prepping for an open house tomorrow.

Angela remembers that tonight her neighbor Jim is hosting drinks on the rooftop, and that makes her happy. She likes to spend a lot of time alone on the weekends, but not Friday. She's still young enough to think of Fridays as the most celebratory of days.

She pulls the mail from the long rectangular box, never big enough to accommodate all the magazines she subscribes to. Even after having most of them sent to her office, still the box is always jammed. Especially today, when the normal mail competes with a large manila envelope that has a San Francisco return address. Her eyes bear down on the handwriting. Is it . . .

It is. Definitely.

CHAPTER 47
Salvador
1994

Hugh and the Canadians have gone to get stoned, so Kate sits alone at the crowded outdoor café, in a cobblestone square in Salvador, Brazil, drinking a beer and trying not to stare at the prostitutes.

Just a few feet away, separated from the café patrons by a rope and stanchion, stand some ten girls in short skirts and brightly colored low tops. They use their eyes, their smiles, their breasts—anything—to catch the eye of any man inside. Technically, these Bahia girls are not allowed entrance into the café, but if one of them gets invited in, the proprietor can't very well kick her out. So there they stand, tall and short, chubby and slim, smiling and preening, young and even younger.

Two girls in particular have caught Kate's eye. Sisters, she thinks. The one in front is taller, older, and confident, wearing a red halter top and silvery skirt. Next to her stands another girl, maybe fifteen or sixteen. She's chubby, awkward, and shy-looking, with a tidy Afro of reddish brown hair. She wears a halter top like the taller girl, but hers is ill-fitting—a hand-me-down?—so that a crescent shape of baby fat mixed with breast threatens to shimmy out the side.

Kate can't stand the feeling of this, so she turns away from the girls, lets her eyes rest instead on the Pelourinho's main square. She leans her cheek against her knuckles, which still smell, though faintly, of business-class hand lotion, rubs the back of her forefinger against her lip, and closes her eyes just a few seconds.

It's pretty, the square, with its shiny cobblestones and colonial buildings the color of Easter eggs. The cathedral's been lit from below, and generously, making it even more special, like the castle at a theme park. In front of the church, which is the square's main attraction, a group of tourists line up to take their shots.

As Kate watches them, one, a tanned blonde who looks like Camilla Parker Bowles, wanders away. So enraptured is this lady by the floodlights, or the warm night, or the escape from everyday life, that she fails to notice the street kid a few feet from her, with hair made opaque by dirt, about to dip into her Louis Vuitton.

Kate considers yelling something to scare off the kid, but before she can, the boy, all of eight, maybe nine, has finished and is running away, waving at the lady as he goes.

Anyway, Hugh and the girls are back. Kate hears a café chair scrape over the cobblestones and turns to see "the jolly English giant," as she calls him, in a white shirt and khaki shorts, plop into a chair as the Canadians, in their khakis and pink layers of T-shirts over beads, hemp bracelets on their arms, stand there, mute-stoned.

"That woman was just robbed," Kate says, and points at Camilla Parker Bowles, still oblivious, now photographing a tall, thin man against the backdrop of the church.

"Weren't we all," Hugh says, and throws a pack of Marlboros on the table. With his green eyes, brown skin, despite living in London, he is the chubby George Hamilton of the medical set. "I want a beer," he says. "But instead, I shall have a Coke. Girls?"

The Canadians plop down in a cloud of tie-dyed clothes and patchouli-scented dreadlocks.

"Beer," says Clarissa, the taller and more mellow of the two, half black and pretty.

"Yeah, me, too," says Lucy, who is short, blond, and a little angry. Probably because of her height, Kate thinks. Hard enough to be a girl, let alone a short girl.

"Did you see all the nurses?" Hugh asks, and points his head at the group of girls behind the rope and stanchion.

"I wish you wouldn't call them nurses. It's so fucking sexist."

"Only because you assume nurses are women. What about doctors? Shall I call them doctors?"

"I would appreciate that," Kate says.

"Consider it done, then."

"I'm already lost," Clarissa says.

"That's because you've had some marijuana, haven't you?" Hugh says, and tries to get the attention of one of only two busy waiters, clad in a white jacket and black bow tie, skirting tables with his silver tray in hand.

"I should go," Kate says, and stands.

"Come on now, come on," Hugh says, and takes Kate's hand in his. "I'm sorry I called them nurses. World's oldest. We know that. Just a job, like any other. Like making hammocks or cars, but with a bit of added physical contact. Come on now, you're stronger than this," Hugh says, and kisses her hand. "Come on, buddy, sit back down."

Kate does sit back down. She wishes she could put it away and stop looking and say to herself, this is the world. This is how the world works—there are lonely men and there are poor girls, and these two groups are able to trade what one has and the other does not. Just a transaction. Like hunter-gatherers of a sort.

Finally, a waiter arrives. "*Sim?*" he says. Hugh orders one Coke and three beers.

Clarissa and Lucy sit rather slumped over, marveling at all this newness.

These twenty-year-old McGill students have come to Brazil for a week to help pass out condoms and give Pap smears and medicine to sex workers, but already they appear way over their heads.

Hugh uses yearly Brazil trips as a sort of escape valve, to release a bit of guilt for making so much money. It might be his last trip. Because of the economy, he isn't making that much more money to feel so guilty about. And because . . . well, probably because he's sixty, he's not feeling that much guilt about anything anymore, really.

This is definitely Kate's last trip. Master's thesis is done. Soon a full teaching schedule, with a book to promote or whatever one does with these types of books—dinner parties, probably, where she will dine on the stories of girls like the ones behind her.

"Listen, ladies, it's been a real pleasure, but I just hit the jet-lag wall. Give my Coke to a worthy person," Hugh says, and stands, puts some money on the table. "And tomorrow, we must be on the road by nine. So, breakfast at eight, yes, kids?" he says, and looks at Kate and the two girls.

"We'll be ready," Kate says.

"Nighty-night, then," Hugh says. On his way out of the café, he tips his imaginary hat to the young prostitutes and says, "*Boa noite.*"

"He's funny," Clarissa says.

"I find him annoying," Lucy says.

Both girls turn to Kate, as if expecting her to issue a finding on Hugh—funny or annoying, which is it? But Kate keeps watching the Brazilian girls.

The older one works it and works it hard, trying to catch an eye. Business-savvy and quick, she doesn't worry Kate. She's also very pretty, which gives her power. It's the younger girl Kate worries about. She looks vulnerable and scared.

Kate sighs so heavily, the Canadians stop talking and stare at her.

"Have you ever actually helped anyone leave prostitution? I mean, have you had any actual success?" Lucy asks.

"Sure, one of our girls is now a vice president at Morgan Stanley," Kate says, and the girls look at her dumbfounded, for so many possible reasons: They don't believe her. They don't know what Morgan Stanley is. They are too stoned to remember the question.

"In Saõ Paulo?" Clarissa asks.

"Yes. She lives in a high-rise and has a doorman now," Kate says, and the girls both nod.

"That's cool," Lucy says.

Was I this stupid at their age? Kate wonders.

"All right, girls, I'm going back to the hotel," Kate says, and gets up. "See you in the morning. You didn't bring purses or wallets out, right?"

"No," Lucy says. She's pouting. Kate could say something nice, let her off the hook. It'll probably take a week for Lucy to figure out why Kate snapped. She'll turn it over and over until she realizes why it was silly, even mean, to ask, in that holier-than-thou tone, if anyone was actually helped by these excursions. But then, eventually, after some rationalizing, Lucy will surely absolve herself. People always absolve themselves in the end. They don't need your help to do it.

"And do you remember where the hotel is, or would you like to come with me now?"

"No, we're cool, don't worry," Clarissa says.

Kate maneuvers her way around the tight tables and chairs and finally gets to the small area that serves as both entrance and exit. Instead of walking through fast, as she should, and heading down the hill to their hotel, she walks by the young girl and stops.

The girl doesn't notice her at first, but as Kate stands there, pretending to have forgotten something and patting the pockets of her cargo pants, the girl turns and smiles at her. She has such thick lips, but they look dry, and it worries Kate that one more smile like this could break skin.

"*É possível falar com você?*" Kate says, asking if she can talk to her.

"*Sim,*" the girl says, and Kate indicates that she should move away from the older sister, who hardly notices Kate, so involved is she in her own plans.

"*Você . . . você . . .*" Kate doesn't know what to say next. The girl looks so sweet, waiting for the question. Kate takes a twenty-dollar bill from her pocket and gives it to her.

The girl looks at the money, then at Kate, clearly wondering what she needs to do for this money. Then the girl reaches out and touches Kate's arm, not sure where, or even if, to lead this woman somewhere.

"Oh, no, no, not like that," Kate says in English. *"Eu no . . . no page porque você. . . ."* Kate tells the girl she didn't give her the money for that reason.

"Why, then?" the girl asks.

"Amigas," Kate says, and points at herself, then at the girl. *"Amigas."*

"Sim, amigas," the girl says, and smiles even more, so that now these heartbreaking dimples appear and the skin on her lips definitely breaks.

Kate shakes her head, embarrassed and wanting, more than ever, to cry. *"Boa noite,"* she says, and walks away. Too much, too horrible, too stupid. Yes, you and me, best friends, so much in common. Maybe we could go to a movie sometime.

"Obrigada," the girl calls out after her.

As she walks back to the hotel, dodging tourists, Kate struggles to put it away. She doesn't want to imagine either girl anywhere except home, in front of a TV or on a phone with a friend. Maybe tonight is an aberration, just a transgression, an experiment. Not for the older girl, but for the younger. Kate tries to picture her at home or with friends—anywhere but in some hotel or alley with some man.

The hotel stairs and lobby floor have been aggressively scented, washed with something that reminds her of Listerine or root beer, a medicinal cleanliness.

Kate opens the door to the room but doesn't turn on the lights, just crosses and opens the French windows to let in some air. So humid tonight. She strips off her clothes and goes to the bathroom, turns on the shower. Tiny and without a curtain, it's at least clean. She made sure of that after checking in. If she's learned one thing about herself, it is that she cannot abide a dirty shower. She washes quickly, covering herself in body wash left on the sink for just this purpose. As she steps out of the shower, a feeling of nausea grips her and she looks for bottled water, then remembers that hers sits in her bag in the bedroom. She figures she must have eaten something that didn't agree with her. Fortunately, the feeling quickly disappears.

Kate strips the bed of its comforter and opens the two tiny bottles of Ketel One that a flight attendant gave her for no apparent reason. He leaned down on his way to deliver someone's warm cookies and opened his hand on Kate's tray table, making a small thud as he left behind the two plastic bottles.

"You are so pretty," he said, and walked off. Gay boys love pretty women, especially if they're lesbians, don't they? she thought.

"You are so pretty," the sweaty, sexy boys in New York would say as the music thumped and pounded their bodies, only they didn't offer tiny bottles of vodka, but lines.

She pours both bottles' contents in a glass and pushes the bed so that it's closer to the French window, then lies there and listens to the music-school groups below.

Every night, two or three of these *blocos* or *batucada* drum bands come to the Pelourinho. Each is made up of several rows of people, mostly women, who dance to the quick, joyous rhythms, then rows of percussion, and finally rows of drummers. The school groups take different routes, each gathering up fans as they go, like pied pipers. The groups and their respective fans all end up in the central square for a sort of competition. That must be where they are now. From this far away, Kate can hear their joyous rhythms.

Why does money for sex still upset her so much? She's studied it, written her master's thesis on it, even spent a whole year working as a cocktail waitress at Swank, in the Tenderloin, studying the politics of sex and money.

And this is her third trip to Brazil. Why does it still bother her?

Kate finishes the vodka but knows it won't be enough. She gets up and finds a bottle of Ambien in her bag, takes two with a swig of bottled water. This should do the trick.

CHAPTER 48

Leaving Ibiza
1994

Louis gets up first, at six, checks his computer, and is quickly rewarded with the documents Mariana, the neighbor downstairs, created or scanned and sent.

"Yes," he says, and takes the laptop to Angela's bed. She's still asleep but rouses herself to look at the computer. "Good news," he says, and points to the screen.

It's a legal document, grayish in color but readable, a marriage certificate with Kate's and Louis's names on it.

"I thought you hadn't done it," she says.

"No. But if you have friends who are good with computers . . . This one is real," he says, and clicks to the next page, a document with the heading "Medical Power of Attorney."

"That one alone should be enough," she says.

The plan is to call Georgina and tell her they're not going to the hospital this morning, then pack up most of their things but leave just enough lying around that the concierge or, more important, Don will think they're still here. Angela will go to the hospital and Louis will head to the airport.

Assuming the morning meeting is daily, Santillan will arrive at seven. So they have until nine, when Kate's parents will return, to convince him to discharge her. It shouldn't be as difficult now, given the possible pregnancy.

When they arrive at the hospital, no staff members are present.

At least they'll be able to visit Kate undisturbed. Angela and Louis stop moving when they see, twenty or so feet away, Don's unmistakable silhouette. He's standing at the door of the room.

"Unbelievable," Louis whispers.

Angela watches Louis walk quickly toward the room. Georgina is already there.

"Come to say good-bye?" Louis asks.

"Why would we do that? We're not leaving," Don says.

"She is. We're having her flown to Madrid," Louis says.

"Nonsense, she's staying right here," Don says. "The doctors won't discharge her."

"Yes, they will, and they should," Louis says.

"We have to do the right thing for her medically," Georgina says. "The hospital chief has assured us—"

"The chief, right," Louis says, hands on his hips, staring at Don and Georgina.

"You have no right to intervene in any way, either one of you," Angela says. "She's a grown woman and neither of you has power of attorney. Only Louis does."

"Does he, though?" Don asks. "Or is he simply saying that he does?"

"Hoping she'll just die here in Ibiza and so will your not-so-secret secret?"

"You're very angry right now, Louis," Georgina says.

"That's right, I am, Georgina. I am very angry at both of you, but especially at you, Don," he says, and steps closer to Don.

"Louis, please," Angela says quietly.

"Come on, Don. Let's go outside."

"I'm not sure that's a good idea," Don says, and pulls at the front of his shirt, inserting a few fingers between the buttons, like some modern-day Superman ready to pull off his shirt and reveal the suit underneath.

"I think it is. I think it's time to talk out some things," Louis says, and walks to the other side of the room. "We've all kept our mouths shut for what . . . almost twenty years now? We know what you did, but we don't talk about it. What, you worried she'll start talking more? You'd rather we just let her go to her grave?"

"Louis, Kate's a very difficult person. You know that," Georgina says. "Those things she said about Don . . . they're not . . . They're greatly exaggerated."

"Oh, is that right? Not real? Some kids have imaginary friends; others have imaginary molesters?"

"Please don't be flip," Don says. "I've suffered a hell of a lot thanks to those things she said."

"You've *suffered*? Oh, well . . . God. Terrible to be slandered like that. Especially since it's he said/she said, right? Two people, contradictory statements? Cancel each other out, right?"

Don hangs his head, as if these accusations are too much, but Louis thinks the old man is simply hiding the look in his eyes that says, That's right. That's why I've managed to get away with it.

"But, guess what, Don, you and I have a lot in common. We both have secrets. Your secret is that you remember how it went, every detail. And so do I. That's your secret. And my secret. How about that? The same fucking secret!" Louis says.

Angela can feel that Louis is losing control. She looks outside the room and sees no staff members in the hallway.

"I remember you doing it, because . . ." Louis moves closer to Don, his arms taut, fists ready. "Because guess who sneaked into Kate's room when she went to the bathroom and hid under her bed, lying there quietly, listening to her play music? Guess who else was there, Don."

Don shakes his head and puts up his hands, palms toward Louis. "You're too angry for civil discourse right now," he says. "If you won't leave, we will."

Louis gets so close to Don, their shirt buttons touch. Louis's nose is nearly touching Don's. His fist is flat against the old man's heart as he pushes him into the wall, a knee in Don's crotch.

"No, you won't go, you fucking pedophile. You won't go, and neither will I, not the way I did when I was a kid. This time, you'll pay for you what you did," Louis says, and grabs Don's arm and neck and pulls him out of the room and into the hall.

As soon as he's in the hall, Louis knows why no one is coming to Kate's room. Doctors and nurses hurry toward a room down the hall, one nurse pushing a red cart. He can hear the loud beeping of monitors and people yelling what sounds like the names of medications.

"Epinephrina, atropina . . ."

Louis considers dragging the old man all the way outside, but it's too long a distance and he doesn't want to lose this opportunity, so he slams him against the outside wall of Kate's room, so that Louis hears the steadiness of her heart monitor as he listens to the old man choking. Louis's fingers push their way into each tiny crevice in Don's larynx. Both women come out of the room, Georgina loudly begging him to stop, Angela trying to pull him and whispering for him to please stop, too.

"You'll be arrested," Angela says. "And that's what he wants."

CHAPTER 49
Kate's Bedroom in Encino
1982

Louis hears the barely audible sounds of the song Kate's listening to on her Walkman. Louis strains until he pieces it together—of course, "Every Little Thing She Does Is Magic," the song she's completely obsessed with.

The last time Louis sneaked into her room, he pushed his hand up against the mattress gently, so that she felt something move. Then he pushed harder, and she ran, screaming, out of the room. It was funny as hell, although she punched him hard in the chest. He figures it would be funny if he did it again, and this time it probably wouldn't scare her quite as much. Just as he's about to push up, though, Louis hears what sounds like scraping and tries to figure out what this is. She's filing her nails. That's totally what it is—file against nail. What if she stabs him with it? Better wait. After a few minutes of this, she grows bored, stands, and takes a book from her shelf, then plops down on the bed to read.

A big smile fills Louis's face as his heart beats a little faster, anticipating her scream when he reaches up and grabs at her ankles. Or maybe he'll start whispering stupid things until she gets on her knees and looks under the bed—not scared at all, just shocked to see him.

And then, there he is—Don. Just a voice at first.

"What are you doing?" Don asks. Kate gets up from the bed.

"Nothing," she says, sounding annoyed. "I was just going into the living room."

"Mom just went shopping. I saw her car as I was pulling up."

"Okay, well . . . I was going to go into the living room," Kate says. She sounds so strange that he lifts up the bed ruffle and watches her feet move toward the door, watches Don come into the room, close the door behind him.

"Give me a hug," he says.

"I was going to go meet Louis," she says, and walks toward him, but Don stops her. "Come on, give me a hug. Aren't you saving up for a new jacket, a ski jacket?"

"Yeah."

"Well? I have twenty dollars in my pocket," he says.

They stand like this in the center of that room, with its beanbag chairs and Police posters, its hand-painted dresser with photos atop it of friends from school, of Kate's father and mother, so long ago, sitting in a frame Kate made in third grade. In that room, with its heady mixture of little girl and burgeoning woman, they stand for what feels like days, Don holding out a twenty-dollar bill as Kate stares at his hand, at the floor, never at him.

"I don't want to."

"Come on, sure you do," he says.

"I hear Mom's car," she says, and tries to walk past him and get to the door, but he grabs her as she goes by, locks his arms around her. "It's so easy, come on," he tells her, and Louis watches her try to pull away. "Come on, look how happy I am to see you," Don says.

Louis keeps watching, thinking that maybe, just maybe, this is only a hug. But they eventually sit on the bed and he's forced to stare at the backs of their legs as he listens and feels the girl he loves give her stepfather a hand job.

CHAPTER 50

Ibiza
1994

"Guess who was there?" Louis whispers. This is it, this is the time. This will be an exorcism for Kate, a way to clean the slate and bring her back. Louis pulls his arm back as far as it will go and hits Don on the side of the head.

This does what he's hoped it would—shocks the man and gives Louis a second to make a fist, pull back, close his eyes, and use every ounce of force he has to land a good punch on Don's face. It works, and Louis feels both the excruciating pain of his own knuckles disintegrating along with the feeling of small bones collapsing under Don's skin. A moment later, he's rewarded with blood.

"See how happy I am to see you," he says to the old man, whose lips curl down, pools of saliva forming in each corner. He's trying to fall to the floor, but Louis won't let him. What he really wants now is to kick Don's balls back up into his body, to castrate him with one swift kick. Louis wants to feel the end of Don, the very end of him, so he waits until the old man's body unfolds a little; then he steadies himself and delivers another kick, which connects with Don's stomach, and the old man collapses.

Georgina is screaming and Angela is pulling at his arms, but Louis hears nothing except Kate crying softly after Don left her room that day, Louis lying very still, very silent, hiding under that bed.

Don's on his side, holding his face and moaning. One more,

259

Louis thinks. He steps back, cocks his leg, and delivers the hardest kick he can to Don's pubis. The old man is crying now, finally. Holding his face with one hand, his balls with the other, he's crying.

Winded, his hand aching, Louis leans against the wall and watches nurses arrive, then a doctor, to tend to Don and the wounds he has just inflicted. Angela looks worried, not scared or crying like Georgina, but worried.

"You knew, too," Louis says to Georgina. "You knew and you let him. You're as guilty as he is."

Georgina looks like a lost dog right now, completely scared, not sure which way to go, uncertain about her future. Two security guards arrive. They handcuff Louis and pull him out of the main area of the hospital, leave him lying near the front entrance, a maintenance man on a cigarette break his guard, as they go back to aid Don.

CHAPTER 51
Encino
1982

Louis stays under that bed for what feels like a lifetime, listening to her cry. He doesn't want her to know he's there, and he's not sure how to get out. After an hour or so, she leaves the room. He listens for clues to where they might be. The house is quiet. Every few minutes, there's a cough or the sound of a fork falling, maybe, into a dishwasher tray, a toilet flushing somewhere in a different part of the house. After a while, he feels fairly certain she's left the house, maybe even gone to find him.

He gets out from under the bed and hurries down the hall, pausing only long enough to see, through the sliding glass door in the living room, that Don sits outside, on his patio, smoking, drinking coffee, and staring intently at his pool.

CHAPTER 52
Ibiza
1994

Don's taken to a room off the ICU and given painkillers and ice. His nose stops bleeding quickly, so the doctor packs it lightly, just a bit of gauze. His elbow is badly bruised but not broken. Nothing broken, just very swollen and bruised. The chief of staff himself, Dr. Mendoza, stands beside him, watching as the doctor finishes examining Don's ribs.

Georgina stands next to the window, trying to clean the blood off of Don's shirt with a small white towel.

"Have you considered that it will be very wet when I put it back on?" he asks his wife, and she looks up quickly, worried, like a child who's just been reprimanded.

"No."

"No," he repeats.

"I cannot apologize enough," the doctor says. "Our security officers were assisting a patient who was being transferred to a nearby clinic—a child—and so they were slightly delayed reaching you."

"Oh, I see, a child," Don says, and gives the doctor the same insincere smile he offered his own wife. "Budgets don't allow for appropriately staffed security, is that it?"

"I think we are well staffed; they were simply busy," he says.

"I completely understand," Don says, and slowly shimmies

off the bed. "I understand, and yet, there I was, beaten for nearly ten minutes, while no one intervened. No one. No security, nothing."

"Yes, but fortunately you are a strong man, and I think you will feel much better tomorrow, with some rest and some medicine," he says, and hands Don a bottle of Percocet.

"Yes, yes, I am indeed a strong man," he says, and takes the bottle of pills. "But I believe that, under the circumstances, you are obliged to help me achieve what I need to achieve because of your incredible negligence and lack of care for patients. I can tie you up in court for a long time."

"I'm sorry you feel this way."

"I'm sure you are. You can be of help, however, assisting me with some things," Don says.

"If I can, I will be happy to," the doctor says.

"Oh, you can," Don says, and smiles at the man.

As Angela stands outside the room, she watches Griffin, who's down the hall, speaking with a uniformed man, a security guard. They keep talking, and Angela has a minute to look inside the room at Kate, who still seems as peaceful as can be. Do you even know what's happening all around you, Kate? she thinks.

After a couple of minutes, Griffin comes over to Angela.

"That was very unfortunate," he says. "They'll keep Mr. Ross until he cools off, just for the night."

"Ted, what if something happens to her tonight? And he's not here? He won't do anything. Come on. It's not necessary. Please don't do this."

"It's not . . . I can't risk it. Why is Mr. Ross so angry at Mr. Williams? Does he think Mr. Williams was abusive in some way?"

"Yes, and he was. In the worst possible way," she says. "Don did things that no father ever should." She watches Griffin for his reaction. He nervously pushes his glasses up, then rubs his chin and his cheek.

"I find that hard to believe," he says. "Mr. Williams seems like a very nice man."

Everyone sees and perceives life through their own filter, don't they? she thinks. Because Ted Griffin is an older man, like Don, he sides with him. He probably projects his own love for his daughter onto Don, in that blank canvas we all make of strangers.

It's hard for Angela not to shake Griffin and tell him that of course it's difficult to imagine Don doing such a thing. It's almost impossible to imagine anyone doing such a thing, yet it happens all the time.

"Kate's been very honest about it. She's talked to a lot of people about what happened. And she might even say that she's forgiven Don."

This interests him. Ted lifts his head and looks at her quizzically. "But Mr. Ross has not."

"Right."

He nods a few times, pretending to understand. "I hope you know that I feel very sorry for Mr. Ross, that my heart goes out to him at this moment. But I have certain duties, and in this case, it is absolutely my responsibility to ensure everyone's safety—Mr. and Mrs. Williams's, yours, Mr. Ross's, and Kate's."

"There may be some extenuating circumstances now. A very good reason she should be in Madrid," Angela says.

"Well, perhaps you know something I don't. I was told to . . . well, that great effort should be taken to ensure that her . . . that her time is peaceful."

Griffin has such a hard time expressing this, she almost feels sorry for him.

"You don't think she'll survive, either."

He looks her in the eyes and nods no.

"Okay, well, she is going to. Look, I know you're doing the best you can, but please release Louis. He can't be in jail right now."

"He'll be out tomorrow. Look, this is . . . this is not the time to fight, but the time to . . . simply not the time to fight."

"Maybe not, but neither is it the time to give up. You haven't known her as long as we have, or loved her the way we have, so maybe it's hard to understand."

"I'm sure that's true," he says, and pushes his fingers through his hair, rubs his neck, and walks away.

CHAPTER 53

Los Angeles
May 1994

Angela takes the package upstairs but doesn't want to open it. She sets it on her kitchen counter and stares at the address. Something so large, it has to be a form of writing. Does her hesitation spring from fear of what it could be—a completely impersonal offering, a script or a story of hers that Kate found in a box and is simply returning, which would be heartbreaking in its own way—or is she savoring the moment before a new connection is revealed, a note, a few warm words, something that points to a new way forward with Kate?

After she's had dinner and showered, she slowly cuts the top of the envelope and slides out its contents—a thick document, and underneath it, a card with her name on it. She puts the card aside and looks at the document: eighty pages of white paper, three-hole-punched, with gold brackets holding them together. It has the clean, almost sharp smell of an office-supply store or a freshly filled copier tray.

The cover page reads "From the Me Hurt to the Me Healed Generation: Redemption and Resurrection at the Local Gentlemen's Club." She opens it and skims a few pages, then goes to the dedication page, where she reads "For Angela and Louis, with love. For Georgina, with forgiveness."

Angela leans forward and just stares at the pages, then slowly runs one forefinger over the words *By Kate Harrington*.

CHAPTER 54
A Room in Ibiza
1994

Angela stands outside Kate's room and watches her, then goes inside and walks to the bed. She touches Kate's arm, then rests her hand on Kate's stomach. With her palm flat against the sheet, Angela presses down just a little. Silly to think you could feel anything. But then, it's not that she wants to feel anything, just the opposite. Angela wants the life inside Kate to feel that he or she is safe and not alone.

Her skin color looks good; her chest seems to rise and fall as it should. Angela takes her hand and holds it, warm to the touch. Then she smooths her hair.

You could argue that Kate has spent her entire adult life stringing together as many moments free of Don as humanly possible, and she has done an amazing job of it, finding more pleasure than most in so many places and so many ways: on dance floors, in beds. She always laughs after she comes, this deep, bawdy laugh, followed by a few quiet ones as she bites your arm or your shoulder, your earlobe. That laugh makes it seem as if she just got away with something.

Kate has succeeded, but you could also argue that he always catches up with her. Whether lying in a bed spent and sweaty, or broken and bruised, whether entwined in the body of a lover while napping blissfully on a sand dune, or so unconscious that only a heart machine's steady beep proves your existence, there he is. If nothing else, thanks to the fact that you are grateful for his absence, there he is.

"You live in the deepest part of me," she'd said. Once you get that deep, physically and otherwise, you find it all, don't you? It's a trove, but not all treasure.

You live in the deepest part of me. And so does he.

Angela quietly leaves the room, then the hospital itself. Louis is in a jail somewhere. Is he even in this town? Or in another, miles away? She has to find him, first, then get him out. Then they have to get out of Ibiza.

Angela starts to walk in no particular direction. The heat is so strong, intensifying everything. She looks down the road and imagines a spot she wants to reach, starts walking there. But then it's no good; she loses steam. The heat or the fact that she's fooling herself shut off her momentum.

She should call the medevac company and change the departure day to—when? Tomorrow? The next day? Or are their plans completely wrecked by what has just happened?

Getting Louis out is most important. She'll just go to the bakery and see. If the kid is there, she'll talk to him and maybe find out where they might have taken Louis. "An unsavory fellow," as Louis had said, will probably know all about the detention system here in Ibiza.

The bakery's door is closed. No lights. Angela presses her face to the glass, looks at the counter. Two orphaned baguettes lie at its center. She then looks at the display case, its white doilies sitting on empty plates, getting rustled by air from above. As she stares, the doilies suddenly stop moving. Angela looks to the back of the room and sees him, the kid, a beer in hand, turning off a switch—to the fan, probably. Angela knocks on the glass. He turns and stares, his face cold. Angela reaches in her pocket and takes out the cash Louis gave her, presses it to the glass. The kid stares and stares for what feels like a minute, until putting together how he knows her, then takes a swig from his bottle and starts to walk toward her.

"*¿Qué quieres?*" he says, asking what she wants.

She tells him what happened and asks if he can help get Louis out of jail. He can try, he says.

"How much, then?"

"I don't know. Two hundred?" he says, and shrugs as if he doesn't care, but the quick look he gives her hand and the way his teeth clench indicate he definitely cares. She gives him three hundred dollars.

"¿Qué más?" Holding the extra one hundred dollars, he asks what else she wants.

"I don't know yet. I'm not sure," she says, and asks for his cell phone number.

As she walks back to the hospital, Angela recalls a visit to the beach in Provincetown, years ago, remembers lying on the sand near the pine tree stands.

A hawk was flying above them, circling over the beachgoers serenely.

"He's looking for something to eat in the fields. Just watch," Kate said.

Angela thought, Why do you have to see it that way—as predator and prey? Why?

But eventually, Kate was proved right, and the hawk flew over with a tiny field mouse in its mouth, the prey issuing a tiny, just barely audible cry, as if it knew there was no point in trying. If you weren't expecting to see this, the hawk with his prey, you would miss it. You might even look and see the hawk but not the mouse in its clutches. And you would just think, Wow, a majestic hawk.

"That's why I don't eat animals," Kate said that day on the beach. "It's one thing to have to do that, for it be instinctual and just a matter of survival. But to prey when you don't have to, I just can't."

CHAPTER 55
Ibiza
1994

Bandaged and bruised but much stronger than before, Don has got the doctor firmly on the defensive, a situation the doctor is smart enough to recognize but not clever enough to undo.

"For starters, you can make sure that her mother and I have some time with her. Alone. Without that very angry man anywhere in sight," Don tells the chief of staff, who says that of course this can be done.

Five minutes later, Don is standing next to Kate's bed. They say that everything happens for a reason, and although he normally detests such Hallmark philosophies, right now Don could almost embrace that particular cliché.

He's pleased and not at all ashamed of the ache in his scrotum, of the memory of Louis's knee almost inside him. He likes what it represents. Louis is in jail now and there he will stay, a young man who, unfortunately, has turned his grief outward, which has, in turn, made him a serious threat to everyone, especially little Kate here. How many times has a disgruntled or jilted lover killed the person he allegedly so loves? Many times, the chief of staff agreed, far too many times.

"In your case, that scenario is avoidable," Don says. "You have to ensure medical power of attorney reverts to her mother and is not held by someone whose capacity to be a good guardian is seriously in question."

"Well, perhaps so," the doctor says, still polite but hating this old man for the control he's trying to exert.

"I know that's what my own attorneys have advised. In fact, they told me to hire a local attorney right away, which I have done."

"Uh-huh, very good," the doctor says.

Don and Georgina return to the hotel in silence. Even now that they are in the room, Georgina says nothing, just goes straight to bed, not even bothering to take off her pantsuit jacket, just kicking off her shoes. Don goes to the phone and orders two of what seem to be the Spanish equivalent of club sandwiches, then to the bathroom, where he wets a towel and fills a glass with water, opens a bottle, and pours out two Percocet, then adds another. He returns to the bedside and says her name, stares at those wrinkled lids covered in gold eye shadow, making them look like the yolk of a hard-boiled egg—as if makeup could possibly make a difference at her age. Those ridiculous lids slowly lift, revealing two light blue eyes he once thought pretty. He shows her the water and pills, then sets both on the nightstand, puts the wet cloth on her forehead.

"I should be nursing you," Georgina says, but she stays right where she is.

Don goes to the closet and pulls out their suitcases, sets one on the bed next to her stockinged feet and the other astride the chair arms, opens the chest of drawers, and begins to fill each case. Easy to do, since they haven't brought much.

After emptying his wife's drawer, he moves to his and picks up the pile of undershirts, his hand feeling the center of that pile, where last night, while Georgina was in the shower, he placed a bright pink G-string taken from Kate's luggage. Georgina had been ever so possessive of the luggage when they got back to the hotel, acting as if it were hers. As if he couldn't have access whenever he wanted. What was she guarding anyway at this stage?

The G-string is his talisman, the item that will protect him in the next hours, possibly the most important of his life. He uses his forefinger to caress the garment, though if his wife were to look up, she would see only a man taking great care to pack his things. But she won't look up, because she will be out by now. All these years of marriage have taught him that pills do not sit for long on any nightstand beside Georgina.

"Done packing," Don says, and closes the lid of each suitcase as his wife lies perfectly still on the bed, a barely audible "Good" coming from her.

Although he doesn't need to look at the nightstand for confirmation, he does it just for fun and smiles at the fact that her greedy old hand has already swept off the pills and popped them in her mouth. If he didn't need her to complete the picture of father, mother, and daughter, he would leave this wreck of a woman right here.

He hears a knock at the door. The food's arrived. Don tells the waiter where to put the tray, tips him, and watches the guy walk off. Then he pulls up a shiny cover, grabs a piece of sandwich, and starts to eat as he dials his assistant on the cell.

"It's me. I need you to do some research," he says, and looks up and watches Georgina's thick fingers entwine around one another and come to rest on her chest, which rises and falls ever so dependably.

"And I'm having some paperwork faxed to you within the hour, some forms, so you'll need to remain on call. . . . She's fine. Thank you for asking."

CHAPTER 56
Los Angeles
May 1994

Angela reads the thesis the very same night but holds off on the card. She wants to call Kate. There's no phone number on the document, but it does contain a return address and with that she is able to call and find a phone number.

But picking up that phone is the hardest thing in the world. She's worried Kate will say she's moved on, that she has a new partner and a new life, putting herself and Angela firmly in the past. In some ways, this would give Angela a solid end point from which to start a new life, but in other ways, it would provide an ending she's never really wanted.

CHAPTER 57
Ibiza
1994

Before starting off on his errand, Rodrigo decides to get some coke for himself. He's earned it for taking this job from two Americans who don't have a clue and will probably get him caught. If this job does lead to a few days in jail, he'll at least have a good high to remember. Anyway, he's cut way down lately, and, even now, he's leaving half the gram wrapped in a photo of his nieces inside his wallet. If this little errand does get him in trouble, at least he'll have a nice pair of lines waiting for him.

And also getting high helps—this is what gives him the feeling not just of strength or invulnerability but of righteousness as well. This is the last bit of reassurance that the American guy is good and the old man isn't.

For that guy Louis, with the soft eyes, the clean hands, to be buying a gun and asking for Rodridgo's help, then the old man absolutely had to have done something for which he deserves punishment.

The first bump burns. He bought it from an Englishman, a deejay at Pacha. Probably cut with something like baby laxative or God knows what. Maybe Paracetamol, whatever that is. English tourists are always asking at the bakery if he carries it.

"Does this look like a fucking pharmacy?" he learned to say in perfect English, only to tire of using the phrase after a few times. Old people with headaches are just not all that amusing to yell at.

He gets on his motorbike and rides through the hot afternoon air, going straight to the police station. He parks a block away and lights a cigarette, then walks to the station and paces outside the glass door, waiting to be seen. It takes two more cigarettes, but eventually he comes out, Juanma Badero, the cop who likes coke almost as much as Rodrigo does.

"*¿Qué haces?*" he says, and bums a cigarette, just to make it look natural that he's out there smoking with a known drug dealer and sometimes criminal for hire. Sometimes snitch, too.

"Is there an American guy in there, in trouble for fighting in a hospital?"

"Yeah." Badero seems surprised at the inquiry. "Friend of yours?"

"No, no, the guy has enough problems. But I need to see him, out here."

"Forget it. The American embassy wants him to spend the night."

"Well, maybe it's like a hotel. He can be gone for a while but then be back later, yeah?" Rodrigo asks, and reaches into his pockets, pulls out a Chiclets box in which he's stashed a gram. Badero looks at it, and a thin layer of lust rises on his forehead. "I just need to see him for an hour," Rodrigo says.

When Louis is brought his lunch, a guy who looks like a detective leaves a sandwich and a Coke on the plastic table next to the chair, then walks out of the cell, leaving the door open. Then the guy walks to the door nearby, opens that, and goes down the corridor to the reception area. Louis walks out of the cell, then through the back door. He looks around and sees, five feet away, a taxi with the bakery kid sitting in the back, smoking.

Don finishes his sandwich and the iced tea, takes the plate to the table by the door, then goes into the bathroom and finally inspects his face. His nose is still swollen and red, so many of the tiny capillaries now burst, he looks like an old Irish drunk. It hurts to the touch, as does his cheekbone. Better put the bottle of Percocet in his pocket, lest his wife use up pills he will actually need for days to come, especially with the way that self-righteous little prick kneed his balls. He'll sue that bastard for everything he has, keep him in court for years, until all his funds dry up, so that he has to sell every precious item he and Kate bought together.

Don smiles, remembering the G-string now securely in his luggage, then turns his face and rubs his cheek. The only piece of underwear in the entire suitcase. Louis surely has the rest. And they say Don's the pervert.

Don thinks of Kate at thirteen or so, maybe a little younger. Beautiful. The perfect age, really, although she only got prettier and prettier. If only society hadn't filled her head with so much negativity about the two of them. He had thought for years that when she got old enough, she would first forgive him for loving her a little too soon, and then, after a time, come to realize that she loved him, too, and that they could have a life. He tried to explain that to her, to say that it's quite possible to remake yourself, to forget that it started in an admittedly less than ideal way and focus instead on what it became.

At twenty and fifty, sure there would be an age difference and people might think it odd, but only that. They could have made a life together, but she wanted none of that. Told him off, called him names, even threatened to go to the police. He was forced to stay away for years, had no choice. And in that time, of course, she made the life she now has, with this Louis.

Don decides to shave, then put on a fresh blue shirt, a tie almost the same color as the shirt, and his good suit jacket. He needs to both look and feel his best for this, possibly the most important errand of his life. Once dressed, he puts a fresh bandage on his nose, combs his hair, and looks through his toiletry kit for the cologne he brought. There it is, Drakkar Noir, what he wore for years, when he first met Georgina and Kate. This will be a good way to let Kate know it's me, he thinks, and puts a few drops into the center of his hands, rubs them together, then rubs them on his face, his neck, and finally through his hair.

Then Don goes to the door and checks his wallet, filled with the hundreds he knows will make things easier here in Spain.

CHAPTER 58
Ibiza
1994

After arranging to get Louis out of jail, Angela returns to the hospital, hoping to find the doctor.

"I think he's gone for a few days," a nurse tells her.

"Gone?"

"*De vacaciones por unos dias.*"

It's not as if they'd made any headway, but she cannot imagine having to start with another doctor. Angela sees Carolina exit a room at the end of a corridor, and she walks over to the nurse, asks if she has any idea where Santillan might be.

"*Tu amigo se enloqueció,*" Carolina says.

"Yeah, he did go crazy, but for good reason. Her stepfather is a horrible person," Angela says, and Carolina nods slowly, waiting for more details, proof to back up Angela's assertion.

"Is there any way you can get me Santillan's number? His cell? I need to speak to him right away." Angela pulls several fifties from her pocket and tries to put them in Carolina's hands, but the nurse shakes her head no, so Angela stops.

"I would be fired," Carolina says, angry but also maybe a little hurt at the implication she would take a bribe.

"Sorry, I'm sorry. I'm just—this is really important. I have to talk to him. This is so important, Carolina."

"It's okay," Carolina says, and tells her that the doctor sometimes has lunch at a Greek restaurant in the old part of the city, on the hill. "You might try that."

Angela has no address, but the taxi driver doesn't seem to need one. Less than ten minutes later, he deposits her in front of a set of French doors framed in wood. She opens one of those doors into a room so white, it seems to be made of cake frosting. Angela looks around the room, then at the wall of windows that look out onto the blue of the Mediterranean just outside.

In a nearly empty dining room, there he sits, smoking, finishing a glass of wine, and working on his laptop, that amazing view seemingly irrelevant.

Santillan nods when he sees Angela, doesn't seem surprised at all.

"I was desperate," she says, and he looks her up and down, then exhales and stands to pull a chair for her.

"It's all right," he says. "Coffee?"

"No, thank you."

She takes a seat and waits for him, but he seems ready to listen.

"Have something," he says, and when she nods yes, he motions to the waiter to bring what he's having. "I assume you are here to talk me into supporting your desire to take her to Madrid?"

"Yes, but there's new information, Doctor. We found a pregnancy test in her things. And we know she took the test. She thought she was pregnant."

"No," he says. "That would have shown up on the test they did before the X-rays. Blood test, I think, maybe urine. Either way, it would have shown up."

"Well, can you please check? I mean, is there any way that . . . It didn't show up?"

"It's possible but not probable. But I will check."

"Thank you. We need to help the baby, if . . . it's possible. Right?"

Santillan leans into his fist and uses a forefinger to rub at his hairline, then takes a sip of his drink. "Even if she is, which I do not think she is, because of the trauma, she could very easily . . . She probably . . . a fetus under twelve weeks would have difficulty surviving this."

"I know, I know that," Angela says. "But it's important to know. And if the baby is alive, then it's important, isn't it, to get her to a hospital with a prenatal-care unit?"

"That is only relevant if she survives the flight and then lives for at least three more months, if she is three months pregnant. Or pregnant at all." The doctor lights a cigarette, then leans into his hand, so that it looks as if his cheek will take the next drag.

"Is that a lot to hope for?" she says, and holds her breath.

He nods yes. "I'm afraid it is, yes."

"She woke up yesterday; she tried to talk. And I think she recognized me."

"I know, and that is good, but it does not mean she is coming back to you."

She stares at that ocean, trying to fish from it some argument with which to counter his pessimism.

"He, your friend, he hurt the old man," Santillan says, and allows his mouth to form the quickest of smiles before looking down at his lap. When he looks back up again, his expression is serious.

"Yeah," she says. "I think he broke his nose."

"Not broken, but close."

"He deserves a lot more than a broken nose."

"May I ask you something very personal? If Ms. Harrington's father was not here, would you want to do this? Are you doing this because of him?"

She takes a toothpick with bits of red cellophane on its end, uses it to poke the tablecloth. The memory of Louis holding Don against the wall flashes in her mind, makes her feel good, actually, the way it did in the moment.

Angela looks around the restaurant, its view of the sea, its shiny wood tables, so much care and reason for optimism in this place, this view. She gets it, sees the irony that, perhaps yet again, Don plays a principal role. Whether you're acting in accordance with or in opposition to him, there he is, center stage, the ringmaster. There seems to be no way of exorcising him.

"I don't know for sure, but I think we would, even if Don wasn't here. Doctor, if she was your wife, what would you do?"

"I would be crazy with fear, like you, and I would want to fly her home, too."

"Is there a benefit at all in flying her to Madrid?"

Santillan shrugs his answer. "Some benefit, yes, maybe."

"Will you help us?"

He nods yes slowly. "I am on vacation starting tomorrow. Someone else, probably Mendoza, will be in charge of her care. But I can call right now and ask them to give her a blood test. If she is pregnant, then my boss will allow the transfer."

"That's . . . Thank you, Doctor. Let's say she is pregnant and you do discharge her. Would you consider accompanying us to Madrid?"

He closes his eyes for a second and nods yes.

"You would, really?"

"Yes."

"Why?"

"I don't know," he says, and shrugs, reaches into his pants pocket for some money, which he looks at briefly, then leaves on the table, stubs out his cigarette, and starts putting away his laptop, folding his glasses—a daily routine, probably. "Against very bad odds, I want you to succeed."

Outside the restaurant, after exchanging cell numbers, Angela tells the doctor that Kate could be flown to Madrid today, before sunset, if everything is ready.

"I doubt we can do this so quickly. Maybe," he says. "Hire Carolina to accompany you if possible. It's important to have a good nurse," he says, closing the door of her taxi. "See you."

Angela's nervous, arriving at the hotel, worried, for some reason, that Don will be there. If she had a gun, would she use it on Don?

She might. She's fired a gun only once, when profiling an actor who took her to target practice. She'd gone with him to a club in the Valley somewhere and shot off rounds from a Beretta, or something that sounded equally Italian and sleek. It was empowering, just as the actor had promised—for both of them. Afterward, eating a spinach salad from which he violently pushed aside almond shavings, the actor finally opened up about his process, his childhood . . . all the memories that shooting a gun seemed to have finally unlocked. She was thankful for the experience, even if her palm was still numb hours later.

Don is not in the room, thankfully, but Louis is. She is so relieved, Angela crosses the room and practically runs to him. She throws her arms around him, and he holds her tight and kisses her shoulder.

"Thank you," he says. "You saved my life by getting me out."

"Santillan agreed to go with us," Angela tells him, and he smiles, nods yes, and looks down.

"God, good news, finally," he says, "Let's get out of here, get her home."

CHAPTER 59

Salvador
1994

"Cakes, cakes, and more cakes," Hugh says, squeezing dainty silver tongs around the waist of a lemon loaf, which he places on a plate and carries in the center of his manicured hand to the breakfast table. It's 8:00 A.M. and it seems as if no one is awake, either inside or outside the hotel.

Kate stands at the wall of windows of this third-floor dining room, huge, many of the panes cracked, and looks out over the tiny streets of the Pelourinho and, beyond that, to the bay, still and blue-gray, with an orange sky above it, like the backdrop for a Broadway show.

The streets below are quiet, and so slick, it would appear to have rained. Did it rain, or do city workers hose down the roads? she wonders.

Kate thinks of a Miami Beach boardwalk where once, as she prepared to go for an early-morning run, she watched a wide, squat tank of a machine roll over the boardwalk, spewing disinfectant from jets along its sides. This happened every single morning right after daybreak. The boardwalk, lined with soft plants and expensive sea grasses, had to be cleaned of all the excess and the stains of the night before.

She goes back to the table, where her coffee and Hugh await.

"Everything is full of bloody sugar," he says. "Don't they know old people like me are watching our figures?"

He's wearing a colorful shirt and looks youthful but incredibly jowly. His cheeks remind her of those fancy draped velvet curtains in old movie theaters.

"How old are you?" Kate asks.

"None of your fucking business," he says, and drinks from her coffee cup. "How can you drink milk in your coffee? Milk is for babies. Which is why decent human beings are lactose-intolerant."

"What about the French? They have milk products at every meal."

"As I said." He takes yet another gulp of her coffee and again makes a face.

"Get your own coffee," she says, and gets up to fetch him a cup.

"You're a dear," he says when she returns.

"And you're a lazy old man."

Kate met Hugh when he was giving a lecture at Berkeley on the ethics of cosmetic surgery.

"To begin as well as conclude, there are no ethics in cosmetic surgery or in any other specialty," he said, pronouncing the word *speciale-ity.* "Thank you. Lovely being with you today. Now, where does one drink around here?"

She took him drinking for hours in the Tenderloin, SoMa, the Castro. Hugh professed that day to have arrived at an age where backgammon on the laptop was about as good as trying to bed women while away in foreign lands.

"My wife, naturally, is disappointed because I come home wanting to have sex with her, but she's a good sport about it. Lies back and thinks of England," he said, and winked at her.

"I bet you do all right."

That very night, Kate asked Hugh if he wanted to get involved with a group of San Francisco dancers and sex workers who wanted to help women in other countries who didn't benefit from the protections of progressive San Francisco.

"I'm a cosmetic surgeon. I could do their tits for them, but other than that . . . no."

"You could learn about sexually transmitted diseases and come help us."

"Oh no, that involves sores and . . . such. Oh no. Also sounds like charity," Hugh said with a completely straight face.

"You'll like it. It'll give you a sense of accomplishment."

"Do you know how much money I have? I don't need a sense of accomplishment."

"Sense of selflessness. Have you ever felt that?"

"No. Not interested," he said.

She laughed and asked for his card, said she would send all the details.

"I'll throw it straight to the trash," he said.

Now, Hugh found a savory option, a croissant, on which he's just spread some butter. He licks his knife.

"Remember the girl from last night, the younger one, the chubby one?" she asks.

"One of the uh . . . doctors?"

"Yes."

"Not really, but what about her?"

"I can't get her out of my mind. I think I want to find her."

"And to what end? To tell her she is your long-lost daughter? That you are taking her to America, where she will now toil cleaning hotel rooms? You out of your mind?"

"I don't know, but I have to do something, Hugh."

"Well, you are. You are here doing something. Look, we've come to do our bit of good. Prevent a few unwanted pregnancies, help some girls live to see another profession, by default if nothing else . . . once they get too old or fat for this one. It's the good we do. We are lucky, as you have told me many times, to have found a way to do something. And that is all. Full stop."

"But if I see her and I can sense she needs help, why is it wrong to try to help her?"

"It's not wrong, just completely futile," he says. "And you know that far, far better than I do."

She stares at him and considers leaving right now, just walking out, down the stairs, onto the street. She knows she could find the girl. In a day, two tops, she could find her.

"Come on, now, let's do be realistic."

He's right. It's better to go and speak with dozens of girls, educate them, "empower" them. She's come to hate that word, with its simplistic concept of power, but their work on Ilhéus just might make those girls stronger, and that, in turn, will help lead some into a different line of work or at least into a healthier way to do what they do. Finding one girl here in Salvador would do nothing.

"Oh, look, it's Paris and Rome," Hugh says about the Canadians, who stand at the door, looking completely confused. "God bless, I think it's their first buffet."

There's a plan and she will stick with it. That's best when you get depressed or crazy-feeling or just lost. Have a plan and stick to it. They'll stay in Ilhéus for three days, pass out the birth-control kits, see any girls who need to be seen, then go back to Salvador, and then she'll fly to Spain for vacation.

CHAPTER 60
Ibiza
1994

They hurriedly pack a few last things, trying to get out of the room as quickly as possible. They move some of Louis's clothes and his laptop to her suitcase, since it's possible he could be stopped and arrested. The plan is for them to travel separately, in case the police are at the hospital. She'll get Carolina to agree to go with them, then meet Louis at the airport.

"I'm going to go to an AmEx office and get about three thousand for you to have," he says, so that Angela can make bail for him if necessary. If it's for more than just a minor offense, she is to call his business partner in San Francisco and his father in Encino and explain what happened, ask them to help.

"One more thing, but I don't know if you'll want it," he says, and shows her the gun. "Do you want it?"

She stares at the gun, then at Louis. "This is what that guy brought?"

"Yeah. Look, I know exactly what he's capable of," he says. "You want to take it just in case?"

She pulls her purse and opens it, lets him tuck it in between her wallet and sunglasses.

"This is crazy."

"You won't have to use it," he says. "Don's busy licking his wounds."

They decide to get something to eat and take a cab to a café four blocks away, near the water. Sitting on big white plastic chairs, a blue awning above and tanned tourists everywhere—only tourists would eat at four o'clock—they feel almost normal.

"You wanna call the doctor? See if there's news?"

Angela rings Santillan, but the call goes to voice mail.

"Is there someone back home?" Louis asks. "You have a girl-friend?"

"No. Not at the moment. I'm married to my work. I have a cat."

"Worse things you could have than a cat," he says. "Are you, you know, that word? Happy?"

"Am I happy? I don't know. I'm not unhappy, a little under-happy, kind of like underwhelmed, but that feels so ungrateful to say, you know? I can feed myself very well. I own my place. My family's healthy. I have nieces and nephews, good friends. I should be happy. Right?"

"Yes, you definitely should," he says, and smiles at her in a way that makes her not just understand why Kate and Louis are together but actually feel some sort of relief over it. "But I still haven't found what I'm looking for." Louis sings the words from the U2 song.

"Exactly."

"I think that's the dilemma of our First World, that it's so good on paper, but then in reality, I dunno, something's missing. But you feel like such a jerk for thinking that. You have no right," Louis says.

"Exactly, and I don't really . . . I don't want to chant."

"No. I'm not a chanter, either," he says, and runs his hands over his head, closes his eyes tight. "She's really proud of you. You know that, right?"

"Even though I'm a sellout. Working for a magazine like the one I work for?"

"Well, you know how she is. The high standards are for her only. The rest of us, you know, we always get a pass. Even when we're wrong."

"Especially when we're wrong."

He nods.

"She defends what she loves."

"That she does," he says as Angela's cell phone rings.

It's a Spanish number. "¿Sí?"

She listens and nods yes to Louis, whose eyes go wide. When she asks the doctor if there's a way to know how many weeks, Louis understands, and he pushes his chair from the table and leans forward, clutching at his head. "Christ. Jesus Christ," he whispers.

Angela covers the mouthpiece with one hand and puts the other hand on his arm. "Six weeks maybe, he thinks."

"Why the fuck didn't they know this sooner?" he says, and people at the other tables turn around to look at them.

"¿Qué pasó, Doctor? ¿Cómo es que no sabían?"

Louis tries to calm down as Angela listens to the doctor. "Ask if they can do a sonogram," he whispers.

She talks a bit, then finally puts down the phone.

"He says they'll do one in Madrid."

"How could they not have known?"

"He said they did a urine test instead of a blood test, and I guess that gets more false results."

"Is the baby in danger, then?"

"He didn't know. In Madrid, they'll know more."

"Madrid," he says, and rubs his eyes with one hand.

"He says everything's set. He can go in the ambulance, once the transfer happens. Meet us at the airport."

"All right. Well, I'm just gonna go to the restroom. Be right back," he says.

Angela watches him, can see perfectly well that he's in the lobby, making a call.

When he comes back, he tosses a pack of cigarettes on the table.

"Who'd you call?"

"A friend. Just want to be sure no one gets in our way."

"We're almost there, Louis. We almost have her out. And you were arrested yesterday, and could be again."

"I know. Look, I don't want to hurt you by saying this, but I want to defend her and I want to defend this child more than anything. I could almost forget Don, forget everything, knowing what I know now. But I have to be sure. I can't leave anything uncertain now. You understand?"

CHAPTER 61

Salvador
1994

Once Kate gets to Spain, she'll go to a pharmacy, get a test, and know for sure. Maybe she'll call Louis and ask him to join her there. She misses him so much. If it turns out that she is pregnant, she knows he'll fly out.

In the cab to the airport, Hugh mutters the entire way about how late they are. What if they can't get on the afternoon flight to Ilhéus?

"We'll stay in the Pelourhino and find the girl," Kate says, and he shakes his head. The Canadians want to ask what girl, but they refrain.

"You know *pelourinho* means 'whipping post.' It's where they whipped and sold the African slaves," Clarissa says, and everyone in the cab nods at her.

"I didn't know that," Kate says. Clarissa looks proud of her knowledge, and Lucy proud of her friend.

Hugh's worries prove unfounded. They have no problem getting on the flight to Ilhéus. Once there, they hire a taxi that takes them to Canasveiras, two hours south.

Because of its proximity to a famous golf course and to popular beaches, at night the little town attracts men seeking comfort.

The local doctors know and like Kate and Hugh, sometimes they have even set a few cases aside—not so much to review with

Hugh, since he's not a gynecologist, but to discuss with Kate. A sort of freelance sociologist, she's tried on many occasions to help various girls conceptualize a different future for themselves.

They arrive in Canasveiras at 8:00 P.M. and drive over a small bridge to the island where they'll stay, just minutes from the center of town. They are staying in a house owned by an American woman who works in the film industry, whom Kate befriended years ago at a restaurant in San Francisco.

The house is white-walled, with dark gray floors, three bedrooms, and as many bathrooms. Each room is simple, with not very thick mattresses on beds draped in yellow-and-pink plastic mosquito netting.

"I thought film industry people were superficial and liked luxury," Hugh says. "She still hasn't bought new fucking sheets."

"She's a documentarian," Kate says.

"Ah." He sighs and looks disparagingly at the bedding.

The best parts of the house are the double doors that open to a terrace with a long cement table, with L-shaped benches covered in thick blue cloth. The owner at least thought to place deck chairs everywhere, and two hammocks. Just beyond the terrace is a narrow dirt path that leads to a wooden gate, and beyond that is the sea.

The Canadians have found a closet with clean bedding and have offered to change all the beds.

"Thanks," Kate says. "That would be great."

They'll see enough on their night visits, no need to feel uncomfortable at the house.

Hugh asks Kate to go for a walk, see the water. He's already changed into a bathing suit.

"When you're done with the beds, come out to see the beach," he says to the girls.

Kate never ceases to feel thrilled at the sight of the beach—so wide, with forty feet of soft sand, then what feels like a mile of darker, wetter sand, cooled by the ocean but packed hard. She remembers riding a bike on this beach once, going up and down it for hours, seeing almost no one, sometimes riding so close to the water that the bottom of the pedal and her heel would graze the sea.

"Amazing, huh?" Hugh says, patting his hairy belly. "Look at this stomach," he says. "I used to be thin."

"Did you really?"

"Yes, I really did," he says mockingly. "To be fair, it is filled with delicious food," he says, and pats it like he's knocking on a wall to ascertain where the studs are. "Pâté corner, here, lamb-roast square right here. . . ." He looks up to see if she's entertained, but she's not even listening. "Be a dear and put the poor working girl out of your mind. This is depressing enough without thinking about it twenty-four/seven," Hugh says, and pulls a joint and book of matches from the pocket inside his bathing suit.

"You flew with that?" she says, incredulous.

"Yes. Up my bottom. Go on, have some," he says, and offers the joint.

She shakes her head no and starts walking into the water. "Why would someone need to go to another country for sex?"

"I thought we agreed to forget?"

"We agreed to no such thing."

"You are the very fucking definition of a bleeding-heart liberal. If your heart bleeds, do you know what happens? You die, and then you are of no use to anyone. Take it from a doctor."

"Why do they come here for sex?"

"Well, because at home, they would feel constrained. Perhaps they live with Mother. Or maybe because their money goes a lot further in a place like this, what with the exchange rate. Who knows. Stop thinking of it as a feeling thing. For these girls, it's like giving a pedicure."

"No. It is not. Have you ever given someone a blow job?"

"Not on purpose," he says.

"I'm serious," she says.

"Oh, I know. I know you are. Maybe they come here because what they like is illegal in their country."

"Exactly."

"Right, well good. Got that noted. Just smoke this, please. And be quiet."

"I don't want any," she says.

It was different in San Francisco. The customers at Swank were honest, straightforward, even nice. Some of the girls felt they were actually doing good with their work, saw lap dances as a form of charity. The guys would walk up to the door with their twenty-dollar entry fee, pockets full of tens and fives for tips, hair combed, cologne on, best shirt, best pants, as if going on a date and way too optimistic about how far those bills and a smile would get them. All they want is a feeling of sexual excitement, she'd think, passing one on the street. Seeing her in a long black coat, boots, and sunglasses, he had no idea that soon she would be in a tiny outfit, serving him drinks. And it wasn't just johns who wanted this.

Every single one of the professors to whom Kate had spoken about her master's thesis had gone to the club. One by one, they stopped by, wearing their finest "sexy outfits" of black turtlenecks and jeans. And every one of them, eventually, had said something like, "You know, you're certainly attractive enough to be a dancer." As if that were a compliment. Every single last one of them, including the female professors, had looked at her at some point with that gleam—Could we, would we . . . should we? Everyone wants a little rise, a thrill, she realized.

Thinking of this now, Kate tells herself she should understand. She herself loves sex, and chases this same feeling unabashedly, thinks of it as a gift. So why does she blame the professors or the johns for wanting what she wants—something essentially normal and good?

"Let's get some rest, shall we?" Hugh says, and offers his arm.

The next day they're awakened by the cleaning lady, whom Kate and Hugh have now known for three years. She's come bearing gifts of rolls, coffee, a pineapple, and mangoes for breakfast. The Canadians seem tired or disappointed and barely touch the food as everyone sits outside at the cement table drinking coffee, smoking, and filling bags for tonight with condoms, lubricant, and alcohol rubs. The cleaning lady, Mireilla, shakes her head and laughs as she walks by and Hugh offers up a condom.

"*A mi edad?*" she says, referring to her age.

"Never too late to start," he says.

Everyone goes for a swim; then the Canadians nap as Kate and Hugh walk, in merciless early-afternoon heat and humidity, to the car rental in town. They're told only beach buggies are left, the open-top dune buggies painted bright primary colors, which tourists love. Last time they were here, they actually considered renting a buggy, because of that very popularity with tourists. Its loud, mufflerless exhaust system would act as a siren song on certain dark streets, telling the prostitutes, Clients coming.

Tonight, when the girls come out of the shadows, they see an Englishman who looks like a well-fed John Kerry, a tall American woman with short hair and a pretty face, and two Canadian girls perched on the back of the buggy, looking . . . scared?

Sometimes the prostitutes look disappointed, other times happy to see the contraception mobile.

"*Para você,*" Kate says. "For you," passing out condoms. Then she asks if they need to see a doctor: "*Quer falar con um doctor?*"

"*Naõ,*" the girls say, and giggle. Some ask if she's the doctor.

"*Naõ, ele,*" Kate says, and points to Hugh.

"*Ele?*" they say, and giggle some more.

Hugh doesn't look like a doctor to them, in his colorful T-shirt and shorts, that smile so big, the eyes too twinkly for him to be a doctor.

"*Loco Ingles, mais boa pessoa.*" Kate explains Hugh is a crazy Englishman but a good person, and he usually winks just about then.

"Might help if you didn't wink like you would like to date them," Kate says.

"I am speaking their language. Who wants to see a serious, old, mean doctor? Why not instead a handsome, jovial gentleman of a certain age?"

Clarissa laughs, and Lucy announces that her best friend back home did some hooking on a phone sex line.

"Very sanitary that way," Hugh says. "Good for her."

Lucy explains that it wasn't on the phone per se, just that she found her clients on the phone.

"Oh, I see." Hugh pretends to just now understand. He thinks these girls are silly, even for twenty-year-olds, and intends not to say one sincere thing to them the entire trip.

They avoid the prettier areas on the mouth of the river, where the restaurants are painted yellow, blue, or pink, just like those in the Pelourhino, and are well lit. Tourists sit outside these establishment and eat nice meals.

Kate, Hugh, and the girls go instead to the center of town, to one of the squares where the locals hang out. Less colorful but just as busy, the plaza is lit by canopies of big white bulbs and surrounded by small bars or restaurants, whose owners stand next to a chalkboard menu at the door, a white towel draped over their shoulders, waiting for customers. Most people, young and broke, buy dinner from the sausage seller and cups of juice or beer from the guy hauling his white Styrofoam coolers like saddlebags.

The people relaxing here are the ones who work in the town's three banks, its two grocery stores, the handful of pharmacies, the dozens of bathing suit or surf shops, and its eight or so big hotels. Most of them are here to meet others of their station, to flirt, start a courtship. But the foreign tourists are also known to come here to look for prostitutes, so they walk around the plaza with a beer in hand, trying to make eye contact with any group of girls they pass, uneducated in the language of young-girl fashion, so that they can't tell the difference between sexy, fun outfits and working-girl outfits.

Kate always begins to feel sick at this juncture, because instinctively she knows she will see something difficult to forget.

"Come on, let's take a break," Hugh says, and buys two beers, one for the Canadians to share and another for him and Kate. The girls lead them to a small wall where a few older locals congregate.

As they lean there, passing the beer back and forth, Kate watches a girl of about fourteen, who stands next to a yellow moped with two other girls, who look older. All three are laughing loudly, for the sake of the men who walk around and around. Kate watches a guy in his forties walk by the girls and say hello, then keep walking. He goes to the beer man and buys four beers, then goes back and gives the drinks to the girls.

"Smooth operator," Hugh says.

The man wears khaki shorts and a Hawaiian-looking shirt; he has a thick black watch on his arm. Kate thinks he looks like a Trader Joe's employee.

Finally, he makes his move, starts talking to the younger girl, paying her the most attention. You can see it from a mile away, the seduction. Within three or four minutes, they're walking down the street together, heading toward an alley.

"I'm gonna follow them," Kate says.

"Why?" Hugh asks. "When she comes back, we can talk to her and all her friends together. The poor girl is working. Leave her alone."

"I can't."

"Oh for God's sake," Hugh says, and pushes himself unsteadily off the wall. "Why are you doing this?"

"I don't know, just to see."

CHAPTER 62
Ibiza
1994

For Rodrigo the plan is simple: get as high as possible, both to make it easier and as a reward. He deserves it. No one arrested him or got in his way at all. On the contrary, fat Badero and his hungry nose caved in minutes, and not only did the American woman give him money to get the guy out of jail, but then that guy Louis gave him a lot more money to come to this hotel and stop the old man from going to the hospital anymore.

Rodrigo agreed and bought a little more coke. All good, except that now he has to get the old man into this car somehow. He could forget it, leave town, go party for a few days. By the time he's back at the bakery, the Americans will all be gone. And if they're not, so what? So he didn't do what he was paid to do? Call the police, file a complaint.

But, at the same time, this guy trusted him and gave him a lot of money—a thousand dollars—to make sure the old man goes nowhere near the hospital. Rodrigo would prefer, if possible, to keep his word.

There they are, the old man and his wife, tipping the bellman, the guy in a nice suit, a Band-Aid on his nose, the woman in a pantsuit, big sunglasses on her face. He watches them for a few minutes. They're tipping the doorman now—oh, everyone gets a little something—making sure all their luggage is there.

Rodrigo puts the car he rented from his cousin, a Mercedes 3000 SL, into drive and pulls fifty feet forward to the curb, then exits the car, pulling the monkey hat over his hair. Amazing that anyone would still wear a hat like this. And the suit hasn't been worn since his father's funeral. Baggy on him, but so what? No one expects a chauffeur to have the best of suits.

"*Buenos días,*" he says, and takes the two pieces of luggage. Fuck they're heavy. Rodrigo moves quickly to the trunk and places them there, one on each side, with plenty of room in the middle for the old man's body. "*¿Listos?*" he says, and puts a big smile on his face, goes to the back door, opens it, then reaches out and cups the woman's elbow, smiling at how much it feels like the end of a baguette. "*Madame.*"

The old man looks at the doorman, who nods yes, it's fine to take this car. Rodrigo nods at the doorman. "*Te veo en un ratito,*" he says, telling him he'll see him in a while.

Don's instincts have always been terrific— about people, about business, everything—which is why he doesn't trust this driver. Why would the hotel hire a man with hair like this—sloppy and long? But he gets in the car anyway, mostly because it's so damned hot outside.

In the car, he gets only more suspicious. The man drives too fast, has the radio on, and smells of cigarettes and even perspiration. It doesn't make sense.

"Is this the way to the airport?" Don asks.

"Yes, yes, the fast way. I am from here, grow up here, in Ibiza, my home," he says, and smiles into the rearview mirror. The old man doesn't listen to anything he says, just mutters "Uh-huh" and looks out the window nervously. How far can he get out of town before this old man starts to get really curious and then angry and then tries to get out of the car?

When that happens, Rodrigo will look in the rearview mirror and say something like, "You are going to the municipal airport, right?" And the old man will say, "No, no, the international airport," and Rodrigo will pretend such embarrassment and apologize so profusely that the old man will calm down. He'll tell them to have a drink, to pop open the bar back there and have a drink, on him. And the old man will do it, or maybe his wife. When they go to open the bar door, he or she won't be able to, because Rodrigo made sure no one would be able to. He'll pull the car over somewhere quiet, then go back there to help open the bar, telling a story about driving some famous American star. As he's talking and pulling out the bar that won't budge, he'll knock out the old lady, then the man. He'll tie up the old man and put him in the trunk, leave the woman there by the side of the road. Then he'll drive the old man far away, where he's not likely to see a passing car for days. Two days, Louis said. Leave him where it will take two days for anyone to find him. He will take the wallet and every other belonging and give it to his friend Jairo, who will make sure it passes through several dirty hands before the cops find it and deduce that the old man and his wife were the victims of a simple robbery.

If only there wasn't a blue light in the mirror, and the low but impossible-to-ignore *waaooo* sound of the cop's siren, pulling him over. Shit! Almost any cop in Ibiza will recognize him. But why is he even being pulled over? He was driving fine. Maybe the car's stolen. Shit. Rodrigo opens the window, takes off the hat, and prays that he will see an unfamiliar face.

Even before the cop has finished arresting Rodrigo, the old man and his wife have taken a cab and left him behind, their luggage, too, not wanting to slow down for anything.

CHAPTER 63
An Empty Room in Ibiza
1994

In the cab on the way to the hospital, Louis and Angela hold hands, like a pair of nervous kids on a first date. The most important thing, they agree, is never to let Kate out of their sight.

Angela goes straight to the nurses' station and is happy to see Carolina there.

"I have to talk with you. I need to ask if you would consider coming with us, right now, to Madrid. We could pay you well."

"To Madrid? Why?"

"We're taking her there, flying her there. Santillan agreed to discharge her."

"Yes, I know, but . . ." Carolina shakes her head no and seems confused by this.

"What? Is everything okay?" Angela asks.

"Yes, but she was already discharged. She was taken to the airport, no?"

"No, she wasn't. No, I don't . . . Who discharged her? Santillan?"

"I think so," Carolina says, and looks for the chart, so nervous, she knocks over two others. "Oh, no. Here, here . . . Dr. Mendoza," she says.

Francisco Carreras Irrigatu Mendoza's signature is there, and next to it is Donald Williams's.

The look in Angela's eyes scares the nurse. "There was a mistake? The doctor said everyone had agreed to take her to Madrid. He said finally the family was not fighting anymore. I think Santillan is with her."

"How long ago did they take her?"

"I don't know. Maybe half an hour. I thought everyone was together now. I'm sorry I . . ."

Angela walks away while the nurse is still talking about how it happened, the way that Don thanked everyone. You couldn't think anything was wrong. Everyone had come to an agreement.

"Louis, she was discharged to Don and Georgina half an hour ago," Angela says.

CHAPTER 64

Salvador
1994

The girl and her john walk a couple of blocks up a slight hill paved with cobblestones, then turn right into a small dark street, at which point Hugh reaches out and grabs Kate's arm.

"Okay, stop right here. Stop now."

"Sometimes you just need to get in the way of it," Kate says.

"No. No, you don't. She's worked to get him here; she's about to finish with this client and get paid. Your efforts will only ensure lots of effort for nothing, and piss her off. I assure you," Hugh says.

He's right, of course.

"If it's not enough to do what we do, then I think you seriously need to think about not coming anymore," he says.

"This is my last trip."

"Good. It really should be your last," he says.

"Come on," she says, and pulls away, starts down the alley. She leans forward and sees them, sixty feet away, standing against a car, next to each other, the girl's left hand still holding the beer. You can just see the shadow of movement that tells you she's using her right hand to pleasure him.

About five minutes later, the girl and the man walk out from the alley, talking. Or at least he's talking, in broken Portuguese.

"I am from a small town but with very nice chocolate," he's saying. "My country is famous for its chocolates."

"Amazing what passes for postcoital conversation these days," Hugh says, and reaches out, clasps his hand around Kate's wrist, a gesture more of restraint than affection. "Now, now. She's fine. Safe. Right?"

They both watch the girl and man walk past them and back to the plaza.

"I guess."

That night, Hugh and the girls drink caxaisa on the back patio, while Kate sips pineapple juice. They light candles and play a guitar with about three strings.

Eventually, Kate slips away and down the path, heading toward the gate that leads to the beach, still upset by the square and the girl, all of it. She pulls hard on the wooden gate, bleached gray by wind and sea, and steps onto that powdery sand. She pushes her feet into its coolness but walks toward the water, where the sand is harder and colder. Above, an orange moon with a halo around it stands watch. Rain tomorrow? Down a few hundred yards, three tiki lights jut from the sand at right angles. Did the wind knock them over? They are meant to light the way into a café with a couple of plastic tables on the sand. Other than the flicker of flame from the leaning tiki lamps, nothing moves.

But then she hears laughter and sees two thin bodies far in the distance. She can just make out their bodies running and angling almost as oddly as the tiki lights. The peals of laughter make her imagine both of them using the sides of their feet to slice at the water and wet each another. She closes her eyes and listens to their laughter, wills it to come inside, wash away these thoughts. But she can't stop the girl from the Pelourinho coming to mind.

Is the girl home yet? Sleeping curled up in some pastel-colored blanket, maybe next to a stuffed animal given to her by someone who actually cared about her? Or still out working?

Hugh eventually comes looking for her, walks out to where she stands ankle-deep in cool water.

"Hello, friend. What're you doing?"

"Nothing. Do you know what grunion are? Do you have them in England?"

"Is that like a bunion?" he asks.

"No," she says, and laughs. "It's a fish, and once a year or so, they come out of the water and end up on the beach, in California anyway, and people, hundreds, come out and grab up the fish. At night, they come out at night."

"Sounds strange, people grabbing at fish," he says.

"It is, but fun, too. My dad took me to do that, when I was little. My real dad. He loved the ocean, everything about it, any water. He was a surfer and a diver. A swimmer," she says, and looks down at the water, wipes the snot trailing down her chin. "I don't think we ate the fish. I think we threw them back. I'm pretty sure we did."

"I'm sure you did. Come on now, buddy," Hugh says, and puts an arm around her.

"Why do I hate the johns so much?" Kate asks him.

"I dunno. Why? I could sort of . . . ask politely, but you know that's not me," he says. "So I'll just come out and ask. Did you ever trade sex for something other than alleged love, something more tangible?"

"Not that I recall," she says.

"'Not that I recall.' I see," Hugh says, and squeezes her shoulder. "So, then?"

She looks at him and shakes her head. "He was in love with me, you know. Proposed marriage at my high school graduation."

"Teacher?"

"No. Stepfather."

"Ah, I see. And how did you . . . What did you do?"

"I told him to go fuck himself. And then we all went for a nice dinner. Because I was, you know, salutatorian," she says.

"Aha, very good. High achiever," Hugh says, and pulls her to him. She cries for what feels like ages and he holds on tight, as if she were his kid to console.

CHAPTER 65
Ibiza
1994

Driving up the small road that leads to the office of the aviation company, Don sees between the brown grass and the heat rising off the tar of the runway a Learjet with the name TRANSPORTE MÉDICO DE EUROPA written on the tail in small elegant letters. Don tried to convince the cop to come with them in case anything happened, but the cop said he had better things to do than drive along beside an ambulance like an escort, didn't believe Don that something about the driver made him distrust everything. He had picked them up at the hotel, probably hired by someone.

"Normal scam. Just another druggie," the cop said.

"A druggie with access to that Mercedes?"

"Believe me. I've worked on this island my whole life."

"Did we do the right thing?" Georgina asks, but she doesn't bother to look at him.

"Of course we did," he says, and watches Santillan absentmindedly run his fingers along the line that hangs from the IV pole next to Kate. The doctor writes something on a clipboard.

As soon as she's in her own room, in London, Don will find a way to take much better care of her, buy lip balms and nice creams, maybe even a nice perfume—things to make her feel good, cared for. He cannot wait to finally have some time alone with her, tell her how he feels.

They pull up between the office and the airplane. There's a man inspecting the plane's tires—the captain, probably, in a short-sleeved white shirt and a tie. Don looks at his watch: 5:10. A bit later than he'd hoped, but so what. That idiot Louis is planning to take off at six. They have time.

"We are meeting Angela and Louis here?" Santillan asks.

"Yes, of course," Don says. "I think the nurse is on board."

"Oh, okay. Who is it?" Santillan asks.

"Someone this company recommended. They hired her," Don says, and starts to leave the ambulance.

Santillan wonders why they didn't hire Carolina, and he decides to call Angela.

"Carolina could not come?" he asks Angela.

"Are you with the parents?"

"Yes," Santillan says.

"They didn't . . . The parents were not supposed to be with her. Don just found a way. Please don't let them fly her somewhere."

"Ah, I see," Santillan says as the captain opens the back of the ambulance to help him take the patient on board. Santillan nods at the captain but stays on the phone, listening to Angela direct him to stall as much as possible. Before disconnecting, he looks at the mother, who is staring at her daughter with the most focus he's ever seen.

"*¿Hola, Doctor? ¿Listo?*" the captain says, asking Santillan if he's ready.

"*No, todavía no, un momento.*"

CHAPTER 66
Salvador
1994

Kate wakes up first, makes coffee, then packs. When Hugh awakens, wild-haired and in his white Skivvies, she tells him she got a call from Spain and must leave early. One of the boys she's meeting there has had to cancel; the other has been left alone. She can change her ticket, not a problem.

"Really?" Hugh says, confused. She can tell he stayed up many more hours strumming that alley cat of a guitar and sipping caxaisa. "Hold on a minute. I have to pee," he says, and goes into the hallway bathroom, comes back out a moment later. "Where are you going? You're not going to Salvador for the nurse, are you? I meant to say 'doctor.' This isn't about that young doctor working in the square, is it?"

"No," she says. "I'm done with doctors and nurses."

"Aren't we all?" he says, but he's squinting at her, trying to figure out if she's telling the truth.

Kate stays at the same hotel down the hill from the Pelourinho. At 9:00 P.M., she goes to the same outdoor café they'd been to days ago, where, once again, a group of girls waits outside, just like the other night. But no sign of the girl. Kate goes for a walk down each street of this square, but still nothing. She comes back, sits again, and orders a soda and a sandwich, eats slowly. Still nothing. At eleven, she starts to head back to her hotel.

The café in front of the church had been getting ready to close, but here it's a different story. The cramped little streets are tight with young European tourists walking with beer cups, and groups of sun-kissed travelers still hoping to dine al fresco at narrow tables pressed to the outside walls of restaurants. The streets really aren't wide enough to accommodate this, but the owners have made it work, staggering it so that everyone can make some money by seating at least a couple of groups outside.

Kate allows herself to be pushed forward by the crowd, still looking for the girl. Eventually, she starts to feel a little dizzy, as she has for several days now, usually only in the morning. Kate picks a small restaurant set just above the street. It has a long bar right near the doors, from which she can see the streets. She orders a soda water and keeps looking through the windows, although hardly very focused. So many people pass by below that it's virtually impossible to find any one person.

Eventually, people at the outside tables start to stand. Inside, too, the excitement is palpable as younger people rush to the windows.

The drums get louder and louder, and more tourists push back chairs and scramble to grab their cameras. Here comes the music school group! Kate goes to the French doors, where they will pass right in front of her.

It's a big one: Some twenty women dance at the front; they're of all ethnicities, between the ages of fifteen and thirty, all moving their hips so fast in what Kate assumes is a samba. Next comes the percussion section, with their beaded gourds and silver instruments that look like shiny rolling pins. Finally, there are three rows of *batucada* drums. Some resemble conga drums; others are big and round, attached to the player's hips with straps and hanging down low near their knees; still others are huge and are pounded on with mallets. The drummers are mostly guys; they're of all types, from white boys with rasta knit caps and David Beckham faces in shorts and tennies to dark black men in jeans and open shirts, wearing woven leather sandals. The drummers start to sway as they play, then step forward at the same time, a bit of choreography that makes the crowd cheer. The dancers, the drummers, the percussionists—everyone gives their all to that music.

Kate's eyes go back to the girls in front, the dancers with the huge smiles. You can't ignore those smiles as they dance to the fast beat.

This is joyous. This is joy, Kate thinks as she watches a European-looking young man with lots of curly blond hair and a Brazilian girl in a minidress dance—the girl pushing and pushing his scrawny little Norwegian or Swedish body to keep up.

Kate's certainly not the only person loving this. At a table nearby sits a family of four. Mom is bouncing a toddler on her lap, a girl of two or three. Suddenly, the little girl grows impatient, kicking her legs out and her arms back, on the verge of crying. The mom, maybe in an effort to change the mood, stands the girl on her legs and points to the musicians.

"Look! Look at that," she says, as if the *bloco* has only just come into sight. The baby seems uncertain whether to fall for this and allow herself to be distracted or throw a tantrum, as planned. Kate watches as the baby turns and looks at her mom, then back to the musicians and points, starts to clap, now showing her mom the very same thing she was shown.

"Yes," the mother squeals, and claps along with her. "Yes! See. Music, yes!"

If a child, any child, your child, saw the dancing and heard the music, she, too, would smile and tap her feet, maybe clap, or even dance.

Kate imagines what it would feel like to hold an infant daughter on her shoulders so that she could watch the parade. Or to let the child dance on her lap, the tiny sandals barely weighing anything on the tops of her legs, her hands firmly gripping those chubby little legs so the little girl can clap and dance and know that nothing bad will happen.

Every few minutes, that baby would probably turn to make sure she was still there, that she was hearing and seeing the same thing. The little girl would want to be sure her mother was still there, enjoying this, too, oblivious to the fact that those very hands wrapped tight around her knees, propping her up, were her mother's.

One moment, Kate is in the Pelhourino, imagining a little girl, and then, the very next day, that girl comes to life before her eyes on the plane. As Kate sits relaxed, watching her fellow passengers walk about the cabin, a guy in his thirties, handsome, dark-haired, and with a thick five o'clock shadow, paces with a little girl, all of two or three, up on his shoulders. The mom must be a redhead, because this child looks nothing like the man, but she is clearly his. This you know from the way she pats his ears, then lays her face on his head, even shakes her face in the curls. He laughs and nuzzles her chubby legs, and she thumps his head in delight. This is my dad. Mine. His head is my drum, his arms my support, his back the wall against which I can throw myself when I'm tired and grumpy; his face is that thing that feels rough on my hand and makes a sound, his nose as pliable and fun as his cheek is rough, until he shaves anyway, and then it's soft. My dad.

Kate smiles and the guy looks away shyly, as if trying not to encourage this lady, who is possibly flirting with him. Louis will be such a wonderful father, she thinks, and takes out a postcard on which she will write him a note. She looks back up, and the young dad is gone.

And what about her mother? Kate tries to remember her mother back when her father was still alive and thinks she can just faintly remember a beautiful woman with a hearty laugh, her body curvy and strong.

The plane tips to one side and Kate sees the lights of Brazil. How do you stop caring about people you don't know in order to care for one who is all yours? Is it enough to promise yourself that you will inculcate in her the desire to know and help others?

"I'm sorry," she whispers to the cold plastic of the window, to the girl in the Pelourhino. I promise to hold you tight in my thoughts, and I will pray that's enough to keep you safe. *Safe.*

As the plane flies away from Brazil and toward Europe and night turns to morning, and a sky full of clouds emerges, a different sensation comes over Kate—one of weightlessness, as if a heavy burden has been lifted. She knows she'll be fine. Everything is new.

CHAPTER 67

Ibiza
1994

Don goes inside and straight to the desk, extends his hand to the man behind the counter, who is slow to take it.

"I'm Don Williams. My assistant called you."

"Yes, hello," he says, and shakes Don's hand. "This is the same patient another man was here for yesterday, yes?"

"Yes, that's right. I sent another assistant yesterday to make the arrangements for me. Is everything in order? I trust we can depart as planned."

"Yes, yes," the man says. "We must just finish signing some things, make sure the address is correct for the clinic where you are taking her. You changed to London, not Madrid."

"Yes. Much better doctors in London."

"Ah, okay," he says. "May I see, please, the papers from the hospital?"

Don sets those on the counter and points to the signatures at the bottom. "You should have received the clinic's address from my assistant Jenny. Did you get it? She did confirm with you?"

"Yes, yes," he says, staring at this older man with the bandage on his nose, who seems annoyed, trying to push him into something. But what? "You must pay the balance, and there is a surcharge for the extra petrol and the change in flight plan," the man says.

"Of course there is," Don says, and goes to pull out his wallet.

It's not in his back pocket as it should be. He checks his jacket. Nothing. That driver.

"I have no . . . Fuck! I don't . . . My wallet seems to be gone."

"Do you have, perhaps, a different credit card or cash?"

"I have . . . No," Don says, and he would love, right now, to reach across and punch the look off this guy's face, the smug look.

What about Georgina? Don looks outside, at the ambulance. Georgina will have credit cards, but every single one has a limit of one thousand dollars, to control her excess spending.

"I'll have to have the money wired to you," Don says. "Give me your bank account number, please."

"What? You do not have a credit card?"

"No. I just explained that my wallet is gone. This will only take five minutes more, I assure you. Call your bank and ask them to expedite the request. I'll pay whatever they want to confirm quickly for you that the money is in the—"

"You don't have another way to—?"

"Do you understand what a fucking wallet is? That my wallet was stolen?" he says, and he can feel his nose throbbing and his eyes stinging. He really hadn't wanted to lose his temper right then. "I'm sorry," he says. "That was uncalled for."

When Angela sees the ambulance, she looks at her purse, thinking of the gun inside. But then she looks toward the office and sees Don there at the counter, his back to her. She takes her cell and dials Louis.

"I'm coming toward you," he says. "I'll be there in five."

Angela stands next to the ambulance, touching the silver square of the door; then opens it and she sees Georgina sitting close to Kate, smoothing her cheek. Santillan sits on the other side of her, checking the medical tubing.

"I don't know what you think you're doing here," Georgina says to Angela.

"Trying to help Kate," Angela says, then looks at Santillan, who nods. "Do you know what that's like?"

"You have no right."

"I have every right. You had a responsibility, as her mother, and you failed her, Georgina. Utterly fucking failed her."

"You don't know. What would you know? It's . . . girls . . ."

"Girls what?"

"Young girls can be very seductive."

Angela can't say anything, just shakes her head. "*Seductive?* How old was she when you married Don?"

"I won't discuss this with you."

"Yes, you will. How old was she?"

"I can't. Don will be very upset with you."

"Go get him, then. Go tell him to help you out of this. If he can. How old, Georgina? Ten? Twelve?"

"No, no," Georgina says, and shakes her head. "I will not have this." She now lifts a hand knotted in veins. "I will not tolerate this."

Santillan looks at both women. The mother should go. This is not good for anyone, especially Kate.

"You don't understand," she says. "Don will be very upset. He can be very angry at times. You won't want that."

"Maybe I do. Go get him, Georgina."

At this very moment, Don and the man at the counter are deciding if this will spill over into a shove or at least more yelled words. The men stand like two mirror images, hands planted firmly on the counter, leaning toward each other—inches away from unleashing all that anger. Then the Spaniard lifts his arm in triumph and says, "Wait, wait. I know! What about the credit card your assistant gave me, the man, when he was here? That had a very high limit, no?" The Spaniard turns quickly and grabs paperwork from his desk, pulls a clip off, and reads the credit card number

"For Louis Ross, company card. Seven point zero. Correct?"

"Yes. Of course. Why didn't I think of this?" Don shakes his head and smiles, wants to laugh, actually. The irony of it. God really does come through sometimes. "Yes, good idea. Use that credit card."

Georgina looks down at her feet, one hand wrapped in a tight fist.

"You don't know," she says, and stares at Kate. "You have no way of knowing." She rocks forward and back.

And then it happens—the heart monitor beeping ever so regularly to let them know the patient is fine stops. Santillan looks at it.

"Shit!" he yells, then cups his hands, centers them just over Kate's chest, and gently presses down. Georgina's head pops up and she looks crazed.

"No," Angela says. "Oh no."

"*No pasa nada pero actua como que sí,*" Santillan says to Angela, telling her that nothing's wrong but to act as if there is.

Angela turns to Georgina. "This is your fault."

Georgina looks scared as her eyes move from Angela to Kate. Finally, she pushes her way out of the ambulance.

"Don!" she yells, running toward the office. "Don, it's happened."

"*Vamos,*" Santillan says to Angela and the ambulance driver. "*A subirla.*" They move quickly to transfer her to the plane.

Georgina has never felt this way in her entire life. The anger literally throws her inside the office and into Don's back, his neck. She hits him with her fists, kicks him, then stops and looks around for something, anything, to use. But on so many painkillers, she's hardly a challenge, and Don quickly grabs hold of her hands, pushes them down to her sides, then maneuvers her against a wall.

"Calm down, Georgina. Calm yourself now," he whispers.

"You did it!" "You finally did it. You bastard. You fucking bastard!" she yells, and frees one hand, with which she tries to hit Don in the face. His bandaged nose is her target now and she uses everything, even her forehead, to get at him, succeeding.

"Oh Jesus fucking Christ!" he yells, and slaps her as hard as he can, aiming for just under her chin, so as to shock her into stopping.

"¡Ya basta!" yells the owner. Enough.

A nurse Angela's never met helps Santillan go over the equipment on the plane. Angela watches Kate's breathing, steady and strong. Or at least she thinks it seems strong.

"¿Está bien?" she says to both Santillan and herself.

He nods yes, she's okay.

Looking out a window, Angela sees a taxi pull up to the tarmac. Louis exits and stands there staring at the plane, then at the office. Only when Don and Georgina step out of the office does Louis start toward them.

Georgina stops walking, turns, and goes back into the office, not for help, seemingly, and not in a hurry, just wanting out of all this. From the plane, Angela watches as Louis quickly gets Don on the ground and, straddling him, hits him once, then again. Don's body forms a tight, seemingly unmoving coil on the ground and Louis leans back, appears to be considering if this is enough. He grabs the old man by the lapels and pulls him up. Don's head is now hanging back; he's completely out. Louis looks up to the plane and lets go of the old man.

Angela thinks of the gun in her purse and understands why he gave it to her—not for her to use, but to prevent himself from using it.

Louis lets go of Don, now immobile, and moves away from him, runs up the stairs. Inside, the captain stares at him for a moment, as if deciding, then asks him to take a seat and closes the door. A moment later, the owner of Transporte Médico de Europa exits the building and walks slowly up to the nose of the plane, directly below the pilot, looks up, shielding his eyes from the sun, and gives a thumbs-up. Five minutes later, the jet is finally taxiing down the runway, cleared for takeoff. And then, five minutes after that, it's in the air.

CHAPTER 68

In a Cove in Blue Water Where All of God's Children
Love to Swim Naked
1994

Angela watches Santillan go through his routines of checking Kate's vitals and noting everything on a clipboard. He then pulls on a sweatshirt and takes a sip from the water bottle he's pulled from a duffel bag. Angela stares at the bottle, which looks old, its bottom opaque from so many washings. He smiles at Angela, then speaks quietly to the nurse. Then Santillan moves back to his seat, opens a bag, and takes out a book.

Angela thinks of the gun and wonders if medevac passengers have to go through customs or security. Probably not within the same country. Still, she'll have to find a way to get rid of this thing. Kate always wanted her to take more action. Stop watching and taking notes, stop reporting. Have an opinion. Indisputable action.

Angela moves over closer to Kate, then reaches under the blanket and feels her hand. "You're safe," she says.

The two silver rings on Kate's fingers—one on her thumb, the other on her ring finger—feel loose, as if poised to fall off the moment she awakens and lifts her hand. Angela pulls back the blanket and puts her arm on the sheet, stares at the rings. Has she lost weight the last few days, Angela wonders, or were they always like this?

She takes a deep breath and puts her fingers around the ring on

Kate's thumb and moves it around as she watches Kate's face to see if there's a change. She wants so much for those eyes to open again.

In the bathroom, Louis splashes water on his face and stares at himself with eyes that look back at him as if he's the enemy. But, for once, you're not, he tells himself. He stares and stares, his hand holding that tiny silver sink, wanting to wrest it from the wall. It is unbelievably difficult to resist the desire to pull at the sink. Slowly, Louis talks himself out of it and begins to control his breathing. In the mirror, his eyes begin to look calm. They did it. Kate is safe. He did it.

He's berated himself his entire life for not pushing hard enough, but in the end, maybe he pushed at just the right moment. Not in Encino, not in New York. In San Francisco, yes. And now, too.

He closes his eyes and pictures the two of them floating over the Palancar Reef hand in hand. If he closes his eyes, he can feel Kate's hand in his, as when they first submerged themselves.

The first few times they dived, she held his hand for about ten minutes because she was afraid. He loves remembering that she never stopped holding his hand, even on the last dives, when, he knows damned well, she wasn't afraid anymore.

They land at 7:00 P.M., the lights of Madrid a relief after so much dark sky. The ambulance awaits, and Santillan, after checking the oxygen supply and heart monitor, directs the attendants to lift her in. From there, it's a half hour ride to Clinica Ruber. By nine, she's in her room, and by ten, the sonogram machine has been wheeled in.

"I've asked Dr. Mantela if we may do this and he said it was fine with him. He will be here early in the morning," Santillan says.

Angela and Louis nod like kids receiving direction.

"I don't want you to have expectations," the doctor says to them in English.

"Don't worry, Doc," Louis says.

Santillan pulls the machine closer and leans against the bed, pulls down the sheet and then gently pulls up the gown, folding it just above Kate's sternum. Her stomach is brown and untouched, a beauty mark near her belly button. This place, this little haven, has seemingly been untouched by any accident.

Santillan squeezes gel from a tube and uses a now-gloved hand to spread it on her belly, then turns on the machine and starts to use it to find the child they hope still lives inside. No one seems to breathe as this wand gently covers the terrain of Kate's abdomen. Then Santillan stops and turns to them, points to the monitor. The cloudy images on the monitor don't resemble anything human, much less alive.

And then the doctor stops, smiles, and points to the monitor. "*Piernita*," he says to Angela, then adds in English, "Leg." Santillan then reaches over and turns a dial on the sonogram machine and everyone in the room can hear the faintest but steadiest of heartbeats. Angela and Louis smile through their tears.

"I think ten weeks or so," the doctor says. He tells them that many challenges remain for Kate and this fetus. They know he's right. But still, after so much angst and so much worry, they can't help but feel optimistic.

Santillan stays at a hotel near the clinic and Louis and Angela get in a cab to travel to their hotel a few miles away. And it's then, as they travel in a taxi through the streets of Madrid, as Santillan walks to his hotel, stopping for a bite on the way, that Kate's heart gives out.

She goes into cardiac arrest and the alarms on the monitor signal for help. Within a minute, the emergency doctor, two nurses, and the crash cart are at her bedside. They perform CPR, intubate her, bag her, administer emergency drugs, defibrillate her. After thirty minutes of unsuccessful attempts at resuscitation, the emergency doctor shakes his head and calls it. There is nothing more they can do. Kate's heart has stopped.

As their taxi pulls up to the hotel, Louis receives a call that goes to voice mail. Angela goes to the desk to check them in while he stays outside to smoke a cigarette. Standing there, rolling his neck, his eyes closed, he feels the phone in his pocket vibrate. He takes it out. A voice mail. As soon as he hears the somber voice asking them to please return to the hospital, Louis knows. He stands there, looking inside at Angela, who's chatting with the receptionist, and he cannot believe what he has to tell her. He cannot yet feel or know or believe what he understands. He just stares at the sidewalk, lets the cigarette burn out, tries to stay standing.

One by one, the doctors and nurses leave the room. The tube no longer in her mouth, she looks like an actress after a night of hard partying. And someone has folded the sheet tightly around her chest. Louis loosens it and pulls her arms out.

"God," he says over and over, and shakes his head, sits down, and stares at her, his face frozen. He can't cry or have any other reaction, because he doesn't believe it.

Angela stares and stares, waiting for something like an exhalation or even, secretly, an inhalation. Then she leans forward, so that her forehead is pressed against Kate's. She closes her eyes, tries to will herself to see or feel one last bit of energy.

Angela laces her fingers onto Kate's and holds them tight. She stays like that, forehead to forehead, for a while, hoping that, like two people on different sides of a dark window, suddenly they will see each other.

Santillan comes in and hugs Angela, then Louis.

"Do you understand what happened? You know the child could not survive?"

"Yes," Louis says, and embraces him. "Thank you so much for what you did, for coming with us."

Santillan nods, tears in his eyes. "This would have happened in Ibiza, too," he says to them both, touching Louis's shoulder. "You know this?"

They're allowed to stay as long as they wish. No one comes to usher them out. They sit, just watching her, no longer hoping for an impossible sign of life from her, but for a sign in themselves that somehow they can leave her behind in this room, that it won't feel like abandonment.

"Should we fly her home?"

"I don't think so. Home is with us, wherever we are."

After about an hour, it feels as if Kate is not in the room anymore, as if this body really is a shell and the woman inside, that amazing woman, has gone elsewhere.

Louis takes Kate's hand and kisses it, then rubs the back against his cheek. "Good-bye, beautiful," he says.

They go back to the hotel, where their bags await them next to the reception desk. Once in the room, they order two bottles of wine and a plate of bread and *jamón* Serrano. When the food arrives, Angela and Louis sit on one bed, staring at the TV, eating and drinking steadily, mechanically, like people driving as fast as possible to reach their destination, only theirs is not a physical place, but a state of drunkenness.

After a while, they turn off the TV and go out on the balcony. It's one in the morning now, and, despite a flash of rain that left the ground shining, lots of people trot by under their perch, feet quick, voices high, laughs easy.

"Such night owls, Spaniards," Angela says, and Louis nods yes.

"She loved that about this place."

They watch the street together in silence for a while.

"So you read the thesis?"

"Yes."

"You talked to her?"

"Yes."

"Did you see her, too?" he says, and looks at Angela in a way that says, Just be honest.

"No. I called her and told her I wanted to see her again. She said she'd think about it. Said she was heading for Brazil, then Spain."

"That's it?"

"That's it."

Angela puts her arm in his and leans in. He rests his head against hers.

"She was doing so much better," Louis says. "Her book, teaching, the diving. All of it."

Angela looks up at the sky. It's one of those nights when the stars look like tiny bright blue holes, as if the sky itself were a black velvet curtain with just enough pinpricks in it to let you see the light burning behind. Not heaven, as much as she'd like to believe in heaven right now, but definitely light.

Four days later, each carrying a small box of her ashes, they leave Spain.

CHAPTER 69
"Home"

The very day Angela returns to work in L.A., she's handed a buyout offer by Bennett, the associate publisher, not Rob, the publisher and her longtime boss and mentor. She can imagine just how excited Bennett must have been planning this moment. She opens the envelope and sees that it's for an insulting six months of severance.

"Is this your way of saying you missed me?" she asks, then laughs. Bennett's face shatters. Laughter was not the hoped-for response.

Angela goes home, uncorks a bottle of champagne someone gave her for her birthday, and goes out on her balcony. She takes with her the card Kate sent with the master's thesis and finally opens it.

The envelope is new, but right away she recognizes the card inside. It's the very same one Angela had left for Kate in Boston when she left.

On the front is a colored-pencil drawing of a regal-looking woman in a long plantation-style dress, a scarf around her hair. Next to her, a man bows slightly as he holds a yellow-and-pink umbrella to protect the woman from the sun—it's a scene from *carnaval*, depicting a lovely lady and her loyal servant. Below the drawing, there's a line from a poem by Mario Benedetti: "After all, you know that the world and I both love you, although me always a little more than the world."

Angela takes a deep breath and opens the card. Her writing is on the left and Kate has written something on the right side. As if standing in the loft again, she can remember exactly how painful it was to write it. "This card reminds me of something you once said. I think the person who truly loves has a way of looking at you that illuminates you from inside. And from that look, from that feeling grows everything else that is worth keeping close. I love you very much, Kate, which is why I have to leave. I hope you'll understand and I hope, with all my heart, this is not good-bye."

She musters up the courage to read what Kate has written, "Ani, if not for you, things would have been very different. You've been part of everything good. I hope you know that. I love you very much."

She looks out at the rooftops of L.A., at the new billboard on Melrose, the mountains to the left.

"Why are you so wild?" Angela asked Kate once as they hid in a closet. They'd fooled around in there, at a party, then got stuck when another couple came into the room and started fooling around on the bed.

"You're in here, too," Kate whispered.

"Yeah, but you're always the instigator. Why are you so wild?"

"To make things different, to make them mine. To make you mine," she'd said, and thrown Angela back down onto a bed of a stranger's shoes.

If Angela had once tried to mix her own happy memories of family with Kate's, like a scientist melding the contents of two beakers, well, Kate had done the same, adding courage and fearlessness and bravado and dancing and ecstasy to the beaker filled with get good grades, make a career, find stability.

She turns the card and looks at the woman, the bright colors of the drawing.

She has to do it, head back along the trail and find the place where she made the wrong turn. Maybe go back to writing and reporting. Maybe she can tell new stories, at the very least find the farmworker girl who went to Harvard. Eventually, she may have to work for a paycheck, but for a while at least, she has to try some-thing else.

You live in the deepest—and the best—part of me.

This time for Louis, there's no ringing the buzzer at the front door, once and then again, no waiting for Kate, or pressing his face to watch her run down those stairs toward him. Louis didn't tell the girls next door what time he was arriving, so as to have a few hours to steady himself. He can't imagine what he'll do when he hears someone say "I'm sorry."

But the girls have already been here, filled a vase with white peonies. It sits on that dark-wood dresser, where Louis puts his keys, his wallet and passport.

He considers whether to go to the living room and lie on the couch or just go to the bedroom and hole up in there, read some book from long ago, drink, pretend to forget.

The girls thought to put on the heat for him. Oh, not just for him, Louis realizes as he looks down and sees that silly cat, whom he'd somehow forgotten about, sitting on the floor in front of him, meowing like crazy.

"Fuck," he says, and stares at Madonna Ciccone.

She doesn't move, just stares at him, a little orange triangle head with blue dots and a voice three times her size.

"I'm sorry," he says. "I came home empty-handed."

He wants to pick her up and cradle her, comfort her, but the idea that she needs comforting, the reason for that scares him be-cause he knows he'll fall apart. Still, he does it, picks up and holds Madonna, who lies back and closes her eyes as he rubs her chin, her ears. A tiny pearl of drool forms at the end of her mouth as tears roll down Louis's nose and onto hers. Madonna opens her eyes as the water falls on her and offers one meow, then closes her eyes again.

Two weeks after he's returned to San Francisco, an attempt is made to deliver a package from Spain, but no one is there to sign for it. He leaves UPS a note on the door and the package is left with Mariana downstairs. When Louis gets home that night, he sees it's from Spain, from some U.S. government office in Madrid. He opens it and sees a digital camera, on it a note that says simply, "This was found under car seat in auto involved in collision. Best."

He wonders if the camera battery will be dead, but when he presses the button, Louis hears a small *ding*.

He takes it and plugs the camera into his computer in the office, goes and fetches a bottle of scotch.

In the months and years to come, Louis will do this a hundred times, often with Angela, whom he'll invite to San Francisco for just this purpose. Both of them will view these so many times, they'll come to know the exact order of the pictures, but tonight, the first time, every one is a surprise.

The first shot is of the guys, Liam and Paul, at breakfast, or maybe dinner—handsome, huge smiles, arms around each other. The next is of Kate, same table. You can imagine the camera being passed over plates, the guys saying, "Here, we'll take one of you now."

She's beautiful, of course, kissing the air, lips pursed, eyes half-closed. Flirting.

Next, there's one of Kate in the hotel, holding a pillow on her head, the round yellow one, a finger near her lip, looking coy, a little like Audrey Hepburn.

Next, it's a movie, taken from the car window, of pines flying by and what seem to be mustard plants. She loved close-ups of flowers, brought them home to him like a child bringing real flowers to her mother, for Louis to use in his graphic design work.

Upon arriving at the cove, they had stopped and marveled at the water: Argentine blue, a color so bright, it seemed to personify optimism itself. Then they'd let go of the bags they'd been carrying, looked around, and saw that everyone was either topless or completely naked, so they did the same, stripping off shorts and bathing suits, then running straight in, like children who know their parents will lay out the blanket, set out the food, even hold the warm towel into which they can later, much later, collapse.

They stayed in for hours, floating around inlets, or *calas,* the temperature warm as half hour–old tea.

"All of God's children love to swim naked!" Kate screamed to no one and apropos of nothing, but the boys got it.

"Yes, they do!" Liam yelled from the hot yellow rock on which he was sunbathing.

After exploring the coves together, they stretched out on the sand and let the sun's heat iron away the goose bumps. Then the heat began to intensify, and with that, the smells: of *patatas* frying at the snack bar; hash smoked by some German hippies clustered by the rocks; cologne-scented European sunscreen. . . . And the sounds got crisp, too: of seagulls fluttering past like feathered kites; Jet Ski bees buzzing around, just past the reef; a radio that searched for and found a station playing an acid jazz tango fusion perfectly matched with the Argentine blue of the sea.

So simple this day, but with staying power—one of those you knew would lie close to your subconscious for years to come, a memory you'd pluck out when anyone said the word *vacation,* when it was raining and you were standing next to the kettle, waiting for the water to boil. For so many reasons, Kate knew she would never forget this moment.

In the car, on the way back to the hotel, she rested her hands on her belly and smoothed it, seeing if anything was visible. It wasn't. Not yet anyway. She closed her eyes and thought of the Brazilians in the Pelourinho, the tourists dancing to the beat of the *batucada* drums. Kate had caught the eye of one of the dancers, a girl of sixteen or seventeen, in a black T-shirt, her hair pulled back tight and a huge, confident smile on her face as she shook her hips so incredibly fast to that samba rhythm, along with the dozens of bracelets on her arms, a sort of percussion. No one watching could ever have replicated her moves, a fact that clearly gave her pleasure, the look on her face triumphant.

I can feel your happiness right now, Kate had thought. I can actually feel it. And, sure enough, the girl smiled right at her and waved.

You can feel it, too, Kate thought, talking to the baby, if indeed there was a baby inside her.

I can do this, she thought. I can teach you how to find joy. I can protect you, as I wasn't always protected, and I can teach you how to find joy. And your little sandaled feet will always dance atop my legs.